More
erotic stories
of Sin City

WHAT HAPPENS IN VEGAS

...AFTER DARK

Jodi Lynn Copeland

Anya Bast

Lauren Dane

Kit Tunstall

Spice

Spice

WHAT HAPPENS IN VEGAS...AFTER DARK

ISBN-13: 978-0-373-60531-6
ISBN-10: 0-373-60531-5

www.Spice-Books.com

Printed in U.S.A.

...AFTER DARK

More erotic stories of Sin City

♣ ♠ ♥ ♦ ♣ ♠ ♥ ♦ ♣ ♠ ♥ ♦

HOT FOR REVENGE

♣ ♠ ♥ ♦ ♣ ♠ ♥ ♦ ♣ ♠ ♥ ♦

Jodi Lynn Copeland

To Melissa, who listens to all my rants and raves and understands the value of a good caramel brownie to make everything shiny and new again.

♣ ♠ ♥ ♦ ♣ ♠ ♥ ♦ ♣ ♠ ♥ ♦

Chapter One

Ryan

Vegas. A hell of a place to call home. At least, until the bill collectors came a-calling.

"Shit." Growling out a second curse, I pushed through the door that connected the garage to the kitchen and tossed the lease agreement for my inner-city rental house onto the table. Jenison Davis, the old guy I rented the place from, had been nice enough to tape the form to the front door so that I saw it as soon as I pulled in the drive from twenty-four hours on at the firehouse. He'd also been nice enough to highlight in yellow and circle in red the surcharges posed for not paying the rent on time. The rent I was almost two grand behind on.

"Yeah. Real fucking nice."

Not that I expected him to let me freeload forever, but, damn, this blew. If I didn't find a housemate to cover the half of the rent my brother, Jack, quit paying when he moved out to settle down with his fiancée, I was screwed.

Of course, there was the option of living at the fire-house full-time. A year ago I would have done so in a heartbeat. Women dug being sneaked into the house and were only too willing to shell out the oral gratitude. But then, a year ago, my guts hadn't roiled with the thought of being bottled up full-time with a couple dozen adrenaline junkies. And a year ago, I wasn't a mental case waiting to happen.

The barely contained nasty shit in my head was the reason I hadn't been more serious about finding a housemate. Now, I didn't have a choice. Even if it meant some stranger moving in, touching my stuff, moving things where they didn't belong, ticking me off in general—I had to find someone fast.

Going to the fridge, I pulled a longneck bottle of Bud from the crisper drawer and uncapped it. Cool, crisp ale slid down my throat, calming my irritation while washing away the sensation that smoke clung to my throat and lungs as much as my body. This morning's apartment fire was the last thing I wanted to think about. The building was located on the opposite side of the city from the blaze that changed my life. Still, it had looked enough like the other building to have guilt chomping a huge hole in my stomach and making me pissy long before I'd gotten home.

I lifted the bottle back to my lips and chugged its contents. One beer wouldn't get me plastered no matter how fast I drank it. But one beer was a hell of a start. Two were even better.

Slamming the empty bottle onto the counter, I grabbed another longneck from the crisper and headed for the stairs sandwiched between the kitchen and living room. Before I could ascend the first step, someone knocked on the front door.

Or make that some chick who hadn't waited for an invitation to enter, but let herself inside. At present, she stood in the open doorway, giving me a visual head-to-toe pat-down. I'd forgive her the indiscretion of trespassing. But only because she had waist-length red hair, huge, barely covered tits, glistening cherry-red lips and slanted ice-blue eyes that were screaming "do me all night long."

Shallow? Yeah. But what the hell, I was having a shitty day.

Those stunning lips curved in a siren's smile. In a voice laced with smoke and sex, she asked, "Are you Ryan Dempsey?"

Before she'd knocked, I'd been in the process of heading upstairs to shower the acrid smell of smoke from my body. Now, I wanted smoke all over me. Or rather that sexy, smoky voice coupled with her hotter-than-a-four-alarm-fire body.

Goddamn, the woman was built!

Feeling like I'd just come face-to-face with my destiny for the next seven or eight hours—or however long it took my dick, which was currently in the process of tenting my jeans, to get its fill of her—I took a step forward. "I am." I flashed the arrogant grin all the chicks dug and the guys at the fire-house nicknamed me "Cock" because of. "Can I help you with something?"

"You can if the housemate position hasn't been filled."

Was I really thinking a couple minutes ago that I loathed the idea of a housemate? Spending my free hours mating in the house with this hot mama had the makings of all kinds of wicked good fun. "It has."

Displeasure flashed in those devilishly seductive eyes. "Oh. That's too bad."

"Not really. Since you're the one who filled it."

Relief took over her displeasure as the siren's smile returned. "You don't want to get to know me first?"

Hell, yeah, I did. I wanted to get to know every tanned,

toned, naked inch of her. First, a little "welcome to the house" gesture was probably in order. "You drink beer?"

She glanced at the bottle of Bud in my hand for a few silent seconds, then closed the door and joined me near the foot of the stairs.

Outside, the temps were peaking in the high nineties. Inside, as she took the beer and proceeded to guzzle it down like a drunk on a bender, it felt twice that hot.

"Love it." Winking, she slid the empty bottle into my left hand, and then took my right one in a shake. "I'm Deitre. Nice to meet you."

Like the air around us, the heat in the connection of our fingers felt electric—raw and primal. The heat in her Southern drawl, which I hadn't noticed until now, was like a physical stroke down my spine and along the crack of my ass.

"Something tells me the pleasure's all mine." Something also told me I was right before. She could touch my stuff all she wanted and I wouldn't mind a bit. The stuff scattered throughout the house and the stuff now nearly stone-stiff behind my zipper.

Up until last year and that day my life changed irrevocably, I was an admitted horn dog. For all the women I'd done, not one had gotten me so quickly and thoroughly aroused with barely a touch.

Sliding my gaze from hers, I eyed her lush red lips. If her presence and a gentle touch had me this hard, what kind of power would her mouth hold?

"Find out."

I darted my gaze back to Deitre's with the unexpected response to a question I hadn't asked aloud. At least, I don't think I had. My mind was doing a sort of tunnel-vision thing that focused entirely on sex with my newfound housemate. "Come again?"

Amusement gleamed in her eyes. "Find out and maybe I will."

Holy shit, I was right a second time. She *was* my evening's, night's and, quite likely, morning's destiny.

Just to be certain we were on the same page, I asked, "Want to be more specific?"

With a slow nod, she thrust out her chest and leaned forward. "You want to kiss me. I'm telling you to go ahead."

She'd only been a foot away to begin with. Now, she was inches away and, with that thrusting move, it was all I could do not to stare at her tits. Better yet, push my hands beneath the sheered hem of her tiny black tank top and see if the generous mounds felt as good as they looked. "You're serious?"

I'd managed to waylay my urge to cop a feel. Deitre didn't bother.

Her fingers dove beneath my dirty gray T-shirt and splayed branding hot over the muscles of my chest. She knocked me back a foot with the press of her palms, far enough I could feel the last step riding against my sock-covered heels.

The strength of her arms was surprising. The strength of her tongue was the stuff wet dreams were made of.

On a husky breath, she drove her tongue between my lips. The urgent grinding of her hips mimicked the actions of her mouth. Through a few-inch-long jean skirt, she rocked her mound against my erection, urgent, needy. Her tongue lashed against mine, demanding, devouring.

Devouring back, I gave in to my initial urge and shoved my hands beneath her clingy black tank top. Obviously the top had some serious padding. She wore no bra beneath and, until her breasts filled my hands, I couldn't tell that her nipples were as solid as my shaft.

She pushed me backward again, catching me off balance and leaving me no choice but to go down on my ass on the staircase. I landed hard on the third step. She came along for the ride, swallowing my grunt with her lips. Then she made me forget about my sore ass altogether as she grabbed hold of the stair ledge on either side of my head and dragged her pussy up and down the length of my cock.

I grunted again, this time with the tightening of my balls. Christ, I'd never had a woman affect me like this. My blood felt afire and my heart pummeled against my ribs so hard they were bound to be left bruised.

At the moment, I could give two shits less. I just had to be inside her. Had to be.

Deitre plucked her tongue from my mouth. Pushing off from the stair ledge, she rolled off me to wedge herself in the foot of space next to my hip. Her jean skirt had come up with her grinding to reveal the visibly damp crotch of her black panties.

With teasing eyes, she studied the wet cotton. "How about the coming again part?"

"Pretty sure you'd have to come a first time," I managed in between sucking in breaths in the hopes of calming the ragged state of my mind and body.

"Make me," she returned in a commanding tone that said she expected me to slip my fingers beneath her panties and bring her to orgasm without hesitation.

After what went down a year ago, I *was* a mostly reformed

horn dog. But that was only mostly. And, hell, I wouldn't be much of a housemate if I didn't live up to her expectations, now would I?

Deitre

I'd been expecting to find Ryan hot—Jada never slept with a mutt a day in her life. I'd also been expecting to walk in his door and want to kill his ass for the part he played in my mortal best friend's death nearly a year before.

But this guy was literally hotter than Hell. At least, the northern stretches of Hell that I'd spent the better part of the last two hundred years frequenting.

The sensuality in his megawatt smile alone had my pulse racing and my nipples standing at attention well before our mouths connected. From the first challenging flick of his tongue, my pussy squeezed so hard I wanted to wrap my hands around his fine behind and deliver death immediately. A minideath of orgasmic proportions.

What the hell. Why not toy with him awhile? Get a few cheap thrills out of the bastard while slowly draining the life out of him?

I hadn't bothered to use seduction powers on him. From the player rep the guys at the firehouse painted for him to the carnal invitation in Ryan's strikingly deep green eyes when he spotted me in his doorway, I didn't think they would be necessary. Considering he was still sitting on the third step, eyeing me dazedly instead of screwing me, I might have been wrong about that.

"Make me come, Ryan." I added a bit of clarification to my initial order, just in case he was finding this all too good to be true and thinking he'd fazed out.

The clarity seemed to do the trick. He lost the dazed look to turn on his hip and slide a decadently callused palm along my bare inner thigh. His knuckles brushed against my mound through the damp cotton of my panties. I sucked in a hasty breath as electric sensation charged through my pussy over what should have been subtle contact. "Inside! Put them inside me."

Eyes sparkling with sensual amusement, he bent his head and slanted his lips over mine. His tongue pushed deep as he worked a finger beneath the leg of my panties and then drove up hard inside my slick sheath.

My sex shuddered with the forceful impaling. I gasped into his mouth and fisted a hand in his sweat-and-smoke-stained T-shirt, silently demanding that his lips remain on mine. And then demanding he add another finger to the first and rock them together in the quick and carnal rhythm I could never get enough of. Ryan did just that and my clit twinged with all kinds of goodness.

Yeah, I was definitely seeing what Jada had seen in him—and that it went well beyond his golden-brown tan, overlong curling black hair, and muscles honed to perfection. Damn, was I ever.

I was also seeing two fingers weren't nearly enough for my dripping-wet core and famished body.

Grabbing a fistful of hair, I jerked his mouth from mine. "I want your dick in me."

His eyes glittered with primal demand. "Get it there."

Typically, I loathed taking orders from any man, be they human, demon or otherwise. Since I planned to stick around awhile and since, going by the quaking in my pussy, I actually liked taking orders from Ryan, I obeyed.

Employing a fraction of superhuman strength, I pulled his fingers from my sex, planted my hands on his chest, and bore him back on the stairs. With my knees straddling his muscular legs on the step below the one his ass occupied, I jerked open his fly. Questions came into his eyes—probably wonder over how a woman half his size could move him about so damned easily. I stole those questions from his mind by filling it with thoughts of all the ways he wanted to do me.

When arousal held him in its grasp, I could see into his head as clearly as if he was one of my familiars. The low-level demons who took the shape of animals and saw to my every beck and call would never be entertaining thoughts of my sucking their cock, though. Ryan was.

I was tempted to relent to the vision as I dragged his jeans and underwear down his thighs and a sizeable purple-headed erection jutted out. But I was even more tempted to climb back up his legs and slide onto his cock.

As a succubus it wounded my pride to admit, but I hadn't fucked a guy in months. My father—might as well call him my boss since he was Prince of the northern stretches of Hell and all who lived within answered to him—had kept me busy with training the younger succubi in the ways of their fledgling powers.

Taking my dry spell out on Ryan, I tugged aside the crotch of my panties and dove onto his prone body. His cock impaled me on the downslide and tears of ecstasy darted into my eyes with the exquisite pressure the move ignited in my core.

"It's been way too long," I panted as I pushed the T-shirt up his body. The shirt fell back down again, obstructing my view of his stunningly sculpted torso. Damn, that just ticked me off.

I took care of it, though, by fisting the shirt in my hands, releasing the tips of my claws, and shredding it off his body.

Ah, much better.

His body went still beneath mine. I jerked my gaze to his eyes to find questions back in them. Couldn't have that. Using my powers to get his mind back on thoughts of sex, I repeated my last words, "It's been way too long."

The questions left his eyes again as wicked heat sizzled into them. His hands slid to my ass. Strong fingers cupped my butt and spread my cheeks as he lifted me up his cock and pushed me forcefully back down again on a groan. "Damn, are you tight."

An extrasnug pussy was just one of many benefits of being a demon. The ability to be in two places at once was another.

I unleashed my second self, surfacing her on the staircase above his head. Fervency shone in her cool blue eyes. Pink flushed her cheeks and neck. The huge breasts I'd always adored peeked from beneath the black tank top to slap against the air with each thrust of Ryan's erection inside me.

Before he could see her and think he'd lost all touch with sanity, I ordered, "Close your eyes and I promise it'll get even better."

Like the good little submissive I knew he would never be without my influence, he snapped his eyes shut. I appreciated the view of his taut features, rock-solid chest, and the slide of his eager dick inside me for a handful of seconds. Then I pried his hands from my butt and handed them over to my second self.

With a keen smile, she grabbed hold of his wrists. She corded the lower half of her waist-length hair around each, binding them with the unbreakable red strands and securing them above his head. And I shuddered around his shaft with the reckless need to feed.

Not wanting to drain his energy completely this first time, I took a small portion of his strength from his cock and a bigger portion from his jugular. Sweeping the tips of my throbbing nipples against the solid wall of his chest, I lashed my tongue across the tightly strung vein in his neck. It corded further with that lick. My heart and tongue pulsed in synchronized anticipation. Elongating my canine teeth into needle-sharp points, I sank them into his neck.

Ryan bowed up on the stairs, driving his cock even deeper inside my soaking body. "Holy Christ!"

He sounded more pained than I wanted him just now, so I hit him with a shot of mental seduction. His hips kept up their wild bucking and he struggled against the bindings of my second self's hair, but the look on his face quickly became raw and endless pleasure.

"That's awesome," he moaned as I rode his cock and sucked his blood, and felt orgasm pooling thick and hungry in my core.

I drank greedily until the pumping of his hips slowed and the struggle to free his arms quit, telling me I'd taken as much blood as I dared. I saved a last mouthful as I sealed the small twin wounds with the damp swipe of my tongue.

Bringing my lips to his, I applied pressure until his parted and then fed him the sweet nectar of his life force. His tongue resisted, pushing back against mine. Then it melted, going soft and pliable, feeding needfully. The bucking of his cock resurged, the fight to free his hands renewed.

Feeling strong for the blood, I slipped a finger between our bodies and stroked my clit in time with the contracting of my vaginal muscles. I felt strong for Ryan's orgasm then, too, as climax ripped through me as a fiercely shuddering wave and he roared with his own as he pumped hot and silky fluid into my passage.

I didn't need time to recharge. My breath was coming fast, but it was mostly for show at this point. Still, I let him have ten seconds to bask in what I knew was the best orgasm of his life before I withdrew my second self and, in doing so, freed his arms.

"So, do I get the job?" I asked in a practiced Southern drawl as I lifted from his lap to stand on the bottom step.

His eyes opened to reveal murky deep green touched with confusion. I dipped a finger into the juices trickling down my thighs, and then sucked the shimmering tip between my lips on a throaty sigh.

His breath caught. His softening cock jerked. The confusion left his eyes and he hit me with an exultant grin. "Welcome home."

I laughed. "I'm already loving it."

I could see myself loving Ryan, too. Right to death.

♣ ♠ ♥ ♦ ♣ ♠ ♥ ♦ ♣ ♥ ♦

Chapter Two

Ryan

I don't know what it was about Deitre, but she removed the nasty shit that had been lurking in my head for months and replaced it with a single-minded need to fuck her. Speaking of fuck… How the fuck had I forgotten about a condom?

Only, I knew that answer. It had everything to do with her open-legged stance on the bottom step and the way her glistening pussy plumped out from the tugged-aside crotch of her panties. Even more to do with the teasing glint in her eyes as she dipped her finger back into the stream of fluid dribbling along her naked inner thighs.

From the second she opened my door, she had me aching for her. And I ached again now, with the want to lean forward and lap at her cream-coated finger.

But, hell, I had to focus. At least, enough to note our oversight. "There's a problem."

"What's the matter, bad boy?" She punctuated the question by rubbing her creamy finger over the peak of an erect, dusky-pink nipple.

I groaned while my shaft pulsed to near hardness again,

like it hadn't just released the most mind-consuming climax of my life.

Strange how completely that orgasm had gotten to me, considering I'd never been all that turned on by dominant lovers. Deitre had let me have the lead for a handful of on-again, off-again seconds. All in all, though, there was no mistaking she liked to be the one in control.

She was in control even now, playing my body like a machine attuned to her every move as her fingers darted down again to trail through our cum.

In search of reprieve, I stared into the living room beyond her. "I lost my head."

She let go a rich, thick laugh dripping with Southern seduction. "I'd say."

Fighting the sensual echo, I sent a pointed glance at my shiny, bare dick. "We didn't use a condom."

A touch of the taunting heat left her eyes, but just a touch. "Not a problem. I can't get pregnant and I'm not carrying any diseases."

Thank God for that. "Yeah, I'm clean, too."

The thing was I did want kids. The desire had grown considerably the last few months, with spending time around my brother and his fiancée and seeing the obvious love between them. But I couldn't settle down and start a family until I got the issues in my head cleared up, permanently. And I wouldn't start one with some random chick I'd barely known fifteen minutes.

Even so, Deitre's comment intrigued me. "Are you sterile?"

"Something like that." The teasing left her eyes entirely. With a sober look, she moved off the bottom step onto the tan carpet, pulling her tank top down over her breasts in the process.

Obviously, I'd hit on a topic she didn't like to discuss. Duly noted. As was the fact that I could sink into her whenever the urge hit and not have to worry about protection. Assuming she planned to sleep with me again.

It was a question to ask later. Twenty-four hours on at the firehouse had apparently just caught up with me in a huge way. Much as I hated to leave her to get herself moved in, I felt like if I didn't get to my bed in about thirty seconds, I was going to pass out on the stairs.

Concern came into Deitre's eyes. She tipped her head to the side, sending the length of her thick red locks cascading over her left shoulder and breast. "You okay? You're looking a little on the pale side."

Not surprising, since I was feeling a little on the pukey side.

Standing with supreme effort, I grabbed my jeans and briefs, but didn't waste the strength to pull them on. "Just tired." I braced my hand against the stairwell wall as a wave of dizziness struck. "I didn't get much sleep last night."

"Right. I heard you guys went up against a major blaze this morning."

I momentarily forgot about my health with the response. Did she keep that close of an eye on the news, or how had she already heard about this morning's apartment fire? "Where did you hear that?"

"Same place I found out you needed a housemate. At the firehouse."

"Were you visiting someone?"

"Yeah." The teasing smile resurfaced. "My new coworkers."

Damn, I never saw *that* coming. I could guess, by her incredible strength and the lean, hard lines of her body, she wasn't hired on as a dispatcher, either.

I forced a smile of my own to let her know how pleased I was with the revelation. "In that case, welcome home *and* onto Ladder 19."

Now could she use some of her incredible strength to drag my exhausted ass up the stairs to my bed?

After I'd slept the better part of the day, we'd spent the night of Deitre's arrival chatting and getting busy. The next afternoon I was on for twenty-four hours again at the firehouse. I learned shortly before I left for work that she was on the same schedule. A good thing after seeing what a prime addition she made to the crew. A couple of the guys had made it their personal mission to heckle her for being the only female in the house. All it took was Deitre dropping them on their ass to prove she had the physical strength to do the job as efficiently as any man.

Of course, our shared schedule wasn't such a good thing when it meant every hour we weren't either on the clock or sleeping, she was sending me fuck-me eyes I had zero tolerance to resist.

This morning I'd headed out before she woke, leaving a note to say I was spending the day at my brother's place outside the city. Probably, I should have invited her along. But then, probably that would have been defeating the purpose of getting the hell away from her.

Sex with Deitre was amazing to the point every orgasm seemed like an honest-to-God spiritual experience. But every orgasm also left me drained.

Despite sleeping a full eight hours last night, I felt weary now as I bypassed the rambling, three-story Victorian estate house Jack had bought for his fiancée, Carinna, to turn into a bed-and-breakfast. The transformation process was complete on over half the house and, judging by the number of cars occupying the back lot, business was good.

Smiling to know Carinna's dream had come to fruition, I continued past a row of trees to the sizeable pole barn they camouflaged. The door was open a couple inches and low music pealed out. The music registered as a tribute song from the eighties as I cleared the door. Jack sat on a workbench a dozen feet away, lovingly working a rag over the chrome bumper of a nearly restored turquoise-and-white Chevrolet Bel Air.

And I do mean lovingly. Since the time we were kids, my brother had a serious chrome fetish. "Betcha got a woody just rubbing her."

He shot me a guilty grin from beneath a black mustache as I joined him at the front of the car. "Don't tell Carinna."

"Like you haven't had her up against the hood a dozen times already."

Not bothering to deny it, Jack grabbed a rag from a pack near his foot and tossed it my way. "I didn't expect to see you until Wednesday."

Since Jack and Carinna had moved out of the city, we'd changed our once-weekly Wednesday poker nights to bi-monthly. Generally, I didn't get out this way on off days. Generally, I didn't have a she-devil acting like she would happily forgo both lunch and dinner to eat my cock, either.

Shrugging, I squatted on the other side of the bumper and went to work on cleaning the over fifty-year-old part. "I had the day off and wanted to get out of the house."

"Just admit it. You miss me."

"I do. Sometimes." Jack had been my coworker at the

firehall for nearly a decade and a father figure for far longer. Afraid of dying on the job and leaving a family behind, the way our father had, he'd quit the crew to help Carinna around the B and B while working his way toward owning a classic car restoration garage. "But actually I wanted some time off from Deitre."

"That your latest woman?"

"She's my new housemate."

"I didn't know you found one." I nodded, and he frowned. "So what's the problem?"

"She's a firefighter. Actually, she's the newest member of Ladder 19."

"Sounds pretty perfect to me."

"She is. Too perfect. I can't stop thinking about her." Even as I said the words, Deitre's sultry smile appeared in my mind. Followed by those vibrant red lips diving down and sucking hard on my bare, stiff cock.

I shook my head against the vision. I'd been having them every few hours or so since I got off work yesterday and each one felt less like a hallucination and more like she really was doing me. Just that quick glimpse had my pulse speeding and my cock pressing semihard against the fly of my nylon shorts.

Jack sent a glare at my hand. "You're cleaning it, not working a hole in it."

Realizing my hand had gone from gentle rubbing to furious scrubbing, I murmured an apology and slowed my pace.

His glare turned to a shit-eating grin. "Baby brother's falling for a girl. About damned time."

"It's nothing like that," I quickly assured him before he bolted inside the B and B and shared the news with Carinna. "I just can't be in the same room with Deitre without wanting to screw her. I mean, she's hot, yeah. But this is ridiculous. I swear all she has to do is look my way and I'm rock-hard and taking her up against the wall. Seriously, Viagra has nothing on this chick."

"Is she not reciprocating?"

"Nah, she is. Whenever I want it and sometimes when I swear I don't."

"Somehow I never thought you'd see sex as a problem."

"It's not a huge deal. Just I've been dragging ass lately. Last night I would have liked to have gone to bed, but then I get there and I hear her voice calling good-night, and next thing I know we were screwing like we hadn't seen each other in months."

Amusement filled Jack's eyes. In a moderately sober tone, he suggested, "Maybe you should get a different housemate."

"I don't want to do that. She *is* pretty perfect." Frankly, the thought of not sleeping with her had my guts feeling just as pukey as they'd felt after she did me on the stairs that first morning. "Maybe I should tell her I'm not quite on par with the guys she's obviously been with in the past."

Bafflement took over Jack's expression as his hand stilled on the bumper. "You—*Cock Dempsey*—are actually going to say that to a woman?"

In the months before Deitre came along, I hadn't been living up to my nickname so much. But neither my brother nor the guys at the firehouse knew that. I didn't want them knowing it, either. Didn't want to come close to them learning how badly I felt like I'd fucked up at that apartment fire a year before and the lasting repercussions it was having on me.

"You're right, bro. I'll just make it a point to pick up some vitamins on the way back to the house." Standing, I tossed the rag back at him. "In the meantime, can I snag one of your spare bedrooms for a few hours?"

"Sure. But let Carinna know you're there. Otherwise she might walk in and think you're me after some morning loving. Then you won't only have more sex to deal with, you'll have a brother with a shotgun aimed at your balls."

Deitre

Wet with anticipation, I hoisted myself up on the firehouse's kitchen counter and untied the sash of my green, ankle-length robe. Then I yelled for Ryan. Mixing business with pleasure wasn't a risk I should take, but I was having too much fun with him to keep the toying confined to the house. Besides, if I really thought we were in danger of getting caught by anyone who mattered, I could transport myself to another room.

He shouted back from the dining room just outside the kitchen door. At last look, a half-dozen guys sat around the long, narrow table, shooting the breeze while tossing back pizzas dropped off courtesy of the Italian restaurant across the street.

"I need your help," I called again. "The knob's stuck on the…hot thing."

Male laughter roared through the door. Most of it was good humor. Some of it was derisive. I could guess the owners of the scornful laughs and vowed to pay them back later. After I finished paying Ryan back.

The door pushed in a half foot and he stuck his head inside, a suspicious look on his face. His gaze fastened on my position on the counter, then quickly slid to the bare portion of my legs and feet sticking out from beneath my robe. Warily, he asked, "Which knob on what hot thing?"

Smiling, I parted the sides of my robe to reveal my nude body. His eyes darted to my breasts, and I took a nipple between my fingers and twisted. "This one."

His eyes slammed closed as the door shut behind him. Opening them, he vowed, "You're going to be the death of me, woman."

If he only knew how right he was…. "Does that mean you aren't going to help me fix it?"

The want to do precisely that flared as dark green desire in his eyes. "You realize if the chief catches us, we could both get canned? Maybe you don't care, but I've been here for almost a decade and this place was in my blood long before that."

Pushing out my lower lip, I pulled my robe back together. "You're right. We shouldn't play."

"Christ, don't pout."

"I'm not trying. You're just so sexy and I can't think about you without wanting you." That much was true. For all that I was making Ryan want me, with both my actions and the visions I planted in his head when I knew they wouldn't interfere with his ability to do his job, he had my mind pretty well taken over in return. It wasn't the first time a male intended as my victim had made me desire him. But it was the first time in fifty or sixty years. "Don't worry about it. As wet as I am, I probably won't even notice if it's your cock or a vibrator inside me."

A pained sort of lust flashed over his face as he eyed my thinly-covered crotch. "How did you get so wet?"

"Like this." Sliding the lower half of the robe apart again

by spreading my thighs, I slipped a finger inside my pussy and pumped.

On a low growl, Ryan strode across the room. He jerked the fly of his jeans down and yanked out his solid cock with a speed and grace even a succubus had to appreciate. "You seriously are going to be the death of me."

Grabbing my butt, he jerked me to the edge of the counter and right onto his waiting cock. I nearly cried out as pleasure, raw and intense, whipped through my body. Then I remembered where we were and that I wasn't yet ready for either of us to lose our jobs.

"How the hell do you stay so tight?" he demanded as he shoved to the hilt, again and again.

I wrapped my arms around his neck and thrust my tongue into his mouth, licking at his tongue and teeth and stealing a bit of his energy in the meantime. I lifted my lips away, feeling revived and eager for orgasm. Truthfully, I said, "I'd tell you, but then I'd have to kill you."

Ryan's chest slammed against my breasts as his breath jerked out like he couldn't get enough air. He didn't attempt a reply, but fixed glassy eyes on my face and pounded inside my dripping sheath like a man possessed. He wasn't. Not at the moment. To know how badly he wanted me, even when I wasn't influencing his thoughts, made me wetter for him yet.

"Cock?" a man's deep voice shouted from somewhere on the other side of the kitchen door.

"God, yeah, it is," Ryan got out in a thin voice.

I stilled the rocking of my hips. I *could* teleport out of here, but I'd prefer not to leave him with a memory loss of the last few minutes if avoidable. "That wasn't me."

"No?" he asked in a dazed voice.

"No." Grabbing hold of the counter ledge, I pulled off from his erection and moved back on the counter. He stood immobile, and I stage whispered, "Ryan, I think someone's about to come into the kitchen."

Shaking his head, he emerged from whatever trance he'd fallen under. "Shit."

"Cock?" the deep voice shouted again, sounding closer this time.

"I'm coming," Ryan yelled back. He pulled my robe around me and secured the sash in a tight knot before tucking his glistening shaft into his briefs and pulling up his pants.

"You almost were," I tossed out flippantly as a funny sensation passed through me over his consideration to see me dressed first.

I diagnosed that sensation then. Not gratitude for his self-lessness. Rather, the mind and body knowledge that he was a fraud attempting to make himself look good for the sake of ensuring I'd continue to sleep with him.

As if in testament to my thought, he sent an arrogant grin in the direction of my breasts. "We'll be out of here in six hours. Keep working the knob till then."

♣ ♠ ♥ ♦ ♣ ♠ ♥ ♦ ♣ ♠ ♥ ♦

Chapter Three

Deitre

A lot of demons felt mortals were good only for feeding. I felt that way about a lot of them, too, but not all. Jada had been truly kick-ass. Karen—a friend I'd met through Jada a few years back—was becoming that way, more and more. In fact, I'd given some serious consideration to letting her in on what I was and seeing if she was interested in being turned into one herself.

Or I had been until I walked up to the bakery-style café she operated in the first floor of the Liege casino and saw her through the nearly floor-to-ceiling and wall-to-wall windows. Two weeks ago, she'd been spewing that men were pigs good for nothing but sex. Now, she was sucking face with some rangy guy whose hair was the same shade of white-blond and as closely cropped as Karen's own. It wasn't just a random face sucking, either. But the kind that involved her arms tenderly embracing his neck in a way that hinted she was seriously into him.

Right there was the reason most demons loathed humans. Far too many allowed themselves to be victimized by their hearts. Today, this guy was tops. Tomorrow, he'd ring her up from some new fuck's bed and tell her they were through.

Hell, for all I knew Ryan was in some other fuck's bed, too. He'd said he had a standing poker date with his brother and his brother's fiancée every other Wednesday night, but since he hadn't invited me along to play, he could've been lying. I could find that out easily enough if I wanted. I didn't want. For one thing, my gut told me that he wasn't lying. For another thing, I was eager for a girl's night out.

I let Karen and her man maul each other another minute, and then gave her a little mental prompting to break things off and usher him out the door. The café had closed a half hour ago. It was high time to get our butts to a club.

With my prompting as an impetus, Karen led the guy to the door. She wore a moony expression that didn't fit with her black near-goth attire of a snug shirt, ripped-hem skirt and clunky combat boots. Though I was standing less than a yard away, she didn't look over as she opened the door, stepped out into the relatively quiet hallway, and sealed their goodbye with another heated lip-lock.

The guy broke things off with a rough laugh and a few murmured words that got Karen laughing, as well. Then he took off toward the casino's front entrance.

"Hey, woman, what's going on?" I piped in, sans the feigned Southern drawl, when she leaned back against the café door and sighed like a love-struck puppy.

I'll admit the guy had a nice set of buns from what I could tell through his jeans. But c'mon!

Karen turned to look at me. Surprise passed through her hazel eyes ringed with a generous helping of kohl, but she played it off like she'd known I was there all along. "Hi to you. I haven't seen you around in—what—a couple weeks?"

"Almost," I said as she opened the door and I followed her back inside the café. "I decided to finally put my training to use again and got hired on at the firehouse across town."

"Now, there's a tough job. Being surrounded by hot, sweaty men with hard muscles and wet hoses." Karen laughed and then quickly sobered. "Seriously, that's great. I'm proud of you. Aren't you a little intimidated by the fires, though?"

Intimidated, no. Intoxicated, yes. Fire fueled me almost as effectively as feeding off blood and sex. "You just have to respect them."

"Mmm…whatever. I still couldn't do it." She slid behind a midtorso-level counter with a built-in glass display case. "Hungry?"

Technically, I never got hungry. Not for food, anyway. But I could eat and I enjoyed the taste of good food the same as a mortal would. Karen's offerings were always top-notch. "Sure." I sank down on one of three backless black bar stools in front of the counter. "Whatever you have on hand."

She bent a little and reached somewhere out of range of the display case's glass. Straightening, she lifted a plate sporting a huge chunk of chocolate cake laced with gooey caramel. My stomach gave an obnoxiously excited rumble as she set the plate in front of me.

Caramel and I were friends from way back.

Practically salivating, I grabbed a plastic spork from a glass jar on the counter and sporked a huge, gooey bite into my mouth. Ooh, yeah… The only way it would be better was served on Ryan's rock-hard abs.

I took another bite, murmuring my elated gratitude before I cut to the chase. "So who's the guy?"

Karen's moony expression returned. "An old boyfriend. He moved back to Vegas a few weeks ago. I ran into him at a club the Saturday before last, and things clicked just like old times. Only, this time they're a lot more serious."

"Like multiple, mutual orgasms serious?"

Her gaze traveled to her left hand and her lips curved in a beaming grin. "Like rings and vows and, maybe, one day kids serious."

My belly flip-flopped at the sight of the rock on her ring finger. Holy Hell, the situation was far worse than I thought.

As much as I liked the woman Karen was on her own, I'd vowed to never use my powers on her aside from in a minor way, like getting her apparent fiancé out the café door. Seeing the ring on her finger, I began to doubt that vow. It was possible the guy would turn out to be worthy, but it was a lot more possible that he wouldn't.

I stabbed the chocolate-covered tines of my spork in the air a few inches from her face. "Last month you swore you never wanted that stuff."

"Yeah, and so did you, but the second I mentioned it, your eyes lit up."

What?

Was Mr. Rings and Vows and Maybe Kids an incubus in disguise, warping her mind?

Karen had to be warped to suggest I wanted a husband. Now, kids… Since being placed in charge of the lesser succubi's education, some latent part of me had been warming to the idea of offspring. I'd suggested to Ryan that I couldn't get pregnant. But I *could* get pregnant, with the right desire and the right sperm.

Snorting over the absurdity of Karen's suggestion, I stuffed another bite of cake into my mouth. Obviously, the caramel was of the highest quality. Even when I was feeling irritated, its succulent taste took a tight third to blood and semen.

"A trick of the light," I assured her after I finished chewing. "I don't do serious relationships. I definitely don't do husbands."

She studied my face, looking unconvinced, and then shrugged and turned to her register. "I'll be ready to head out in ten minutes. Brian's got plans with the guys. Want to take in a club with me?"

Going clubbing with her had been my point in coming here. But now I wasn't in the mood for a girl's night out with a moony mortal. I needed the kind of place where I could let my wings out and relax. The type of laid-back yet feel-good atmosphere guaranteed to be found at Darkness—the club across the street from the Liege. Unless a supernatural being deemed it otherwise, Darkness was visible only by nonhuman eyes. In other words, Karen and most every other moony mortal weren't allowed.

I took another bite of cake, and then pushed the plate to her side of the counter. "Thanks, but I think I'll call it an early night."

Concern entered her eyes. "Work catching up with you?"

Damn, she would have to break out the sympathy. It almost made me want to disregard the love-struck vibes coming off her to accept the clubbing invitation. Almost. "Something like that. But don't sweat it. Once I get into my stride, I'll be fine."

Ryan

I *could* handle Deitre, I reminded myself as I pulled into the garage of the two-story rental house. Our first week together had been a little taxing on my system—even with my most sexual of lovers I'd never screwed so much. But the last couple days I'd been adjusting to her strenuous expectations and those she had me expecting of myself.

I'd also come to appreciate how well she erased my negative thoughts.

Yeah, the occasional nasty shit still entered my mind, but all in all, I was feeling good. Feeling like I could keep up with any guy from her past. Feeling overly aroused from not having seen her for almost thirty hours now.

One of the guys had come down with the flu, so I'd had to pick up an extra twelve-hour shift. I'd gotten the call while out at Jack and Carinna's place for our bimonthly poker night and had headed straight to the firehouse. Though I'd had the nearly unstoppable urge to speed home as soon as my shift let out at ten this morning, I didn't want to scare Deitre off by making it seem I couldn't handle being without her.

Christ, it was scary enough for me to think that.

Of course, it wasn't that I couldn't handle being without her. I could. But why bother when coming home meant spending the morning making up for all the sex we'd missed out on in the last thirty hours?

Grabbing two small, brown bags of goodies I'd picked up for her while killing time after work, I got out of my Jeep and headed for the door that led from the garage to the kitchen. The door opened when I was a foot away. I expected

Deitre to be standing there, waiting to jerk me inside with a blood-boiling kiss and grope. But she wasn't in sight.

Hoping to hell she was somewhere inside, for how anxious I was to see her, I moved through the door. Aside from the dim light filtering in from the garage, the kitchen was mostly dark.

"Welcome home, bad boy." Her sultry twang came from the direction of the living room.

My eyes adjusted to the blackness as I moved through the kitchen to find her standing a few feet from the stairs. A halo of fiery light sliced up from somewhere behind her. The halo shape mocked her demonic horns and tail while the light illuminated the tauntress's smile curving her shiny red lips and the glimmering red leather that made up her miniscule, skintight she-devil costume.

My heart and cock throbbed in tandem as I slid my gaze along her body.

Nipple holes had been cut out of the low-riding dress's top and thin black rope crisscrossed over her belly. The dress's hem had to damn near skim her pussy. Red fishnet stockings dipped down to four-inch-heeled black-and-red lace-up spikes, and would keep her crotch from being completely nude. Somehow the knowledge her sex wasn't completely bare had my dick pulsing even harder.

Feeling like I was hovering a couple inches off the floor for the magnitude of pent-up lust rocketing through my system, I went to Deitre. Dropping the goody bags, I tugged her bodacious bod against my own. She purred out a sexy little growl, and I crashed my mouth over hers like a starving man.

She tasted like heaven and hell all in one. Too damned good just like she was too damned perfect. Almost perfect.

She still had that whole need to control me thing going on, letting me have the ropes just long enough to pacify me.

Tonight, that was going to change. Tonight, I showed her who the man was in this relationship.

Coming up for air, I fondled her velvety tail. "All this is for me?"

She tossed back her head, slapping the weight of her lustrous hair against the air while she moaned like she could feel my fingers' stroke and was majorly getting off on it.

Freeing her tail, I cupped her backside. And what a delectable treat that was. Like her nipples, the leather over the curves of her butt had been cut away, and smooth, muscular ass filled my palms.

Circling her groin against my erection, she brought her head back up and smiled knowingly into my eyes. "Like it, do you? I saw it while I was visiting a friend at the Liege and thought of you."

So I was sticking in her head during our time apart, too. I could take a small measure of comfort in that. Maybe.

Damn, but this thing we were doing felt like it was getting complicated.

If one of us could leave after the sex ended it might not seem like more than the physical was happening. But we never went further than our respective bedrooms, and even then Deitre spent the night invading my dreams.

Focusing on the present—and she *did* look like a present gifted straight from the gods—I said, "Carinna, my brother's fiancée, used to work at the Liege. I visited her plenty and I don't recall ever seeing anything like this for sale."

She glanced down at her nipples, stabbing erect through their holes and gleaming in the fiery halo light like they were coated with some kind of gel. "You just weren't looking in the right places."

My mind painted the gel as cum from some earlier masturbation exploration, and my balls snugged tight.

Glancing at the floor had the forgotten goody bags coming into view. I picked up one at random and held it out to her. "I got you something while I was out, too."

She took the bag, unwrapped its neck, and pushed her hand inside. Licking her lips excitedly, she pulled out a container of lube and a silver-sparkled butt plug. Her eyes—ice-blue even now when rapturous anticipation claimed them—swept up to mine. "Can I use it on you?"

My sphincter muscles tightened with the enthusiasm in her question. Maybe I couldn't handle Deitre, after all.

Feeling like my ego was about to shrivel up and die, I stepped back from the temptation of her barely clothed body to confess, "I should've told you from the start, but I'm not up to the level of the guys you've obviously been with in the past. Maybe a year ago, I would have been. But my life has changed since then. I need some downtime now and again." I eyed the anal toy and winced. "And probably not a butt plug stuck in my ass during the up time."

Smiling wide and wanton, she stroked the shaft of the plug. "So that's not a no?"

"Not a definite no." Her smile grew, and I realized what I'd said while my logic was clouded with her sexy stroking. "Also, not a probable yes."

"What happened?"

With effort, I yanked my gaze from her finger play. "When?"

"A year ago. Why the changes?"

The anxious beat of my heart went from that of arousal to that of unease. I hadn't told anyone the answer to her question. Not even the department shrink we were required to see once a year to ensure dealing with casualties on the job wasn't affecting our mental health. For whatever reason, and despite my unease, I wanted to tell Deitre.

Guessing that lust was continuing to cloud my judgment and responsible for that want, I offered a partial response. "I did my job. Part of me knows that. Part of me is convinced that I screwed up."

Deitre

The way this week was going I would soon be adding myself to the list of demons who loathed all mortals.

First, Karen had to go and get all moony. Now, Ryan was acting like he actually felt remorse over Jada's death. His body was aroused to the point his thoughts were once again clear to me, and there was no doubt that it was her death he was referencing.

I was fully aware of his thoughts, but he was managing to hold back his emotions. That withdrawal made it likely that his behavior was nothing more than another attempt to keep me around by acting like he had a sensitive side. Even so, I couldn't convince myself to lead him into the kitchen and feed him the drugged stew I'd made for dinner. Normally, I would never rely on mortal pills to help drain my victims. But, like his ability to keep his emotions from me, Ryan had started to resist the full effect of my feedings. I still left him tired, just not nearly as much as he should be.

Sniffing, he glanced into the kitchen. "Something smells incredible. Did you cook?"

"Yes." I feigned a pout. "But we're not eating it. I tried a new recipe and it didn't turn out."

"No need to pout, devil girl, I've got a present number two." He squatted to grab another small brown bag from the carpet.

Ignoring how much I liked his incredibly accurate endearment and, more, his desire to see me happy, I took the bag from him and unrolled the top. And, ooh, yeah, he got me happy with that gift.

My pussy tingled as I pulled out a bottle of edible caramel body sauce. "Can you read my mind, or how did you know what a sucker I am for caramel?"

"Honestly?" I nodded, and he got a sheepish look complete with a lopsided smile. "You're not the only one with a weakness for caramel. I bought it for you to put on your body so that I can lick it off."

Like I'd noticed from day one, the guy was hotter than Hell. What I hadn't noticed that day was that he was also cute in a boyish sort of way.

A boyish sort of way? What the fuck was *that* about?

It was the kind of thought for a moony mortal, not a she-devil who got off on screwing the life out of her lovers.

Soon, I would screw the life out of Ryan. Tonight, I was just going to forget that cute concept ever entered my head and let him stroke my tail some more.

My sex spasmed with the remembered feel of his callused fingers caressing my tail. Clearly, he believed it part of the costume as I'd intended. But it was part of me that I'd kept secreted before this and my biggest erogenous zone by far.

Or maybe not where he was concerned.

One second I was standing there preparing to seduce him. The next second he had me on my back on the couch, and was pouring the caramel sauce between my spread thighs. The diamond-shaped openings at the crotch of my fishnet stockings added remarkable friction against the slippery glide of the sauce. His fingers, as he bathed my otherwise naked labia with caramel, added a thrill so primal and delicious, it had my pussy burning with need and me considering that my sex might just be my new favorite erogenous zone.

Flattening my palms against his chest through his T-shirt, I prepared to flip him onto his back, strip off his clothes, and cover his rod with sauce. He grabbed my wrists and met my eyes with command in his own. "*I'm* in control tonight, Deitre."

Someone really should've told him the number-one way to piss off a succubus was to order her around sexually. That someone should've probably been me. But like that first day, shudders of expectation pulsed through my groin with the idea of letting him take the lead.

I couldn't hand it off without a bit of a fight, though. Or, at least, a threat. "Fine. Have the lead. But do it right, or I swear you'll pay."

The arrogance he'd lost when admitting that he didn't think he was up to pleasing me as well and as often as my past lovers returned as a cocky grin. "I'll do you right, devil girl. I'll do you so right you can't stop from screaming my name."

There was cocky and then there was annoyingly cocky. Ryan was stepping awfully close to annoying terrain. Since he was cute—and I swear to Lucifer if anyone got wind I believed that I would claw out their tongue—I would let his arrogance go.

For now.

Everything about this situation was temporary. I hadn't forgotten about getting my revenge. And I wouldn't, no matter how hard my hips darted off the couch as he took my bent legs in his rough hands, spread them even farther apart, and slipped his tongue through one of the open diamonds at the crotch of my stockings.

Caramel sauce sluiced up into my sheath with the lash of his tongue. Cool at first, it warmed near instantly. He rocked back on his knees to pour more of the sauce over my sex and then licked that up inside my opening, as well.

Sighing out a shaky breath, I fisted my hands in his overlong black curls as tumultuous pressure shook through my dripping-wet core. My vaginal walls contracted greedily around his eager tongue. It was tempting to let my second self out to play. But I'd given him the lead and so far he was earning it. That being the case, I shared my sight with him, planting a carbon copy of his every move as I saw it into his head.

Ryan's tongue stilled for just a second, and then it returned to its vigorous lapping as his mouth fitted tight to my sex and he fed hungrily from my pussy.

One of his hands left my thighs to move beneath the dress's übershort hem and tease along my crack. The tip of his finger, wet with caramel sauce, dipped past a diamond opening to nudge at my anus. At least, I thought it was his fingertip. I recognized the butt plug's small, rounded head about the time its caramel-lubed shaft eased inside my anal passage one ecstatic wail at a time.

I howled like a werewolf bitch in heat as he worked his tongue and the plug into my juicy openings in tandem. I'd been handled this way before, but there was just something about him that made it seem new and truly un-fucking-believable.

Then it got even better, when he pulled his tongue from my sex to replace it with his cock.

Obviously, he had me seriously gone with lust that I'd missed the point at which he'd unzipped his fly and took out his dick. I got even further gone with lust as the fiery halo of the energy burst I'd conjured up just before I ordered the kitchen door to open, illuminated his face. Deep green eyes unquenched with raw desire bored into mine as he bent his head and took my mouth in an urgently demanding kiss.

The mingled taste of delicious caramel and salty cum sent my senses on a wild ride of seduction. A starburst of sensations whipped through my body. Every filled orifice dripped with tingling, primal need.

I came instantly. Screaming his name, just as he'd vowed I would do.

♣ ♠ ♥ ♦ ♣ ♠ ♥ ♦ ♣ ♠ ♥ ♦

Chapter Four

Ryan

I pulled out of Deitre and collapsed on the floor in front of the couch. It was a damned good thing we didn't need to use condoms—from the first sweet lick of her pussy, I would never have remembered to put one on. I didn't even remember to peel the red leather from her body so I could get my hands on her beautiful tits.

Of course, there would be another chance. Probably in a half hour, knowing her appetite. The butt plug would be carefully hidden by that point in time. I was plenty comfortable with my sexuality, but there was still no way I was letting her stick that thing in my ass.

Silky, red locks slipped over the edge of the couch to stroke against the side of my arm. I jumped with the contact, still too keyed up despite another of those almost spiritual orgasms. I was dragging butt again, too. Not nearly so bad as I had last week, not getting that pukey sensation, but my breathing was coming out as wheezes and I felt like I could do with a twelve-hour siesta.

Deitre popped her head over the side of the couch. I

expected her to be smiling. All right, I feared that she would be smiling. That sexy-as-sin siren's smile that would no doubt have my dick swelling right back to hardness.

She wasn't smiling. She wore a look so serious I pushed to a sitting position despite my body's aching plea to remain on the floor. "What's the matter?"

She swiveled around, until she was sitting on the couch with her megaspiked heels digging into the carpet. "What you said before, about your life changing so much a year ago, I can't forget that."

Hell, she sounded sad. And like a total asshole, I was staring at her nipples peeking out from the holes in the low-cut top of her skimpy red dress.

Cursing the single-mindedness I struggled to shake around her, I met her eyes and focused on her words. My gut clenched as they settled. She wanted to know more about what happened the night of the apartment fire. Part of me still wanted to share the information with her. Another part was scared shitless she would agree, that while I had done my job by the book that night, I'd still fucked up in the long run.

All of me feared that the admission would be enough to make her walk away.

It wasn't just the fear of losing her as a lover, either. Somehow, in less than two weeks, she'd worked her way into my mind as much as my heart. I didn't get that somehow. And I didn't want her in my heart. At least, I shouldn't. Not when I wanted kids and she couldn't get pregnant.

Of course, we could always adopt. And I was putting the cart way in the hell out in front of the horse…

Tucking both cart and horse into the back of my mind, I affected a calm tone. "Why can't you forget it?"

Sorrow entered her eyes. "Because mine changed a year ago, too." She looked down at her lap where she worked her joined fingers anxiously. "My best friend was killed."

I went the asshole route again by breathing a sigh of relief to know that she wasn't talking about my past, but her own.

Regaining a bit of nice-guy ground, I took one of her hands into mine and gave it a supportive squeeze. At least, I'd planned to gain some nice-guy ground with the move. Even that subtle touch had sensual heat arcing in the air between us and the fiery halo of light expanding until the living room was as bright as if the shades were drawn and sunlight flooded the house.

I wanted to question where she'd found whatever was giving off the light—it could make for an invaluable tool while searching smoky and night-blackened fire scenes. But right now, all that mattered was soothing her grief. "I'm sorry to hear that, Deitre. We have to face loss as a part of our job, but it never gets any easier."

She looked up and pinned me with an impassioned glare. "She was killed because of *our* job."

My want to comfort her combusted as an eerie sense of foreboding started a vicious roiling in my gut.

Our pasts couldn't be intertwined. Not the way my suddenly spinning mind was considering. "What happened?" I asked, unable to keep a tremor from my voice.

"Jada was trapped on the top floor of a burning apartment building." Deitre's voice shook twice as badly as mine had, and tears glittered in her eyes. "Supposedly, the fire crew on site did everything they could to get her out—I mean, I *know* they did—but I still can't help but feel like they should have done something more. She was such a good person."

Sniffing, she sent me a wobbly smile. "Actually, I could see the two of you getting along well."

Ironically, so could I. Because Jada and I *had* gotten along well, right up until the day I decided she was getting too clingy and I ended our relationship.

That was about two months before Ladder 19 was called out to her fire-ravaged apartment building and I was left with the choice of saving her, or a stranger down the hall before the roof collapsed. I had no idea if Jada was even still alive. The stranger I was guaranteed was alive because I could hear him screaming for help. The stranger lived. Jada hadn't.

Fuck.

My guts clamped tight and bile rose up in the back of my throat. How could this be happening? How could the woman who was so completely perfect for me that I'd fallen for her without even trying be the best friend of my dead ex-lover?

Yeah, I had a generous supply of ex-lovers and most were from around the Vegas area. Still, it was too coincidental. It had to be a mistake. Some other Jada and some other fire. Because Jada was such a common name and there had been so many massive apartment blazes in the city a year ago.

"Ryan?" Deitre's voice piped through all the nasty shit that had returned to my head as a near-deafening roar. "You okay? You look pale again." She gave a soft laugh. "I swear sex with me really *is* too much for you to handle."

"I'm fine," I snapped back. Fine as goddamned shit.

"Is that why you're trying to break my fingers?"

My gaze cleared and I recognized the death grip I had on her hand. The blood had drained out of her fingers to the point they were stark white.

"Sorry." Feeling like I might crumble from the weight of

guilt riding on my shoulders, I released her hand and came unsteadily to my feet. After tucking my shaft into my briefs and zipping my jeans, I started toward the kitchen with the fervent hope she wouldn't follow. "I need to find some real food. I didn't have a chance to eat lunch."

"I'm the one who's sorry. Talking about my friend has clearly upset you."

"Nah, it hasn't." Seriously, I wasn't upset. I was well past that point.

She gave a quirky laugh. "Because big, tough firefighters aren't bothered by the thought of someone perishing in a fire, right?"

"Not when we've never met the person," I said without turning back or breaking stride. "It's a necessity if you want to stay sane on the job. But then, I don't need to tell you that."

I also didn't need to tell her it was a lie that firefighters weren't bothered by the thought of death by flames. It bothered us so much that we made it a point to never consider it an option until destiny deemed it otherwise.

Destiny. Two weeks ago my only clear one had been mind-blowing sex with Deitre. Tonight, my destiny was figuring out how the hell I could ever own up to the sins of my past while keeping Deitre by my side and in my arms.

Deitre

After the way Ryan had intimated three nights ago that he'd never met Jada, I should have let him eat the poisoned stew. I hadn't. But now, tonight, I was getting a second chance at seeing to his demise and without having to lift a finger.

A mortal wouldn't be able to make out the face of the

fallen firefighter past the shroud of heavy black smoke and the high-licking orange-blue flames that filled the basement of the processing plant.

I wasn't a mortal. I also, clearly, wasn't in my right mind for considering saving him from a perfectly agonizing death.

A massive wooden support beam had snapped without warning, knocking him off balance and onto the oxygen tank secured to his back. The lower half of the beam came to rest against his upper thigh. Between the weight of the tank and the beam, he was immobile from the waist down.

Essentially impotent.

It would be easy to leave him there. Let the fire reach him in another couple minutes, and watch as it slowly devoured his turnout gear and facepiece, and then went to work on burning away at his skin and muscles. The beam didn't just trap Ryan in place. The top half butted up against the door we'd entered the basement through moments before, blocking the rest of the crew from coming inside.

He was such an easy target. The revenge couldn't be any more exact.

Deitre!

He didn't attempt to shout my name and break the seal on his respirator. But even without his body being aroused, I could hear my name screaming in his mind. See the plea for help in his fear-filled eyes past the glass of his smoke-filmed facepiece.

Sorry, bad boy. Not gonna happen today.

Ah, hell, I already knew better. It *was* going to happen.

Just like three nights ago, my heart was slamming with the thought of not having him around to toy with a little longer and my sex fluttering its loss because, by mortal standards, he was an incredible lover. And my mind, my freaking mind couldn't stop from thinking what a shame it would be to burn off that endearingly lopsided smile he got whenever he was feeling out of sorts.

Hoping to Hell, literally, that my father wasn't watching over me, I hurried across to Ryan. I knew fear was flooding my eyes to match his own, and I also knew that my concern was only partly pretense.

With my eyes, I questioned his condition. In answer, he wrapped his left arm around the side of the beam and attempted to push it out of his way.

I almost laughed at that. I mean, what an arrogant bastard to think he stood any chance of moving the thing on his own. We also had no chance of moving it together without me employing my supernatural strength. That he'd tried to move it on his own suggested he had no idea how much weight he was up against, so I circled my arms around the beam from the other side and acted like we were about to make an amazing team.

I waved my right hand to signal his attention and then stuck up three fingers. At his nod, I bent them one at a time. My third finger folded over, and his features contorted behind his facepiece as he pushed for all he was worth. Popping a little sweat out on my brow for effect, I gave a gentle tug and then stepped aside as the wooden beam went crashing down in the opposite direction.

The beam was out of the way of the door now, as well. The odds were favorable more of the team would be filing into the nearly fire-engulfed basement in search of us in about ten seconds. If I had any chance of fixing whatever damage the beam had done to Ryan's leg before they arrived, I had to work fast.

Dropping down on my knees, I yanked off my gloves and palmed his right thigh through his yellow rubber trousers. With adrenaline cruising through his system, he wouldn't be able to feel the extent of his injuries. I could feel his crushed femur as acutely as if it was my own. Healing wasn't a gift I'd ever owned up to possessing—succubi were meant to harm, not fix. It also wasn't a gift I'd used before today, at least not on anyone other than my favorite familiar, my cat Tinder, who I'd planned to move into the rental house this coming weekend.

Praying the gift—holy fuck, I wasn't just thinking the guy was cute, I was actually praying for his pathetic ass—would be strong enough to heal him, I closed my eyes and focused my energy into my fingertips.

Heat so intense it singed my fingers shot down my arm and momentarily turned the leg of his trousers neon orange. Both the heat and the color disappeared then, and I felt like they took every ounce of my strength with them.

The turnout gear and oxygen tank had always seemed light as a feather. Now, they seemed to weigh a ton, or probably, rather, what they really did weigh to the rest of the team. I swayed against Ryan. My helmet rammed into his midsection as I shot my palms to his thighs and just stopped my face from planting in his crotch.

On second thought, that sounded like an excellent place to be. Snuggled up tight against his solid shaft, lips wrapped around the bloodred corona, and pulling back his delicious seed.

I closed my eyes on a comforted sigh. Just a few sips from his cock and I would be as good as new.

Ryan

I hadn't saved Jada. I also hadn't loved Jada. Whenever it happened, I'd fallen fast and hard for Deitre, and I was saving her even if it meant dying in the process.

Huffing with the exertion, when I already felt wiped out and too aware of the flames snapping barely a yard away, I pushed to a sitting position and eased her onto her side on the floor. Behind her facepiece, her eyes were closed and she looked serene in unconsciousness. Vowing to see her serene again for real, I held on to the front straps of my oxygen tank's carrying frame and came to my feet.

I expected my freshly freed leg to buckle, or at least for pain to rip through it. The support beam obviously hadn't weighed as much as I thought, though, because my leg stayed locked and felt fine.

The rest of me didn't feel fine.

My pulse was speeding and my mind circling with the wonder of how we were going to get out of this damned basement alive.

The football-field-size plant's twin furnace and boiler systems were less than twenty feet away and primed to explode and unleash all hell. We should never have come down here, but a worker who'd escaped upon hearing the explosion that started the blaze swore someone was trapped in one of the four refrigeration rooms that snaked off from the basement's central area. We hadn't made it as far as the heavy wooden doors of the refrigeration rooms. If someone was in one, it was already too late to help.

"Ryan?" The unexpected sound of Deitre's voice came thick and raspy from her prone position on the floor.

My heart skipped a beat with my gratitude to hear her talking. Living. Then I realized she had to have broken the seal on her respirator to be speaking so clearly. Which meant she was even now sucking in toxic fumes.

Son of a bitch.

My heart beating harder, I squatted beside her, intending to hoist her into my arms and perform an escape trick worthy of the world's finest and fastest magician. Through her facepiece, her gaze locked on mine. Her eyes held something I'd never before seen in them. There was affection but, more, there was the kind of trust that went beyond what one firefighter felt for another.

With the breath staggering in my throat, I stroked the glass over her cheek. *I'm here, baby. I'm going to get us to safety.*

"We're already there," she murmured back.

She'd spoken quietly enough that it was possible I'd heard her wrong. It was just as possible that she was hallucinating. Worry sailing through me and eating at my gut, I slipped my arms under her legs, tucked her against my side, and stood. And then I toppled right back to the floor, dropping her flat on her back from five feet up, as something crashed into the side of my helmet with the force of a semi.

I caught Deitre's smile, still so trusting despite the fact that I could have broken her in half by dropping her onto her tank. Then my eyes shuttered closed and my mind was consumed with nothing but thoughts of her hot body, naked of the tank, turnout gear and everything else, as she rode me to another of those truly divine orgasms.

♣ ♠ ♥ ♦ ♣ ♠ ♥ ♦ ♣ ♠ ♥ ♦

Chapter Five

Deitre

It shamed me to realize I'd passed out for a few seconds. It shamed me more to acknowledge how ridiculously soft and moony Ryan had me feeling. I should have left him to die. But I hadn't at the first opportunity and I couldn't at the second. I also couldn't erase the whole fire scene without my father finding out and raising hell when he discovered the reason behind my actions.

Since none of the other crew members had arrived to assist us, the only viable course of action was employing my second self to knock Ryan out while I fed him seductively sweet and dirty dreams.

Tucking my second self inside my mind, I removed my face-piece and oxygen tank and then called out my wings. I could walk through the inferno sizzling and popping all around us without a problem. He wasn't liable to make it unscathed.

Scooping Ryan into my arms, turnout gear, tank and all, I soared to the ceiling and surveyed for potential exits. The door wasn't blocked by the support beam any longer, but the fire was eating its way through the entry. Small windows lined the top of the basement walls, letting in shafts of oncoming twilight.

The windows were too small to fit his body through.

Shit. I didn't want to teleport. Mortals had a way of not making the transition so well. It affected their minds, which was one part I knew I couldn't heal. But then, the side effect of a little lunacy was better than the death I should have let him succumb to.

Holding him close against my body, I retracted my wings and teleported us to the processing plant's semidark parking lot. We reemerged behind the camouflage of a ladder truck. I laid Ryan down on his side on the blacktop, and then tugged off my helmet, and ran around the truck to shout for a paramedic from one of the waiting ambulances.

A woman in white-and-blue EMT gear raced over and jogged with me around to the backside of the truck. Together, we removed his oxygen tank and then carefully rolled him onto his back.

"He got hit by flying metal," I said in a shaky voice as she eased off his facepiece and checked his vitals.

I wanted the tremor in my voice to be feigned. But Ryan's face was sickeningly pale, and I was seriously afraid for the harm I might have caused him. Shivers ignited deep in my belly and swept through me as a tidal wave of terror. I could feel my entire body attempting to slip into shock.

Like some common freaking mortal.

Damn, but he'd gotten to me these past weeks. By making me feel like more than a demon. By treating me like both a sexy woman, inside and out, and a colleague whose hands he'd place his life into without a second thought. By making me go almost as moony over him as he so obviously was over me.

"I have to check on the rest of the crew," I offered the medic. Like a complete chicken shit, I didn't even look back at Ryan's face, but rounded the ladder truck and hurried over to the first of a trio of water trucks.

"What can I do?" I shouted to Landen Vernelli, a beefy blond guy in his midtwenties. His reputation as a playboy was well noted, and I might have found him appealing in that way if he hadn't made it clear he thought I belonged back at the firehouse, answering phones.

He turned to glare at me. "Where the hell did you guys go?"

"We had to get out a back way. Ryan was knocked unconscious on the way out."

Surprise entered Vernelli's eyes. "You carried him all the way around from the back of the building?"

"You got a problem with that?" I snapped.

"Not at all. I'm impressed."

Though I shouldn't have cared, I basked in the glory of his approval for a few seconds. Then the enormity of the harm I might have caused Ryan came slamming back. "Don't be. I have no idea how he's going to be when he wakes up."

If he woke up.

Ryan

Deitre entered my hospital room, and I shut off the wall-mounted TV to grin at her from my semisitting position in the narrow bed. When Vernelli stopped in this morning, he'd mentioned that she planned to come over as soon as her shift ended. I'd spent the fifteen hours since being carted via ambulance to Sunrise Hospital & Medical Center last night, convincing the staff, as well as a number of my coworkers, that I was fine, and all I wanted was to see my devil girl.

Right now, she wasn't looking like a devil girl, though.

Standing just inside the door, she wore faded jeans and a loose-fitting, white pocket T-shirt. A navy blue, unadorned ball cap covered her head, and a waist-length red ponytail stuck through the ring at the hat's back.

Nah, right now, she was looking even better than a devil girl.

She looked like someone I could take home to meet my family. Someone I could understand why I loved for more than the sex. Someone I could settle down and adopt a couple of kids with.

Presuming she stuck around after I owned up to my past with Jada.

I'd let sharing the information slide the last few days, while I silently battled the mind-swamping guilt made better only when Deitre had her hands or mouth on me, or spent the night infiltrating my dreams, the way she'd done again when I'd been knocked unconscious last night. But I couldn't continue to let it slide. I had to tell her the truth. I would do it as soon as I gave her a more complete look at the man beyond the cocky grin and turnout gear.

"Thinking about making a break for it while you still can?" I teased when she continued to stand a few inches from the doorway.

She gave a weak smile. "Just making sure that you look okay."

I glanced down at my half-dressed body. Not buying my confirmation over the phone that I was fine, Jack had dropped by last night. Since I hadn't been so sure I would be fine back in the basement of the processing plant, I'd been damned glad to see him. Almost as glad to see the sweat-pants he'd brought me so I didn't have to lie around in a hospital gown with my naked ass hanging out.

Of course, Deitre would have enjoyed the view. Or maybe not.

For only the second time, outside of while we were on the clock and she generally behaved, I wasn't getting the vibe that she wanted to do me.

Her gaze returned to mine, and I asked in a light tone. "Did I pass inspection?"

"You look good."

"I feel good. I'd feel even better if you closed the door and came and lay down with me." Recognizing how that sounded, I clarified, "Not for sex."

Like the word *sex* was her cue, a devilishly wicked sparkle moved into her ice-blue eyes. Her smile peaked into a sultry one. "You really think I can handle lying beside you without wanting you?"

Five seconds ago, yes. Now, as she closed the door and then started toward me, not in the least.

With every step she took, the room temperature seemed to notch up another ten degrees. My breathing sure as hell picked up by a good ten anxious inhales. She slid onto the bed beside me, and I jerked at the brush of her hip against mine. Two layers of cotton separated our skin, yet my cock roused to instant hardness; an obvious fact since I hadn't worn underwear beneath my sweats.

Running her hand along my thigh, she eyed the bulge of my groin. Her tongue slipped out, dabbing at her lush lower lip, not quite that deep shade of cherry-red today and still way too tempting.

Yeah, I could see where this was about to go. The thing was, I wanted it to go there. I wanted her with such an instant and intense desire that it had perspiration popping out on my face and chest. I also wanted to get some conversation in before we had life-confirming sex.

Lifting Deitre's hand from my thigh, I curled her fingers in my own. "I hear congratulations are in order."

She turned her attention from my crotch to my face. "For what?"

"Winning over Vernelli."

"Whatever. I was just doing my job."

"Were you?" Despite a good deal of what happened in that basement last night being patchy, I could remember the gut-level fear in her eyes when I'd become trapped under the support beam and then later that breathtaking trust. I practically ached to believe those emotions meant that she was feeling more for me than lust.

Deitre frowned. "What do you mean?"

"Saving me didn't mean anything more to you than rescuing a victim while on the job?"

Her frown deepened. "What was it supposed to mean?"

I wanted a straight-up answer, but not at the cost of killing the moment and the weekend plans I'd yet to share with her. Reverting to the teasing tone, I supplied, "Thought maybe you were afraid of losing me before you had a chance to track down the butt plug and stuff it up my ass."

Her frown evaporated on a debauched laugh. "You really would enjoy it if you gave it a chance."

"I'll take your word for it." Fisting the end of her thick,

silky ponytail, I pulled her flush against me, torso to torso, face-to-face. "And enjoy these killer lips for a while."

Her mouth opened on a throaty sigh. I slipped my tongue inside and caressed her moist inner cheeks and gums. Over her teeth. Against her own tongue. She responded, but not in her typically fierce style. Rather, soft and slow and easy, and with just a little wiggle of her mound against my erection.

She was giving me the lead without my having to ask for it. That alone told me I was coming to mean something to her. Instead of ravishing her, the way my throbbing cock would have liked, I broke the kiss to send her a smug smile. "You know, *I* would have saved *you* if you just left me alone long enough to regain consciousness."

"Of course you would have. Right after you walked on water."

We shared a laugh that felt almost as good and not nearly as draining as sex with her had a habitual way of being. Before Deitre stopped laughing, I said, "Jack stopped by last night. He invited us out to the B and B for dinner on Sunday."

Her laughter died short. "You're going to be out of here by then?"

I breathed a sigh at her tone. Not wariness to think I wanted her meeting my brother and his fiancée, but relief to know I really was going to be all right. "They're discharging me after lunch."

"So it didn't have any adverse effects?"

"Nah, the metal didn't even dent my helmet. Mostly they kept me overnight for observation and to check for smoke inhalation." I gave her a reprimanding look as the memory of the panic I'd known for her returned to quicken my pulse. "They should have held you, too, for that stunt you pulled."

"What stunt?"

"Breaking the seal on your respirator. Those fumes could have killed you."

"I didn't break the seal on my respirator. You must have been hallucinating." Concern came into her eyes. "Are you sure you're okay?"

Like I said, last night was patchy. Maybe I'd only imagined Deitre's voice, though I swear I heard her talking. Since it wasn't important enough to argue about, I took her face in my hands and her lips in another blood-sizzling kiss.

This time she met me lick for hungry lick, slide for needy slide. Her sex rubbed against my cock and her warm, soft palms worked their way up the sides of my bare torso. I had no idea how she kept her hands so soft, considering the demands of our job. I just knew I liked her touch a hell of a lot as she slipped her hands between us and circled the tips of her fingers around my nipples.

She took my nipples between her thumbs and forefingers and pinched the small, hard discs. White-hot electric sensation pulsed in my nipples and darted to my groin.

I pulled from her mouth on a hiss. "Oh, yeah, I'm *way* okay." She let out another laugh, this one low and rich with lust, and I pressed, "So are you free on Sunday?"

The amusement left her face again. She wasn't exactly frowning, but I could feel her body go tense against mine. Placing a hand on the bed on either side of my head, she rocked back on her bent legs. "Actually, I'm not. I have plans with a girlfriend. The one who works at the Liege."

"She could come along."

A hint of an impish smile played at her lips. "Hoping for a threesome?"

I was hoping to see her interact with two of the people I was closest with and have the three of them get along as well as Deitre and I did. So as not to look too eager, I again kept it light. "If she's as demanding as you are, that *would* be the death of me. I don't want your girlfriend. I would like for you to meet Jack and Carinna. You know how it is, with family worrying about the people you hang out with."

"Not really. My father isn't around often, and I've never much known my mother. I have sisters, but they're mostly off doing their own thing, too."

I countered the loss of her smile with a knowing one of my own. "In that case, you definitely need to come along. The four of us can be one, big, happy family."

"I actually *prefer* not seeing my family."

"Okay, then, you don't have to pretend like my family is yours. They can just be your new friends."

She frowned. "I'm telling you, Ryan, I don't do families. Not mine or anyone's."

"And I'm telling you I'll make it worth your while." Taking my smile from knowing to wolfishly naughty, I slipped a hand between her spread thighs and petted her mound through her jeans. "C'mon, now, what's it gonna take? A little pussy worship?"

Interest flared in her eyes with the rising of her eyebrows. "Right here on your hospital bed?"

"If it gets you to agree."

A few silent seconds passed. Then a wickedly carnal grin curved Deitre's lips. She moved off the bed, brought the jeans and underwear down to midthigh with a single, graceful push, and then climbed back onto the bed and lay down on the cramped space beside me. "Start worshipping and I'll think about it."

Even if the stakes weren't so high, I would have risked being caught for the sake of getting my tongue buried inside her pussy. Like every orgasm I shared with her, the taste of her cum was pure heady indulgence. Better than caramel. Better than most anything I could think of save for the tantalizing taste of her mouth.

Going up on my knees, with my stiff cock doing a flagpole number at the front of my sweats, I worked the jeans and underwear down her legs the rest of the way. After depositing her clothes on the tile, I centered her on the bed. She spread her legs, affording me a breath-hitching view of her sex. Her pussy was freshly shaven. The tender skin, past the gently parted lips of her labia was a glistening, slick pink. The scent of her arousal perfuming the air with a sweet and sexy musk was too inviting to keep from tasting a second longer.

"Hey there, gorgeous," I coaxed her cunt with a smug, rough voice as I slipped my hands beneath her and cupped the silky, smooth skin of her butt. "Looks like you're in need of a tongue fuck."

To the sound of Deitre's laughter, I lifted her ass off the bed an inch, tipped her hips and fitted my mouth to her succulent sex. Her amusement faded to a throaty gasp as I impaled her pussy with my tongue.

I groaned back, struck once again at her tightness. Either she was a master of Kegel exercises, or she had to use some kind of tightening herb or gel.

Whatever the case, the powerful clenching of her sheath as I corkscrewed my tongue up inside her moist inner walls had my balls snug and my dick quivering its need for release.

Writhing on the bed, she grabbed hold of my head and ground her mound hard up against my face. Greedily, her sex sucked my tongue even deeper inside her as she panted out, "Throw in the butt plug."

I pulled my tongue free of her sheath to lift my head a few inches. Her lips were swollen and back to that shimmering, lush cherry-red. Her eyes half-masked and shiny, cool blue marked with the sizzling heat of ecstasy.

Gorgeous, yeah. Out of her mind, yeah, that, too. "You're crazy."

With a primal grin, she jerked the ball cap from her head. She sent it sailing across the hospital room and her luscious, long red hair feathered all around her body. Her grin grew even wilder then, as she pushed the hem of her T-shirt up to expose her big, gorgeous and awesomely bare tits. Another mystery—how she managed to keep the erect state of her nipples hidden when she never wore a bra. A mystery I could have given two shits less about right then.

Deitre took the heavy mounds in her hands and fondled the rosy flesh. "Throw in the butt plug, or it's a no. To dinner on Sunday and sex with me tonight."

"Ah, fuck." It was almost illogical the limits I was willing to go to for her. But I was clearly willing to go just about any damned where and try any damned thing if it meant we had a chance of ending up together. "Fine." My sphincter muscles squeezed. "On two conditions. It happens after we do dinner on Sunday…and I get to control the lube."

Deitre

With the way Carinna insisted I help her grab beer from the B and B's extensive kitchen while Jack dealt the cards for the next round of pinochle and Ryan, apparently, assisted by keeping the private dining-room table occupied, I could guess a grilling was in store. That might be okay. She had the tall, stacked build of a succubus to complement her Latina coloring and the sort of no-bullshit attitude that I'd always respected. Jack maintained an arrogant charm similar to Ryan's while making it clear he had eyes only for Carinna. Despite my qualms about coming here, I'd been relaxed and enjoying myself from nearly the second we walked through the B and B door.

"How long have you and Ry been an item?" Carinna tossed over her shoulder. Bypassing a ceramic-tiled island, she went to a double-wide, stainless-steel refrigerator and pulled open the right-side door.

"A few weeks. He seems great." Frowning at my automatic and irritatingly adoring-sounding reply, I came to a stop behind the fridge door.

Ryan *was* charming. He made it seem like he cared about me until I had moments where I was convinced that he really did. But he'd made Jada feel the same. She'd been head over heels for him when he dumped her cold. He'd cared about her so little he'd allowed her to die in order to save some guy he'd never even met. Given the opportunity, the odds were favorable he would let me die as easily as he had Jada.

Except, he hadn't let me die in the basement of the processing plant.

He'd silently vowed to save me and had been attempting to do just that before I knocked him unconscious.

Carinna reached around the side of the refrigerator door, two longnecks of Bud dangling from her fingertips. "He used to be a cocky little shit. But yeah, he's really come around."

My relaxed feeling a thing of the past, I accepted the beer. I hadn't been able to see her face when she'd spoken, or now, as she reached back into the fridge for another set of beers, but the honest affection in her voice knotted my belly with guilt. It wasn't a sensation I knew a lot about, and it also wasn't one that I planned to hold on to.

Moving back to the island, I set Ryan's beer down, and uncapped my own. "Have you known him long?"

The affection was evident in Carinna's nearly smoke-gray eyes now, as well, as she joined me at the island. Smiling, she repeated my move, setting down one beer and uncapping the other. "Pretty much his whole life. The three of us grew up together."

I pulled back a long, cold drink as the information settled. Just because she knew him, didn't have to mean she really *knew* him. After all, she hadn't seemed to know how long Ryan and I had been screwing. "Any notable skeletons?"

"Since you work at the firehouse, you must know that he has a reputation for getting around." I nodded, and she continued, "He can also be pretty narrow-minded, though he hasn't acted that way in months." A thoughtful frown formed on her lips. "Actually, he hasn't mentioned sleeping with anyone in months, either. Maybe it's just because Jack and I are together and we don't share our sex stories with him for obvious reasons, but we used to hash on the details of our love lives as part of our Wednesday-night poker routine."

So he'd broadened his horizons and potentially quit sleeping around. Damn, so much for skeletons, not to mention obliterating my guilt.

"Has he changed in any other way?" I pressed, all but hanging on the hope of a negative find.

Carinna took a pull from her beer as she considered the question. She set the bottle back on the island. "He is more affectionate with Jack. They've always been close, with their dad dying young and Jack basically being a surrogate dad for Ryan, but you know how guys can be about their fear of getting too touchy-feely with other guys?"

Not to mention their fear of butt plugs.

I nodded. "I do."

A conspiratorial smile returned to her lips. My guilt finally ebbed, and I gave in to my own smile over thoughts of the night that lay ahead.

As soon as we got home, I was seeing that Ryan made good on his promise from the hospital. If only because it meant showing him the best of pleasure tonight before I doled out the worst of pain someday in the near future, he was going to experience a G-spot orgasm like nothing but a butt plug and a woman who knew how to use it on her man could deliver.

"Well, Ry seems to have gotten over his fears," Carinna continued. "He'll actually hug Jack goodbye when he takes off now, or if they talk on the phone, he'll say that he loves him before he hangs up."

My smile had quavered a bit with the thought of Ryan as my man. It quavered a bit more as Carinna's words sank in and my guilt once again flowed freely. I could see him acting a fraud to a woman he hoped to fuck, or keep fucking. But he had no reason to act that way around his brother.

Did he truly feel remorse over what had happened with Jada and was shaping himself into a nicer guy for it? And, if so, did his regret haunt him enough that I should let him off the hook?

Wanting my mind off thoughts of Ryan and my mood back to relaxed, I took in the expansive kitchen done in all-natural hardwoods and trimmed with a deep shade of green that would be a perfect complement for Ryan's eyes. "This place is gorgeous."

Carinna beamed with pride. "It's a work in progress, but it is coming along a little more every day."

Apparently, getting my mind off Ryan was also a work in progress, that checking out something as routine as kitchen trim could make me think of him. Whatever my plans for the guy, I had to get them figured out pronto and my mushy, moony ass back to Hell.

♣ ♠ ♥ ♦ ♣ ♠ ♥ ♦ ♣ ♠ ♥ ♦

Chapter Six

Ryan

"Ready to suffer?" Deitre asked the instant we cleared the garage door and stepped into the kitchen.

Today with Jack and Carinna couldn't have gone better. For all her claims that she didn't do families, Deitre had meshed with mine from word one. She'd admitted to what a great time she had when I pulled out of the B and B, and both my brother and Carinna commented on how much they liked her while she was out of the room. Somehow, I'd managed to keep from commenting on how much I loved her, in return.

I let those three words become a mantra in my head now, as my anus clenched its anxiety. Not bothering to hide my grimace, I turned around midway through the kitchen. "Could you make my ass pucker a little harder?"

Amusement gleamed in her eyes with her laughter. She stopped laughing then to cross the few feet to me. Pressing her bountiful breasts against my chest, she wrapped her arms around my neck and met my lips with a soft, sweet openmouthed kiss.

A tender smile curved her lips as she eased her head back a couple inches. "Sorry. I couldn't resist. Seriously, though, if you can trust me enough to relax and do as I say, you're going to love it."

If I didn't trust Deitre, I would never have agreed to be in this position in the first place. And if I didn't love her already, I would have fallen for her the second that tender smile emerged. Her kiss had been just as gentle. Both seemed packed with affection.

I let that thought warm me as I accepted my fate. "Where do you want me?"

Approval flashing over her face, she unroped her arms from my neck. "Get naked and lay on the couch. I'll be in to join you in a minute or two."

The one time I would expect to hear command in her voice, there was none. Just more of that gentle persuasion that managed to soothe my frayed nerves, if only partway.

I started to backstep toward the living room, then stalled to ask, "Do you want me on my front or back?"

"It's up to you. The element of surprise can be nice."

My nerves reared up full steam as I stripped off my clothes and lay naked on the couch. Folding my arms beneath me, I tucked my face into their opening. I wasn't convinced the element of surprise would be a reward for lying on my front, but I knew I didn't want her seeing my face when she jammed that plug up my ass and I started bawling like a baby.

Closing my eyes, I pulled in a few deep breaths and attempted to relax. A half minute later, the flat of a hand swatted across my ass, jarring my eyes back open and jerking the air from my throat.

With her voice once more dripping Southern seduction, Deitre remarked, "Stellar view, bad boy."

Stifling a cry, I squeezed my butt cheeks as a sting raised

on their surface and dull ache shot through my groin. Ache that was just going to grow increasingly worse. *Fuck me.*

My voice muffled against my arms, I said, "Where's my lube?"

"Tonight, I'm in total control, Ryan." Her hand contacted with my butt again, this time as a warm caress. "All you're going to feel is ecstasy."

Ecstasy was about as far removed from my mind as possible. Or so I thought until she kept up with softly petting my ass. Her fingers dipped down to push between my thighs and stroke along my perineum. By rote, my legs spread farther apart and my hips canted an inch off the couch as a zing of awareness rocketed to my cock.

Her breasts rubbed against my bare back. The press of her warm, hard nipples suggested she was naked, as well, at least from the waist up. My shaft roused a little more with the thought. Then more still, as she purred, hot and husky, in my ear, "Just relax, Ry. This is going to feel *sooo* good."

Ry. She'd never called me that before. It wasn't exactly an endearment. But it felt that way as she lifted her breasts from my back and slipped her fingers to my balls. She fondled the sac with the skill of a woman long in the know about pleasuring a man. Cupped and massaged my testicles until my cock was rock-solid and damned uncomfortable wedged beneath me on the couch cushion.

I groaned with the tension against my dick, and Deitre released my balls to nudge the tip of something tiny almost to the point of being undetectable into my anus.

All thought of my aching cock ceased as liquid squirted hard against the inner walls of my rectum. I contracted my sphincter against the invasion. And then felt the muscles soften with my shocked gasp over how damned good that liquid felt. Not like an invasion at all, but totally erotic in a way that had my blood heating and my thoughts snapping right back to my near painfully trapped shaft.

"If either of us ever plans to use my cock again, I should turn over," I suggested in a rough voice.

"You're fine. Perfect. Stay right there and relax."

Relax, right. Obviously a woman who'd never experienced the discomfort of an all-but-crushed erection was making that proposal.

Lifting my head from my arms, I glanced over my shoulder. I could see just enough of Deitre to make out a portion of the right side of her body—fully nude so far as I could tell—and the butt plug in her right hand. It wasn't the small, tapered silver-sparkled plug I'd expected. Instead, she held something that resembled a deformed gray hot dog with a handle on the narrower end.

I was guessing it was a handle, anyway. One side curved up at a ninety-degree angle while the other curved down in a tight, almost flat semicircle. Both had round, flat tabs at their ends. "That's not the plug I bought for you."

"Of course not." She sounded amused. "This one's made for a man."

"What kind of man?" And how the hell did she get so educated?

I had no room to talk when it came to having a thoroughly notched bedpost. But for Deitre's incredible appetite and all that she knew about sex, she'd obviously done more than her fair share of men. I also had no right to feel jealousy—hell, I'd slept with her best friend a year before—but a part of me did.

"One who's in touch with his sexuality." Her right hand moved out of view. An instant later, her fingers returned to stroking my perineum. "Put down your head, close your eyes and focus on the area my finger is petting. You do that, and I might refrain from paddling your ass, good and hard, once the plug's inside."

The emergence of Jada in my mind couldn't have come at a worse time. I hadn't wanted to tell Deitre about our shared past before we spent today with Jack and Carinna. Still, I should have told her immediately thereafter.

Or maybe somehow she already knew. Maybe effectively taking me in the ass and making me feel about as unmanly as possible, in the process, was my penance.

If it was and, after this, I would be off the hook from the mountain-size load of guilt and, God help me, be able to get the nasty shit out of my head, once and for all, then it would be worth every second of pain and humiliation.

With a quick prayer to above to help me endure this without crying, I tucked my face back against my arms and shut my eyes.

Deitre's fingers retained that soft caress along my perineum as the tiny tip of whatever she was lubing me up with nudged deeper inside my anus and ejected another squirt of the fluid.

The first squirt hadn't been heinous like I'd expected. The second squirt knocked all other thought from my head as it felt like it somehow shot directly up the center of my cock. Unable to contain a whimper, I squirmed against the couch. Mind-numbing sensation vibrated through my ass and shook deep into my groin, almost cutting the circulation off in my powerfully hard dick in the process.

"Remember, relax and focus down here." She pressed hard against my perineum, and I bit back my wail over the intense pressure that felt anything but bad. "Not up here." Her hand shoved beneath me to stroke the root of my constrained shaft, and the vibrations zeroed from my butt to my cock.

I barely had a second to take the change in, let alone draw a wheezing breath, before the tip of something new pressed against my anus. This time it wasn't small, but closer to an inch around and wet with fluid. The amazingly good vibrations quit as my pulse roared between my ears and panicked tension mounted in my gut.

I wanted to do this for Deitre. I wanted to show her ultimate trust. I wanted to earn her forgiveness over the part I played in Jada's death, if that was what this was about.

But, Christ, I couldn't handle being taken in the ass.

Unwrapping my arms from beneath my head, I tightened my butt cheeks, in the hopes of barring entry, and pushed off from the couch. "I'm sorry. I can't do this."

She placed two hands at the top of my back and shoved my face down hard against the cushion. "Of course you can. You're going to love it."

How could she have two hands on my back, one stroking my perineum, and another guiding the butt plug up my ass?

The question flitted through my spinning mind as the tension in my gut fanned out to every limb and orifice.

Then the question was forgotten as the rounded head of the plug pierced my anal canal. For the space of a heartbeat, pain zinged through me, rendering my body rope-tight and screeching every nerve ending to standing attention as the breath hissed ice-cold from my mouth. Wickedly clever fingers found my balls then, kneading the heavy sac as more of the lube fluid gushed up and around the plug.

The pain became a shallow ache. And then that ache

became something else as the plug glided past my sphincter muscle and the vibrations started back up in my ass. These ones came from the plug itself. They quivered through my anal canal, hot, carnal and astonishingly pleasurable.

The tension sucked back into my lower abdomen as a quivering, pleasing kind of tightness. Fisting my hands next to my head, I smiled without even trying. Then I laughed, thick and coarse, against my crooked arms for no known reason at all.

Damn, it just felt so remarkable. Like nothing I'd ever experienced.

The plug moved deeper inside my canal and that awesome tension moved from my stomach to my butt. Quakes shook through my ass and shot down my legs. Waves of pleasure rippled through my body, sizzling my blood while somehow managing to miss my cock altogether.

Or maybe it hadn't. I couldn't focus on my shaft anymore. Every thought in my head was on the feel of the butt plug vibrating inside my asshole.

"Good, huh?" Deitre's thready voice came from next to my ear. "You might not ejaculate. You *will* experience orgasm like never before."

I couldn't feel her breasts pressing against my back, but I also couldn't feel her hands on my ass. And I also couldn't find the energy to open my eyes and locate her whereabouts.

The plug traveled another quarter inch inside me. The vibrations grew stronger. Pleasure built to an intensity where my only response was a desperate hum.

Warmth tingled from my head to toe. The heat increased from steamy to scalding, and my entire body spasmed. I moaned without trying. Groaned to the point I was nearly screaming as the plug must have reached its limits and the inward-facing round, flat tab swiped across the hypersensitive area south of my balls.

Goddamn, how could I have ever doubted her when she swore this would be incredible?

The tab below my balls pressed harder and vibrated faster. Sweat broke out on my body, soaking my chest and rolling from my upper lip into my mouth.

"Open your eyes and look at me, Ryan!" Deitre commanded.

The order came from beside my head this time. It took every ounce of my waning strength, but I opened my eyes and turned my head. She sat on the floor a foot away, eyes drenched with sensual hunger and her swollen lips that captivating shade of rich cherry-red. The length of her hair twined around one stunning breast while she worked its mate in her hand. Her other hand was buried between her succulently parted thighs, fingers ravenously stroking the cream-slicked folds of her labia.

"Tonight, we come together." She shoved two fingers into her passage with the words that were a command no matter how softly spoken.

Her pussy ground against her hand, and a keening cry spilled from her lips. My eyes slammed closed again, and I mimicked that cry as the butt plug mimicked her fingers, driving hard up inside my anal canal, vibrating tremors of red-hot sizzling sensation like nothing I'd ever known into my ass and throughout my entire body.

I could all but feel the cum shoot from my constrained dick as orgasm crashed over me as a long and continuous wave that felt like it could go on and on and on.

Past a blinding haze of rapture, I was distantly aware of

Deitre shouting with her climax. Even more distantly aware of time passing and the continual shudders that coursed through my butt. A minute might have passed, or maybe ten or twenty, when fingers stroked against my anus and then slowly eased the plug out. Another round of minivibrations started off with the move, and I sucked in a gasp with my disbelief.

Orgasms with Deitre had always felt spiritual, but this felt like I was as close to Heaven as I could go without dying. Even as some part of me ached for another climax, I felt at complete bliss and like I might never find the strength to move again.

She took care of that by grabbing my hips and rolling me onto my back like I weighed as much as a newborn. Sensual hunger still drenched her eyes. Wicked want burned just past that as she straddled my lower thighs. Gliding her wet pussy along my heated skin, she took my cock in hand and stroked.

Some small part of me had been aching for another climax. But damn, a guy deserved a few-second recoup break before he should be expected to get hard again.

"What are you doing?" I asked in a near whisper, all that I could manage just yet.

In response, she draped her breasts against my chest and teased me with the erect tips. "Making you come. Unless you want another G-spot orgasm first."

My shaft surged in the circle of her fingers. Desire rolled through my groin thick and lusty. She straightened with a feline grin, and I glanced down at my cock and sucked in a breath at the unbelievable sight. My rod was still rock-hard and bucking for attention. I swear to God I thought I'd come from the plug up my ass.

Deitre laughed. "You climaxed. You didn't come."

She took my cock into her tight channel then, and I thought I would make up for not coming before by coming instantly. I made a feeble attempt at lifting my hips to meet hers on the downslide, and then groaned with the realization I was more winded than she'd ever made me feel before. I was also stiffer than stone, my balls drawn tight as hell and feeling like they would release at any second.

"I can't take this long, Deitre," I ground out.

"I don't plan to let you." Riding me fast and hard, with those luscious tits jiggling all over the place, she reached a hand on either side of her body.

She fingered her clit with one hand and my balls with the other. Orgasm took me over from the first caress. I came hard, shouting her name and filling up her pussy even as she tightened around my shaft and cried out with her own release.

Breathing hard, she collapsed against my chest. A handful of seconds passed and she asked, "Happy you trusted me?"

"Happy you walked through my door," I managed in a pathetically thin voice.

As feeble as she'd rendered me tonight, I had a feeling that would be nothing to the pathetic pile of shit I would become if she dared to walk back out my door.

Deitre

After leaving Ryan asleep on the couch last night, exhausted both from sexual strain and from the energy I'd drained from him in the process of delivering his orgasms, I'd gone up to my bedroom. Like was true with food, I didn't need sleep to survive. But I enjoyed the break from the cognitive most nights.

Last night, there had been no break.

I'd lain awake considering my options. If Ryan deserved to live. If I dared to stay with him any longer when it was clear I was starting to lose all objectivity. If there was a chance the mortal feelings of affection coursing through me were authentic, and if he truly did care for me in return.

No answers had come to me last night. But now, as early-morning light streamed in past the thin white curtains covering my bedroom windows, I was going to get my answers. At least, I was going to give Ryan a final chance to provide them.

Tossing back the top sheet, I climbed naked from the bed. I didn't bother to dress, but made my way downstairs to find him passed out on the couch, sunny-side up. I lifted him from la-la land with a hard slap to the right cheek of his far too appealing sunny side and a little mental stimulation of the magical kind.

Jerking awake, he rolled over and right off the edge of the couch. He winced as he slammed ass-first into the floor. That boyishly lopsided smile appeared on his face then, spreading into his deep green eyes as he pushed up on his elbows. "Good morning to you, too."

I was beginning to hate that smile. Hate even more the way it raised a gush factor I had no idea existed until I entered his life.

Focusing on his involvement with Jada, I kept my lips from smiling back. "I've been thinking about Jada."

Losing his smile, he sat bolt upright. "What about?"

"I'm surprised you don't remember her death. I couldn't stop thinking about her long enough to fall asleep last night, so I went online and I found some old news threads on her apartment fire. Ladder 19 was one of the crews that responded to the blaze."

He looked thoughtful for a few seconds before glancing away with a shrug. "I probably had the day off."

Damn, I didn't want Ryan's denial. But that he was giving it to me was the answer I needed. He was a fraud. A smooth player who, if he cared at all, would have the balls to trust me with the truth as fully as he claimed he did with his body.

For the sake of my fiercely beating heart, I pinned him with an expectant look and gave him one more chance. "Did you?"

A hundred different responses raced through his eyes. Was the truth in there? I couldn't tell. I could only hear the detached tone of his voice as he gave a resolute nod and said, "I'm sure that I did."

Fuck. Fuck, and yet, I should have expected no less.

Every bit of the hatred I'd lost for him the last weeks resurged as an acidic burning in my belly that quickly ate its way outward. That he could act so aloof about Jada's death… it proved him the bastard I'd always known. Coldhearted and deserving of a death just as agonizing as hers had been.

Flashing a supreme smile even as my belly quivered with loathing, I went down on my knees in front of him and took his cock in hand. A dose of mental stimulation had his shaft rousing to hardness in seconds.

I bent to swipe my tongue across the pre-cum oozing at the tip. Despising how much I still loved his taste, I feigned an eager grin. "What do you say to a welcome-to-the-morning blow job?"

"I could use more sleep first."

Now that he mentioned it, he did look tired. Too bad for

him I no longer gave a shit. "Just shut up and enjoy the entertainment, *Cock*."

Hitting him with a heavy shot of seduction, I wrapped my lips around his dick and took it deep into my mouth. I licked at his rod as my lips worked up and down the steely length. All the while, I concentrated on stealing his strength.

Ryan had done incredibly well at resisting my attempts to drain his energy and take over his mind the last while. But I knew now that was only because I hadn't been trying hard enough. I'd wanted to like him. Maybe I'd even wanted to love him to the point of rings and vows and, one day, kids, regardless that our progeny would have been far less powerful Damphir for their half-human blood.

Now, my illusions of love, lust and offspring burst.

Now, I turned every ounce of my power on him with the plans to render him unconscious and then take him to the one place on Earth I could count on both my powers being at their strongest and an audience eager to view the demise of a mortal with bloodstained hands and a vicious heart.

Ryan

"Open your eyes, Ryan."

Though I couldn't recall closing my eyes, or for that matter falling asleep, Deitre's sultry voice taunted from the fringes of my subconscious. There was also pain there. Too damned much pain. And exhaustion.

My pulse beating slow and thready, I shut out the ache to open my eyes. The lids wouldn't budge. I couldn't lift my hands, either. Solid weight trapped my lower half in place, and I wasn't even sure if I could move a muscle.

"Open your goddamned eyes!" she barked this time.

Like they were controlled by some external force, my eyes snapped open. Hurt, raw and consuming, ratcheted through my head and along my prone body. Blurred faces swam into view against a backdrop of semidarkness. Deitre's face hovered a foot or so above me. Dozens of others registered past the smog that could be a film covering my stinging eyes as easily as a fog of humidity. I couldn't make the faces out down to the detail, between the darkness and that film, but what I could see resembled a hodgepodge of the impossible.

Some misshapen, ears with points instead of curves and multiple eyes where there should have been a lone one. Some covered with dark, coarse hair that resembled that of a wolf. Some pale green to the extent I expected to see Frankenstein scars covering their temple and plugs sticking out of their neck.

All were faces I'd only seen in movies or imagined in my worst nightmares.

I had to be dreaming. Some twisted nightmare of a dream that was a side effect of letting Deitre shove that butt plug up my ass. Any moment now I would wake. She would be sitting on the living-room floor, naked and with her thighs spread to reveal her slick sex, looking hotter than sin and ready to climb onto the couch and do me.

I had no energy to do her. Would she let me off the hook this time?

"There is no hook!" The words snapped out from above me.

With effort and a resulting stab of hurt in my temple, I pulled my gaze from the creatures around me to Deitre's face still hovering a foot away. Now, it was more than her face, though. Her entire nude body was there, those gorgeous tits on full display and her hot, toned thighs straddling my upper legs and registering as the weight that trapped my lower half in place.

A devilishly wicked smile curved her lips as she took my cock in hand. My naked cock. My *hard* cock.

Yeah, this had to be a dream. I could never feel such intense pain and fatigue and still have an erection bucking for more than just her fingers.

Her smile intensified with every fervent stroke and each of my shaft's eager pumps. The carnal edge vanished completely then, and it seemed only evil turned up her glistening, cherry-red lips.

"You're not dreaming," she voiced tauntingly, the wickedness in her smile reflected in her hostile tone, the Southern seduction missing in action. "This is happening. *All* of this is happening."

What was "all" supposed to entail?

Hell, it didn't matter. Neither did my exhaustion nor the pain. I had to be seconds away from succumbing to alertness.

Waiting out my escape from a bizarrely hellish slumber, I turned my head to the right and assessed my surroundings again. More pain sizzled through my neck with the move. Only, Christ, this wasn't just pain. This felt like someone had driven a set of nails through my jugular and left a chunk missing from my neck in the process.

"There is no waking, Ryan. There is no better," Deitre goaded, again in that chillingly hostile tone, as she leaned forward.

Pressing her breasts against my chest, she did something with the wet flick of her mouth at my neck that increased the sizzling pain until my eyes clamped shut and my breath hissed out on a ragged exhale.

Against my will, my eyes slammed back open a second time. The hazy film was gone. A hundred mingled voices and the throb of blatantly carnal music lifted on the air as my surroundings came into detailed view. A club of some type, furnished richly, the walls and trimmings set in shades of black and deep bloodred. A lengthy balcony raised up ten feet overhead, more freakish faces watching over its railed side. Some focused on the dance floor teeming with other-worldly bodies. Most focused on me and Deitre atop the long side of an oval wet bar.

A big, burly guy stood in the center of the bar. With the gnarled face I could imagine only a demon would possess, he growled at Deitre, "Finish him!"

She lifted her mouth from whatever the hell she'd been doing at my neck to render the kind of pain that had nausea swimming in my gut. Her eyes met mine from a few inches away. No longer were hers that cool ice-blue, or tinged with tenderness or even sweet-yet-naughty seduction. Reddish-orange, the same fiery shade as the half halo of hair cascading around her nude body, centered them.

The malicious smile slipped from her lips with the opening of her mouth. Her teeth flashed. Teeth appeared incredibly long. Jagged.

Stained with crimson that looked a whole hell of a lot like blood.

This was a dream. This *had* to be a dream. But would I feel such extreme pain in a dream? Would my mind be able to race with the impossible even as it swam with faintness? And why would I turn her into a bloodsucking monster in a dream?

Maybe it wasn't a dream. Maybe not owning up to the truth about my past with Jada had finally pushed the shit in my head so far to the forefront that it turned me into the mental case I'd been a step away from becoming for months now.

Just in case it was neither of those options, which made it something too implausible to fathom, I demanded, "Who the hell are you?"

I meant to snarl the words. They came out as a whisper that sounded a hundred times more feeble than I had following that session with the butt plug. I felt a thousand times more winded. And then I felt a hundred thousand times more fearful as Deitre sank her chest back against mine and the warmth of her mouth closed over the area of my neck that already felt torn apart.

White-hot pain sliced through my neck. Tears of agony stung my eyes. My guts roiling bile up the back of my throat, I struggled to lift my hands. My feet. Anything to get her demonic mouth off my neck, to end this goddamned anguish. This woman I thought I trusted. Loved. This woman who wasn't a woman at all.

What the fuck was she?

A nightmare. I still wanted to believe I was either asleep or insane, but that seemed less of a possibility all the time. It seemed this really was happening. That she really was ripping into my body and slowly tearing me apart.

Blood dripping from her fangs, Deitre rocked back on my thighs. Even as my mind rejected her touch and her viciously ravenous smile, my gaze zeroed uncontrollably on her bare, bouncing breasts. Movement at her back had me looking to either side of her body. To wings.

Black and huge, they were nothing I could think to dream of. Nothing I could know existed on Earth. If we were even still on Earth. Maybe I hadn't lived that night of the processing plant fire.

Maybe I was in Hell.

Smaller wings emerged at the sides of her head. A tail curled up from her ass—a tail I'd seen once before but had written off as part of a fantasy costume.

I knew now that it had been no costume accessory. Her tail was real and coiling deadly tight around my throat as she shoved her hands against my chest and impaled her ever snug pussy onto my cock.

Claws extended from the tips of her fingers. Nipping them into my forearms, she ground her pubis against mine. "You're not in Hell, Ry, baby. Not yet. But if you're lucky, maybe as soon as your she-devil finishes fucking you to death."

♣ ♠ ♥ ◆ ♣ ♠ ♥ ◆ ♣ ♠ ♥ ◆

Chapter Seven

Deitre

It should have been perfect. The owner of Darkness, who was pulling double duty as a bartender this morning, was pissed about me using his place of business to kill my latest victim. But other than that, Ryan's murder should have been perfect.

Unlike the owner, nearly every patron in the club was keyed up by my performance on the bar, watching in raunchy, rapt anticipation as I dug my claws into Ryan's forearms, tightened my tail's grip around his throat until his eyes bulged and then again slammed closed, and rode his cock for what would be the last time.

That it would be the last time was the reason his murder wasn't going perfect. Or, rather, my moony, mushy, guilty-as-hell feelings about killing him.

What I needed to focus on was that he'd been a driving force behind Jada's death. For weeks before that, he'd been the primary reason for her sorrow by making her believe that he loved her and then leaving her without a backward glance. For those reasons and many more, he deserved to die.

The excitement lifting off the throng of supernaturals

grew from anxious chatter and shouts of encouragement to a steady, throbbing chant of "Kill him!"

I let that chant fuel me. Let the taste of Ryan's blood, still so fresh and warm on my teeth and tongue, obliterate my guilt as it called forth my natural instinct. I was born to seduce men to their deaths. This was my calling. One that I'd always loved. Almost as much as I'd nearly convinced myself I'd come to love Ryan.

Fury over my stupidity screamed through my head. I took it out on him.

Lowering my breasts to the sweaty, solid-packed wall of his chest, I uncoiled my tail from his throat, fitted my mouth to the unmarred side of his neck, and punctured a fresh vein. The blood here wasn't as sweet, and that meant I'd already taken too much. I didn't want him unconscious. I wanted him cognitive for every excruciating second of his end.

Only, shit, I didn't..

No matter my calling, no matter how I'd operated for nearly two centuries, I didn't want his sorry ass dying.

Using my wings, I shifted on his cock and cocooned his body against mine, shutting out the incessant chanting and the aroused, blood-hungry eyes of dozens of onlookers. Freeing my teeth from his neck, I moved my head back a few inches and mentally forced his eyes to open.

Ryan eyed me through glassy green, his pupils dilated with a haze of confusion and pain. His breath pushed out as feathering exhales and his normally golden tanned face was near paper-white.

My guilt returned, lashing through me to an extent I'd felt only one other time, that night I had to teleport him out of the burning processing plant. Then, I'd held on to the hope of letting him live. Now, I might have already pushed him to death's door.

With my heart knocking against my ribs and my belly turning somersaults over the idea of never again seeing his ridiculously cute lopsided smile, I demanded, "Tell me you knew Jada, Ryan! Tell me what you did to her!"

His features contorted with the parting of his lips. I waited, goddamned broke out another prayer. If he just told me the truth, I would save him. Heal him. Go against every facet of my calling and training, and love him.

"I…" He got out on a rough whisper. His head whipped to the side on a tortured cry then, and he emptied the contents of his stomach against the web of my wings.

I threw my wings back on instinct, breaking the make-shift cocoon. The owner-bartender's furious glare shot to the mess that encroached upon the bar's teak surface, and he barked, "Finish him the hell up so you can clean up that mess!"

On a keening whimper, Ryan's head fell backward. His throat lay open, blood trickling from twin holes on either side of his pale neck, soaking his thick, black curls. His eyes rolled back into his head, the lids fluttering closed seconds later.

Oh, no, he didn't!

Forcing the lids open, this time with the prying of my freshly declawed fingertips, I shoved my face almost tight to his. "Tell me the truth!"

His eyes rolled forward again, with the subtle shake of his head. It was barely a movement, and yet it felt like the biggest signal of my life.

He wasn't going to say the words. The bastard was going

to make me kill him. Loathing channeled acid up my throat and my heart lurched with remorse as I snarled, "Then you're going to die."

He didn't say a word in his defense. Maybe he couldn't. Maybe he really was already too far gone, his soul departed and his body kicking with final nerves.

If he was still here, it would take no more than resuming the slide of my pussy along his stiff cock to drain the frail remnants of his life force. It would take no more than that if I wanted him to continue to suffer.

Ryan had left me no choice but to exact my revenge. But I would take it as swiftly and painlessly as possible from this point onward.

Rocking back on my bent legs, lifting free of his erection as I went, I cracked my wings against the air. Dual energy bursts emerged at their tips. The chanting of the crowd of supernaturals fell to a chorus of anxious gasps.

The large, fiery, furiously spinning circles that hovered an inch from my wings weren't like the harmless energy burst I'd raised in the rental house as a source of light. These ones were all-powerful, and laced with enough dark fury and concentrated acid to turn their target into a boneless, blood-less pile of ash on contact.

Pulse thrumming at my neck, regret eating at my belly, I brought my wings back and took aim. His eyes flickered open. Honesty filled them. Honest and open love that stilled the air in my throat.

"Deitre," a low voice rasped.

I thought it was his. That he'd somehow managed to in-filtrate my mind, because his lips sure hadn't moved. Then I recognized the voice.

Zipping my attention over my shoulder, I met with the impossible. With Jada. Only, not the Jada I remembered. But a shimmering, nearly translucent gray version of her head and a small portion of her upper body.

What the hell, was I the one that was dreaming? I'd heard of the dead returning as vapors in times of extreme need, but I'd always believed it nothing more than hearsay.

"Jada?" Her name trembled from my lips.

She didn't nod. Didn't flinch. Her gray-washed eyes didn't even blink as she offered in that same, low raspy voice, "It wasn't his fault. He didn't kill me. I was already dead."

I had to be dreaming. Making up words I yearned to hear. "No. It was his fault. If he'd gotten you out of there, they could have revived you."

"They couldn't have," she argued without emotion, without expression. "I set the fire, Deitre."

My pounding heart missed a beat. What was she suggesting? Why was she? "It started on the other end of the building. You were asleep."

"I wasn't asleep. I was dying. I wanted to die."

Shock slid over me. I gasped, "You killed yourself?"

"Yes. I set the fire and then went back to my apartment and took a bottle of sleeping pills. I wasn't happy. Not even when I thought Ryan loved me. Don't blame him, Deitre. He did nothing but his job."

"You can't believe—" My fervent reply stopped short as Jada's ashen face and upper body vanished in a flash of yellow-orange smoke.

It wasn't friendly smoke, but the toxic kind from the fire at the processing plant. It drained me in an instant. Left me to fall helpless against Ryan's dying body. Left the energy bursts I'd forgotten all about in the wake of Jada's appearance, to unfurl on their target.

Before, that target had been Ryan. The bursts were still directed at him. But now, my body was between him and the bursts. Now it was my wings and back they slammed into as a maelstrom of singeing light and acerbic power too strong for even a succubus to withstand.

Ryan

"Open your eyes, Ryan."

They were the words that Deitre had spoken to lift me from unconsciousness into a hellish nightmare that had morphed to hellish reality. But these words weren't hers. These words were spoken by a man.

I could feel his hands on my body as I surfaced from a trancelike sleep. Huge and rough, his fingers ran over every inch of my nude frame. They lingered on the pain that seared the sides of my neck and then moved south to caress my softened cock.

As was the case when it had been Deitre's hands on my body, I wasn't sure that I had the strength to open my eyes. Adrenaline changed that. Adrenaline born of disgust had my eyes snapping open. My surroundings hadn't changed. I was still flat on my back on the bar. The blatantly throbbing music was gone, but excited voices still filled the semidarkness and a hundred-plus supernatural creatures still eyed me from the dance floor, the balcony and other vantages throughout the club.

The fingers circled around my shaft, and the man stroked my cock with intensity. I turned my glare on his face. Then looked higher when my eyes met with his chest. He was a huge black being, his body roped with muscle and his stance at least seven feet. His dark, narrowed features resembled those of a hawk, and I could guess he had wings similar to the ones I'd seen on Deitre retracted into his body.

He could snap me in half easily. But then, I'd already written myself off as dead once. Somehow, I hadn't died. And I wasn't dying while some hulking birdman attempted to get me off.

Glaring, I pushed to a sitting position and fisted my hand around his wrist. Christ, my fingers barely even folded halfway around. His slanted pale blue eyes landed on mine, and I growled, "What the fuck are you doing?"

"Healing you." His voice wasn't deep and coarse, as expected, but soft and low. He looked past me, down the bar top. "It was her dying request."

Even as I acknowledged that my pain was gone, that he somehow had healed me, my gut roiled with viciousness. I knew what would be on the bar behind me before I turned to look. *Who* would be there.

Deitre.

Her wings and tail were gone. Though she lay naked, someone had arranged the length of her thick, red hair around her body to cover her breasts. The pasty shade of her skin and her unblinking eyes pushed bile up the back of my throat.

Jesus, she couldn't be gone.

"She's dead?" My voice shook.

I should have been thrilled to see her lifeless after what she'd revealed. That I'd never truly known her. That the only reason she'd entered my life was to render my death. That she really was some kind of she-devil. But I wasn't thrilled.

My heart squeezed painfully, and I felt like I was going to be sick again.

Looking back at birdman, who'd finally released my cock, I shook my denial. "She *can't* be dead. You *have* to save her."

"My magic is no match for her powers."

Dammit, how could he sound so sedate when a woman, or demon or whatever the hell she was, lay dead a few feet away?

Rage cruising through me, I shoved off the bar to land on my feet. Now, birdman looked even bigger. More than twice my weight and closer to eight feet than seven. Ignoring his size and the ogling of my naked body by our creature audience, I demanded, "What *is* a match for her powers? Something has to be."

"You're the only one here who can help her now," the big, burly demon-looking dude behind the bar offered. His voice wasn't dripping concern, either, but at least he'd given me something to work with.

It was up to me to save Deitre. The question was how and, deep down, did I even want to do that?

I couldn't remember much after she'd slipped around my cock and suggested she was going to fuck me to death. Just traces of conversation I hadn't been able to open my mouth to respond to, and then a flicker of Jada's face. Only, it hadn't been her flesh-and-blood face. She'd looked like a film on the air. She'd given me absolution.

Relief to know that I hadn't been the reason for Jada's death washed over me. Then it was forgotten as my tension and terror remounted.

Jada was dead. I refused to let Deitre be, as well. Maybe I hadn't known her. Maybe I had no reason to believe I'd ever loved her. But saving lives was all but innate in my blood and

I knew I would never be truly free of the nasty shit in my head, which had started with that fire a year ago, if I didn't attempt to save Deitre.

Going to her, I slipped my arms beneath her body and tugged her to the edge of the bar top. She was limp in my arms, but she wasn't cold.

I looked back at birdman with pleading eyes. "How do I save her?"

"Her powers aren't as strong on her own body as they would be on others. The energy bursts didn't burn away her muscle and bone, but they did steal her blood. The only blood that runs through her body now is that which she drank from you. If she has any chance, then she needs more of your blood. Much more."

In other words, I had to walk right back into the sizzling hell I'd experienced when she'd sunk her fangs into my throat. Shuddering with my fate, I again turned to the birdman. "How do I get her to drink?"

"With your wrist to her mouth. If she can sense you, she'll drink. If she can't, no one can help her."

Breathing a sigh to know it wasn't my throat that would be involved this time, I brought my free hand to Deitre's mouth and used my wrist to part her lips.

Unlike her body, her mouth was cold, numbly so. It didn't warm as I kept my wrist there, pressing it hard against her lips, considering biting into it myself to get the blood flooding. "Drink, dammit!"

Her eyes remained unblinking, her body limp in my arms. Her lips moved. Her teeth nipped at my skin. A delicate touch at first, a tender caress. And then jarring, searing pain as the blunt edge of her front teeth broke into my skin.

I winced as the ache intensified, burning throughout my arm and into my entire body, swayed a bit as a wave of dizziness moved through me. Birdman was behind me in an instant.

Pressing his hulking body against my naked back to stabilize me, he explained, "She lost her fangs. She has only mortal teeth to rely on now."

Yeah, and mortal teeth obviously weren't meant for tearing into flesh and sucking blood.

Closing my eyes, I shut out the morbid pain, the feel of birdman holding me upright. The knowledge the creature crowd was probably enjoying the hell out of their entertainment. Seconds turned to minutes and then more. Finally, birdman said, "That's enough. Any more and I won't be able to heal you again."

I opened my eyes to look back at him. My pain was still there, but it was more of a dull, throbbing ache now. Apparently, I'd adjusted to feeling like a piece of human meat. "*Is* it enough?"

"Only time will tell." He brought his beefy hand over mine and lifted my wrist from her throat. The rub of his thumb across the ragged teeth marks sealed the skin in an unbelieving heartbeat. "Sit now. You need—"

"I'm fine," I snapped, shaking my shoulders to get his body away from mine. He stepped back with a grunt. I swayed instantly to the right, catching myself on the lip of the bar seconds before my face would have rammed into the teak. Straightening, I shook off the dizzy spell. "I'll be fine. I don't belong here."

Birdman nodded. "Then go. But know that you can't come back. Once you pass through the door, this club will cease to exist to your eyes. You may never know if she survives."

"Good." It was better that way. As much as I wanted Deitre to survive, needed it with an intensity that was illogical, I didn't want to know that she had.

If I didn't know that she was alive, I wouldn't feel the need to go looking for her. I wouldn't wonder if anything we'd shared the last weeks had been real. I wouldn't have to face the fierce beating of my heart that suggested even now, after all that happened, I still loved her.

Deitre

The reason most humans were scared of the unknown was because it was just that, unknown. Personally, I'd always thrilled in it. I loved being a succubus. I loved the reality that nothing was beyond the realm of imagination.

But I wasn't a succubus anymore. And I was scared shitless of the unknown.

Karen had been nice enough to let me shack up with her the last few days, on the pretense that I'd made the moony-ass mistake of moving in with some guy and had immediately regretted it and had given up my old apartment in the meantime. In between swapping spit with her fiancé and running her café in the Liege, she'd fed me enough calorie and carb-laced sweets to have my mortal backside spreading.

It was going to take some getting used to, this whole human thing. But it wasn't that unknown that scared me as I turned Karen's hatchback onto Ryan's street. It was the unknown of how he would respond when I showed up on his doorstep.

Probably, I was crazy to be going to his house. But I couldn't leave things the way they were now. At the very least, I had to let him know that he'd saved me.

My belly flitted with butterflies as I pulled into his drive and stepped out of the car. Getting used to these new emotions was going to take some time, as well. I'd experienced emotions as a demon, but never this intensely.

Feeling like tears of apprehension were about to burst from my eyes, I bypassed the garage entrance to cut across the grass to the front door. Before I could knock, it opened. Ryan stood there, looking so good, with his breeze-tousled black curls and nothing covering his killer bod but a pair of gray cotton shorts, it took my breath away. My pulse pounded at my temples until I was squinting with the force of the pressure.

Concern flashed in his eyes. Then he seemed to remember who I was, that I didn't deserve his pity, and he crossed his arms over his scrumptious chest and leaned against the doorjamb. Stiffly, he asked, "Feeling better?"

I swallowed hard against the lump of panic in my throat. Not bothering to feign the Southern drawl any longer, I nodded. "Much. Thank you. What you did—"

"Was asinine." He smirked. "I should have left you dead, the same way you would have me."

"Why didn't you?"

He gave a detached shrug. "It's my job to save lives. I did my job."

Just as he had with Jada.

He didn't need to voice the words. I couldn't read his mind now, whether he was aroused or otherwise, but I could easily guess what he was thinking. Did he get that I'd been, more or less, doing my job, too? "It was my job to kill you. But I didn't want to do it, not after those first few days. I don't think I could have."

Ryan's smirk deepened. He let out a boisterous laugh

without a trace of mirth. "What's the matter, your demon sense slipping?"

"I'm not a succubus anymore."

His smirk turned to a wary look. He straightened from the doorjamb, visibly tensing in the process. "If this is some sort of trap to get inside so you can give fucking me to death another go, don't—"

"It's not a trap," I rushed out. "If I were still a succubus, I wouldn't need to get inside. I could teleport myself there. The same way I teleported both of us out of the processing plant basement that night."

Surprise widened and then narrowed his eyes. "*You* knocked me out?"

Guilt reared up, merging with the anxiety clawing at my throat. "It seemed the only way to get you out of there alive."

"Why would you want me to get out of there alive?"

My nerves feeling like they'd been rubbed raw, I chanced a soft smile. Damn, if that didn't make me feel all warm and tingly inside. I'd always thought those corny love-struck smiles were a bunch of crap, but then I'd been doing a lot of reassessing as of late. "I got moony." Emotion shook the words. "I don't know why now, after two hundred years of screwing with barely a care, but you did it to me. I couldn't let you die that day and I really don't think I could have let you die three nights ago."

Ryan studied my face long and hard, making me want to squirm with the intensity of his eyeing, before asking, "So you're human now?"

A huge sigh slipped from my lips. He still wasn't smiling, but at least he hadn't shut the door in my face. Letting my own smile grow, I admitted, "You turned me."

"What, with my unrequited love?"

Despite his sarcastic tone, my heart did a little flip-flop number of hope. "*Do* you love me? Is that why you saved me?"

Emotion to rival my own entered his eyes. Snorting, he looked away and then back again. "I don't even know you, Deitre, how the hell could I love you?"

Hope surging through me now, I gave him my most tender smile. "You know me better than most anyone ever has, Ry. You obviously care, as well, or you wouldn't have saved me. You turned me into a human by giving me your mortal blood when I was drained of my own. And your love wasn't unrequited. It still isn't."

He uncrossed his arms, and I considered that now he might slam the door in my face. But he just returned to studying my own. The seconds ticked on again. Finally, he spoke, letting his feelings come through in his voice. Not loathing, but warmth that slowly slid into his deep green eyes and emerged in that adorable lopsided smile. "Where do you expect to go from here?"

God, anywhere, now that he was back to smiling.

Feeling capable of flying even without wings, I went for it, pressed my body tight to Ryan's and answered with the press of my mouth. His lips parted instantly, his tongue going wild against mine in a heartbeat. Cupping my ass in his palms, he lifted me up his body. I'd never used much in the way of seduction powers to make him want me. Our chemistry had always been explosive on its own. Explosive and burning thick in my blood as he ground his growing cock against my mound.

Shivering as my sex went liquid with longing, I pulled from his lips to offer a teasing smile tinged with love. "Where do we go, bad boy? How about multiple, mutual orgasms, and then maybe rings and vows and, one day, kids."

I waited, hoped—all right, I prayed—for his smile to grow. Instead his expression went stone sober. "About Jada—"

"Her death wasn't your fault."

"I know that now, but I thought it was. I didn't admit to knowing her, because I was afraid you'd realize I was there the night of the fire, that I hadn't been able to save her, and that you would hate me for it." His voice broke a little on the last words. In a tone wrought with emotion, he admitted, "I couldn't handle the thought of you walking away. Because I got moony, too."

Every ounce of my panic fell away as my heart gave a furious clenching of happiness. I laughed as the tears I'd been holding back for three days welled in my eyes. Flippantly, I tossed out, "Well, aren't we just a couple of love-struck puppies?"

Ryan let out his own laugh, deep and rich and wonderful. Then he sobered again. "So you're okay with adopting?"

"Yeah, but we don't have to."

"The human version of you can get pregnant?"

"The demon version of me *could* get pregnant, but only at my command and only when the right sperm was involved." Winking, I slipped a hand between our bodies to pet his shaft through his shorts. "Don't think just because I'm not a succubus anymore, I plan to go easy on you, though."

Love, tender and amazing, filled his eyes, and he gave me a wicked grin that warmed me from the top of my mortal head to the tips of my mortal toes. "Don't you, either, devil girl. Because I plan to go hard on you." Rubbing his cock against my fingers, he brushed my mouth with the most gentle of kisses. "Very hard."

His lips grew firmer, hungry, parted my own to slip his tongue into my mouth and devour. And then he jerked me inside the house and spent the rest of the night showing me exactly how hard he planned to go on me.

SENSUAL MAGIC

♣ ♠ ♥ ♦ ♣ ♠ ♥ ♦ ♣ ♠ ♥ ♦

Lauren Dane

ACKNOWLEDGMENTS

As always—without my wonderful husband, Ray,
none of this would be possible. Thank you for putting up
with a wife under the influence of book deadlines
and the messy house that comes with it.

Thanks most righteously go to Laura Bradford,
agent and friend. I've rarely come across people
who work as hard as she does. She's shiny and a joy
to work with, even when she sends me revision notes
she says herself contain "a million nitpicks."

Thank you to Susan Swinwood for giving Nell and William
a place to tell their story.

Writers live in their heads a lot, so it takes friends to keep us
grounded, laughing through the rough times and kicking our
behinds when we get whiny. Megan Hart—brrrrring me my
hooooookah! Anya Bast—you may eat my candy house except
for the peanut M&M's. Ann Aguirre, thank you for listening to
me blather daily. Renee Meyer—you're made of awesome for
more reasons than I can articulate in this space.

And to my readers—seriously, thank you each and every one.

♣ ♠ ♥ ♦ ♣ ♠ ♥ ♦ ♣ ♠ ♥ ♦

Chapter One

In the narrow alley, Nell crouched, turning her face to the stiflingly hot blast of air apparently referred to as a breeze in these parts. She shut out all other stimulus, simply waiting for the magic to come to her. Tendrils of energy hung in the air, spicy and unique to the individual who worked the spell. The taste of it wove through her system. Nell's own magic broke it down, analyzed it, identified the owner.

It was her particular talent. Hunting. Tracking. A family trait she inherited from her mother. Not just a gift, but a calling. Who she was, as well as what she did on behalf of her Clan.

She stood and tapped a finger against her iPod. Music filled her senses, drowning out all other noise. Dio's "Rainbow in the Dark" kept her company as she made a few notes before tucking the pad into the back pocket of her jeans.

Mage magic. The metallic flavor identified it as *other.* Not the earthy tang of her own magic. Witch magic like hers was inherent and came from the earth beneath her feet, from the air around her and the water under and above-ground. Mages weren't born with magic, they traded for it. Most of the time with the kind of creatures best left alone.

It cost a lot to trade for power. It cost in lives, energy, dark gifts and money, too. This Camarilla was on Nell's shit list because they were in possession of nearly a hundred thousand dollars belonging to the Owen Clan.

The Owen Clan—a circle of witches and the Clan Nell belonged to and worked for—didn't take thefts of any kind lightly.

And what they took seriously, Nell took seriously. Frankly, this Camarilla, their little name for a group of them, seriously pissed her off. She'd spent the last two months traveling from city to city until she'd finally locked onto Las Vegas. Summer in Las Vegas was not Nell's idea of pleasant and she planned to take her annoyance out in someone's hide.

A man stood just a few feet away, eyes warily scanning the area, body taut, ready to spring should it be necessary. Galen, Nell's partner and the physical muscle to her magical strength.

"Got it?" he asked as he stalked toward her, golden skin rippling over roped muscle. His hair was close-cropped, pale blond against his skull. He slid dark sunglasses up over his eyes, all velvet cool and alluring.

A smile canted the left corner of her mouth. "They're here. We need to get in to see that ex-boyfriend of hers. It can't be a coincidence she's in the same city."

Galen shrugged, his dark sunglasses reflecting her face. "Dunno, Nell. From all accounts she screwed him over but good. Could be a coincidence. She might not even know he's here."

Nell rolled her eyes. "Please. How could she not know? That bitch knows where the money is. He's got it big-time. Of course she knows. Right now though, I have a trail, let's follow it to see where it leads."

Opening herself up again, she caught the scent of mage

magic and let it lead her. She knew Galen would watch her back.

"Ah, there you are." Even in the devastatingly bright light of the midday sun, she caught sight of the shine of her quarry's aura.

She nodded in his direction and Galen moved to flank them. The mage, a low-ranking minion from the feel of his magic, stood leaning against a concrete pillar bracketing the entrance to the escalators up and over the Strip. Middle-aged, slightly balding, his vitality leaking from him and speeding his aging process. Stealing magic instead of letting it move through you tended to eat you alive.

Flipping two buttons of her shirt open, Nell shook her short curls out and approached, spilling sex with calm self-assurance. His head snapped up, his attention snagged.

Close. Nell sidled up to him, standing so near her lips touched his ear. "I have a room just across the way." Confidently, she walked past and up the escalators, knowing he'd be right behind her. And he was.

Three hours later, fortified with some information, a shower and a change of clothes, Nell slid onto a padded bar stool and raised a brow toward the bartender.

He moved to her with a smile. "What can I get you?"

She looked him over. They sure did have some pretty people in Las Vegas. Everyone working in the bars and restaurants in the upscale casino/resorts on the Strip looked like an ad from a lifestyle magazine.

She considered the way he looked, the openness of his expression. He was young. Twenty-three maybe. His dark hair was tipped into fashionable little spikes. A band of barbed wire was inked into his very solid biceps. His eyes were slow and very interested.

One tip of her chin and a murmured word or two and she could go in the back with him right then and fuck. She could rip his sexy low-rise jeans open and suck his cock. Shove him to his knees and press his face into her pussy. It would be…thrilling. Unlike her, but perhaps that was why it seemed so alluring.

Or maybe it was because she felt as if she'd jump her skin. Anxiety, no, expectation coursed through her as sure as the beating of her heart. It grew every day. She'd been patient with it until the last week or two, but it rode her now until it distracted and annoyed her. She wanted to fill the uncertain space within, wanted to pull deep emotion into herself for just a short while, so her jangled senses would have something else to soothe them.

But she had the sense it would leave her feeling even emptier once it was over. Still, what did it hurt to flirt a bit? Nell leaned toward him, canting her head and sending him a seductive smile. No magic, just her. "What do you suggest?"

He leaned a hip against the counter and one arm on the bar. "Well, now, let's see. What do you like?" He definitely flirted right back.

"I like lots of things. I like it strong." Her resolve to just let it go began to slip from her fingers.

"Do you like it slow and building up to strong? Or hard right off?"

She laughed then, settling more comfortably into the high-backed stool. "Oh, it's hard to say until I get to know the drink. I do like staying power. Can you give it to me?"

His bottom lip caught between very white teeth for just

a moment, sending a shiver through her. "I might be able to deliver."

Someone at the other end of the bar called a name and her pretty bartender reluctantly tore his gaze from hers. "I'll be back with something strong with staying power."

But before the bartender returned, Galen entered the bar and motioned her to a booth in the far corner. Reluctantly she moved to sit with him, noting the bartender's shrug and wink.

A waitress delivered a tall glass just moments later. "Strong and hard," she said and Nell laughed.

"Just how I like it. Send my thanks." She put a bill on the tray and Galen ordered a beer.

"Nell, you're not... You seem a bit uncontrolled this week. First today with the mage and now with the bartender? This isn't you. What's going on?"

She looked at Galen, followed the planes of masculine cheekbones and hardened jaw. She'd used a lot more magic than normal that afternoon on the mage. Had broken into his shields and spilled her magic through him until he sweated and begged her to touch him. It wasn't as if she'd have harmed him, but she knew the magnitude of her abilities and took an oath not to abuse them.

"It won't happen again. He was weaker than I'd expected. I overcompensated." All she said was true. "And with cutie over there?" Nell jerked her head toward the bar. "I didn't blow him, I just flirted." She paused, sipping the drink. "I've been patient. Waiting. It's coming and it has been for a while now. But suddenly I'm restless, Galen. I'm itchy in my own skin."

"Last time I saw her back home, Meriel told me to keep an eye on you."

"You know, how fair is it that Meriel is pretty much the total package? I mean, she's beautiful and smart, she's full-council. All those perfect genes." Nell snorted a laugh.

"Nice, too. Even if her judgment is poor in choosing you for a best friend." Galen took a few pulls from his beer.

Meriel Owen was Nell's best friend, lead counsel to the Clan and Edina Owen's oldest child. Also unlike Nell, Meriel was a full-council witch. Meaning there was a bond-partner who'd bring Meriel into the full power of her magic, like a key in a lock. Once she was fully bonded, it was highly likely she would take over the leadership of the Clan.

Nell wasn't full-council. She was powerful, yes. Good at her job. So much so the Clan gave her free rein in most situations. She was paid well and in general, life was good. But something was missing. And as she'd told Meriel on the phone that very morning, whatever it was, she had the feeling she'd find it there in Las Vegas. Or at least would be led to it.

"I called the club the ex owns. He'll see you tomorrow afternoon. We've got suites set up at the Liege and our belongings have been sent over. With what our little friend told us this afternoon, I think we can do some digging."

"All right. Party pooper. Let's go on over, get room service and start digging."

♣ ♠ ♥ ♦ ♣ ♠ ♥ ♦ ♣ ♠ ♥ ♦

Chapter Two

William Emery walked through the club, *his* club. The rip in the upholstery of one of the VIP booths had been repaired nicely and the tabletop scarring had been polished out.

He liked when his orders were followed. It made everything much easier.

"I'll be in my office," he called to the floor manager who'd been speaking with Roseanne, his lead dancer. The Dollhouse was a burlesque club. While in the over two years since he'd opened, several others had cropped up in Vegas, the Dollhouse still reigned. It was his club people waited in line to get into. His club whose bottle service tables were booked up to six months in advance. His club the young, rich and hip had made their living room while in Las Vegas.

And to think he'd nearly opened a dance club in Boston. Another techno club with overpriced drinks. He'd have made it a success, it was who he was. But if that faithless bitch hadn't tried to con his mother, he'd have never made this dream come true.

A steaming mug of tea waited for him on his desk as he let the leather of his chair embrace his body. His kingdom.

William had learned the hard way just how closed off you had to be, just how distrustful, to hold on to what was important.

A knock on his door sounded and he didn't bother to look up from his computer screen, instead, just waving whoever it was into the room.

And when he looked up, everything stopped for long moments.

She was long and lean. The short cap of pale blond curls should have made her girlish, but William wagered there wasn't much girlish about the woman standing in his doorway.

Stylistically, she wasn't a woman he'd normally have looked at twice. Faded jeans and a button-down short-sleeved shirt, cowboy boots. In Las Vegas. In August? Not much makeup and her nails were bare, no polish. And yet, whatever it was she exuded was pure sex.

"Can I help you?" He hoped she was there to apply to be a dancer. She had that certain something he knew would amplify up on stage.

"William Emery?"

Her voice was whisky-rough, smoky. Christ.

"Yes. You know, we don't have any positions open right now, but I'd love to see you audition. Did you bring your clothes with you or is that your costume?"

Blinking slowly, she stilled a moment before she laughed. Deep and velvet seduction. Her laugh brought his already interested cock to full attention.

With a sigh, she dropped gracefully into the chair across from his desk without invitation and pulled a notepad from her bag. When she looked back up at him again he caught bright green eyes and cinnamon lashes.

"Such a kidder. I'm Nell Hunter. I work for Owen Group

International and I'm looking for this woman." She slid a photograph across his desk and his enchantment with her ended when he saw who it was.

Well, that was unexpected. At the sight of Leah's face, his cock lost all interest. "What do you want her for? Why are you here? I haven't seen Leah in three years."

"She's here in Las Vegas. You haven't heard from her?" One of her eyebrows rose slowly, as if taunting him.

"I just said that, didn't I?" Why did this woman have to be so tantalizing?

"You did. Can you tell me about the last time you saw her?"

"No. I think you're going to do some telling just now. Why the hell are you in my office, in my club, asking me about a woman I broke up with three years ago? What did she do?" he asked, suspicious.

"Why do you care? Are you protecting her?" Her lazy manner only barely hid the sharp attentiveness just beneath the surface.

He leaned back once he knew she was as much a shark as he was. William knew how to play this game. This Nell Hunter amused him, fascinated him even. Why not fence a bit with her?

"You know, pretty won't get you everything, Ms. Hunter. You're going to have to work for it. Now, I believe I asked who you were and why you were here."

He didn't mistake the glimmer of a smile at the edge of her mouth. Her mouth, God. What would she taste like?

"I'm chief of security for my employer. Your fiancée worked for a company we've done business with for eight years. Through this company and her position in it, Leah Mathers is believed to have embezzled one hundred thousand dollars from the Owen Group. Naturally we want our property back. You were engaged to marry the woman. She's suddenly in the same city you are when we're very close to finding her. You can see how this might be just a few too many coincidences for us to let pass without some questions."

She sat back in her chair and he caught the smattering of freckles across the bridge of her nose.

"How do you know she's here?"

"Mr. Emery, I'd like to repeat to you your wise words of just moments ago. Pretty won't get you everything. I gave you some, now it's your turn. Or, don't you believe in equal gratification?"

Was the lovely Ms. Hunter flirting with him? Even Leah's apparent dedication to her life of graft couldn't sour his enjoyment of Nell Hunter.

"As I said, I haven't seen Leah in three years. I kicked her out of my house. The last time I saw her was at a court hearing when she attempted to wring money from me for breaking off our engagement. After that, I had my attorneys file for a restraining order. I received it and I never laid eyes on the traitorous bitch again." The humiliation at least had been burned out by his rage at her gall.

"Did she steal from you?"

He clenched his jaw. Time had healed the romantic hurts, but it hadn't fully assuaged the humiliation Leah had brought into his life. "No. But I have no problem believing she'd steal a hundred grand from your boss, either." He hesitated a moment and then shrugged. "She attempted to extort money from my mother."

Both of her brows rose this time as she shook her head

and clucked her tongue. "My goodness. Well, then, she's an idiot. Do you have any idea where she could be here in Las Vegas? Any family or friends?"

"Did you just compliment me, Ms. Hunter?" He smiled at her, feeling like the cat who ate the canary. She may have been long and lean, but her tits were gorgeously lush. A brief mental picture of her long, pale legs wrapped around his waist slid through his head.

"You're very sure of yourself, aren't you?" She stood and he did, as well. A business card landed on his desk. "If you can think of anyone or any other details, please let me know. I'll let you get back to—" she looked at the large framed photographs of his dancers on his wall "—work."

He watched her walk from his office doorway and listened to the click of her heels as she headed out of the club.

"Oh, yes. I am sure." Smiling, he sat back in his chair and turned her card over between his fingers.

Two nights later, William sat surrounded by women as he watched the action onstage. For a brief moment, he wished a blonde with short hair and wild curls worked for him. Wished he could see her every day, get to know her.

Nell Hunter had been living in his head since the moment he'd met her. In every woman's walk, he looked for her, compared, found them all wanting. In every woman's eyes he searched for green, intelligent depths and got brown or blue.

She'd imprinted him in some way. Laid her existence on his skin until it fit him. The feeling was stifling and exhilarating all at once. To feel such an intense draw to another person with a sort of longing was an entirely unfamiliar thing to William. He'd felt lust, desire, even love, but not whatever it was plaguing him right then.

She returned to his thoughts like a song he couldn't get enough of. And like that experience he kept waiting for the annoyance to set in, for his subconscious to move on to another, new shiny thing. But it had not happened. Instead, the longing spread, deepened.

He toyed with it, with thinking about it even though it made him wary. He approached thoughts of Nell Hunter and the way she made him feel, knowing aversion was better. He thought on it anyway.

In truth, the depth of whatever they'd shared in his office scared him right down to his Prada loafers. He loved women. Loved them in volume, the more the better he'd always felt. He'd settled in with Leah because she'd interested him, matched him in bed well enough and seemed to share his passions about business. And she'd ripped him apart by attempting to destabilize the one unshakable foundation in his life—his family.

Since the day he'd listened to his mother tell him about Leah's blackmail attempt and then Leah herself on the tape, he'd always had a yawning distance between his emotions and anyone else. Even his younger brother, Nash, had trouble getting past his defenses and Nash was the closest confidant William had.

No one would ever have that kind of power over him again. The power to lay him low. Love wasn't important enough to him to risk that sort of exposure.

In truth, he continued thinking while the woman next to him stroked long nails over his trousers and alert cock, the more he thought about Nell Hunter, the more she seemed to have wormed her way under his skin.

Which could not happen.

No. The woman was way off his to-do list. Pretty, sexy, definitely smart, but not for him and that was all there was to it. He would help her find Leah if he could because Leah was an infectious disease and needed to be removed from humanity before she brought any more destruction. But there would be no fucking of the aforementioned Nell Hunter with her long legs and high, delicious breasts. No matter what color her nipples were. No matter how much his mouth watered as he imagined the taste of her neck just below her ear. He really wouldn't think about what it would feel like to sink his cock deep into her cunt. He shivered for a moment and nearly groaned at the phantom, wet squeeze of her pussy as he slid into her.

Wrenching his attention away, he sent a subtle rise of his chin to the brunette next to him. All he needed was to get laid and Nell Hunter would be out of his head.

♣ ♠ ♥ ♦ ♣ ♠ ♥ ♦ ♣ ♠ ♥ ♦

Chapter Three

Nell walked past the shimmery doormen and through the club's doors. Immediately the magic of the space responded, closed around her and allowed her to pass.

Darkness was a bar, a dance club, a place to hang out for the paranormal population in and around Las Vegas. Its location was cloaked by a fairly powerful spell the local Clan laid over it.

It seemed a small thing, a bar. Nothing so lofty really. But it was a safe haven. Like hallowed ground. No fights were allowed and the demons who watched the doors would take care of anyone who broke the space's neutrality. Having to hide one's otherness in everyday life became burdensome at times so places like Darkness were a welcome reprieve. Several such clubs/gathering places existed throughout the world.

"Nell! I'm pleased to see you," Alex Sampson, a member of the Lee Clan, the witches who held Las Vegas, hailed from a nearby table.

She grinned as he pulled her into a hug before they sat. Alex had a platinum-blond mohawk and pale blue eyes. During the time when he wasn't on official Clan business, he worked at a tattoo parlor near Freemont Street with several other witches. He was a picture of total rebel cool sitting there in his faded jeans and tight black T-shirt.

"Lovin' the hair, my man. So, tell me, any word on the woman?"

"You're not even going to flirt with me first? Come on, now, Nell. You know I like it when you're flirty." He flashed a smile.

"This woman makes me very unhappy. I want her to go away and I want to bag these mages and get this done with. I'm remodeling my kitchen and if I'm not there to guard the contractors, my dad comes by and tries to help. Now that my mom has retired from hunting she's glad to foist him off on me to get him out of her hair." She bracketed the word *help* with finger quotes. Her dad was an astrophysicist, but he could not deal with hammering and basic stuff like that. Which drove him nuts, so he routinely took classes and harassed all manner of handymen and woodworkers to let him help.

Alex snorted and sipped from his glass. "Mango smoothie. Want one?"

She nodded and after a brief interchange with the server, a tall glass of frothy orangey-yellow goodness appeared before her. "Holy crap, that's good," she moaned. "It's, like, eight hundred degrees outside today. What *is* with the heat? It's still, like, a hundred at 2:00 a.m. I live in Seattle to avoid the heat."

"Pussy." He pushed a file toward her. "Here. One of my people saw your little friend out with some of the high rollers over at Mandalay Bay. Don't know if she's working them or if she's just on holiday."

Nell rifled through the pictures and the attached notes.

"This is excellent work. Why Lucas doesn't have you working for him anymore, I don't know."

"Puhleeze. Lucas's current paramour is not okay with our past history. She's jealous. So he's pretending and keeping all manner of temptation away."

"Well, that's a very pretty picture. And you are very tempting." Nell took another drink of the smoothie and let herself imagine Lucas's long dreadlocks trailing over Alex's tatted belly. "Sorry, I was in my happy place for a moment. But I don't believe it. You two have been friends since your breakup." A breakup she couldn't really understand because they'd always seemed good together.

Alex shrugged. "Moving along. You want to come back to my place? If I remember," he leaned forward and drew two fingers down her thigh, "you like it in the middle of the day."

"Tempting. Truly. But Galen is expecting me for a conference call to the full council in less than half an hour. If I recall correctly, you like to take your time." Alex was a very inventive guy between the sheets. Still, despite her general sexual frustratedness, and hello, Las Vegas was filled with pretty, nearly naked people, she sensed Alex was looking for something to fill the emptiness hinting at the corner of his smile. A lovely afternoon fucking wasn't going to do it.

"You know my number if you change your mind. You can bring Galen." He winked.

"Ha." She stood and tossed down some money. Holding up the file a moment, she hugged Alex briefly. "Thank you for this. You should come visit. I keep telling you, you need to see Seattle. My friend Meriel is single, you know."

"I've heard all about Meriel Owen. And the last thing I

need is that kind of business. I keep my partners away from full council, remember? Too complicated otherwise."

He walked her out and they separated at the crosswalk. "Say hello to Lucas." She waved and jogged across Las Vegas Boulevard toward the Liege on the other side where she'd meet up with Galen.

They would catch Leah Mathers or someone would die trying.

During the phone conference, or rather as they waited for what felt like years to be heard by the full council, Nell thought about William Emery.

How could she not?

He got to her and she liked it. What was it about a cocky, arrogant and slightly cold man that made her all sweaty? In William's case, she didn't sense his coldness as something natural, but more of a defensive behavior.

She didn't need to have special gifts to have felt the pain radiating from him when the subject of Leah Mathers came up. Nell saw the shock on his face when she handed him the picture of his ex-fiancée, heard the slight hesitation in his voice and then the anger that flattened out the upper-class Boston accent he'd had only moments before. But he'd recovered quickly, his cocky veneer sliding back into place. She liked that sort of resilience.

Still waiting, she returned to musing over his mouth. The man had a very nice mouth. He tried to be hard, but his mouth said otherwise. His mouth said he could kiss a woman for hours until she was drunk with his lips, until his taste led her into all sorts of delicious trouble.

Galen caught her eye and raised a brow in her direction. She shrugged with a smile. He'd caught her, no use denying it. She'd tell him later—he'd pester her until she did anyway, so it was useless to resist him when he wanted to know something.

Finally they were able to report on the status of the investigation and ring off. Nell hated the politics of the job, hated having to think about every word and movement, always being careful about who you addressed when. Witches had crazy hierarchy and if you didn't follow it, people got miffed.

Now that they'd finished up and had disconnected, Galen turned to her and simply made a *get on with it* motion with his hand.

"We're walking and talking. I need to squeeze into some ridiculous dress for the club Alex's spotter saw Leah in. You need a tie. Hmm. Suddenly I'm feeling better. Knowing you'll be as uncomfortable as me makes me happy. I'm petty that way."

He grumbled as they headed toward their bedrooms from the main area where they'd been on the phone call.

She left the door open as she dressed and called out to Galen. Somehow telling him about her crush on William Emery was easier that way.

"Hang on," he said as he entered the room, already dressed and looking handsome. "Just as I thought. You're hopeless, Nell."

He reached into the neckline of her dress and adjusted her bra.

"Hey!"

"You have nice breasts, use them. We're going into this club filled with singles and you need to sex it up a bit. You're wearing makeup, right?"

"What? Why? Come on, my boobs are hanging out and

everyone's gonna stare at them as it is. What difference does lipstick make?"

He just stared at her until she sighed and pointed toward her overnight bag.

"This stuff is still in the original packaging." Galen struggled to open up the plastic.

"Yeah, Meriel gave it to me before I left. She's always on me to girl up a little." It partly amused, but also rankled. She wasn't horrible to look at just because she didn't have her best friend's elegant beauty and perfect hair. It wasn't that she never ever wore makeup or dressed up, but when she was in the field or doing research she didn't have much call to get dolled up.

She sat still while Galen primped, brushed, lined and generally worked some everyday cosmetic magic on her face.

When he finished she opened her eyes and inspected his work. She couldn't help but smile at her reflection. "Nice work. I suppose it's a testament to how many women you bed when you can turn a pumpkin into the princess's carriage."

"Why, yes, I've learned much from the lovely women I encounter. Also doesn't hurt when your mom did theater for thirty-five years. But cut the crap. You're a naturally beautiful woman, Nell." Galen looked into her face as he inspected his work. "All I did was shine you up a bit. Meriel thinks so, too. She just likes to give you things."

She stood and kissed his cheek, careful not to smear. "Thank you. Goodness, you look pretty delish." She looked him up and down as they headed out to the hall and toward the elevators. "It's a shame you're practically my brother or I'd jump on you every chance I got."

♣ ♠ ♥ ◆ ♣ ♠ ♥ ◆ ♣ ♠ ♥ ◆

Chapter Four

After a rather illuminating few hours at the nightclub Alex had sent them to, they'd headed straight to the Liege. They needed to stop by the Dollhouse to see if Emery was there.

"You know, I didn't say much about it back in the room, but from what you said, this Emery guy is totally wrong for you. Which means you can't get enough, I'm sure. Just watch yourself." Galen said it without judgment, but it rankled that he was right anyway.

"I'm a big girl, thank you very much." She paused and turned toward him. "This is just business. I need to follow up with Emery with what we learned at Club Indigo."

They'd heard a few things from some of the staff at the nightclub and Nell thought it would be wise to see if William could add anything. It wasn't that she wanted to see him or anything. Not like she'd been thinking of him pretty much nonstop in the two days since she'd seen him last. Not at all.

Light strobed from the entrance. There was a line of people, but Galen just rolled his eyes and she straightened her spine and thrust out her boobs. Together with a subtle persuasion spell and her cleavage, the doorman seemed to find a way to fit two more people inside and let them pass.

"You stay here. I'm going to talk to him alone." The woman checking coats and bags informed her William was either in his office or at the VIP table.

Galen shrugged. "I've got your back. Be careful, Nell. Not just about this guy, but these mages are too serious to ignore."

William looked around the lounge area. The dancers were between sets so the lights were up a bit and slow, throbbing electronica filled the air.

He missed a woman he'd met two days before and had been with for a grand total of perhaps half an hour.

His vision snagged on a pair of long-as-sin legs and his gaze traveled up lean thighs to the hem of a very short black dress. He took his time when he arrived at some stellar breasts, up the long line of exposed neck to a lovely face punctuated by glossy lips and big eyes. Looking right back at him.

One of her brows rose and he realized it was *her.* "Excuse me, everyone. I've got some business to attend to." He stood and made his way toward Nell with every intention of killing anyone who got in his way.

Taking advantage of the noise, he leaned in close, placing his arm around her waist. "To what do I owe the honor of this visit?"

"I'm sorry to bother you at work, but I found out some things about Leah and I needed to see if you could help."

Even though she was speaking about Leah, William's body, his brain all thrilled to see Nell, hear her velvet voice.

"Come on back." He kept a hand at her back to guide her through the crowd and down the back hall where his office was located.

Once he'd closed the door after them, his hearing took a

moment to adjust. He motioned her to the chairs bracketing a small table in the corner.

"Would you like a drink?" He sure needed one. Seeing her dressed up this way discomfited him. She was beautiful sitting there, poised but humming with energy. Still, oddly enough, while he couldn't object to the amount of bare skin she showed, he apparently preferred her the way she'd been in his office before. Go figure.

"I've already had a few, but thanks. I'm not good with a lot of alcohol in me."

He looked at her as he sat, sipping his Scotch and taking her measure. Bright green eyes met his, shooting right through him.

"Really now? Good for whom? Do you get wild and dance topless?" William really had no idea why he teased her—she was off his to-do list and everything.

She blushed, which, God help him, just made it worse. He hadn't been around women who genuinely blushed in a long time. Unless you counted his sister-in-law who was one tough woman, despite those blushes she occasionally gave when Nash said something particularly racy.

"Stop that," she said without any real heat. "You said before you didn't know of any family Leah might have in the area. But how about friends named Jonah Cutler or Randy Bane?"

Right to the point. He sighed and thought. "I really don't think so. Randy sounds sort of familiar, but not the last name. We've got a distributor here named Randy Johaness so I may be thinking about him. Why are you all dressed up?"

Her eyes widened a moment. "Is that your totally random question for the day or does it have a purpose?"

"I'm not trying to start a fight." Although if she was mad she wouldn't be so appealing maybe. Or at least she probably wouldn't want to get naked with him. Which was a good thing. Absolutely. "It's just you look so different tonight than you did the other day when you were here. Just curious. You look lovely."

"So is patronizing your fallback personality? Can't a woman dress up? The other day I was in the field, it would have been silly to wear something like this. But tonight I went out. It's Las Vegas. I see women out there, including the one who was practically kissing your zipper, dressed in far less."

"Patronizing? Because I complimented you? Is bitchy *your* fallback personality? And she wasn't kissing my zipper."

"Sure she wasn't. I'm sure she was looking for her encyclopedia in your pants. Your cock must be taking a class or something. Oh! I know, she's the cock whisperer, right?"

Nell knew she'd gone too far when she saw the light in his eyes. He was *enjoying* their little interplay as much as she was.

He stood and she did, as well, not knowing what he was up to. In quick work, he'd moved very close. She took a step back and then another and one more until her back was against the wall and he bracketed the front of her.

Her heart thundered as he moved so near she caught the flecks of gold in his eyes. His scent wrapped around her. She wasn't afraid of him physically, but a jolt of awareness shot through her. He was meant to be someone important to her. She simply knew it as much as she knew her PIN number or that it was warm or cold or whatever when she went outside.

Everything stilled for a moment. Fate. Not like she could tell him that without him flipping out or thinking she was nuts.

"Damn, but you lure me," he murmured softly before his lips touched hers.

Leaning his weight against her body, he held her in place with his body while he coaxed. Seduced. Tantalized with his mouth on hers and she opened to him. Her hands, which she'd had fisted in his lapels, slid up and around his neck. Nell wanted him so badly she had to lock her knees to keep them from trembling. How had it come to this so fast?

She'd expected him to be a different kind of kisser. She knew he'd had those lips on a variety of other women, but he didn't rush. He pulled her in slowly so that when he finally drew his tongue over her bottom lip all she could do was groan and let him in.

Not that she regretted the choice. His tongue skillfully roamed into her mouth and darted out. He nipped her bottom lip once and then again.

With her heels, they stood nose to nose so he fit her perfectly—hard to soft. He rocked his hips, dragging the length of his cock over her pussy and she gasped when the head of him brushed against her clit.

She sucked his tongue, reveling in his taste. He wanted her so much she caught the flavor of his desire and it stoked hers.

His hands, which had been on either side of her waist on the wall, slid against her at last and she writhed at the energy of his touch.

He broke the kiss, breathing hard. She stared at him and licked her lips, wanting more. She caught the intake of his breath at the sight.

"Look, this can't be… I'm not looking for anything permanent here." His hands still roamed her waist and up and down the small of her back. "We should stop."

Nell laughed. There was nothing else she could do with his cock pinning her to the wall like a butterfly in a case. Of course he wasn't looking, but they'd found each other nonetheless.

She slid her hand down into his pants and grabbed his cock, squeezing just so. "Yeah? So stop." Letting go of him, she shoved him back and stayed leaning against the wall. If he thought he could walk away when Fate had other plans, he was wrong.

Still, a little incentive never hurt and she needed to come. Slowly, she inched the hem of her dress upward. He stood frozen, gaze rooted to her movements.

"What do you think you're doing?" He sounded rusty, dazed even.

"Just go about your business. I'll…mmmmm…close the door when I leave." Widening her stance she petted over the front panel of her sheer panties and unsurprisingly, wetness greeted her.

William leaned against the edge of his desk, stunned by Nell's behavior. Her long legs spread, dress around her waist, all he could see was her. Her creamy, pale skin. The contrast with the sheer black panties made him even harder.

And he was hard enough as it was while he watched her pull the panties down, leaving them around one ankle. Her cunt was bare and smooth so he could see the glisten of her honey on her labia.

What the hell was she up to? Need hobbled him. More than mere lust, something akin to craving coursed through him. He'd wanted women before, but he'd never felt as if he couldn't draw a breath if he didn't touch her.

"Show me, Nell. Spread your cunt and show me your clit."

"I thought you wanted to stop." Her bottom lip caught between her teeth a moment as her middle finger disappeared between the lips of her pussy. The scent of her arousal reached him like a punch.

"Are you teasing me?"

"No, I'm fingering my cunt so I can come. You made me this way so I have to finish. Mmmm." She arched her back and added another finger, apparently not caring he'd nearly swallowed his tongue. Her hips slowly rolled forward and then back again and her eyes slid partway closed.

Did she think she would come and walk away? And wasn't that what he should want? What he didn't want was for her to come by her own hands. He wanted her orgasm, damn it.

Turning, he leaned and swept everything from the surface of his desk and when he faced her again, she'd pulled her fingers from her pussy and began to raise them to her mouth.

Nell knew she was playing with fire and she loved it. Loved the way his eyes had widened and then narrowed as she'd fingered herself. Loved the way he'd absently stroked over his cock through his pants as he'd watched her. And then that bit of violence as he'd cleared off the desk she hoped like hell he planned to fuck her on. Delicious.

Before she could tease him by licking her fingers, his hand wrapped around her wrist. "No," he rasped out. "That's mine. For now, it's mine and I'll take it."

Her entire body stretched taut as he drew her fingers into his mouth and sucked, slow but hard. His gaze remained locked with hers as he did it, as she felt the tug in her cunt. His tongue was warm and wet as he licked between her fingers. All she could do was imagine him buried between her thighs, licking and sucking on her pussy and she couldn't stop the groan from escaping her lips.

"You taste better than I imagined."

"Oh." Articulate, she knew. But how to respond to something like that?

He laughed as he reached out and grabbed her waist, spinning her and taking a few steps until he deposited her on the desk. Bare-assed.

"Shy now? Too late, I mean to have you."

He dropped to his knees and pushed her thighs wide and without any preamble, shoved his face into her cunt and began to lick.

The breath whooshed from her lungs as he took a long lick from her gate to her clit.

She leaned back on her elbows, arching her spine, too turned on to be embarrassed about how she pressed her pussy into his face. He felt so good, his slight beard shadow rasped against the bare skin of her inner thighs, contrasting with the smoothness of his tongue.

Skillfully, he knew just how to drive her up and keep her there for a while, just hovering inches away from coming. But he didn't tease, it was a seduction with his mouth and she gave over to it.

"More," she whispered. A deep moan broke from her lips when he slid two fingers into her gate and pressed in and out. He focused his attention on her clit, steady with just the right amount of pressure.

Before long, she shuddered and stuttered a breath as climax

sucked her in, pulled her into a maelstrom of emotions, and all she had to save her was him. His presence there, a hand on one thigh, his mouth on her pussy.

It meant so much she had to close her eyes and will herself back under control. He wouldn't understand it and she wasn't in a position to explain. For the time being it'd have to be a quick fuck for her, too. Even if inside she was ready to explode.

Nell opened her eyes as he leaned against her body, reaching out to rifle through a drawer behind her head. He cursed a few times until he straightened with a triumphant cry. "Gotcha!"

He held a condom in his hand and she just barely held back a frown. Why did the man have condoms in his desk drawer? Did he fuck women on his desk just like this all the time? Was she so totally meaningless to him?

"During the Mardi Gras celebrations here at the Liege, the management sent out these huge baskets of swag. I just tossed a lot of the smaller stuff into a drawer and gave the good stuff to the girls. Glad I kept the condom."

Oh. Well, then.

She levered up and had his pants unzipped and his cock out in a flash. She tried to move to take him into her mouth, but he held her in place with his body. "No. I need to fuck you. Now."

Nell didn't fail to see the way his hand shook a little as he rolled the condom on and hoped it meant he felt it, too. Whatever connection they had, whoever they were meant to be to one another.

William looked down, entranced by the way his cock disappeared into her cunt, by the way her body opened to admit him.

Christ, she was hot. Hot and beautiful and alluring. Addictive even. Her taste lived in him now, like it was meant to be there, and he knew he should be disconcerted by it, but he couldn't find the place to feel it.

Instead all he felt was the velvet-inferno clasp of her inner walls as she adjusted around him. Until that moment he'd avoided looking her in the eyes, but once he did, she snared him and he couldn't look away. Even as it felt like she saw straight to his very soul.

He thrust deep, aching to bury himself in her as completely as he could and not knowing why. Over and over he pistoned into her cunt, wishing the complicated bodice of that sexy dress she wore could open so he could see her breasts bounce with the movement.

Next time. Next time he'd peel every article of clothing off. Take his time as he tasted every bit of her beautiful body from her toes to the top of her head.

Christ, where did that come from? No next time! There shouldn't even be a this time, but he'd be damned if he hadn't taken her when she'd stood, her fingers buried in her cunt, begging him to.

What sane man could turn down this woman beneath him? Her green eyes, pleasure-blurred as she looked up at him, *into* him.

She wrapped her long legs around him, holding him close, keeping his thrusts as deep as he needed. William was glad they were in accord on that issue.

She writhed, her back against the cool, hard surface of the desk as he loomed over her. His handsome, elegant face morphed into a mask of savage, feral sexuality and she loved it. Wanted more. Loved knowing she brought that change.

He fucked into her body with hard, deep thrusts, delighting her. Many men didn't fuck that hard, or if they did, they lacked the finesse to give that little rotation of the hips he gave on each forward thrust so his pubic bone crushed into her clit over and over.

"Finger your clit. Make yourself come, Nell. I got impatient before, but I want it now."

Nell watched, fascinated, as a bead of sweat rolled down his temple, even as she brought her fingers to her mouth, wetting them before she took them to her clit.

Their gasps were in unison as she made that first contact, felt her inner muscles contract around his cock.

His eyes were beautiful and filled with so many things. Pain. Fear. Lust. Amusement. Arrogance. All Nell could hope was that the latter were due to her, but not the former. She didn't want to make him afraid, she wanted to make him want to take chances and leap even when he'd only known her a few days.

Her system responded, nerves quickening as her pleasure built. "Harder."

He cursed, but kept his pace.

"Don't hold back. Harder." She didn't want his control. Wanted him to stop hiding behind it, wanted to see him crack and show how much she affected him.

With a moan laced with surrender, he pulled nearly all the way out and plunged in again, moving her body up and pulling her back down as he retreated. Bright spots of pleasure burst against her momentarily closed eyelids. Over and over he drove into her body, hard and fast, his control ribboned away. When she opened her eyes again he'd let his head fall back.

The wall holding her climax back fell and it filled her, coursing through her system until she knew nothing but that exquisite contact made from cock to cunt and her soul to his. She breathed him in as he groaned and came, leaning over her, his mouth next to her ear.

Not caring what he thought, she gave in to temptation and licked up the line of his neck from the collar of his shirt. Salty, warm, a bit spicy. Oh, sweet heaven, she was a total goner.

Once he got his breath back, he straightened and moved to get rid of the condom. He really would have to send a thank-you for that swag basket. As he looked everywhere but at her, he noted his office was a mess, the items from his desk scattered all over the floor.

He didn't say anything as he cleaned up a bit and got himself in order and she did the same. She primped her hair, but not with the sense of ease the other women he usually dealt with did. Her dressed-up act was total bullshit, a costume to put on and play pretend. Part of him was relieved. He liked her more natural and at ease, but another part was turned on that she was playing a game. Role-playing. He did so very enjoy it, and not in the naughty-secretary sense. In the sense that role-play, even just to pretend you don't know your girlfriend, pick her up in a bar and fuck her in the parking lot in the car, was hot and it kept a sense of fun in a relationship.

Of course, relationships and girlfriends were something he didn't allow himself and didn't miss. And the woman now pulling her dress back down over her newly restored pantied ass was a nice, quick fuck and that was that.

"While I'm thankful for the enjoyable interlude, I

already told you I'd assist you if I remembered those names." He smiled arrogantly. He needed to keep her at arm's length.

She merely returned the smile, but hers was…well, serene. *Serene?* He'd just eaten her pussy on his desk and fucked her senseless and she looked like that? Even as the scent of sex hung between them, beating at him, she calmly grabbed her little sparkly bag and headed for the door.

"I'll be in touch before I leave Las Vegas."

Speechless, he watched as she left.

Nell wanted to laugh out loud when she noted the look of shock on his face when she didn't rise to his little jab. Amateur. Oh, he was scared because he'd felt it, too, the depth of this thing between them.

His sort of grumpy behavior after he'd given her so much pleasure and had clearly taken his share, as well, sort of amused her. Dear God, she may have even been charmed by it.

It was probably love, then, since in any other situation if a man had said that he'd be spitting out his teeth.

Galen saw her approach and snorted. "Well, I guess I don't have to ask how your meeting with him went. He's standing in his doorway looking at you, by the way."

"He's a tool. Come on, let's roll."

Galen put an arm around her shoulder and walked out with her. "You all right? Do I need to beat him up for you?"

"He's meant for me, Galen," she said quietly once they'd left the noise of the club. "I know it. He feels it, but he's scared."

Galen paused and then took a deep breath. He touched her face briefly, smiling. "Ah, darlin', I wish this moment could be easy for you. You're going to have to take some stick while he figures it out. That's going to suck. Humans, Christ. You couldn't get some nice male witch?"

She laughed. "Fate, you can't fight her or she'll kick your ass. He's—" she paused with a shrug "—it. But yes, he's trying to push me away with his reactions. It won't work and frankly, he's the one who's going to come for me in the end."

Galen wrinkled his nose. "Too much info there, Nell."

She tsked. "Shaddup! You know what I mean. To my door, to me. Perv."

"I expect you'll take a few knocks between now and then. He's not going to accept it the same way we do. But he'll come around. How could he not? You're wonderful. And if he doesn't, I'll kill him."

She grinned and hugged him briefly. "You're so awesome. Come on, let's get some sleep, shall we?"

♣ ♠ ♥ ♦ ♣ ♠ ♥ ♦ ♣ ♠ ♥ ♦

Chapter Five

He tried not to watch her with that other guy after she'd walked out. But he'd not only stood in his doorway, he'd followed and taken in their easy interchange in the area outside the front doors.

The sight of her hugging the other man had remained burned into his brain, kept him from getting much sleep and agitated him even the next evening as he sat at his desk and pretended to work.

Damn it, what was up with the way he could not stop thinking about her? Even after a hot shower when he got home and another one before he came into work he still smelled her on his skin. As he sat at his desk, all he could remember was how she'd looked there on it while he'd been buried deep inside her.

A physical ache lodged in his gut as he remembered the feel of her body, the sound of her responses, the taste of her pussy, the salt of her skin. Craving. He craved her. Tossing his pen down, he scrubbed his hands over his face.

She drew his thoughts. Had done so since the moment he met her. Like the wisp of a voice here and there, always occupying part of his attention. Why? She wasn't exceptionally beautiful, although those breasts were delicious. She wasn't a sex kitten or a skilled seducer. She seemed a bit hard, more so than his usual type, that's for sure.

Whatever the reason she lay on his mind, he most definitely wanted to help her get Leah. That bitch had taken advantage of her last mark if he could help it.

He'd made some calls to old friends of his back home to see if they knew anything about what Leah might be up to these days and he was able to get a few names. Something he felt ridiculously proud of, like he'd championed Nell in some way. The need to show off for her made him want to poke an eye out.

"You rang?"

He looked up. As if he'd conjured her, Nell stood in his doorway, back in her jeans, boots and a pretty, faded blue blouse. Her hair was pinned away from her face and she looked, well, wholesome. Or she would have if she didn't give off some air of potential violence.

He sat up, interested in his own train of thought. Why did he think of violence? She didn't seem physically aggressive although certainly sexually so.

"Why do you have that look on your face? Do I have catsup on my shirt?" She looked down and irritation slid through him that she'd charmed him.

"Sorry, you caught me when I was thinking about something else. Come in and shut the door."

She laughed as she closed the door and entered the room fully. It was already nearly eleven so the show had started and the club was packed and loud.

"I don't have time for a captivating quickie on your desk

tonight. I have errands to run. Also, I have a pen-shaped bruise on my ass."

"Maybe next time I'll spread you out on a bed. I think I'd like to have about four hours to spend on your body."

She cocked her head, eyes glimmering with sexuality so raw he felt it, electric, riding up his spine. Her tongue darted out, sliding along her lips until he squirmed in his seat. "Is that why you called me, Mr. Emery?"

He took a sip of his mineral water and tried not to smile. "I took the liberty of asking a few friends back in Boston about those names you gave me last night." He pushed the papers toward her and she took them, looking through them. "That may give you something. Not a whole lot, but hopefully a bit of help."

She smiled. "Thanks, William. I appreciate it." She stood and he followed, not wanting her to go yet. He reached her quickly, before she got to the door.

"Where are you headed?"

She stopped and he angled her body with his own, backing her against the door.

"Hmm, against this door, apparently. Déjà vu?"

He moved so close his body rested against hers. The sun-warmed scent of her skin rose to his nose and he breathed deep. Leaning in, he nuzzled her neck softly and she sighed, melting into his touch.

He skated his lips up, under her chin, his teeth nipping at her jaw. Her mouth was waiting for him when he got there, her lips parted, breath mingling with his as he slid into the kiss.

Her hands smoothed up the front of his shirt and he shivered when her nails scored over his nipples. Their tongues tangled, flirted, teased back and forth in an easy dance. It felt as if he'd kissed her a million times, her taste was so familiar and at the same time, like he'd never been kissed before. Their connection was so unexpectedly moving. He knew it would be, and yet found it surprising, too.

Need slammed into his gut, his cock, his heart. His fingers fumbled with the buttons on her shirt and she stayed him.

"You know you want this as much as I do," he said as he struggled for breath.

"I do. But not here. Not now. I really do have to go. I'm expecting to meet someone and I can't be late."

He took a step back, feeling like a toddler who'd been told no. He wanted her, damn it! Why did any woman have the ability to do this to him? This wasn't who he was.

He gave her a smile, easing back, using his feigned nonchalance to build a moat between them before he did something stupid like beg.

"Okay, then. You know it's not fair to give me a taste and then deny me. But fine. Call me before you leave Vegas. Maybe we'll get together before you go home."

Her lips tightened into a line for a brief moment, but instead she breathed out and then shrugged. "Okay, then. Have a good one and thanks for the help." She hauled the door open and he was, yet again, watching her leave. That's all she had to say? *Okay, then*?

Oh, no! With a muted growl of frustration, he stormed after her. One of his people saw her walk out and handed her a note.

"What's that?" he nearly barked as she read.

"A piece of paper with words on it. Don't you have, like, eleventyfourteen women to blow before you turn into a pumpkin at midnight?" She tucked the note into her bag and headed toward the door.

"Let me walk you to the elevators at least. You're staying here, you said. It's getting late." He quickly told the bouncer he'd be back shortly and hustled to catch up with her.

Nell wanted to rap him over the head with her bag. Oh, he'd see her again before she left Vegas all right. He was an idiot and willfully blind to what they had between them. Or, well, not so blind, which is why she knew he played it all cool after she'd called a halt to that kiss. She'd moved him, he wanted her and he didn't like that he did. Well, tough shit. He was hers, the stupid twit. She wasn't going to engage and let him goad her, though.

"Hey, wait, those are the elevators to the parking garage," he said, trying to steer her like she was an idiot. Her legs still felt like rubber after that kiss. God, he'd felt so good there, his mouth on hers like it was made to be there. He had no idea how hard it had been to stop it. But she had to meet with Galen and Alex.

She rolled her eyes, exasperated. "I know. I need the elevators to the garage. I'm meeting someone down the Strip so I need my car. Thanks for walking me to the elevators. Have a good night." She walked into the elevator, just waiting for the door to close so she could fume a bit, but he had the nerve to follow her in. Hmpf. He couldn't bear to leave her. Ha!

"Why didn't you say that? I'm going to walk you to your car."

"This place is totally safe." Not like she'd be worried if it wasn't. She could handle herself quite ably against most threats.

"Of course it is, but I'm not letting a woman walk to her car alone this late. What sort of gentleman would I be?"

She refrained from answering that question and got out when the doors opened.

"You know, do you take these sorts of risks in… Where did you say you were from?" William's legs were as long as hers and he didn't have heels on, so he kept up nicely.

"I didn't, but I'll give you a freebie. Seattle. We've both already said this hotel was safe. And by risks do you mean fucking a near-stranger?"

He didn't want to know. Oh, hell, of course he did. He wanted to know if she did this sort of thing regularly or whether it was special between them. It was still a one-night stand though. Just a special one.

"Do you?"

"Walk to my car in hotel parking lots?"

"Are you sulking? Because I told you up front this wasn't going anywhere."

She stopped next to a deep green Mercedes and he approved mightily. Until she turned to the shiny black car next to it.

Her annoyed look, the one she'd tried to hide when he'd jabbed at her with his last comment, smoothed into amusement.

"What? Don't tell me you expected the Mercedes?" She laughed, putting her bag, much larger and far less useless than the one she'd had the night before, on the seat.

Speech eluded him. The car was beautiful in its own way, but not sleek. Not new and elegant. It didn't have air bags and heated seats. It was a muscle car.

"1969 Camaro. Beautiful, isn't she?" She said it with pride.

He circled it. "Gotta admit, it's fucking gorgeous. Someone really gifted did this work." He looked up to catch her surprised look. "Now I surprise you. My father loved classic cars. He passed that love on to me and my brother." He wished she'd be around long enough for him to show her his collection.

She'd moved to join him at the blunt nose end. "I am not mechanical at all. I just knew I wanted one so I spent six years until I found her. There's this guy in Oregon, way up in the mountains."

"Pete Simpson. I just went up there last year to buy a Jag. A '68. Drove her back here in the late summer and it was perfect."

"Red, right?" At his nod she continued. "He'd just finished it when I went down on my way to San Francisco midsummer last year. He said he had a buyer. Congratulations."

"So do you or not?" he burst out and she stopped, fisting her hands on her hips.

"We're back to that, are we? Do I fuck near-strangers on a regular basis? That was the question, yes?" She paused. "Well, here's the thing, bucko, you made sure to tell me several times since last night that this wasn't going anywhere. You wore a condom, so I don't think you have a right to ask that question."

♣ ♠ ♥ ♦ ♣ ♠ ♥ ♦ ♣ ♠ ♥ ♦

Chapter Six

Before Nell could smirk, she felt the sharp metallic bite of magic on the back of her tongue. Mage magic.

"Get down, now!" She shoved William down behind the shelter of her car and his mouth, opened to argue, snapped shut as a sizzle of offensive magic hit the ground nearby. Quickly, she spelled the security cameras in the area to a continuous loop. They couldn't afford to be seen if they could avoid it.

Still crouched, she grabbed him by the shirtfront and hauled him close. "Stay your handsome ass right here. If you get in the way, we could both get hurt. Do not call the authorities."

"Are you out of your fucking mind? Stay here!"

She shook him off even as she let the magic fill her, opened her othersight and hunted for the mage nearby. When she turned back to him, she knew her eyes reflected her power, knew he saw it in the way his own widened and the restraining hand he'd had on her ankle fell away.

She quickly reached inside the car, grabbing her bag and opening it. The reassuring cool of gunmetal touched her hand.

"A gun? What the hell?" William asked in a sharp whisper as she made sure the clip was full and the safety was off.

"You're in over your head and I need you to deal. Now

listen to me. Stay down. You can't help me, but you can hurt. So shut the fuck up and keep out of harm's way. I'll be done in a few minutes. The door will shield you."

The gun was nice and all, but she'd do as much as possible with magic. Discharging weapons was a pain in the ass—the sound drew attention. Magic was cleaner and more easily hidden. Still, she'd shoot that damned mage assassin in the head if need be.

She inched her way around the back end of the car, tracking the mage with her othersight. She used a simple diversion spell, one that would make sure the mage heard her from another direction, and stood.

There were two; a human also stood several feet away. He was well armed. She needed to take out the mage first. After that, the human would be easily dealt with. One-handed, she drew her magic and sent it toward the mage, knocking him down.

He writhed, screaming in pain and the human turned and a spray of automatic weapon fire peppered all around her. With a quick look at the expiring mage, she turned her attention to the human who continued to shoot.

She hissed when a bullet just barely missed her arm and reached out to slam him with her energy. She'd used a lot on the mage—when this was over she'd need to rest and recharge.

William watched the entire exchange, totally shocked and shaken by everything he saw. The gun was one thing, although why anyone would be trying to *kill* them was bizarre enough. But her eyes. The subtle movement of her hands and the blurred wave of…whatever the hell it was, as it had hit the other guy and knocked him down in obvious great pain.

And now she did some stuff with her hand, her *gun* pointed down, as she walked to the other guy. He'd fired an automatic weapon at her and she didn't look hurt. What was going on? Was he being punked? Were there hidden cameras?

In a blinding flash, the two men were gone and she turned and stalked back toward him.

"You…you want to tell me what the hell is going on here?" He shook now that it was over, whatever it was.

She sighed, putting her gun away, and then loaded him into the low-slung passenger seat. She got into the driver's side and closed the door.

"I'm not going anywhere with you right now."

She turned to him and pressed a bottle of water into his hand. It was warm from being in the car, but it felt damned good as he drank it down in giant gulps.

"I'm not *taking* you anywhere without your permission. Why don't you go back to the club? Or can I get you home?" Her voice was soft, calm.

"Tell. Me. What. Is. Happening!"

"I'm a witch." She shrugged. "The one man was a mage, which is sort of like a witch, only they're not bound by the same principles we are and they get their magic differently." She paused at his look and smiled sheepishly. "Not that you care much about that or need to know anyway. Your ex helped them steal a great deal of money for the Clan I serve. Sort of an, um, city-state government of witches. They know I'm here, obviously, and they came to take care of me. But I took care of them first."

He just stared at her as the sounds of night, which he only then noticed had been totally silenced during the fight, sounded around them.

"Am I on one of those practical-joke shows? Did Nash put you up to this?"

She sneered a moment. "Do you honestly think I'd *fuck* you for a television show? Did what happened out there seem like just special effects to you?"

"Don't get bitchy with me. You, well, stuff came out of you and it knocked the other guy down and he's not there anymore. Where did they go? What did you do?"

"They don't exist. Best to think of it in those terms."

He scrubbed his hands over his face. "So this is, like, Wicca? But with, like, death shock fingers?"

She sighed. "It's not like that. A few of us are Wiccan, some are other types of pagan, some are Christian, Jews, Muslims, even a Zen Buddhist here and there. Wicca is different than what we are. We're born with our magic. It's inherent. It doesn't need to be invoked or brought by ritual. It's just there. I don't know how to explain it to you. But I can tell you I took a risk just now by confiding in you. What we are, who we are is not common knowledge."

"What did you do to them?"

"Do you really want to know?"

He nodded.

"I set off a chain reaction in his DNA. It unraveled until he was nothing."

"Like one of those curses that kid warlock did in those books?"

"Wizard, and sort of. I mean, not really, but it's the closest you need to get just now."

His brain could sort of grasp it, but he didn't want to. "This is fucking crazy. You murdered those men!"

"One of them shot energy at me and the other used an

automatic weapon. They wanted me dead, I defended my-self. This isn't some shiny television show, William. The members of this Camarilla have shown a predilection for extreme violence and what they're doing with this money is a big concern. They're bad people and if it's between me and them, it's going to be them."

"All I wanted was to fuck you. Just some hot sex to get you out of my head. I want a *normal* life. Normal women. Plural. How did it get to this?" He opened the car door and stepped out. "I want you out of here. I'm going to have the hotel management get your things and send them elsewhere. I'll have them secure you rooms at Bellagio. I won't tell anyone. Who'd believe me anyway? But you need to get the fuck out of my hotel and my life right now."

He walked quickly back toward the doors and tried to ignore the way it felt when he heard her start the engine and pull away.

Nell hated the slice of pain at his words. Hated the empty spot in her gut as he'd told her to get out. She didn't know what she expected. She never dated human men, not wanting to hide her life from anyone. But he'd appeared repulsed, horrified by her admission.

She pulled into the lot at Bellagio—nice coincidence since they were apparently staying there now—and headed inside to meet Galen and Alex.

"What the hell happened to you?" Galen rose as she approached their table in the bar.

"It's taken care of. We've been kicked out of the Liege. Emery saw more than he could deal with apparently. Our things are being sent here. We should check shortly to be sure he didn't just toss our stuff into the street." She sat and Alex handed her his drink.

"You look like you need it more than I do."

If she talked about it she'd cry. Cry like a fucking girl, and she wasn't going to indulge just then, couldn't afford to.

"I don't want to talk about it. Tell me what's going on." As she said it, she pushed out a dampening spell to cover what they were saying.

"Word on the street is the mages know you're here and they've taken out a contract on you." Alex's pretty face was serious.

"They have indeed. I just took care of that problem in the parking garage at the Liege. Well, two problems. It's cleaned up. I really don't like being shot at, even more than I don't like being stolen from by some human con artist. Makes me shirty. Alex, I want you to put out the word that I'm gunning for these mages and that human bitch Leah. I'm coming for them and they can't hide." It might even make her feel a bit better to scare someone after the night she'd had.

Alex nodded. "Okay. That should shake things up a bit. You may want to hang out at Darkness a bit more. All kinds of info floats around in there." He paused and touched her hand. "You sure you're okay?"

She shrugged. "Nothing some sleep won't cure. Thank you."

After she and Galen checked into their rooms, she sat on her bed and looked out over the Strip. The rooms at Bellagio were nice, she gave them that, and the view kicked ass, but even that couldn't make her feel better, damn it.

She *knew* William Emery was meant for her. He was

meant to be in her life. Fate brought him to her, or her to him. It didn't matter how they met, it was that they did meet. She also understood this wasn't something William could understand and accept at the same level she did.

It wasn't like she expected him to be all, "Whoo, jim dandy, you're a witch!" or anything, but his revulsion and fear hurt. Yes, it wasn't every day you saw a witch essentially dissolve another person and all, but she'd done it to save their lives. He had no idea just what these mages were capable of. Which, she admitted, was part of why he was probably so freaked out.

How she'd get him to come around on the point she didn't know, but she would. And then she'd make his ass pay for being a twit. Hmpf.

It was too late to call Meriel and bounce the whole thing off her. The sun would be rising in a few hours anyway. She finished off her chamomile tea and snuggled under the fluffy comforter. The air-conditioning was set to extra chilly, just how she liked it. She willed sleep to come so the look on William's face would just go away.

♣ ♠ ♥ ♦ ♣ ♠ ♥ ♦ ♣ ♠ ♥ ♦

Chapter Seven

Three days later, Nash opened the door to his house and took William in with a raised eyebrow.

"I can't believe I'm even here," William mumbled.

Nash yanked him into the house and shut the door. "What's going on?"

William groaned and went into the large living room. Everywhere in the house he sensed Dahlia's touch. Vivid colors, but simple, classic lines. A little bit Old World and a little bit new. Sort of like his sister-in-law. A woman he'd been dead set against Nash marrying and had been proven wrong about.

He sighed and threw himself onto a couch, tossing an arm over his eyes. "I need your advice. I can't believe I'm here, but you're the only married man I know with a hot wife who isn't cheating and has a relatively normal life."

"Well, with flattery like that, who can resist? I take it we're talking woman trouble?"

He sighed. "Yes. Nash, I met this woman and it's only been, like, a week, but I can't get her out of my damned head."

"Have you nailed her yet?" Nash laughed. "Sorry, Dahlia and I have this thing. You don't want to know. Anyway, have you had sex with her? Maybe you just need to get her out of your system that way."

"I fucked her on my desk five nights ago and I would have the night after that all over again if I hadn't been interrupted."

Nash went silent and William peeked from under his arm to see his brother's look of surprise. "Your desk at the Dollhouse? You had sex at work? You never do that. Your office? Your desk? *I've* had sex at the Dollhouse, but you? This woman is more than just a fuck, William. Who is she?"

That was the damned truth. "You've had sex at my club?"

Nash waved it away. "We're talking about this mystery woman who got you to break your code. Who is she? What's she like? How did you meet?"

"She's chief of security for some corporation Leah embezzled a chunk of money from. Leah is apparently in Vegas and Nell, that's her, came to see me about it. She's…she's not a woman I'd normally look at twice. She has Scorpions and Judas Priest CDs in her car. A '69 Camaro, by the way. She's a jeans and T-shirts woman, but she cleans up rather well. But Christ, I actually prefer the faded jeans and boots. Boots, Nash. And *buttrock*. She's hard." He paused a moment. He couldn't very well tell his brother Nell was a witch warrior of some type. "Not the kind of woman who appears to be given to shopping and manicures. She doesn't even wear much makeup."

"So what? You've known her a week, you said, and you broke your no-sex-at-work rule with her. She's not your usual type, but damn it, have you considered the reason you prefer that other type is that those women you involve yourself with are shallow? You get to have sex, you don't have to love them, you give them shiny things and move on. Is this Nell a woman of substance and *that's* what's got you all knotted up?" Nash took a deep breath and William sat up to look at his brother better.

"William, you should be happy. Let go and let yourself enjoy this Nell. Stop questioning why you like a woman in a T-shirt and realize she's got excellent taste in cars and apparently men. Is it so awful to think you might want to spend more than a few days with a woman?"

"She doesn't live here anyway. I don't even know if she's still in town. Okay, that's a lie. I got mad at her and kicked her out of the Liege even though I really didn't have the authority. Anyway, she's at Bellagio. I checked to see if she's still there. Like I've done every day since our fight three days ago. I am so fucked."

Nash laughed. "My advice, since you asked, is to let go and see where this thing could lead. And we want to meet her, too. Not right away, so get that look off your face. But soon. Now, have you eaten today? I was making lunch. Come on back to the kitchen and we'll keep talking."

Nell stepped out of the cab at the hotel nearest Darkness and smoothed her very short skirt into place. As she walked, the click of her tall high-heeled boots sounded against the pavement.

It wasn't often she played the sex-kitten part, but it was fun to try on every now and then. She had to meet a contact in the club so she thought she'd tart it up a bit to blend in. It was Saturday night and Darkness would be filled with paranormals of all stripes out to have a good time.

One of the doormen was waving her through when he

looked up and then put a hand out to stop her. "A human called to you. Our spotter says he saw you come this way. You have to deal with it."

"Care to be specific? Where? I didn't hear anything." Damn and double damn. She'd have to go and make something up to smooth things over. If she ignored it and whoever it was came to investigate, they wouldn't get in, but it would be trouble.

"Across the street. A male."

The Liege was across the street and there happened to be a male over there who knew her.

She turned and carefully exited back to the street and saw William standing on an outdoor plaza on the retail level of the Liege.

He saw her, too, and waved like he hadn't chucked her ass onto the street and then hadn't bothered to call to apologize in the five days since. Hmpf. She did know he'd called to see if they were still staying there, though. She'd gotten that little snippet from the concierge whose mind was very susceptible to magic.

By the time she made it to him he'd procured a frosty glass of something and handed it to her when she approached. "It's hot, so I thought you might appreciate something cold to drink. Would you like to go inside?"

"Why?"

His smile slipped a few watts. "Why? You came over here."

"Because you called my name."

He looked confused for a moment, the spell clouding his mind until he remembered calling for her. She was an idiot for reminding him. She needed to deal with this thing between them. Nell couldn't afford to make these kinds of rookie mistakes.

He took her arm and led her off to the side of the wide plaza, away from prying eyes and ears. "What the hell did you do to me?"

She shook herself free. "Look here, Emery, I didn't do anything to you. You called my name, I came over. If you didn't want me over here, if you didn't care about my where-abouts, why call Bellagio every day to see if I'm still staying there? Don't play games."

William wanted to shake her for looking so good. Wanted to stop the way she made him feel. Vulnerable. Christ, he needed her and he did not want to.

He clung to his anger to keep him afloat in the sea of her; the scent of her, of her essential being, wafted through the air between them.

"Bullshit. Something happened. I know it did. You did something to my head."

Her eyes widened and then narrowed. "I didn't touch your head, asshole." She paused, looked from side to side and then the background noise died down to nothing but their breathing and the beat of his heart pounding in his head. "There. Feel that? *That's* me doing something. Before you run off squealing like a girl, I just put a little protection around us so we can't be heard."

"Squealing like a girl?"

She waved a hand and took a sip of the iced melon drink he'd brought out for her. After he'd seen her across the street and called her name. But then he hadn't. Or had he?

"You messed with my memory!"

"I did not." She sighed loudly. "I'm going to explain and you're not going to repeat what I tell you to anyone. If you do—" she held up a hand, fingers pressed over his lips to stay his interruption "—if you *do,* my friends and family would be in danger, so you won't. I'm telling you now, if I give you these words, you won't be able to share them unless I let you. Do you understand? I'm going to use magic on you, but only if you agree."

She waited while he thought it over. Did he trust her enough? When it came right down to it, he supposed he did. He'd seen what she'd done in the garage to those people who'd tried to hurt them. She could have easily done the same to him if she'd wanted to.

At last he nodded and she relaxed.

"Now, across the street there's a club of sorts. A club where my kind can go and be safe. The entrance is warded in a sense by spells so humans don't go bumbling in. That's what happened. You saw me and then once I'd entered the wards, you forgot. If you were walking past, you'd feel a need to keep going. All you'd see is a wall. Now that you know, I'm meeting a contact about your fiancée, so I've got to get moving."

He took her arm again, not wanting her to go. "You used a spell to make me forget? How is that not you messing with my head?"

"The spell isn't mine. Spells like that one have been in place for longer than you've been alive and they're in place to protect my people and those like me. Stop acting so wounded. What is your issue anyway? You're, like, this super-successful man. You're handsome, well-spoken, obviously educated, rich, successful, people with pink parts seem to like you. So what is your deal? Does this Eeyore thing you're doing make the ladies all hot and bothered? Because, I have to tell you, it makes me want to sneer at you and steal your lunch money. Buck up and stop being a pussy. This isn't about you. Now, if you've wallowed enough, I have to go to work."

She shoved the now-empty glass at him and he only barely swallowed the snarl that rose as a result of her provocation.

"Fine. I don't like being toyed with. I'm sorry if I accused you personally. Let me come with you. Keep you safe. I promise not to say anything about what I see."

She paused a moment, a half smile perched on her lips. "That's quite sweet, Eeyore. But I'm good. I have it handled. I'll see you around."

He sighed, annoyed with her refusal and his need to be with her just a few more minutes. "Humor me."

"You're going to see stuff you've never seen before. Can you deal with that?"

"Like what?"

"Vampires. Demons. Weres of many stripes. Mostly they'll look just like you and me, but they're not. I need you to understand that right now. They are not fluffy bunny paranormals like you might read about in some novel. They're predators."

"Like you?"

"To a certain extent, yes. Witches organized into clans do adhere to the basics of the Rede even though we're not Wiccan. We do not use our gifts to harm or bully. But if I have to harm to save myself or protect my people, I will. I don't feel guilty for what happened in the garage, William. It was kill or be killed." She shrugged. "If you want to come with me, you have to take responsibility for whatever you see."

He looked at her. A warm wind blew her curls around her heart-shaped face. Challenge glinted in her eyes and he knew if he went with her, he was taking another step into…well, into whatever the hell they had, or were building. Or whatever.

He should say no. Turn around and walk inside. Go on with his Nell-free life. She'd go on and do her business and eventually be gone from town and he'd never see her again.

"All right, then. Let's go. They let, um, humans in?"

She took his hand. "If they're with one of us, yes. Don't look at anyone for too long, okay? And trust me. It's different in there, but it's safe."

He let her lead him and it changed his entire life.

♣ ♠ ♥ ♦ ♣ ♠ ♥ ♦ ♣ ♠ ♥ ♦

Chapter Eight

Nell spoke quietly with her contact, getting the information on where Leah and the mages were holed up. She passed him some money and walked back over to the table where William sat quietly, pretending not to be fascinated by the place.

"Come on upstairs with me. It's quieter and you can look at the place from a better vantage point."

She led him to one of the balconies that framed the second story of Darkness. Up there it was lush. The ultramodern chrome of the downstairs area was still there, but plush, thick banquette seating lined the walls and the railing was built in such a way that one could sit, drink and still see much of the action below.

"So? What do you think?" she asked after they'd sunk into the cushions.

"I just had no idea. This whole universe exists and I didn't know about it. I'm fascinated and repulsed all at once."

She nodded. "It's always here, just beneath the surface. Most of the time people see it and because it's so strange their brains just reject it. I suppose that's what keeps us safe. Those wards aren't to harm your kind, they're to protect us."

"From what? You're the ones with superpowers. I mean, if anything, we're the ones who need protecting."

"From that very attitude. There are billions of humans on the earth. There are millions of us. Not hundreds of millions, either. We keep to ourselves and hide our abilities because there are those who'd hang us, put us in camps, round us up and use us if our existence was well-known. We're wary for a reason." She shrugged. "We have rules. We don't harm you all unless it's in self-defense. Some of us need more policing than others, like vampires who can pass on their state via fluid transmission."

"There are, like, what? Cops for you guys then? More than what you do?"

"I'm a cop of sorts for my Clan. For witches. I don't go out and hunt werewolves or vampires who go rogue. There are those who do that though, yes."

"Tell me about it."

She laughed. "I really can't. In the first place I don't know that much and in the second place, it's not my story to tell." She shifted, putting her beer down on the low table, feeling the pulse of the music low and deep, in the same place where her need for him resided. Her skirt rode up to just below the fold of her lap and she let it.

"Why are you here with me now, William?"

He put his drink down, sliding his palm up her thigh. "I don't know. I can't not be. I want to touch you so bad. What is it about you that draws me this way?"

She widened her thighs in invitation, and in the low light she noted his pupils swallowing nearly all the color in his eyes.

"If I told you, you wouldn't believe me. So just touch me and let yourself want. Give it free rein. You've got nothing to lose." Her voice was a whisper, but she knew he heard her, even above the music.

He closed his eyes a moment, the war within himself clear on his face. But when he looked at her again, it was clear which side had won.

"Open all the way." His normally smooth voice had gone rough, sending a thrill through her.

His fingers glided up the supersensitive skin of her inner thigh, his eyes still locked on hers.

"Are you wet?"

"Touch my pussy and see for yourself." *Please.*

"Here?"

"Why not? We're alone up here. For now. It is Las Vegas, after all." That, and if he didn't touch her she thought she might die.

He got to his knees, pushing hers wide until her skirt hiked up, exposing her panties. "I find myself needing to own you, Nell. It's…unusual for me. I don't need to possess the women I'm with. But *you're* unusual."

The tips of his fingers brushed against the slit of her pussy, sliding gently back and forth. Even through the material of the panties she knew he felt how wet she was. For him.

"Well, cat got your tongue then, witch?" A smile canted his mouth and the suave veneer slid away just a bit, exposing the more carefree man just beneath. Crap, she was in deep with him.

"I could ask if you need help getting those off. But I figure you've got more than enough practice in the removal of panties department."

"You're quick with the comments there for a woman whose pussy is wet and ready." He raised a brow at her.

Reaching down, she made quick work of removing her panties before taking his hand and putting it back over her cunt. "Whatever it takes to get you working."

Spreading her pussy wide open, he leaned his head down and took a taste, just the barest whisper of a tongue flick against her clit. It sent her up an inch with a gasp.

William heard nothing more than her breathing, felt nothing more than her flesh against his hands and mouth. Her taste filled his senses, her scent drowned him. She was everything as he knelt there and worshiped her. Her body was magic, wending her taste through him, addicting, sharp and ultimately her. So unique he knew he'd miss her every time he took a breath for the rest of his days.

The idea of her walking away gripped him, scared him, made him want to ask her to stay so they could explore what they might make together as a couple.

As if she felt his panic, she reached down and sifted gentle fingers through his hair, soothing even as they inflamed his need for more.

Nell felt the cool air against the flesh of her slick pussy as he ran his thumbs through her, bringing her honey up and over her clit. William didn't just touch her, he consumed and she didn't know what do to with it all.

A groan from deep inside pushed through her lips as he began to lap at her. Slowly, gently, but voraciously.

There weren't any words, but they didn't need them. He told her how he felt with his mouth against her as surely as she did by offering herself to him so openly. Whether or not the other fully accepted that, she didn't want to face just then.

William told her so much in his touch. With the slight rasp of the shadow of his beard as he ran his chin against the sensitive skin where thighs met body. Delight trilled through her when he began to flick the underside of her swollen clit quick and hard with the tip of his tongue like some secret language.

She'd ceased to notice they were in public, ceased worrying about whether anyone would come up the nearby stairs. All that mattered was his mouth, his hands, their union of the physical and emotional.

Nell knew she was sliding quickly toward an orgasm—not just any orgasm, but a big one. It built in her toes, slid down from her scalp. Her thighs trembled against his palms as he held her open.

His top teeth abraded, ever so lightly, over the hood of her clit, against the bare, sensitized clit itself as he stroked his tongue against the underside at the same time. She'd never experienced anything like it. Like this man. She didn't know what to do or even what she was feeling.

Nearly frozen, totally overwhelmed by sensation and emotion, noises came unheeded from the back of her throat as she opened her mouth to speak but had no words.

A flash of pleasure so exquisite it was nearly pain sliced through her and suddenly she drowned in her climax. But he didn't stop; his mouth stayed on her, kept moving as his fingers slid into her.

Finally she moved up a bit and kept her hand on his shoulder to hold him off. Her eyes remained closed because she was afraid of what she'd say if she saw him right then.

William sat back for a long moment, wondering what the hell had just happened. It shouldn't be so much, this thing between them. This hunger for her shouldn't be there, not like a swell that threatened to swallow him whole. This started as joking and now he was under her spell.

He paused. Was he? Had she done something to him? He looked at her and knew that wasn't the case. Her eyes held the same surprise, the same skittishness at the depth of what lay between them that he felt.

Shoving it aside to puzzle over later, he stood. "Stand up. Go to the rail and hold on. How far are you willing to take this, Nell?"

Her eyes opened and met his challenge head-on. She stood, leaving her panties behind. "You're the one hesitating. I'd fuck you down there on a table if you asked. I want you, William. And I don't care who knows it."

She sauntered past him and went to grip the railing, her ass so very tantalizingly on display. Would she?

A clear vision of spreading her out on the table downstairs, sliding his cock into her cunt in open view of every man in the place, shook him. He'd not considered himself an exhibitionist before, but making such a clear mark of his possession appealed to him. They'd all watch, cocks hard, as he fucked this gorgeous, willful woman. This woman who gave herself to him in full view.

Christ.

Moving to her, he dug into his wallet and found what he needed. The bass of the pounding house music in the club throbbed neatly with his pulse, driving him on. Strobes backlit her body, the smooth line of her bare ass and legs to the top of her boots. Conversation, music, the scent of cigarettes and alcohol, of sex and sweat burned his senses.

The sound of foil being torn open sliced through her,

bringing a small echoing gasp from her lips. Anticipation coiled low in her belly as she heard him roll the condom on.

A gentle but firm hand arranged her so that she was wide open to him, hips tipped so her ass canted high, thighs spread wide. She loved the way his hands on her felt. Loved that he touched her not with disinterest, but with intent. With possession. That touch from any other man would be infuriating and humiliating, but from him? Pride warmed her that he'd want her so deeply.

She closed her eyes a moment as the broad head of him brushed against the slick, hot gate to her pussy. Opening again as he pushed in slowly, her gaze locked on the people below.

She sucked in her breath sharply as she caught the eye of a man at the bar. *Oh my, what a lovely experience* warred with her fascination at being seen this way. Her grip on the railing tightened at the pleasure of his thickness filling her up, stroking those nerve endings deep inside her.

Wickedly wanton, Nell rolled her hips back and pushed against him to meet his thrusts. The man at the bar had turned fully to stare up at them. She caught the glint, knew he was a Were of some sort and had the vision to see just exactly what was happening.

"Yeah. So tight," William said softly as he'd worked all the way inside her. He didn't thrust for long moments, instead, running his hands along her back and around to her breasts.

"He's watching us," she murmured, tipping her chin at the male below at the bar.

William chuckled, leaning around her. "Mmmm. Does that bother you?"

"It should. I don't do this. Fuck in public. But," she swallowed hard, "it makes me hot."

He hissed, taking in his breath. "Me, too, beautiful." He pulled out and pressed all the way in so hard her breasts nearly bounced out of her bodice. "Let's give him something to remember, shall we?"

He filled her in more ways than one, his cock, his body, his presence smoothing over an ache she'd had since their argument in the garage the week before. When she wasn't with him she was empty. It should frighten her, the way he made her feel, like the absence of it would gut her utterly. But it didn't. Nell was *sure* of this. Of him and his place in her life. When this was over, when she'd dealt with the human and the damned mages, she would grab William Emery and not let him go. There'd be work, she knew that, but she knew what they could build would be worth it.

She arched when he reached around and slid a hand into the bodice of her blouse, palming her nipple. Shivers rippled through her, straight to her pussy as he drove into her hard and fast.

"He's still watching," William said in her ear.

Indeed, the man below still stood watching, having turned to face them. A smile broke over his face and he tipped his glass toward them. Even in the dark she knew she blushed at that, and yet, it still turned her on.

"He can watch all he wants, but he'll never have this. This bounty. You're magic." He snorted. "I mean it."

How would he feel a week from now when she wasn't there anymore?

"Finger your clit for me. Let him know you can't get enough of me."

The muscles in her arm corded as she leaned more fully

on it to remove the other to reach to slide her free hand between her thighs.

The tug of her pussy around him and then the brush of her fingers against his cock for a few brief moments let him know she'd obeyed. And then, as she touched herself fully, her inner walls clutched him, squeezing tight.

"Fuck. Fuck! So good. What you do to me, Nell."

Through her curls, she saw the desire in the eyes of the man below, saw the envy, felt the rush of pride that she was William's. *His.*

She cried out softly. Felt her nipple stab into his palm as her cunt slickened, heated, spasmed around his cock until he nearly lost his mind with just how good she felt when she came around him.

She didn't want this moment to end. Wanted him to stay buried in her forever and that's why it *had* to end. He pushed one last time, hard and deep.

Nell felt the rush of intensity as he came. His emotions spoke loudly through the way he touched her, through the change in his breathing. It didn't take a magical gift to know she touched him. But would it be enough or would he force her to push?

She opened her eyes as he stepped back. The man downstairs forgotten, she smoothed down her skirt and turned, but William had already put distance between them and her heart sank.

"William," she started, but he held his hand out. She waited while he tossed the condom into a nearby trash can, covering it with napkins before draining his drink.

"I…I have to get back to the club. Let me know what happens with Leah."

She stood there, livid and hurt as he rushed off, his anguish written on his face.

"What the fuck!" Snatching up her panties, she shoved them in her bag and rushed after him.

Oh, she was so going to make him pay for this when she finally won him over!

♣ ♠ ♥ ♦ ♣ ♠ ♥ ♦ ♣ ♠ ♥ ♦

Chapter Nine

Nell trailed him, wanting to make sure William got back to the club safely.

Her contact said the mages knew of William and he was at risk from them, too. She didn't want him to get jumped by something he couldn't handle before she got the chance to wipe the floor with the fools.

William's reaction was sort of cute once she got over her initial hurt. He'd touched her with tenderness, spoken to her with possession in mind. He wanted her, was moved by her, no doubt. It wasn't that surprising it freaked him out. The differences between the way she saw the world and he did were vast. Her rational mind knew it. Knew his understanding of Fate wasn't similar to hers in any way, no matter what his heart and soul told him. He was a businessman, he believed in the bottom line.

Lucky for him and for her, too, being together was the bottom line in their situation. He'd just have to accept it.

Smiling, she kept some distance, thinking she'd have to give him a few lessons on self-defense and how not to get followed. That smile died when he got to the doors of the Dollhouse and he was met by two women. Two women who instantly began rubbing all over him and worse, he ate it up and even played a bit of grab ass as they entered.

Oh, that prick! She narrowed her eyes and after one last sweep through the area, she headed back to Bellagio.

William's head swam. What the fuck was he going to do? He'd never, ever felt that intensity of connection when he'd been with anyone. Every time he touched Nell, thought of her, he warmed inside.

He wasn't some untested boy. He'd been with plenty of women, but he'd never had a reaction to any of them the way he did for Nell. What they had—chemistry or magic or whatever it was—he knew at some elemental level was different from anything that ever had been or ever would be.

He'd gone to that club, stepped firmly into her world and he'd gotten off on it. Moving aside one of the women who'd attached themselves to him when he entered the club, he ran a hand through his hair. Licking his lips, lips that still tasted of her salt, of her tang, he groaned.

"Ladies, if you'll excuse me. I just remembered something I need to take care of. Please enjoy the evening. I'll have a bottle of champagne sent over." He said it absently, not even noticing the features on their faces. He'd intended to fuck the pain away, to wash Nell from his skin and soul with the bodies of other women and he knew it would be useless.

Worse, it would be a mockery of the heat he'd shared with Nell, and that would betray not only her, but himself, as well.

Heading into his office, he tossed himself onto his couch with a growl of frustration. The interlude on the balcony had been meant to be lighthearted. Hot and fun. But it backfired. It backfired because fucking her, touching her there had sent him headlong past pretensions of extreme lust into the seeds of love.

He sat up. Love? No. Fucking. Way. Sure, he liked Nell; he'd liked her more each time he'd seen her. Each time he'd thought about her he'd recalled something else he admired. Not just the way she felt while he'd been inside her, not just the way she matched him sexually, although admittedly that was huge. He'd never had that sort of parity with anyone sexually. But in truth, he loved the way she held herself, the way she was so strong and in control, the way she smiled and laughed. Hell, even the fact that she was some witch bounty hunter made her special and strong and it attracted him, impressed him and made him proud.

He pushed off the couch and began to pace. She'd settled inside him. Not as a weight, not as a burden, but as part of him. As much as he wanted to deny it, to be frustrated and angry and pretend she was nothing more to him than a few hours' worth of fun, she was more. She was everything and he supposed he'd reached the stage in his life where he simply couldn't ignore it.

Stock-still and struck dumb, he faced it. He didn't understand it at all. He didn't know her! He'd met her less than two weeks before. How could it be? He wasn't a woo-woo type of guy. He didn't believe in karma or soul mates or hell, and until the first time he laid eyes on Nell Hunter, he wasn't sure he even believed in love.

"Too damned bad." He clenched his fists. He didn't want to love anyone and the only way to resolve this stupid mess was to get Nell Hunter's delectable ass out of Vegas posthaste.

★ ★ ★

Nell stomped into her hotel room and threw her purse against the far wall with a curse. Galen had gone out to do some reconnaissance work near the area they'd thought the mages had been holed up.

She snatched up her phone and dialed the familiar number.

"You will not believe what that *fuck* did!" she said without preamble when Meriel picked up.

"This is about William Emery, our boy hero?" Meriel's voice held amusement, but also concern.

"Meriel, I don't care what Fate has in mind, he's a gigantic tool and there is simply no way I can deal with being shackled to such a twit. Fate has to be wrong."

She unzipped her boots and tossed them to the side.

Meriel sighed. "Tell me what he did."

Nell recounted the evening, including the whole balcony episode and then the way he'd let himself get jumped on by the women back at his club.

"Here I am, even after he fucked and ran, making sure he's safe and all he can think about is dipping his cock into yet more women? I'm not enough? He sure came like I was enough. Meriel, how dare I not be enough!"

She wadded her skirt and threw it in a far corner.

"In the first place, of course you're enough. He's an idiot and he's running from a very scary truth. I know you understand that even as it hurts."

"He's gonna be the one hurting if he has sex with anyone but me, I'll tell you what. Punk. Idiot. Prick. Oh! He's just an ass." She failed to hold back the tears.

"He's totally a prick. And I'm going to kick him so hard when I meet him for making you cry. Do you want me to come down there?" Meriel's sarcasm smoothed into soothing tones.

"No. I'll be done in a day or two if everything goes as planned anyway." She sniffled and her blouse and bra followed the skirt. She planned to burn the whole ensemble later.

"You're not giving up on this butthead. We'll make him pay, of course, but you love him. And Nell, Fate is female. She won't take this lightly and you know as well as I do, he's so going to pay for making you cry." Meriel laughed and Nell wiped her nose on the sleeve of the robe she found hanging in the bathroom.

"I hate him."

"No, you don't. If you hated him, he couldn't make you cry. You love him and he loves you, which is why he ran like a little girl after that thing that happened in Darkness. He'll come knocking soon enough. Then you can make him pay. You sure you don't want me to come down there? I feel awful to hear you so upset."

"Save me a pint of Cherry Garcia. I'll be back soon. I have to go. I need to shower and sleep. Or try to sleep. I love you, thanks for listening." Nell slumped onto the bed.

"I love you, too. It's going to be fine. Call me tomorrow."

She hung up and threw herself onto her back for a moment, giving in to a miniwallow. She planned to throttle the hell out of these mages and the woman when she hunted them down the next day. Just to make herself feel better if for no other reason. Hmpf.

William stalked down the hall, annoyed with himself for even being there. He should be back at his apartment with a woman or two, fucking this one out of his head. Fuck it, he had to get her out of Vegas before he did or said something stupid.

Agitated, he pounded on the door, softening as he remembered it was after one. He waited, hearing her approach on the other side.

"What do you want?" Her voice came, muffled through the door.

He leaned in close to the door. "Open up, Nell."

"No."

"Damn it. Open the door."

"Go away, William. I can't deal with you right now. I'm tired and I don't have the energy to fight with you or take your insults." Her voice caught. He heard it through the door and regret crashed through him.

"I need to talk to you. It's important. Open up. Please." His hands fisted with the need to pull her close and make that catch in her voice go away.

She opened it hard, stood there in a tiny pair of pink panties and nothing else. He pushed his way inside and closed the door, locking it. It was then he really saw her face. Her beautiful eyes sparked with temper, but they were swollen and red.

She'd been crying? Tenderness unfurled through him, pushing aside his anger, his frustration. "What's wrong?"

She put a hand on her hip and try as hard as he could, there was no way her near total nakedness couldn't attract his attention. He'd been inside her twice, thought of her in hundreds of sexual situations, but he'd never seen her totally nude. Her breasts were fucking amazing. The rest of her was long and lean, toned and creamy pale. She shone like the moon, nearly stopping his heart with her own unique beauty.

Never in his life had he been so moved by a woman's beauty. No one was like her.

Still, tears. Focus on the tears.

"I'm trying to sleep, in case you haven't noticed. You got what you wanted back at Darkness. Why are you here?"

That hit him like the slap it was. Landed true because he knew he'd run out and made her feel used. He'd done it to hide from what she made him feel and instead he'd damaged her. The wall he'd erected just two hours earlier continued to crumble.

"Doesn't look like you were sleeping. It looks like you've been crying. And I *didn't* get enough of what I wanted at Darkness." He paused and walked down the hall into the room. He'd meant to just tell her to get out of town immediately and instead found himself standing stock-still, breathing deep. Her scent hung in the air, wrapping around him and squeezing until he had no choice but to abandon his stupid plan. "Damn it. Damn it, Nell, I don't feel like I can get enough of you. Ever."

She'd grabbed a robe and was attempting to put it on when he spun and caught her. Emotion clouded his gaze and something deep inside her squeezed.

"What now? What did *I* do?" She left her robe open, daring him not to look.

"Fuck. Fuck. Why? What did you do to me? Why do I love you?" He reached out and pulled her to him and she growled in his face.

"Do you think I need magic to be alluring? You're such a *prick!*"

"I am. I know I am. It's served me well, kept me away from feeling deeply about other women like Leah! And you come along, I barely even know you and I can't stop thinking about you."

Anguish poured off him in a wave, catching her, tugging at her emotions, her need to soothe him.

She pulled herself loose, needing some distance. "I would not use magic to manipulate your feelings. That's not how it works. I use it to defend myself and my people. I don't use it to play with men who I'd be way better off without. You don't know what an insult it is to accuse me of that. There are no love potions, no spells to make another person love you and if there were, I'd still not use them. I wouldn't cloud your will."

He sat on a nearby chair and looked up at her. "I'm sorry. It… I know you wouldn't harm me like that. I don't know why I know it, but I do. I'm just… I don't know what to do with all this emotion."

Unbidden, laughter bubbled from her and she bent, kneeling before him, giving in to her need to touch him. "You think I do?"

A smile tugged at his mouth and she had to kiss it. His hands cupped her cheeks gently as he tasted, teased, returned the kiss.

"I love you," he murmured against her lips.

"I love you, too."

"I didn't want to. I didn't want to love anyone, but I can't resist you and I don't want to. I don't know what this will all mean tomorrow other than that you're mine and that's not going to change."

He said it so surely, so laden with possession and utter maleness it made her shiver.

"Yeah? So take me then."

★ ★ ★

William stood, but she stayed on her knees, leaning in to rub her cheek over the ridiculously painful erection he'd had ever since he'd gotten on the elevator to her floor.

"Let me take the edge off."

He watched her hungrily as ripples of sensation slid through him every place she touched him. He nearly growled when she undid his jeans and finally freed his cock.

"I've not been able to see it this closely," she said, amusement clear in her voice and he laughed.

"Take all the time you want to check it out."

"Well, the first order of business is to determine where it's been. I noticed your *company* when you went back to the Dollhouse earlier."

He blushed, mortified she'd seen it. "Ah. I imagine you were following to keep me safe, huh? I'm a prick, remember? But nothing happened. I ordered them a bottle of champagne and stewed over you for hours until I came here. I don't want any woman but you. I'm sorry I hurt you."

"I considered maiming you for touching the redhead's ass. You'll pay for that, Mr. Man. But for now I'd rather suck your cock."

Nearly choking when she licked a line from his balls to the slit, he simply took her in, so beautiful there on her knees. The shock of heat from her mouth when she took him inside made him ache.

She took it slow, savoring every inch of his cock, licking and sucking, stroking with clever fingertips. What a fucking amazing feeling to be swallowed not just physically but emotionally. The intensity of the moment amped up a thousand times simply because of how she made him feel inside, as well as outside. This love thing sure made the sex hotter.

Orgasm built quickly, gathering at the base of his spine, pleasure seeping through every part of him as she took him into her mouth.

"Stop, Nell, stop. I'm close and I want to fuck you."

She pulled off, leaving his cock shiny and her lips swollen. A pang of desire pulsed through him at the sight. "Do you have slow recovery? Like, once and you're through?"

Horrified, he nearly gasped until he caught her smile. "You're a wicked thing, aren't you? For your information I have wonderful recovery, thank you very much."

"Then shut up and come in my mouth." Before shock and then the flush of heat at her words could register, she sucked him back into her mouth, deeper than she had before and he had to lock his knees before he collapsed.

Her short curls felt soft and cool as he slid his hands through her hair, cradling her skull. Instead of letting his head fall back, eyes closed as he might have done with another woman, he let himself be mesmerized by the sight of his cock sliding into and then pulling out of her mouth. Over and over, each time pulling him in deeper and deeper until he gripped her hair and he came so hard he saw stars even with his eyes open.

He sank to his knees when she pulled back, leaving him with a kiss on his belly. Without words, he pulled her close, one arm banded around her waist, and pulled her to him, pressing his mouth to hers to steal a kiss.

She consumed him like fire, her touch ate him up, the taste of her mouth spiced with his own essence drove him mad. He tore his lips away and stood, pulling her up with him.

"Off with the robe and panties. I want you totally naked and on that bed."

"You, too," she said, tossing the robe to the side. Her panties fluttered to the floor as she threw them over her shoulder when she climbed on the bed.

"Lamps don't do you any justice." He stalked to the windows and used the button to open them wide, letting in the lights from outside and the full moon above.

"Beautiful. God." He worked the shirt up and over his head and toed off his shoes to get rid of the jeans and boxers. She lay on the bed, watching him with a smile. Long and muscled, breasts high and round, her big green eyes taking him in, she was everything he never knew he wanted until he saw it.

"William Emery, you have a wonderfully sexy body. Why do you hide it under all those clothes? Well, scratch that, I'm glad you do. Come over here and fuck me already."

He laughed and jumped on the bed, wondering when the last time he'd been so carefree during sex, or any time really.

Nell took in the tanned, firm skin, the muscles of a man who worked out regularly. He had an elegant body, tall, lean and muscled just right. Thank goodness he didn't shave. She moaned to herself as she slid her hands up his chest, through the light smattering of hair. It was his turn to moan when she slid her fingers around and around his nipples until she pinched them, just hard enough that he jumped, but not hard enough to hurt.

"Christ," he hissed and moved closer, kissing her shoulder. "I have work to do. Back off and stop tormenting me." He grabbed her hands and put them above her head. "Stay. I told you I needed some time with you on your back and here we are."

She smiled, stretching under his touch, loving the way he felt, loving that they were together and not fighting. After he got on all fours over her body, he ran his hands from her ankles to her thighs, skimming featherlight over her mound.

"Wet." He groaned softly. Leaning down, he nuzzled and breathed in at the hollow of her throat. "Why do you smell so good?"

"William." She paused a moment as he traced his fingers down her shoulders, bringing gooseflesh.

"Hmm?" His tongue left a warm, wet trail southward.

"This is probably just going to sound all mystical and stuff, but we're meant to be together. It's Fate."

He shrugged as his mouth left hot kisses against the top curve of her left breast. "At this point, I'm pretty much just giving in. Whatever it is, I believe it."

"Oh." Well, that was anticlimactic.

"Your breasts are so fucking gorgeous. Have I told you that?" He tested their weight, drawing his thumbs back and forth across her nipples as she squirmed.

"I can't really recall right now. I'm sort of distracted. Oh!" She gasped as his mouth surrounded one of her nipples and drew hard. A shock of pleasure shot straight to her clit.

"You like that. I love how responsive you are." He spoke around a nipple, nibbling on it.

"Have you met a woman who didn't? Wait, I don't want to know." Nell writhed beneath him, struggling for breath.

She stretched to touch as much of him as she could, smoothing her palms down his back down to his ass. Spectacular.

He shifted his attention, and his mouth, down her breast, not ignoring the sensitive skin just beneath.

"I like finding all the places on your body that make you tingly. I can see I need to devote a lot of time to this project. I do like the noises you make. Gets me so hot, my recovery time is much improved."

Nell laughed. "Just, you know, do something! You talk too much."

He moved down her body and shoved her thighs open to lie between them. "Even in the moonlight I can see your cunt, glistening and wet for me. Makes me feel invincible that I can do this to you."

He opened her to his gaze and then used one hand to slowly make lazy circuits from her gate up to her clit and back again, just following the furl and line of her labia.

She gasped when he slid two fingers into her, feeling her internal muscles clutch at the invasion, wanting more than fingers.

As if he'd read her mind, he gave her a kiss, a full deep kiss, using his lips and tongue and teeth. He kissed her pussy like a lover, like he'd kissed her mouth just minutes before. Nell grabbed the coverlet to keep from yanking his head closer.

And then he focused on her clit, flicking it with his tongue slowly at first and then speeding his pace. The two fingers inside her became three, stretching her, readying her for his cock.

He sucked her clit in between his lips—in and out, slightly abrading it with his teeth until she was ready to beg. Only to back off, blowing warm air across the slickened flesh of her pussy.

Words escaped, fluttering from her reach until all she could do was issue breathy moans and incoherent pleas.

He hitched her thighs up onto his shoulders then, going in for that final pass. The blood rushed in her ears, roaring as climax circled, descending so that she felt nothing else but him, his mouth on her.

Finally, all his work came together just perfectly and just for a moment it felt as if time had stopped altogether until it rushed back with blinding intensity as she exploded into orgasm, back bowed, arching into his face.

She wasn't aware of much more until some time later when he moved back up and placed a kiss on her lips. She wound her arms around his neck and held on as he devastated her mouth, feasting on her.

"I like the way you taste," she said as he finally pulled back.

"Funny, I like the way you taste, too." He rolled away to rustle in his pants and came back moments later, holding a condom. "Now, I think we've arrived at the fucking portion of our program."

He rolled to his back and pulled her atop his body.

"Oh, I see, you want me to do all the work?" She grabbed the condom and rolled it on his cock quickly. "You didn't lie about that recovery time."

Without any more chatter, she rose up, guided him true and slid back down, taking him into her body as she did.

He lay there and looked up, watching the sway of her breasts as she rode him. Once he'd given in to how he felt about her, truly gave in, it was like everything clicked into place.

They'd have to work at a relationship, but they would, he didn't doubt it. He certainly had a lot to learn about her world.

Taking her breasts into his hands, he pinched and rolled her nipples, delighting in the way her cunt tightened around his cock.

"I like it when you do all the work. You fuck me and I just look up at you and play with your nipples. Life is very good."

They remained that way, gazes locked, her body rocking over his for some time. Neither said much, but at the same time, everything was expressed.

Once he neared orgasm, he slid a hand between them and found her clit, sliding a knuckle back and forth against her as she ground her body down and against him, driving herself higher and him, as well.

When he finally came, it was on the heels of her climax and he welcomed her body as she slumped down with a satisfied sigh.

♣ ♠ ♥ ♦ ♣ ♠ ♥ ♦ ♣ ♠ ♥ ♦

Chapter Ten

The ringing phone woke William up, along with the warm press of Nell's naked body as she leaned over him to grab it. While she was there, he put his arms around her, keeping her in place.

He heard her say she'd be right there, noted the seriousness in her tone and let go when she hung up.

"Everything all right?"

She rolled off the bed and he smiled, watching the way she looked as the sunlight touched her bare skin.

"Galen found Leah. Galen is my partner," she added at his blank look. "Anyway, he's tailing her, and I need to get out there. I'm sorry, I didn't want to have to rush out."

"Good, because I'm coming with you." He picked his cell up and she started to argue. "Don't bother. I'm going to call my manager to let him know to take over for me at work."

Ignoring him for the moment, she rushed into the bathroom, shoving her legs into jeans and quickly brushing her teeth with her free hand.

When she came back out, she caught sight of him standing at the door once her head popped through the shirt's neckline.

"Look, William, this is serious shit. You can't come. I'll

call you when I get back." She moved past him quickly once she'd grabbed her weapons and left the room.

"I'm not arguing with you. I'm coming."

She sighed and sped her pace, but he kept up. Skipping the wait for the elevator she ran down the stairs, her heavy boots thudding on the concrete.

The heat of the garage hit her, staggering her for a moment as she headed to the car.

"I'm going to grab on to the hood if you don't let me in. I mean it. We're together, Nell. Together. I'm not letting you do this alone."

"Oh, my God! William, this is my job. I have to go." She got in, but he simply dove around her and landed in the backseat. Starting her car with a heavy sigh, she seat belted in and tore out of there with squealing tires.

"Does this mean you're letting me come?" he yelled from the backseat over Judas Priest booming from her speakers.

"You will stay in the car. You will follow my instructions. You will not argue with me. I mean it. This isn't just about your safety, but mine and Galen's, too."

She locked in to the GPS on Galen's phone and pointed her car in that direction at a very high rate of speed. The engine roared, purring through her bones as the music amped her up, helped her focus, prepared her to do whatever it took to take these people down.

"Talk to me," she said over the line once Galen answered.

"They've pulled into some luxe mansion thing out here. Magical wards all over the place. Nasty stuff out here, Nell. Be ready." He gave her the general directions to where he parked his rental.

"All right. I should be there in a few minutes. Call Meriel

to let her know we're moving. I've got a civilian with me. Yes, don't ask. He'll keep out of the way. Don't move without me unless it's absolutely necessary." Galen was strong, but not as strong as she was and these mages were nasty. Plus, she wanted to pop that bitch Leah in the face—this was personal.

From the backseat, William watched her. Eyes shielded by dark sunglasses, the music pounding, her face was a mask of severe concentration. Now he knew where he got that air of danger before. She was a dangerous being. And he liked it. Holy shit, she was hot when she got all tough. Who knew he had some secret fetish for tough women?

She'd been right. He should have stayed back at the hotel, but he couldn't bear to let her go, not knowing what would happen to her. That was something they'd have to deal with if they meant to make this thing between them work. The distance would be an issue, as well, but it wasn't that far and they'd make it happen. He wasn't going to just let her go, not now that he'd found her.

She was a damned good driver and clearly the car had been modded. He noted the reinforced roll bars even as he fantasized about fucking her again, this time by candlelight and with no interruptions. Sometimes a man had to multitask.

"Okay," she finally spoke as they slowed and she turned the music off, "I mean it, William, you have to listen. I can't…I can't bear the thought of anything happening to you so you need to stay here. Do you know how to use a weapon?"

She took a side street when they approached the entrance to a gated community, looking at some notes she'd taken.

"Um, yes. I'm not an Olympic gold medalist with a rifle or anything, but I know how to use a handgun."

She stopped at a cul-de-sac in a new development, pulling up next to a rental car where a muscular man with very short, pale blond hair got out. A sliver of jealousy worked through him as he noted the concern on the other man's face and Nell's smile at him. It was the man he'd seen her with at the Dollhouse right after they'd had sex the first time.

She got out and William followed.

"William, this is Galen." They shook hands and looked each other over warily. "He's staying in the car. I'll leave him a weapon and a phone." She turned back to William and pulled a handgun out, handing it to him. "The clip is full. When you get in the car, I'm going to do something to it so you won't be easily seen and hopefully the shade of the houses and these trees will keep you cool, as well. Water in the trunk. If we're not back in an hour, take this car back to the city and someone will contact you."

Fear, real true fear for her safety shocked him into realizing what he felt was beyond what he'd imagined. Yes, he'd said he loved her, but this was striking. He wasn't quite sure what to do with it.

So he nodded and grabbed her, delivering a hard, possessive kiss. "You'd better get back here, Nell. You don't have my permission to get hurt."

She smiled and kissed his forehead. "Gotcha, tough guy. If anyone does see you and asks what you're doing here, you're a developer. You're supreme with the bullshit—I'm sure you'll work it out." Making a waving motion, she ushered him back into the car and then stood back. The air around them shimmered a moment and then he watched her walk away with the other dude at her side.

★ ★ ★

"Stupid to have brought him."

She looked at Galen as they circled the long way around the giant gated community. "I know."

"Are you centered?"

She stopped and then boosted herself up and over the fence easily. "You're a dick. You think his cooties will mess with my mind?" She bent, looking in between nearby cars to see the supermansion just up the street where the mages had gone. "Maybe I'll have to take breaks to write his name on my binder?"

"Fine, fine. Made your point."

They walked closer, snug up against the house next door and she opened herself up to use her othersight. "Five people inside. One human, four mages. Let's try not to hurt anyone. Or not hurt them too bad anyway. I want to bring her back to Seattle today."

She stood and they fanned out, Galen circling around the back of the house, using his magic to short out the security cameras.

Nell went to the front door and with a wave of her hand, the locks disengaged. Much to the surprise of the two men in the front hallway.

"Why, hello there! I'm Nell Hunter, I expect you probably know my name, but in case not, I'm the hunter for the Owen Clan. As you might imagine, my boss is not pleased you've absconded with our money. That makes me very sad, boys." She gave them an exaggerated pout and then shot her magic at them, knocking them both down.

"Did you think you could just come in here like this?"

Nell looked up, easily sidestepping the sizzle of magic sent her way. The air in the house hung heavy and wrong. "Oh, my. Well, look at you. Ben Healy, I wish I could say it was nice to see you, but I'd be lying. And why yes, I do think I can walk right in here. In fact, I did. Now, hand over your human lackey and our money." She tossed some magic his way, but he blocked it. Ben Healy had been a member of the Owen Clan. A natural witch with not a whole lot of ability, but quite of bit of ambition, he repudiated all they'd stood for and joined up with the mages.

"Nell Hunter, still a bitch I see."

She moved up the stairs where he stood, shooting her magic to try and disable him and ducking his. Dimly she heard Galen shout in the background and the sound of breaking glass.

"I'm better than you. I'm cuter than you and darn it, people like me." Nell huffed as she forwent her magic and threw a solid right hook to Ben's jaw.

It knocked him back, sending him bouncing off a table. He scrambled to his feet and that's when Nell saw Leah, cowering in a far corner. Ben ran at her, shoved Leah toward Nell and continued down the stairs.

"Fuck! Galen, get him!" Nell yelled and caught Leah by the upper arm and hauled her down the stairs toward the open front door.

A squeal of tires and the sight of a car racing out of sight greeted her as she got there. Galen came running back.

"You got two of them, I got another. Was that Ben Healy?"

"Yes. Forget it for now. Let's get Alex in here to clean up. You stay behind and supervise. I'll be taking this piece of shit back home."

"I have rights! You can't just take me like this." Leah

struggled, but she was shorter than Nell, petite and while she might have been good at ripping people off, Nell was better at keeping them in line.

"I can do anything I want and you'd best remember that. I am Owen Clan and you have stolen from us. You'll face our justice. Now come on and shut up or I'll have to deal with you in an unpleasant fashion."

Galen got off the phone and turned back to her. "Alex is on the way. I'll stay here. The mages are all incapacitated. Get her back." He paused. "Do you want me to get William back to town?"

She sighed. "I don't know. Hang on here with her. I'll be back with the cars in a few." Nell shoved Leah into Galen's grasp and jogged back to where she'd jumped the fence.

♣ ♠ ♥ ♦ ♣ ♠ ♥ ♦ ♣ ♠ ♥ ♦

Chapter Eleven

William made himself try and rein in his impatience as the plane taxied down the runway in Seattle. It'd been two weeks since he'd last seen Nell and he'd been dying without her.

The last time he'd seen her, she'd come around the corner after being gone for forty-five minutes and he'd let out a breath. He'd been terrified, every minute feeling like an hour since she'd walked out of his sight.

It had been harder seeing Leah and not slapping her. But as he told her with some satisfaction, as he'd watched Nell load her into the back of the car, she'd brought Nell into his life and for that, he'd be thankful.

He *hadn't* been thankful to stay in Vegas while Nell high-tailed it back to Seattle, but he had to get some coverage in place so he could visit her and she had to do whatever the hell she did with Leah. He found he didn't actually care what happened to Leah. Trusted she'd been brought to whatever justice the Clan had and that she hadn't been hurt. Nell was a warrior, but she wasn't a thug.

Finally, they were able to get off the damned plane and he hurried toward baggage claim where she'd be waiting.

Every afternoon before he went into work, he called to

check in. It was during those calls when he'd really come to know Nell. Appreciate her sense of humor, which ran toward Monty Python and Lewis Black. He respected her sharp mind and the openness with which she let him poke at this connection they had without being defensive.

Every night as he'd locked up, the weight of what he felt for her coupled with her absence bore down on him, making it hard to breathe. And she'd be there, a message on his voice mail, the sound of her soothing the ache of her absence.

Her hair was the first thing he saw as she towered over most of the people standing around. And then he noticed the pale blue dress, the long legs and those green, green eyes.

He went straight to her, into her arms, and breathed in deep as he arrived in the place he'd needed to be but had circled aimlessly his whole life.

Her fingers slid into his hair and her mouth pressed the side of his neck. "You're here."

"There's no other place I'd rather be."

He kissed her, softly, almost chastely as they grabbed his bag and headed to her car.

"It's beautiful here." But he only looked at her.

"The mountain is out today. Nice weather. After we have sex for a few hours I figure we might actually do some sightseeing. On the way to my parents' house for dinner and all." She chewed her bottom lip as they took a big hill and she pulled into a driveway.

The house was simple. Not overly big. Greenery exploded all over the landscape. Butterfly bushes, flowers of all hues, planters full of all manner of living things hung from the trees and along the pretty front porch. Mount Rainier took up the horizon.

"This is amazing." He hadn't imagined her to be a gardener, but she'd talked about doing some planting at some point the week before. "I've underestimated you."

She laughed and opened the front door. "My brother did most of the work. He's amazing with green stuff. But I like to get out and work in the dirt. It's a way to relax, I suppose. Our power, my magic, comes from the earth." A blush bloomed on her cheeks.

"Give me the tour." He held out a hand, and she took it.

"Are you nervous?" he asked.

She cleared her throat. "I guess I am. I…" She flapped her hands around, not quite knowing how to say she didn't know if he still loved her, but would break into a thousand pieces if he didn't.

Instead, she looked at him. Took in his face, the beard stubble she thought was so sexy, the curve of his bottom lip, and sighed, smiling.

"Living room." Dragging him outside to the deck she paused. It was a gorgeous day, one of those perfect Seattle days that made living in the Northwest such a joy. Warm. The air smelled rich with living things. Bees hummed, birds sang, everything was vibrant with color and the sky was so blue it hurt to look at overlong. "The backyard."

She showed him the newly remodeled kitchen and her home office and at last came her bedroom where she'd dithered and dithered until Meriel had taken pity on her and shown up with fifteen huge bags of bedding and other decorative crap for the room. She'd stayed the weekend and had helped her make it just right for William.

"I like it in here." He slowly turned in a circle. "Red and

gold, it works for you. Regal, but old-school. Strong." Reaching to her, he pulled her close. "I've missed you. I never imagined I could miss a person as much as I missed you."

The knot inside her loosened. "Me, too."

"So tell me what's wrong and why you're nervous. Do you…have you changed your mind? About us?"

He looked so lost for a moment she touched his face. "No. I guess I was worried you'd changed your mind or maybe once you got back to your club surrounded by willing and normal women you'd start to think I was a mistake." She wasn't used to being anything but totally confident; it was disconcerting.

He smiled. "Ah, yes. I did say that normal thing. But in all fairness it was before I appreciated the spice of unique. And now everything else is bland. You're all I want, Nell. I don't know how we're going to make this work with the distance. But we will because I simply can't imagine my life without you with me."

He kissed her and freed of her panic, she ripped at his shirt, pulling it off and kissing down his neck.

"Take your time. I'm here. I'm yours. We have all the time in the world." He grinned.

"I need you, William. I've masturbated so much it's not funny and nothing helps. I've been so lonely without you."

He groaned. "Way to torment me."

"I'm not trying to torment you. I'm all about gratification." She untied the halter of her dress and let it fall to her feet. He bent and picked it up as she stepped out of it, bringing it to his face to inhale deeply. The gesture brought moisture to her pussy, hardened already-peaked nipples and warmed her all at once.

"God, you smell good. Good enough to eat. I've missed your scent so damned much." She closed her eyes a moment at the words, loving them, loving him as she divested him of shoes, socks, pants and underwear.

"Much better." She grinned. "You really are too gorgeous for your own good."

"Thank you. I think. Now," he said, pushing her back on the bed. "I mentioned something about you smelling good enough to eat. I'd like to test that theory." He smiled at her lazily and knelt between her thighs. The heat from his skin rose in waves along with his scent and she sighed, contented and aroused, stretching like a cat.

"Two weeks, Nell. Two weeks of sleeping alone and wishing like hell you were beside me." He raised one leg, kissing her ankle and moving his lips down, bending both legs at the knee and holding her wide open. It left her breathless and feeling vulnerable and yet, totally adored as he looked for long moments at her pussy.

"Talk about being too beautiful for her own good." His gaze shifted from her cunt to her face. "Arms above your head and hang on."

An involuntary moan escaped as she followed his directions. Her eyes never left him as he settled and opened her up as widely as possible and then bent his head to taste her. Shards of pleasure broke through her at the contact.

His mouth was soft against her, tongue pressing hard over her clit, alternating quick flicks with swirls around it to draw the flesh of the clitoral hood to caress it. She wasn't far away from coming. Just the sight of him walking into baggage claim had made her wet. His mouth on her, working her up, hands holding her open, she was helpless as pleasure, sharp and intense, burst through her, blinding her to everything but him.

Her pussy was still fluttering from climax when he flipped her over and put a pillow beneath her hips.

"I do love you like this," he murmured and licked the line of her spine from the small of her back to her shoulders, delivering a sharp nip to her shoulder.

A crinkle of foil and then the press of the blunt, wide head of his cock at her entrance, pausing just a moment before he thrust deep with one movement.

She groaned into the pillows and scooted back to take more. The windows were open and a breeze blew the curtains gently, the sound of summer layering over his grunts each time he pressed home fully.

"Since you can't reach your clit, let me help."

She dug her fingers into the coverlet when his middle finger danced ever so lightly over her clit as he fucked into her body.

"I want to see your face," she managed to gasp out.

He'd pulled out, flipped her over, tossing the pillow aside and thrust back in before she could take another breath. "Better? Now you can play with your clit yourself while I watch and I can see those gorgeous tits, too. I'm a lucky man."

"I'm the lucky one," she said softly as she touched his chest over his heart with one hand and her clit with the other. She wrapped her thighs around his waist to angle herself higher. His cock stretched her, making her clit hypersensitive and she gasped as he sped his pace.

"I need to come."

She saw the flash of need in his eyes, saw the anticipation and she squeezed his cock with her inner muscles as she let go and embraced her second orgasm with a soft cry of his name.

"Christ," he whispered and thrust into her hard, a feral intensity etched into his features that brought an edge of delight in her. That glimpse of the uncontrolled man just beneath the suave veneer he wore, that glimpse *she* brought on, swelled her pride and made her smile.

His eyes lost that intense focus and blurred as he thrust once more and came deep within her.

After rolling out of bed and coming back shortly, she'd brought iced tea for them both and he'd gulped it down and settled back, holding her against his body.

"I'm apparently going to be opening up another Dollhouse up here and you'll have to get used to the drive south or load up on frequent flier miles."

She craned her neck to look at him, her skin still pinked with a post-orgasmic glow. "Oh, yeah?"

"You're home to me. I've lived in several states, I've thought I've loved a time or two, but I've never been home, not really. And you give me that. I know this is new, but I just feel it's right."

She laughed. "I've known since about ten minutes after I met you. Each time you acted like a prick to push me away I knew somehow or other we'd end up back with each other because we're meant to be. I have to travel for my job, but most of it is West Coast oriented so we can see each other frequently. I don't expect you to just move up here and I can't totally move down there."

He kissed her, enjoying the knowledge that they had several days to spend like this. "We'll meet halfway. I'll take over part of your closet, you can have half of mine and we'll do it. Because I love you. I'm not even scared to tell you that." He snorted.

"Good. Because you working with all those damned gorgeous dancers all the time without your admitting you loved me was really getting on my nerves. I love you, too. Now, I think we can fit in another orgasm and a shower before you meet my parents. And by the way, your mother called me earlier today. She's, um, quite a character."

He cringed. "Sorry. She means well most of the time and she lives in Boston so there's a whole country between her and us." He laughed. "My brother married one of my dancers who's now a CEO and I am going to marry a witch bounty hunter. She'll be so pleased."

"Marry?"

"Yeah. We live in Vegas, I'm pretty sure we can find a way to plan a wedding of some kind. I've got a ring in my carry-on. I'll give it to you." He paused and she laughed. "After you know, I give it to you."

"Mmmm, yes to both."

DIVINE DESIRES

♣ ♠ ♥ ♦ ♣ ♠ ♥ ♦ ♣ ♠ ♥ ♦

Kit Tunstall

♣ ♠ ♥ ♦ ♣ ♠ ♥ ♦ ♣ ♠ ♥ ♦

Chapter One

Malkiel Nixa exited the astral portal in a flash of light, marveling that a little less than two hours had passed since he had received the frantic call from his elder brother, Eli. Mal had been in bed with a stunning blonde whose name he had already forgotten in the time it took for her to approach him at the nightclub where his band had just finished their performance, proposition him, and take him back to her apartment. She had been upset when he'd answered his cell phone, but the blonde had been extremely angry when he rolled out of the bed and threw on his clothes. In his need to get to the ancestral home and the center of the Nixa Coven, he hadn't been tactful in prying himself away.

With a rueful shrug, Mal pushed the woman from his thoughts, knowing there would be an endless number of others just like her, parading through his life night after night. However, he had only one father, and that thought focused him sharply on the task at hand. He pushed back the sense of helplessness that assailed him, knowing it would do no good to give in to the emotion. It was up to Mal to acquire the only antidote to whatever poison some cunning bastard had used on his father. That task had led him to Las

Vegas, and he set out through the desert just beyond the Strip, his leather boots stomping through the loose sand. He dodged an occasional palm tree and wished it had been possible to materialize right on the Strip. He daren't risk that, since people would notice the flash of light and his sudden appearance through an astral doorway. Las Vegas was a city where just about anything could happen without anyone blinking an eye, but someone would have noticed his dramatic entrance.

By the time he traversed the few miles to the Strip, the sun had set long ago, and sand had seeped into his boots. Mal cursed the annoyance, but didn't pause to empty his boots when the flashing neon finally bathed him in its garish glow. Without moving, he stood where he had entered the Strip, orienting himself and allowing the invisible tug of the spell that he had performed in L.A. to lead him to the antidote. After a second, the cord binding him to the object of his mission tugged him south, and he joined the crowd of people strolling the Strip. Though only a Thursday night, there was a bustling crowd, and he was inconspicuous among them.

As he neared the nightclub for paranormals, Darkness, the hairs on Mal's neck rose, and his gut tightened in response to the feeling of the pressure dropping. The vortex of various powers mingling in one location was almost strong enough to break the connection of his spell, but he focused on maintaining and strengthening the link. Once he was past the club, the connection returned with nearly enough force to knock him off his feet. Mal stumbled and might have fallen if not for a friendly hand bracing his shoulder.

"Bit too much to drink?" drawled a cowboy type with a knowing grin.

Mal nodded, said a word of thanks, and waited for the man and his companion to pass before turning to cross Las Vegas Boulevard. There were no crosswalks leading from Darkness to the Liege casino, but he walked between the cars as they waited impatiently for the light to change. When Mal stepped onto the curb in front of the Liege casino, the cord pulsed, urging him to rush inside at a pace that earned a few askew looks. Caught as he was in the grip of the locating spell, he was powerless to resist the compulsion to break into an almost-run. Just as Mal was afraid he would have to dash recklessly through the promenade of shops, he skidded to a halt, drawn to an abrupt stop by an invisible string. He stood outside the door of a tattoo shop. A purple-and-gold sign labeled the shop as Divine Inspirations. With a deep breath, he walked inside. The woman behind the desk failed to register any reaction or tug of the cord, so he knew she wasn't whom he sought. "I'd like a tattoo."

She nodded, tucking a stray strand of purple hair behind her heavily-pierced ear. The rest of her hair was mousy brown and as unremarkable as her features. In stark contrast, the woman who appeared from the back of the shop at the girl's page was anything but ordinary. Unlike the receptionist, this woman hadn't made her body a shrine to bizarre body art and piercings. She didn't need to, he conceded with purely male interest that had nothing to do with his reasons for seeking her.

She was slightly shorter than average, with deep ebony skin. The simple white tank was a perfect foil for her dark skin, as was the intricate white tattoo adorning her left bicep. The small flowers and curves teased his fingers, making them itch to trace each line of the band of ink. His gaze slid to the right to check out her breasts without his permission, and he exhaled raggedly. The beaded nipples pressing through the layers of fabric tantalized him, making him as hard as he'd ever been in a split second.

With some difficulty, he forced his gaze higher. Her delicate features and generous lips were worthy of hours of inspection, but he contented himself with mere seconds. The sight of her bald head gave him a moment's pause. Curiosity made him want to ask why she had opted for the style, but he bit back the question.

It struck him that she was standing there awkwardly, looking a bit confused, and he realized he had been gaping at her like an idiot. A flush of embarrassment warmed his cheeks, and he tried to pretend it wasn't there. Plowing a hand through his long hair, he said, "I'd like a tattoo."

"Of course." Her husky voice sent shivers up his spine, and his intense reaction mortified Mal. It took a concentrated effort to follow behind her without looking like a damned fool. Once seated in the room where she'd led him, he relaxed only slightly. It wasn't at all as he'd expected. The chair was much like one he'd see in any dentist's office, but the plush white suede bolstered calm—even in one who was practically terrified of needles, like Mal. The plan had seemed much better before he confronted the reality of voluntarily subjecting his body to multiple punctures with a tattoo gun. Feeling almost faint, he leaned his head back and breathed raggedly.

She was there in a moment, leaning close enough that he could smell her perfume. The subtle, feminine fragrance somehow soothed him, even as her proximity agitated him in an entirely different way than his needle phobia. He was suddenly optimistic about successfully completing his objective to acquire this latent vampire's power-source. Before he had seen her, he had known there were only two ways to drain her power—through killing her or through seduction. He had refused to kill anyone, but the prospect of seducing someone to whom he felt no attraction had him questioning his ability to complete his mission—especially if the latent had turned out to be male.

Her soft hand made his skin tingle when she touched him. "Are you okay? Having second thoughts?"

Mal nodded. "I think I'll skip the tattoo."

She smiled, her chocolate-brown eyes warm with sympathy. "It happens all the time. Have a nice evening, sir."

Acting on impulse, letting attraction guide him, he touched her hand as she moved it away from his arm. "It would be a better night if you'd join me for a drink."

Sparkling white teeth flashed when she drew her lower lip between them, clearly uncertain. "I don't close the shop for another hour."

He shrugged. "I'll wait."

"What's your name?" She cocked her head, examining him. When her teeth released her lower lip, he assumed he had passed inspection.

"Mal Nixa." He held out his hand, encompassing hers when she extended it. The cord binding them tugged sharply, and he took a step forward. Her aura brightened when he did so, telling him she was equally attracted.

"I'm Devi Madigan."

"Devi." He drew out the syllables, enjoying the sound on his tongue. Not as much as he'd enjoy her taste on his tongue. The accompanying image made his cock spasm, and he had to wrest his mind from playing out all the erotic possibilities. "So, will you have a drink with me?"

After a long second, she nodded. "I'll meet you out front in two hours."

He quirked a brow. "I thought you closed in an hour?"

"I do." Devi winked. "I need time to get ready."

Time was the last thing he had, but he couldn't object to waiting. As Mal walked away, he had a feeling Devi would be more than worth the wait.

Devi finished dressing ten minutes before she'd expected, but found Mal already waiting for her when she closed up the shop. The black dress and leather jacket she'd changed into were appropriate for any club he might choose, but the clothes left her feeling exposed as his gaze devoured her, examining her from head to toe. The naked desire in his eyes made her shiver. It was good to have a man desire her. It wasn't a novel experience, but had happened too rarely for her to be nonchalant about male appreciation.

She fumbled with the shop keys, and her heartbeat quickened when Mal took the ring from her. His touch ignited her senses. His long, nimble fingers sorted through the keys, and he deftly engaged the lock with the one she indicated. A small leap of imagination had her picturing those same lean fingers exploring her body, dancing over her skin, tracing every curve, niche and convexity. The way her body reacted to the fantasy of his touch left her breathless, wondering if the reality could compare.

As he slipped a casual arm around her waist, his hand splaying across her lower back, Devi decided she would do her best to find out. Mal Nixa was a sexy man. His long hair, almost touching his waist, invited her to thread her fingers through the silvery-blond strands. The light green of his eyes made her think of tropical grottos she had seen in magazines, while his pale skin suggested nights spent in darkness. She hadn't dated a white guy before. The opportunity had just never arisen. If all went well on their date, she intended to see about making it happen. Why deny herself any pleasure? Life, in general, was too short to live void of fun. With Devi's health, it was much too short to pass up a chance of sex with a man like Mal.

"Do you know Vegas very well?" she asked in an attempt to distract her thoughts from purely sexual imaginings.

Mal shrugged. "I'm here four or five times a year, usually for a show."

She nodded. "There are an infinite variety of shows, aren't there? I'm obsessed with Cirque du Soleil and have to see all their new performances."

Mal arched a brow. "I've only been to one of their shows. Not my thing." He half shrugged. "I actually meant my band's gigs."

A nervous giggle escaped Devi as they exited the main entrance of the Liege for the neon brilliance of the Strip at 4:00 a.m. "I didn't know you had a band."

"Why would you? We aren't famous or anything." He grinned. "Yet."

"What's your group's name?"

"DisHarmony."

The realization they were about to join the foot traffic on the Strip distracted her from asking how the group got its name. "We can catch a taxi over there." She pointed to the taxi line, where a line of cabs waited for fares.

He shook his head. "The club I have in mind is within

walking distance." Mal steered her to the Strip, away from the crosswalks. Devi frowned as they jaywalked across the crowded Strip with only one car honking at them. Where was he planning to take her? She couldn't think of a club nearby, and the nearest casino with a bar was the opposite direction. As she opened her mouth to question him about their destination, she saw a door she had never noticed before, sandwiched between two buildings. Oddly enough, it appeared to be just a door. She could see no building supporting it. The architecture trick fascinated her until they neared the entrance.

A willowy blonde and her companion awaited entrance as Devi and Mal stepped into line. When she caught Devi's eyes over her companion's shoulder, the blonde parted scarlet lips to reveal gleaming white teeth, complete with the best pair of costume fangs Devi had ever seen. She flinched when the blonde hissed at her. "What a weirdo," she said softly as the couple passed security.

"Hmm?" asked Mal as he handed a key card to the extremely tall, solidly built bouncer.

"Nothing." Devi blinked, half convinced she had seen horns on the bouncer for just a second. When she looked again, he had a gleaming head, as bald as hers, with no trace of horns. The surreal experience occupied her thoughts as they stepped through the red door with the word *Darkness* burnt into the wood. Once inside, the décor had her questioning the club's theme. Darkest red blended with ebony to form a moody, dramatic atmosphere. Her curious gaze raked over the patrons, finding them a curious blend of people. While of varied composition, the crowd all seemed to have one thing in common— they matched the melodramatic color scheme and furnishings.

Mal led her to a table on the second level. Here, the lighting was dimmer than on the first floor, making it almost impossible to see more than two feet in front of her. Peripherally, Devi saw couples dancing close, and a few seemed to be doing more than dancing, judging by their writhing shadows. She kept her gaze focused straight ahead until they sat at a table. He leaned toward her, and her posture naturally matched his, though she was feeling hesitant about her initial plan to spend the night with Mal. His taste in clubs had her wondering what other odd tastes he had. Some strange experiences might be fun to explore, but she wasn't into anything seriously freaky.

"Drink?"

She nodded, and a waitress appeared, as if summoned. She was a tiny little thing, and her skintight red vinyl costume left little to the imagination. "Great contacts," she said to the server. "I have never seen such a dark red."

A sultry smile curved the woman's mouth. "I bet there's a lot you haven't seen, honey." She brushed a hand across the nape of Devi's neck, making her shiver. "What'll you have?"

"Cranberry juice." Alcohol didn't mix well with her biology. It affected her much too quickly, dropped too many inhibitions, and left her feeling more wretched the next day than a simple drink was worth.

The server took Mal's order for a Manhattan efficiently, with little interest. Devi couldn't shake the sense that the woman was watching her the entire time, even though her gaze never left Mal. Perhaps it was the strange contact lenses that made Devi feel like the eyes could see everything around the server, regardless of which direction she faced.

Once she had left, Devi was unable to hold back the need

to ask Mal about the club. "What is with this place? It's creepy." That wasn't the right word, but she didn't know how to describe how she perceived her surroundings. Her nerves were tingling, and the air seemed thick, though she had no trouble breathing even in the thick shroud of smoke. Beneath the pounding music and raucous cacophony of voices, she could almost hear another beat, a simple one-two that reminded her of a heart pounding.

He frowned. "I don't know what you mean."

She decided to let the subject lapse, since she couldn't seem to verbalize what she wanted to say anyway. "How did you find this place? I've lived in Vegas all my life and owned my shop at the Liege for ten years and never knew it was here."

"It's members-only. I guess you could say I am a legacy member. My family's had membership for ages." He touched her hand as he spoke.

That didn't explain why she hadn't noticed the club, but Devi acknowledged she didn't really care. His touch reminded her why she was there, and conversing about the strange nightclub was at the bottom of the list of things she wanted to do with him. "You said you aren't from Vegas, so where do you live?"

"L.A. My entire family lives there." His lips twisted slightly, betraying that wasn't necessarily a good thing. "How about you?"

Devi shrugged, wishing she could avoid the brief explanation that always accompanied meeting new people with whom she might have some kind of deeper connection than acquaintanceship. "Who knows? My mother died when I was born. I have no idea who or where my father is, and I grew up in foster care."

Mal patted her arm lightly. "I'm surprised you weren't adopted. Aren't infants in high demand?"

"Not ones like me." She managed a light tone, not wanting to ruin an evening of potential debauchery with serious conversation. "Do you want to dance?"

"Sure." He took her hand, but the return of their server interrupted their exodus to the dance floor.

She was hot, and not just from the temperature in the club, which was somewhere between tropical and a balmy day in the seventh level of Hell. The cranberry juice was tart, but refreshing, and she drained half the glass in one drink. When she returned the glass to the coaster, she found Mal studying her intensely. His lips were moving, but he wasn't saying anything. The temperature seemed to rise another degree, and she slipped off the leather jacket. The spaghetti straps of the dress burned her skin, and it took a tremendous amount of willpower not to rip off the dress and run naked through the club in search of cooling relief.

Devi couldn't take her gaze from his lips. "What are you doing?" As he continued, blue lights started pulsing around him, and she was dizzy. She fanned herself with a menu of appetizers she took from the table, but found no respite from the heat. It dawned on her that he was making her feel this way. Something Mal was doing was affecting her. She pushed back her chair, needing to escape. "I have to go now."

"Stay." He tightened his hold on her wrist, his authoritative voice making her freeze to her seat. "Stay with me, Devi," said Mal in a softer tone, as he stroked her arm. "Bind yourself to me. Give me your power-source. Do you yield?"

Her head was spinning like a centrifuge, and it was so hot that sweat streamed down her body. "Please stop."

"I can't." He seemed regretful. "Give yourself to me. Do you consent to a power transfer?"

"I don't care what you do. Just make this stop." Buzzing filled her ears, drowning out whatever words he spoke next. Lights flashed around her, and a white light engulfed Devi, sucking her inside its cold radiance. "Mal..." She reached out for him, and his hand was there, an anchor in the storm consuming her.

"Just relax. Let it happen." His voice seemed to be coming from far off. She tried to focus on his words to resist the pull of the light, but couldn't stand fast. Unconsciousness swept over her, and she had no choice but to yield to it, wondering as she passed out just what Mal was, and what he had done to her.

She came to a few minutes later, finding herself on Mal's lap. His face revealed his concern, and she wondered what had happened. The last few minutes were a blur, and she couldn't recall how she had ended up on his lap. "What's going on?"

"You fainted." He touched her neck. "Pulse is strong, so I think you're okay." Mal stroked her throat. "That was scary."

Devi shrugged. "I probably got too hot." She had fainted a few times before, so it wasn't so scary now that she knew what had happened. In the past, she had been too hot, or sometimes too weak, and had lost consciousness. "I'll be fine."

"Dare I hope you'll still be up for a dance in a few minutes?" Concern still shadowed his eyes, making them bottle-green.

She nodded. "I'm fine now." Really, she was. Whatever had made her faint didn't seem to bother her now, and she was able to stand with no difficulty. Devi accepted Mal's hand and walked with him to the dance floor. A glance around at the other dancers showed they were too preoccupied with each other to pay attention to anyone else. That freed her remaining inhibitions, and she curved into Mal without hesitation, enjoying his solid body against hers. He was hard where she was soft, and she wriggled impatiently, wanting to spend the night exploring their contrasts and complements.

His hands were insistent and commanding as they roamed her body, but she yielded without protest to his touch. Mal seemed to be exploring every inch of her, and she had no objection, despite their short time of acquaintance. "Kiss me."

Mal obeyed without question, lowering his head. She parted her lips and met his mouth, their tongues touching. He kissed with the same mastery that he danced, and she melted against him, pressing closer. He nibbled her lower lip, and Devi traced her tongue against the roof of his mouth. Her lips curved to his, forming a seal, and they devoured each other. His taste was unique, spiced by a hint of cinnamon and alcohol. Addictive. That described him perfectly. Mal had an addictive taste and presence. She wanted to lose herself in him, and right then, she didn't care if she ever found the remnants again.

He cupped her breasts through the silk dress, his thumbs expertly chafing her nipples until they were firm buds. Devi's pussy spasmed each time he abraded her nipples, and she arched against him, wanting to feel his cock inside her. She wasn't a prude, having done her share of reckless things, but having public sex on a dance floor was something she had never considered before. With Mal, it didn't seem crazy or impulsive. What seemed nuts was wasting any of their time together to go through the rest of the date, or even holding off until they found a bed or more privacy. She needed him right then, with a compulsion she had never experienced before. With that thought in mind, she tore her mouth from his. "I want you, Mal."

He nodded. "I want you, too. Let's get a room. There are some private ones available here in the club."

"Later." Boldly, she cupped his cock through his tight jeans. "I want you right here, right now. Fuck me, Mal. Bury yourself inside me with all these people around us."

For half a second, he hesitated. Then, with a nod, he pushed down the straps of her dress. "Whatever you want, love. Whatever you want."

"Just you." She tossed back her head as the dress inched lower. "Only you."

♣ ♠ ♥ ♦ ♣ ♠ ♥ ♦ ♣ ♠ ♥ ♦

Chapter Two

If anyone realized or cared what they were doing, there was no indication. Devi drew in a deep breath, steeling herself for the moment when the dress would pool around her waist and bare her nipples. Mal stroked the skin around the straps as he pushed them lower, until the bodice started to droop. He froze, a small gasp escaping him. She looked down with a frown. How could she have forgotten? "It's my port-a-cath." Her attempted nonchalance didn't seem to end his hesitation.

"Should I…?" He trailed off, clearly not sure what to do.

Devi experienced a moment of pity for him. She hadn't thought to warn him about the catheter, and there hadn't been time to introduce her medical history in their short date thus far. Previous sexual encounters with men had been confined to established relationships, so her partners had been forewarned. This was a downside to one-night stands, she decided with a sigh. "It's not a problem. Really," she said more insistently at his frown. "I have it there because I need weekly blood transfusions. Just ignore it. Please."

He nuzzled her neck, his mouth close to her ear. He still seemed intent on making love to her, but she could feel the air hum with his unasked questions. Devi put a hand under his chin to encourage him to lift his head. Mal stopped kissing her throat and raised his head to look down at her. "I guess I should explain a bit more."

"If you want to."

No, she didn't, but did she want him to change his mind about sleeping with her because of whatever he might be imagining was wrong with her, either? "I have a genetic disorder, so my condition isn't contagious. I could only pass it to my offspring." She hid a pang of regret as she uttered the words, having long ago decided she would never risk passing this curse to a child, even if she were strong enough to bear one. "Oh, and it doesn't have a name."

"Why do you need blood?" He asked the question with interest, but a strange light in his eyes suggested he already knew the answer.

She opened her mouth to ask about that, but he blinked, and the glint was gone. Devi shook her head, deciding she was imagining things. "It's part of my condition. My blood doesn't properly replace itself, so I need a fresh supply every few days. I'm also allergic to sunlight." When his eyes widened, she added with a trace of self-deprecating humor. "Before you ask, crosses and holy water don't repel me, though I am allergic to garlic. I'm a quasi-vampire, I guess."

That strange, knowing glint flickered in and out of his eyes as Mal laughed. "Do you bite?"

All the heat coursing through Devi must have reflected from her eyes when she met his gaze. There was no way to hide the intensity of her desire. "Only if you ask me to."

"I'll take my chances." In a smooth motion, he lowered his head to kiss her once again. His tongue plunged into her mouth, and he paid special attention to her canines, as if verifying for himself that they were no pointier than they should be.

Soon, they were immersed in each other again, and Devi reveled in his hands roaming her body. As if the previous interruption hadn't occurred, once again Mal pushed down the bodice of her dress, not stopping until it fell at her waist. The design of the dress allowed for no bra, and her bare breasts swelled when he cupped them. His thumbs provided perfect friction as he circled them in concert. Her lower body had a mind of its own, surging against him as close as it could. There was no space between them aside from a few layers of clothing. The fabric was an intolerable barrier separating her from the feel of his hot skin against hers. Devi whimpered her frustration, and his mouth swallowed the sound.

Surprisingly steady in light of how exhilarated his touch had her feeling, Devi peeled off his jacket, letting it fall to a heap on the floor. Next, she attacked the black shirt underneath. The silk was soft against her fingertips and provided little resistance to her fingernails when she raked them over his nipples. Breath hissed from him, into her mouth, and he retaliated by pinching the firm buds between his fingers. She arched her back, eager for more of the pleasure/pain of his touch.

Devi gasped when Mal suddenly lifted her by the waist. Instinctively, she locked her legs around his hips as he carried her through the club, negotiating the writhing bodies in the shadows. The cool desert air washed over her, sending a shiver throughout her body, when he stepped onto the balcony. The artificial lights of the club offered a backdrop for their tryst. A few other couples were in various stages of the same activity, and they paid little attention to Devi when she looked around before returning her focus to Mal.

Instead of setting her on her feet, Mal propped her buttocks on the railing. The cold metal was a delicious contrast to the heat consuming her, making Devi wetter than ever. As if aware of that, Mal slipped a hand under her dress, expertly honing in on her pussy. She arched against the fingers stroking her through the thin scrap of her panties. "Please touch me."

He pulled her closer. "I am." Slowly, he breached the silk, and she gasped when his finger stroked around her opening, teasing her clit as he pushed his thumb against her slit. "You're so hot and wet. I can't wait to feel you wrapped around my cock."

Devi couldn't seem to breathe as he hovered on the brink of entering her with his fingers. A moan of protest left her when he withdrew his hand. "Please." Never had she needed a man so urgently. More than desire compelled her to fuse with Mal, though she couldn't identify what it was.

"Shush." He brushed a kiss against her eyebrow. "We have all night, love."

Mal lifted her from the railing, and she wound her legs around him again. This time, he lifted her higher, bringing her breasts to the level of his mouth. She buried a hand in his hair, the other clutching his shoulder for support. The sight of him leaning closer to catch one puckered bud into his mouth was erotic, exciting and artistic. Briefly, she entertained the thought of them taking up performance art with their lovemaking, but the silly musing left her as he sucked her nipple fiercely, causing her to go rigid in his arms. He applied pressure until the bead swelled to the point of pain with each touch of his tongue.

As Mal laved her nipple, she arched her shoulders to push

her breast deeper into his mouth. Unable to reach any of his more tempting areas, she stroked his hair and gyrated her hips against his stomach. She longed to stroke him the same way he was stroking her. At the same time, she didn't want him to stop sucking her, ever. Was Mal feeling the same powerful drive, the pressure to join with her, that she was? They were more like wild animals compelled to mate than two civilized human beings—or was that more of her passion-induced flights of fancy? She didn't care.

His tongue forged a wide swath down her skin as he licked her from nipple to navel. Devi clung to him as he somehow managed to divest her of the dress with one hand. It was as though he had more than two hands as he pulled the underwear from her, leaving her only in black heels. "This isn't fair."

"What isn't fair?" asked Mal as he lowered her bottom to the railing again.

It was colder than before, without even the layers of the dress and underwear to protect her, but the sensation didn't distract her from her intentions. "I'm practically naked, and you're still fully clothed."

"Not practically." In a lazy motion, he cupped her mound, squeezing gently. "Completely naked."

She wiggled a foot. "I'm wearing my shoes." Sticking out her tongue at him earned a nip, and she yelped in surprise. Mal's hands anchored her to the railing, leaving her free to lean forward precariously in order to unbutton his shirt. He made no attempt to deflect her efforts, and she soon had him bared to the waist. "Beautiful." To her artist's eye, he was a study in perfection. Each ripple and bulge was proportioned and symmetrical. His pale skin shone like silver in the neon lighting, and it spasmed as she ran her fingers down his stomach. Devi smiled when his stomach muscles tensed as she neared his waistband.

Fumbling in her impatience, it took longer than she wanted to undo his pants. Apparently, Mal felt the same, because he put one of his hands over hers, stilling her movements. "Let me." In seconds, he had unfastened the button and zipper. From there, Devi took over again, pushing the pants to midthigh. She couldn't get them lower without toppling off the metal railing. The position of his pants served to limit his mobility while still allowing her full access. He wore silky black briefs. "Black must be your color."

"It's sexy and dramatic. Good for performances." If he planned to say more, her actions prevented it. He lapsed into silence after a single grunt as she took his shaft in her hand. He was long and thick, with a generous head. Hard and straight, his penis seemed to be straining to reach her.

"I don't think you need any stage props, Mal. You're damned impressive all on your own."

"And you're stunning." He cupped her chin to bring her closer for a long kiss. Devi licked his lips, enjoying his taste and the sense of anticipation.

When he lifted his mouth, she was unsurprised when he took a step back. She gripped the rail on either side of her thighs to prop herself up as Mal finished removing his shoes and clothing. "I appreciate a man who comes prepared."

"I'm ready for any eventuality." He crooked his lips into a half grin as he ripped open the condom he had taken from his pocket. In seconds, he was covered, and he lifted her from the rail. Devi wrapped her legs around him as his erection nudged her opening. She arched against him, taking in most of his head, and Mal met her efforts with equal fervor. Shivers coursed through her as his cock filled her. Her sheath expanded to accommodate him. They were perfect together, as if two parts of the same machine.

He thrust into her, pressing Devi against the rail. She pushed forward, matching his pace. Mal's hands squeezed and caressed her buttocks as he held her against him, and her skin contracted with each stroke. Heat suffused her, burning from the inside out, and she gasped for air. Every feeling Mal inspired seemed magnified beyond what it should be. Never before had a man had her so excited, so passionately turned on.

With a small shout that she couldn't contain, Devi came. Her pussy clenched around Mal, and she tightened her legs around him. Stars danced behind her eyes as she climaxed, and she arched harder against him, riding the wave to a new level of arousal. Another orgasm overtook her, followed by a third. She was gasping with the onslaught, unaccustomed to multiple orgasms. Each one seemed to build on the previous one, bringing her to new heights. She lost count after four, and it seemed like ages before Mal finally gave in to his own release. His hoarse cry and rigid posture betrayed his climax as his cock convulsed inside her. She came again as he did so and couldn't tell where his tremors ended and hers began.

When the passion storm passed, she sagged against him, feeling wrung out. Devi didn't think she would be more exhausted if she had run a marathon. At the same time, she was elated and somehow renewed. "How do you feel about encores?" she asked in a raspy voice.

Mal stared down at her, completely serious. "I never do them. It's always best to leave the audience wanting more."

Devi grinned. "You've certainly done that."

"An encore is out of the question, but I can offer a new performance with a change of venue." With obvious reluctance, he separated himself from her, easing her to her feet. "Should I see about booking a private room?"

Impulsively, she shook her head. "Skip the room and come back to my place."

He nodded. "If that's what you want."

"Honey, that's just one of many things I want tonight."

Divine Inspirations did well, aided by both its location in the Liege casino and Devi's renown as a tattooist. She had a healthy bottom line each year, but her income wasn't nearly enough to finance living on the Strip. Instead, she had a quiet little house just ten minutes' drive from her reserved spot in the Liege's parking garage to her driveway. The first tendrils of dawn were streaking the sky as she parked her Saturn in the garage, and she was relieved to make it home before sunrise. The burning, itching sensation that accompanied any sun exposure was the last thing she wanted to deal with when Mal was hers for the taking.

As though it was the most natural thing in the world, he took her hand as they walked to the door to the laundry room. Devi's heart rate sped up just from the casual touch of his fingers entwined with hers. She led him through the nondescript laundry room, utilitarian kitchen, and average living room. Her bedroom waited down the hall, and there was no reason to pretend that she had brought him into her home for any other reason.

She flipped on the light, relieved she had taken time to tidy up that morning. The bed linens were fresh, as if she'd known she would be bringing home company. Of course, she hadn't, but was pleased with how it had all turned out.

Was turning out, she amended while turning to Mal. She wondered if she looked as disheveled as he did. His hair was wild, and the buttons on his shirt didn't match up properly. The jacket he'd worn earlier was long gone, as was her underwear, both abandoned at Darkness. It was a simple matter for her to strip. She took off the dress in seconds and kicked off the heels. Mal followed suit, and they were both naked again.

In the light of her bedroom, he was even more perfect. She marveled at his male beauty as she grasped his fingers to take him to the bed. Devi lay down first, and he came down atop her. She buried her fingers into the light hair on his chest as he framed his hands on both sides of her face to support his weight. His mouth was sweet, his lips pure temptation as they stroked hers. Devi nibbled on his lower lip before sucking the spot. Mal's chest vibrated when he groaned. She reveled in the proof that he was just as affected by this intense passion as she was. Devi doubted the sex was filling a void for Mal the same way it was for her, but he was definitely enjoying it. So was she, so much that it scared her. If she thought too much about how physically and emotionally satisfying their coupling was, she might be tempted to stop, just to regain some sense of reality. Instead, she suppressed the thoughts and returned her attention to seducing Mal again.

Mal cooperated when she shoved against his chest, making him sit up more. She slid her foot across his thigh and naked ass. "Roll over." His brow quirked, but he complied. Once he was on his back, Devi shifted positions so that she was straddling him. His fair skin was a delicious contrast to her dark hands as she explored his chest, arms and stomach. "You're so strong." She squeezed his bicep. "All big and manly." Her other hand cupped his shaft. "Everywhere." A grin of satisfaction passed her lips when he grunted in response to her stroking his length. Leisurely, she moved her hand lower to cup his testicles. She caressed them in her palm while flirting with his shaft by rubbing the base with her thumb. With a twitch that made his entire body jump, his erection hardened further. "I wonder if you taste as good as you feel?"

"You can find out later." Mal seemed to be gritting his teeth as he grasped her waist to lift her up his chest.

"What are you doing?" Devi wasn't sure if she liked Mal's ability to easily lift her and put her where he wanted. It was heady to be at his sensual mercies, but slightly annoying when she was intent on being in control this time.

"Ladies first," was his explanation as he settled her into a new position astride his face.

She gasped when his breath warmed her clit a scant second before his tongue invaded her slit. The appendage seemed to be everywhere at once, tracing the contours of her pussy while filling each recess. Abandoning the idea of directing this encounter, she gave herself up to the pleasure his mouth evoked. Mal licked and sucked her expertly. Her hips seemed to have a mind of their own, forcing her to buck and arch against his mouth with abandon. Devi's hands found purchase on her thighs, and she dug in her nails in an attempt to maintain her balance.

"Come for me, love," he said. The words disappeared into her slick heat, but she heard them. His breath stirred up all kinds of sensations as he deliberately breathed in and exhaled heavily. She came undone when he sucked her clit into his mouth, his tongue feathering around the most sensitive areas with light perfection, making her scream. Devi let the orgasm wash over her, able to ignore the accompanying wave of fatigue in the heat of the moment.

Before she had even finished coming, Devi found herself astride Mal's cock, poised to welcome him inside. He lifted his hands, and she grasped them for support. Their gazes locked above their joined hands as she sank onto him. A trick of the light made his eyes glow silvery-green, with a brilliant intensity that wasn't physically possible. She tightened her hold on his hands. When she blinked, his eyes were back to normal.

"You feel so good around me, Devi." The cords in his neck stood out as he thrust into her. Other evidence of his exertion was the way his temple pulse beat visibly, and his ragged breathing.

She was in a similar state, with her heart racing in her ears. Her lungs seemed coated in syrup as she struggled to draw breath, and she was hot everywhere. Devi knew her physical state was a combination of the amazing sex and her fragile health, but refused to end their encounter in order to sort out which symptom came from what. Instead, she blocked out everything except riding Mal, concentrating on his gaze, grasping his hands, and matching his thrusts. Her first orgasm literally took her breath for a long second, and she had just regained the ability to draw air when another washed over her.

Shuddering, Devi tightened her sheath around Mal's cock as he came, milking him for each drop of satisfaction. The glow was back, and she lost herself in the depths of his eyes, vaguely aware of another orgasm as they came together. His eyes were tantalizing and mesmerizing, making it difficult to look away until he eased her off him. Only when Devi curled against his side did she find herself able to look away. When she glanced at his eyes again, they were the light green they had been at their first meeting. She blinked in confusion, certain the odd chameleon quality of his irises had been more than the way the light fell.

A wave of dizziness distracted her from the thought, and she shook her head. "Whoa."

He propped himself up on his elbow. "What's wrong?"

Devi tried for a dismissive smile, but the muscles in her face seemed uncooperative. Bone-deep exhaustion was taking over, and she had no way to repel it. "I guess I just need a little break."

His expression betrayed his disappointment. "Of course." He brushed a kiss to her forehead. "You should sleep." With a glance at the clock on her table, he asked, "Do you want me to leave?"

Finally, she was able to smile. "No." Devi put her hand on his chest, slightly alarmed by the expenditure of energy such a simple task required. "Please stay. I'd like to wake up next to you."

"I'll be here." It sounded like a promise when he uttered it so solemnly. She clung to the idea, taking pleasant images of how it would feel to wake up beside her lover with her as she gave in to her body's demands for rest.

♣ ♠ ♥ ♦ ♣ ♠ ♥ ♦ ♣ ♠ ♥ ♦

Chapter Three

Mal lost track of time as he held Devi, watching her sleep. Blackout curtains prevented even a crack of light from getting into the room, so he kept the overhead light on. It was a distraction to sleep, but he didn't care. At that moment, he had no interest in slumber. Devi captured his attention completely.

She really was beautiful. Her beauty was unique and striking, but he knew on an instinctive level that he would have found her just as alluring if she looked just like every other woman. More than her beauty spoke to him. Something drew her to him, and it was more than the spell. The binding spell supported only a purely physical exchange, allowing one person to become the vessel of the other's power-source. It had no power to twist perceptions or emotions. It sure as hell didn't make a guy feel like he was starting to fall in love.

"Perfect timing." His lips twitched, but he didn't laugh. There was no real humor in the situation. Here he was, in bed with a woman he could envision spending a long time with. Their future would be bright and optimistic, if only he hadn't seduced her under false pretenses and was currently stealing her power in order to save his dying father.

Thinking of that, he checked her pulse. It was slow and

thready. Her breathing was deep and even, but her color was slightly ashen. It was obvious she couldn't take another round of lovemaking for several hours. If he risked it, she could die.

If he didn't, his father certainly would. Mal quietly cursed, torn between his father and the woman lying beside him. How could he risk killing her by taking more of her power before she had a chance to recover from the amounts he had already drained?

As he mused, his cell phone rang. The personal ring tone for Eli blared from his pants, and he carefully eased away from Devi to retrieve the phone from his pocket to answer it. "How's Father?" he asked in lieu of a greeting.

"Deteriorating," said Eli, sounding unemotional. That was typical for his elder brother. "Have you located the latent?"

"Yes."

"Well, have you had success?" Eli's impatience was clear. Mal ran a hand through his hair. "Of sorts. I've made contact and begun the process of draining her power-source."

"Excellent. How long until you finish? An hour? Two?"

"I'm not sure." Mal had no intention of explaining the delays to Eli, and he steeled himself for his brother's reaction.

After a pause, Eli asked, "I am only asking for an estimate. I don't expect you to know exactly. Even if you'd taken the easy way, it can be a time-consuming process. I expect even you know that."

"Yes, I know." Mal gritted his teeth to keep from responding to the subtle reference to his lack of formal education in magic, having refused to spend years at one of the archaic institutes where the greatest warlocks studied. He had natural aptitude, but little interest in learning the ways of magic, much to his father Saul's frustration and his brother's delight. Eli enjoyed knowing Mal would never be a rival for succeeding their father as Magister, and it seemed to please him that Mal fell short of Saul's expectations. With a sigh, Mal tried to push aside the thoughts, having accepted long ago that he would never be the son his father wanted him to be, and thankful that Eli was what Saul needed.

"How long then, Malkiel?"

"A few hours yet."

"Might I remind you that our father has precious little time? We don't even know what his enemies used to poison him, so we're having no luck creating any sort of antidote or way to slow the poison. If the Nixa Coven learns he's been poisoned, there will be chaos. If other covens find out—"

Mal cut off his brother's tirade. "I know what's at stake. I'm doing the best I can."

"How reassuring," said Eli mockingly. "The future of the Nixa Coven is secure."

"Call me if he worsens." Mal omitted a parting word, barely restraining the urge to slam shut the phone. With several deep breaths, he regained control of his anger and set the phone gently on Devi's nightstand.

He returned to the bed, crawling in beside her. She made a sound in her sleep and turned toward him, but didn't waken. It was completely natural to hold her against him, and with Devi in his arms, Mal felt complete in a way he hadn't before. She curved against him as though tailor-made, making the moment bittersweet. With his purpose for being there, he knew there was no possibility of continuing a relationship with her beyond the rest of the day. Each time he made love to her, he weakened her further and betrayed her more deeply.

He could only imagine her reaction if she ever found out what he was doing to her. She would never forgive him.

If he hurt her, he would never forgive himself, either. The sobering thought kept him awake for a long time as he watched her, brooding about his choices. Finally, he surrendered to the call of sleep, resting more deeply with his lover in his arms than he had any right to.

Devi woke sometime in early evening. She knew the time of day before ever glancing at the alarm clock. It was the way she had always been. According to her foster records, she had always been a child who fell asleep before the dawn and woke within an hour of sunset. That quirk had probably saved her life, according to her doctor. Otherwise, she would have had much more extensive exposure to the sun before medical tests diagnosed her with an allergy to sunlight.

Something was different, and it took a moment to realize she was in Mal's arms, held tightly against him. His soft snores made his chest rumble, and she smiled. Deliberately, she moved with exaggerated care to avoid waking him. For a long second, Devi stared down at him, still amazed by his male beauty. She found herself hoping he was as genuine as he seemed, and that his true self was as beautiful as his outer shell. So far, she had no reason to think otherwise, and it was odd for her to wonder about such things since they had known each other for just a short time. Devi shied away from confronting why she was questioning such things. Firmly, she reminded herself their affair was purely physical and would stay that way. She refused to entertain ideas of anything else and be disappointed.

Stretching, she padded from the bedroom to the bathroom. After a quick wash, Devi was refreshed and looked almost human again when she saw her reflection in the mirror. Water beckoned, and she left the bathroom to go to the kitchen. Mal had turned on his side, his arms stretched out in front of him, as though reaching for something. A fit of romantic whimsy had her thinking he had noticed her absence and was reaching for her in his sleep.

With a dismissive shake of her head, Devi went to the kitchen for a glass of water. Automatically, she started the coffeemaker and poured a cup for herself when enough had brewed to fill it. By the time she finished that cup, the pot was finished, and she poured a mug for Mal. When she carried it back to the bedroom, he was still sleeping.

Devi set the cup on the nightstand by an unfamiliar cell phone. There were two ways she could wake him. With a gentle shake, she could offer him freshly brewed coffee, or she could be more creative.

A surge of desire warmed her belly, and Devi decided to take the second approach. With care, she climbed back into bed, kneeling between Mal's legs. He stirred, grunted, and resumed snoring. With a small laugh of delight, Devi leaned forward, bracing her hands on his thighs. She didn't wait to see if that awakened him. Instead, she lowered her head, placing her lips around the head of his semiflaccid shaft. His cock jumped at the light touch and was instantly hard.

She licked the underside of his shaft, paying special attention to the V of sensitivity. Mal jerked, and she felt him sitting up as she swallowed his erection, taking the full length until he settled at the back of her throat. Looking up through the veil of her lashes, she reveled in his expression of stunned confusion, quickly followed by a contortion of pleasure when she sucked.

"Oh, God, Devi." He groaned as she bobbed her head, her tongue constantly moving over his head and shaft. "That feels so good, but you have to stop."

To her delight, he seemed to be having trouble speaking. She ignored his request to stop and twisted the base of his penis with one hand while bobbing and sucking the remainder of his member as though she'd never tasted anything so delicious before. In actuality, he was delicious, and she had never enjoyed giving head like this. Devi sucked her boyfriends' cocks to please them, usually, not herself. While she enjoyed bringing them pleasure, she had never loved the feel of an erect penis in her mouth. Until now. She could have spent hours sucking Mal to completion.

He put a hand on her head, but didn't push her away or pull her closer. Devi kept going, spending a long minute laving the corona of his cock and the bundle of nerves, grinning bigger with each twitch of his body and thrust of his hips.

"I'm coming."

She nodded to show she had heard the warning, but didn't stop. Mal shared his gratification with her in streaming spurts, and she took every drop, not lifting her head until the last spasms had faded. Discreetly, she wiped her mouth. "Good morning," she said demurely. "There's coffee if you want it."

Mal blinked, seeming to have trouble switching gears. After a hesitation, he reached for the coffee. She waited until he had taken a sip and returned it to the nightstand before rising to a crouch, legs parted, with a hand between her thighs. Devi spread her labia wide to show him her pink temptation. "I feel so empty without your cock, Mal. Can you handle another round?"

"No." His penis belied his refusal by hardening again. It

seemed to be straining toward her, and she pushed her hips forward slightly to show him more. "No," he said again, but sounded weaker.

With a finger in her mouth, she surveyed him. "I don't know. You look pretty ready to me, love. Hard, hot and ready to pound my pussy."

"Don't do this, Devi."

She frowned, puzzled by his reluctance. "Do what?" Feigning innocence, she trailed the finger from her mouth downward, grazing her chin and neck before slowing down to trace the outline of one of her breasts. His gaze followed each motion of her hand, and she stopped to circle her nipple, then pinched it lightly between thumb and forefinger. "This is nice. It feels good to touch my nipple. It's hard and so sensitive. I'd love to have you touch it. Maybe you would lick my nipples? If you're flexible enough, you could suck my nipples while you put your cock inside me. I can lock my legs around your waist and ride you into oblivion while your mouth is on my tits. Would you like that?"

"No." He nodded. "Yes, of course. I'd love that, but you need to rest."

Devi shrugged. She was still tired and more drained than usual, but could definitely muster the energy for another round of sexual escapades with Mal before leaving to open the shop. "I'm fine, except for feeling neglected." She squeezed her nipple. "I'm starting to think you don't want me anymore."

With a moan of surrender, he lunged toward her. "Never think that, love. I want you so much. I just don't want to hurt you."

She had to blink away a veil of tears that unexpectedly

obscured her vision at his show of concern. "You won't. Fuck me, Mal. Show me how much you want me. Over and over."

His weight crushed her into the bed, but it was comforting, not suffocating. Devi locked her legs around his waist and lifted her receptive pussy to meet his entering cock. He surged deep inside her while bending awkwardly to reach her nipples. She helped him by lifting her breasts higher, squeezing them together. As he plunged inside her, his tongue pleasured her nipples simultaneously, pushed together as they were. She whimpered in protest when he lifted his head. "Don't stop."

"I don't want to hurt you," he said again as he thrust deeply into her. "Let me know if you need to stop."

"I don't ever want to stop." Utter conviction rang in her words, and she meant them on a level deeper than reference to their current encounter. It was all too easy to imagine spending the rest of her life with Mal, in and out of bed.

She wrapped her arms around his back as he embraced her, pulling her tightly against him. He thrust into her, and she tried to meet each one. Heart racing, she stared up at him, once again captivated by his eyes. This time, she knew she wasn't imagining it when they started to glow. The color was an intense amber instead of the silvery-green from before, and as she watched, the color darkened, taking on a chocolate hue. As the tint changed, she seemed to be falling into a vortex. Her head spun, and Mal's sounds of passion came from a long distance. She was falling into somewhere, but didn't know how she had gotten there. She didn't care. All Devi wanted was to be in his eyes, and she was convinced she would join with him forever if she could find the way.

An orgasm rocked her to the core, and she cried out. Her voice sounded faint, as if coming from that same distant place. The pleasure engulfed her, pulling her down into an ocean of oblivion, where nothing existed aside from Mal's eyes and the ecstasy humming through her. As she let herself sink, Mal's eyes went almost completely black, filling her with a sense of completion, even as a gaping void she couldn't identify opened inside her. It was as though someone had ripped open her soul and yanked out a chunk.

As Mal came, he realized Devi had gone limp. It took a moment to force himself to withdraw from her pussy, but as soon as the pleasure faded, his ability to focus returned. Cursing, he checked her pulse, relieved to find she still had one. She seemed to be in a coma. He had taken too much of her power-source, too quickly. "Wake up, baby."

Mal closed his eyes, feeling for the cord that had bound him to Devi from the moment he cast the spell. It was thin and weak now, and he could feel her power inside him. "You have to have some of this back, Devi. I can't let you die." Not sure if it would work, Mal imagined the cord was a conductor, withdrawing some of the massive supply of power he held inside and sending it back to her. The cord pulsed with a flash of light, and her eyes opened. He nearly sobbed with relief. "I thought I'd lost you."

She was clearly confused and barely with him. "What's going on? I don't feel like myself."

"I'm going to fix it." He kissed her face several times, grateful to have her back with him. "I'm sorry, but I'll fix it. I can't do this."

"Mal?"

With determination, he met her gaze. "I'm a warlock, Devi, and I came here to steal your power-source."

Her eyes widened, and a hint of fear appeared. "What are you talking about?" she croaked in a raspy voice. "That's crazy."

"My father…someone poisoned my father. Eli told me to find the closest latent vampire. Eli's my brother." Pent-up energy threatened to explode, and Mal got to his feet, pacing restlessly. "I'm making a mess of this. I know it. I found you. Do you see?" He returned to the bed, grasping her hand. "I found you." Her skin was clammy when he rubbed the back of her hand against his cheek. "You're everything I've ever wanted."

Devi seemed to be having trouble keeping her eyes open. "I need a doctor or something. Help me, Mal."

"I'm going to." In a rush, he released her and threw on his clothes. "I have to get you back to Darkness."

"The club?"

"Yeah. It's the only place where there's a high enough concentration of power to reverse the binding spell." Mal flipped through the clothes in her closet, selecting a light sweater and jeans for her. A quick forage in her dresser yielded panties, and he didn't bother with trying to find a bra. "I can't do it here. I might lose control, and there are no perimeters to hold in the power. If I lose it before returning your power-source, it will be gone. I can't let that happen. I can't let you die."

She was able to provide some assistance as he dressed her, but he could tell she wanted to push him away. It hurt him to see the fear in her eyes when she looked at him. What had he done? In one night, he had found someone he could love and had been the catalyst to ensure she would never love him in return. "I'm a damned fool."

"Yeah." Her chapped lips started bleeding in spots when

she spoke. "Me, too. There's a good reason to avoid one-night stands with strangers. I wish I'd remembered that."

"I'm not crazy. You'll see after I reverse all this." Mal wrapped her shivering body in the blanket and lifted her into his arms. "I don't know if you can ever forgive me, but you'll see I'm not nuts, at least." He clung to the hope that maybe she could understand why he had done what he'd done as he whisked her to the car. Mal thought of his father as he settled Devi into the car, and a pang of guilt struck him. He was sacrificing his father for his lover if he reversed the spell. If there was even time to find another latent vampire, the only way to take their power-source would be through murdering that person. The thought made his stomach roll, and he had to bite down the bile. It was abhorrent to him to think of killing someone else, but if he didn't return Devi's power in order for her to recover, he would be murdering her. After she was safe, he would figure out how to help his father. Right now, he had to focus on Devi.

♣ ♠ ♥ ♦ ♣ ♠ ♥ ♦ ♣ ♠ ♥ ♦

Chapter Four

She was quiet as he drove her back to the club. Devi had lots of questions, but no energy to voice them. Instead, she conserved her energy and tried to think of a way to escape this madman when he stopped at the club. She needed an emergency department, not some hocus-pocus magic trick. Surely, one of the beefy bouncers would find it suspicious if he carried her in wrapped in a blanket. She would just have to find the strength to struggle out of the covering and get the bouncers' attention. They would help her. Clinging to that plan helped her maintain consciousness as they pulled into the parking garage closest to the club.

"They need valet parking," said Mal as he came around the car to open her door. "If you weren't so weak, I would have used an astral portal, but I don't know if you could take that right now. It's daunting having your molecules stripped apart and rearranged."

"I'm sure." It was easier to agree with his ramblings than to try to argue. What was the point? It didn't matter what he believed once she was free of him. She'd never see him again. The thought brought an accompanying pang in her chest, and she chastised herself for her lingering attraction.

Mal Nixa was certifiably insane. While she didn't expect perfection in a partner, since she had so many challenges herself, insanity was just too much to deal with. There was absolutely no future possible with this man, and she had to accept that.

If she didn't get help soon, she might not have any future. That sobering thought had her struggling against him, trying to free herself from his hold.

"Shush, just calm down, Devi. I'm going to take care of you."

"I'm certain that eases all her fears," said a mocking voice from the shadows.

Devi lifted her head in an effort to identify the speaker. Slowly, he coalesced from the shadows, revealing a man strikingly similar in appearance to Mal, though older and somehow…dimmer. Age had touched his temples with strands of gray, and heavy lines underscored his eyes. "Who're you? Mal, who's that?"

"My brother, Eli." Mal seemed displeased to see him.

She was relieved. "Please help me. If he's really your brother, you have to know he's insane. Just get me to a hospital. Please."

Eli stared at her with cold eyes. They were the same shade as Mal's, but with none of the warmth. When he spoke, his gaze shifted to Mal. "I counted on you failing, and you have done so spectacularly, haven't you? Muck-up Mal. That's what I used to call you, wasn't it?"

"I don't have time for this, Eli. I have to reverse the binding spell, or she's going to die."

Eli didn't move from their path. "I really don't care what happens to your little whore."

Devi winced when Mal laid her on the hard cement. "What's happening?" He couldn't just leave her there. She couldn't possibly make it to a hospital on her own, weak as she was.

Mal ignored her. "I can't let you have her power, Eli, even to save Father. He wouldn't approve of killing someone to save himself."

"I'm sure you're right. He is a bleeding-heart old fool." Eli examined an overly long fingernail, as if bored with the conversation. "He's weak, just like you. It was so easy to slip the poison into his nightly glass of port. Anyone could have done it, as lax as he is about security." A cold smile split his face into a chilling expression. "I did it myself, though. I knew it would be done properly if I put in the poison. That, and there's the personal sense of satisfaction I get from knowing I have single-handedly set in motion the events that will lead to my immediate ascension as Magister."

Devi watched the exchange, growing more confused by the moment. Either Mal and his brother were both delusional, or Mal had been telling her the truth all along. How could that be? It was crazy to contemplate the existence of warlocks, covens and magic. Wasn't it? And if she accepted that part of Mal's story, she had to believe it all, right? It was impossible to imagine she was a latent vampire. Suddenly, it was difficult to breathe when the full impact of events hit her. Mal had deliberately chosen her and seduced her in order to gain some kind of power from her, not because of any desire he felt for her. She shook her head, rejecting that. Still, the realization pounded at her. Whether or not Mal really was a warlock, he thought he was and had taken her to bed because he believed he could drain her magic. He had never really desired her.

The epiphany came to her in an instant, but Mal's reaction

to his brother's words pulled her back from the thoughts. Visibly shaking in his anger, each word Mal issued came in staccato bursts. "*You* did it? *You* poisoned Father? But why? You're going to become the Magister when he dies. Why couldn't you wait a few years?"

Eli seemed on the verge of yawning. "Let's just say, I'm tired of waiting. Certain political alignments are open to our coven that Saul has ignored."

Mal launched himself at Eli, making Devi gasp at the quickness of the attack. She could see his eyes glowing again, this time a chilling green that sent a frisson of ice up her spine. Finding a reservoir of strength, she sat up, pushing away the blanket. Her intent was to stand, but that proved impossible, and she soon collapsed to the ground again. Now would have been the time to escape if she'd been able to manage it, but Devi found herself glued to the drama unfolding in front of her.

"I've never wanted to kill anyone before, but now I understand the impulse." Mal knocked Eli to the ground, and they wrestled, each vying for the dominant position. "You've always been a cold, selfish bastard, but I never expected you to stoop this low."

Grunts and the sound of blows landing filled the air for several seconds before Eli replied. "I have been methodical and calculating, while you have been weak and ruled by emotion." With a vicious expression, he flipped Mal, pinning him to the cement. "Father indulged your weakness by allowing you to become a musician, living in the *human* world. He caters to Sabine's desire to play artist, but I was groomed to be his replacement from birth. When did I have the choice? Never! I am the future Magister, and I can't allow Father to pass up a chance to increase our power base."

Devi gasped when silvery-gray bands of light snaked around Mal, holding him in place. He struggled against them, but seemed unable to free himself. She feared for his safety, wondering what Eli would do to him. That changed to fear for herself when Eli stood up and walked her way without another look at Mal. She tried once more to stand, but couldn't muster the energy. A feeble scoot backward was all she managed and soon bumped into the wall of the parking garage. "What do you want from me?" she asked when Eli stopped walking, towering over her. "If you don't want to cure your father, why do you need me?"

That same chilling smile curved his lips. "I don't need you."

A scream escaped her when he revealed a steel dagger taken from the pocket of his trench coat. The handle's elaborate carvings were beautiful, but didn't detract from the deadly sharpness of the silver blade. She brought up her hands to shield herself when he knelt beside her. Eli subdued her struggles easily with one hand. Devi met his gaze, hoping she looked defiant instead of terrified. Though she tried to hold his gaze, the sight of the blade nearing her throat forced her to close her eyes instinctively. Her spine was rigid from pushing herself against the wall, and there was nowhere else to go. The blade sank through her throat with a hot, sharp flash. Once more, she screamed, but had no voice to give life to the sound.

The first pulse of light made her think she was already dead, but the second cleared her thoughts. A spark of hope surged as Mal rose into the air, the bands of power that had confined him gone. Her eyes widened when scarlet light raced from his hands and hit Eli in the back. Her attacker shouted and reeled away, leaving the job of slitting her throat only half-finished.

In a millisecond, Mal was out of the sky and crouched beside her. "Hold on, love." He gathered her into his arms, and before she could process what was happening, a bubble of silver engulfed them. She had figured out they were in an astral portal just as they appeared in the center of the dance floor.

Unlike their passionate encounter earlier, when no one had seemed to give a passing glance to them, all motion stopped. The music screeched to a halt, and the babble of voices was indiscernible.

"I need a vampire." Mal spun in a circle, still clutching Devi.

From the corner of her eye, Devi saw the blonde from earlier shrink into the shadows. She pointed in her direction, remembering the bared fangs and willing to entertain the possibility they hadn't been an elaborate costume prop after all.

Mal turned toward the blonde, but another man stepped into their path first. He was tall, with skin almost as dark as Devi's. Though he appeared to be no older than thirty, something about him suggested ancient wisdom. "What does a warlock need with a vampire, Nixa?"

"It isn't me who needs you, Anai Shol. It is this woman, this latent vampire."

Devi squeaked in protest when the stranger lifted her from Mal's arms. She reached for him instinctively, and he grasped her hand.

"It's okay, Devi. Let Master Shol see what he can do for you." Mal's voice was soothing, but the fear in his eyes did little to calm her.

Master Shol cupped her bald head in one of his large hands. The touch was startling, but somehow relaxing, and the tension flowed from her. With wide eyes, she stared up at him, caught in the hazy golden glow of his irises. Peacefulness radiated from the man, flowing into her. She ceased to be aware of the hot blood flowing down her neck, or the pain from the wound.

"I can help you, miss, but it requires a full conversion." He must have seen the confusion in her eyes. "I must fully make you a vampire, or I cannot save your life. Your power-source is depleted from something, and you are too fragile to heal the wound even if I found a way to replenish your power. Do you consent to the conversion?"

Devi started to nod, but Mal interrupted. "You can't do that. She's too weak. The conversion will kill her."

Master Shol nodded. "She might die, Nixa, but this one has a strong spirit, and she is half vampire. If I don't attempt to transform her, she will certainly die."

"Do it," Devi rasped, barely managing to make sounds. Apparently, Master Shol understood her desire, either by her tiny voice or some other means, because he nodded once more.

She braced herself as he lowered his head. Uncertain what to expect, she was surprised to have warmth flood her when his mouth touched her wound. The area was numb, and she couldn't know for certain what he was doing, but imagined he was biting her and drinking her blood. The thought was both repulsive and appealing, leaving her to wonder how strong the latent vampire side of her nature was. Latent no longer, she reminded herself with a twist of her lips as a fog descended over her.

Adrift in a state somewhere between consciousness and unconsciousness, Devi let herself float, making no attempt to move toward either state. Eventually, Mal's voice intruded into the blissful oblivion. Much as she tried to ignore it, his words soon drew her back to him. Opening her eyes, she found herself staring up at a velvet expanse of darkness. Her other senses told her she was lying on a soft bed, and she felt around with her palms, finding the cover under her was buttery-soft leather. "Where am I?"

Mal loomed over her, gathering her into his arms. "I thought you were gone. Master Shol said you could go either way, and I thought you'd left me."

Devi frowned when drops of moisture fell on her cheeks. She lifted a hand to feel her eyes, finding them dry. It took a moment to sink in that Mal was crying. Automatically, she put a hand on his back, patting lightly. "I'm fine." She was, Devi discovered after a mental inventory of her physical state. Strength flowed through her. *Robust.* That was the word to describe how she felt. Never before had she been so alive. All her senses were keener, and the sense of weakness that had plagued her all her life was gone.

When Mal finally released her, she sat up. Something slid down her chest and dropped into her lap. Puzzled, she lifted the item, finding herself holding the port-a-cath. Her hands caught her attention, and she examined them in wonder. Where there had once been bitten, ragged nails, she now had perfectly shaped, long fingernails. With wonder, Devi lifted a hand to her head, finding a profuse growth of tight black curls springing where no hair had ever grown before. Driven to look for a mirror, she climbed from the low bed and walked around the lavish room. "What is this place?" Only the smallest touches of dark red enlivened the matte black décor. Shivering, she wrapped her arms around herself, aware of an underlying chill permeating the room. It didn't seem to come from the room's temperature so much as from a presence in the room itself. "I don't like it." All she wanted to do was escape the bedroom, her quest for a mirror abandoned.

Mal followed her headlong rush to the door, intercepting her as she opened the glossy black knob. "This room belongs to the owner of Darkness. He kindly loaned it to you for your recovery or crossing over." He grimaced. "He's unreadable, so I couldn't tell which outcome he hoped for."

"I have to leave."

He put a hand on the wood to hold the door shut. "Just wait. Please. We have to talk."

She shook her head. "I think I've figured out everything. There's another world of which I remained unaware until tonight. One of my parents was a vampire. I assume my mother wasn't, since she died at my birth. I have an undead-beat father, and now I'm a vampire."

"But—"

She lifted her fingers, pushing them down as if bulleting her speech. "There are also warlocks and who knows what else? You needed my blood to save your father, so you dragged me into all this. Have I forgotten anything?"

"Your power."

"What?"

Mal raked back his hair. "I needed your untapped power, not your blood."

"Whatever." She shrugged.

"You're forgetting that I changed my mind and was trying to undo the spell."

She refused to let the hardness suffusing her heart to dissipate in order to soften to him. "Have you?"

He nodded. "The spell is broken. Your power is your own again."

Reluctantly, she asked, "And what of your father?"

Lines creased Mal's face, making him look older. He seemed to crumple in front of her. "He will die soon."

"Dammit." She cursed her own emotions as surely as she cursed Mal for putting her in this position. "Can my power save him?"

It seemed to pain him to shake his head. "No. It's too late, and you no longer have the reserve of power now. Once you became a full vampire, the power suffused you. There is no way to separate it now, save for another vampire draining you."

"Yuck." She recoiled from the thought. It reminded her there would be new rules to learn and live by, probably chock-full of equally morbid addendums. The words gave her an idea though. "What if we made your father a vampire? Could that work?"

"I don't…" He trailed off, clearly lost in contemplation. Slowly, his eyes warmed with a trace of hope. "It might work. He is in a weakened state, and the transformation isn't an easy thing. It might kill him."

"But he'll die if we don't try?" she asked softly, moved in a moment of compassion to touch his arm.

He nodded, but the spark of hope fizzed out, making his eyes dull green. "Master Shol has already departed for wherever he dens. By the time I find him, it will be too late for Father."

Devi sighed, marveling at the man's thickheadedness. "I'm a vampire now, aren't I? Can't I change your father?"

"In theory, but you don't know how."

"You saw how Master Shol did it, right?" At Mal's nod, she said, "I'm sure we can figure it out."

"We'll have to arrive before sunrise, which means an astral

portal. If you're caught out in the sunlight, I don't think you'll survive."

"Great." She sighed. "I guess this means my allergy has been upgraded?"

Mal nodded. "I don't know all the rules of your new existence, but I do know that only a few vampires can walk in sunlight. Master Shol is one of them, but he is thousands of years old. All others are destroyed within minutes."

"Just great." Devi squared her shoulders, pushing back the fear and uncertainty that accompanied her change in lifestyle. "Let's go then."

Mal seemed like he wanted to protest. He took her hand, holding it between both of his. "I don't want to put you through this, Devi. I know it isn't fair to ask it of you, especially after everything I've put you through."

She put a finger to his lips, unsurprised by the tingle the simple touch gave her. Even knowing he had never truly been attracted to her didn't kill off her attraction so easily. "You can thank me later. Time is wasting." Devi stiffened when Mal embraced her. "What're you doing?"

"Portalling. You have to be close since you don't know how to create your own portal."

The pounding of her heart made it difficult to ignore her reaction to his proximity, but she managed to feign indifference. "Okay."

Before, she had been so exhausted and drained that she hadn't really been aware of the experience of traveling through an astral portal. This time, she was awake and unnerved. Barometric pressure dropped drastically, and the air seemed thin. She dragged in deep breaths, but still didn't have adequate oxygen. Her body tingled everywhere, and cold spread through her. As the light surrounded them, it was as though she could feel every molecule in her body separating from each other. She might have screamed, but couldn't be sure as her body ripped apart, absorbed by the light.

The transition was timeless. It could have been seconds or hours between leaving Las Vegas and arriving on the grounds of what she presumed was the Nixa estate. After they stepped out of the portal, Devi clung to Mal for several seconds. Ostensibly, she was regaining her equilibrium, but she had to admit part of her motivation wasn't nearly so practical. Her body still responded to his as though the passion between them was real and tangible for both of them, not all one-sided.

Mal's cursing startled her, and she stepped away as he pushed her behind him. The combined effort nearly sent her sprawling, but new, catlike reflexes saved her. Devi twisted, landing in a crouch beside him. "Whoa." Being a vampire was definitely going to have some perks.

Someone in a red robe came toward them, hands held out in front. Devi looked at Mal, who seemed clueless about the other man's identity. She approved of him attacking first, binding the other in scarlet bands of energy before the man could do the same to Mal. They stood over him. "Do you know him?"

Mal shook his head. "He's probably one of Eli's men. Judging from the emblem on his robe, he's from another coven, maybe the one that Eli seems so gung ho to join with." His foot against the other man's side made the robed man grunt. "Who are you?"

"Tam Rippa." He spat his name at Mal.

Devi didn't like Mal's frown. "What is it?"

"The Rippa Coven is even older than the Nixas. I don't know a lot about the composition of the Council, but I know my father displaced a Rippa when he achieved Chief status."

Devi massaged her temples, overwhelmed by the information. "I thought your father was the Magistrate?"

Mal grinned as he stepped over the Rippa Coven member, offering her a gentlemanly hand to do the same. "He's the Magister of our coven. That means he leads our coven, which is not just Nixa family members, but other witches and warlocks who have chosen to band with us. I think there are six hundred or more members of the Nixa Coven." His posture straightened, and his voice dropped as they rounded the corner. "The various covens draw up laws to abide by through a council. The Magister of each coven attends Covens' Council once per year."

A pause followed as Mal dealt with another of the red-robed warlocks, leaving that one bound as he had the last. They moved on at a cautious pace. "The Chief of the Council referees the meetings, I guess you could say. It's a prestigious position, though I don't know how much added power there is with the title. The Chief is elected."

"Hmm. It all sounds as complicated, futile and pointless as American politics."

His laugh was barely above a whisper as they made their way through garden hedges to close in on a rear entrance. Devi ducked instinctively when they neared the edge of the topiary, and she saw several men and women in red robes milling around the patio. "Is there someone else you can call for help?"

Mal arched a brow. "What do you mean?"

"You're kind of outnumbered. There must be six or seven

of those coven people out there." It was impossible to hide her exasperation. "What about Sabine? Who's she?"

He frowned. "How do you know about Sabine?"

"Eli mentioned her during his villain rant."

A crooked grin lightened his expression. "Sabine is my little sister, currently in Paris."

"Can't you just portal to her?"

With a shake of his head, he said, "The longer the distance, the more draining it is to create the portal. I could portal to my sister, but by the time we portalled back, neither of us would have much strength left for fighting."

"What about friends? You need some help."

He looked away from the tableau to meet her gaze. "I have you."

"That'll be a lot of help," she muttered under her breath as Mal stood up, hands poised to do his magic trick to bind the enemy. How was she supposed to help him, being the newbie vampire that she was?

♣ ♠ ♥ ♦ ♣ ♠ ♥ ♦ ♣ ♠ ♥ ♦

Chapter Five

Devi followed Mal's lead. When he burst out of their temporary hiding place, powers blazing, she ran beside him. He managed to restrain three of the seven people on the patio before they had a chance to react. By then, Mal and Devi had reached the melee. One man jerked toward Devi, hands extended. Acting purely on instinct, she lunged at him, lifted the man, and tossed him several feet over her shoulder, all with minimal effort. For a moment, she marveled at her own strength.

Mal's struggles with the remaining three brought her back to the moment, and she hurried toward them. A woman spun from Mal to face Devi. Before she could duck or block, a bolt of energy hit her in the stomach. Devi howled with pain, dropping to the ground. She curled up like an infant in the fetal position, cradling her sore stomach. Her enemy approached her, standing over Devi with her hands extended. Contempt visibly distorted her features, motivating Devi to compartmentalize the pain and spring to her feet. Her body responded effortlessly to the thought, and as she gained her feet, only a lingering discomfort remained.

The woman's surprise indicated she had underestimated

Devi. "You aren't a human," she said, sounding accusing, as she backed away a step.

Without bothering to respond, Devi punched the woman. Her fist landed solidly against the woman's face, and she dropped to the ground in a pool of her own red robes. A slight sting from the impact dissipated when Devi shook her hand as she turned back to where Mal had fought with the other two.

Except there was no battle. The other two were at Mal's feet, one unconscious and the other groaning. Bands of scarlet encased them. Devi walked toward Mal. "Not bad."

He shrugged. "I'm not as inept as Eli thinks I am."

His tone revealed more than he'd probably intended. There were traces of bitterness and uncertainty. She slipped an arm around his waist. The gesture was meant to be supportive, but passion flooded her, making her thoughts hazy. Before she could control the impulse, she fully embraced him, stretching her neck to find his mouth. Her lips curved to his, and every nerve in her body sang from the light contact.

Mal lifted his head, pushing her away a step. "I can't do this. There's no time."

"Of course." Devi nodded. "I'm sorry." Inside, she was a ball of misery. What a fool she'd been to forget that the attraction between them had been all one-sided. Mal never would have entered her life if he hadn't needed her for his father's sake. How could she sacrifice her pride by throwing herself at him, knowing he didn't want her?

There was no one else blocking their path into the house, and they crept in together. Devi stayed just behind Mal, senses alert. The new level of acuity amazed her. She could hear a cacophony of sounds, all underscored with the *lub-*

DUB of beating hearts in the house. Unfortunately, she couldn't distinguish each one in order to determine how many individuals were in the building.

The mansion that served as the Nixa family home and seat of power for the Nixa Coven overwhelmed Devi with its luxury. The hardwood floors shone with the patina of well-maintained age. Priceless Persian rugs added warmth to the rooms they passed through. Elegant décor and furnishings bespoke a limitless budget and a taste for nothing but the best.

Mal led her to a set of curving stairs, and she matched his rapid pace. Her physical state was amazing, and she couldn't wait to have time to test her new limits properly, once she had converted Saul to a vampire. After that, she would walk away without seeing Mal again. Devi tried to convince herself that was a good thing, after the way he had tricked her, made her care for him, and had seduced her to get what he needed. His actions should repulse and anger her. She was angry about the circumstances behind his feigned interest, but couldn't regret the sexual bliss she'd found with him. Nor could she regret that he had helped her discover the missing half of her identity and caused her transformation into a vampire. Her life would never be the same, thanks to Mal Nixa.

Trying to determine if the changes were worth the heart-ache of having and losing Mal, Devi stumbled into him as they emerged onto the second-floor landing. He had halted, and she peeked around his shoulder to find out why.

Eli stood before them, looking quite different than he had from her memory of the encounter in the parking garage. His street clothes were gone, replaced by a resplendent velvet robe of sparkling sapphire. A celestial symbol on the chest made her shudder with awe and a tinge of fear, though she had no idea what it represented. The reaction was purely instinctual. Around his neck, he wore a silver pendant as large as his fist, fashioned in the same symbol.

Mal shook his head, disgust dripping from his tone. "I see you've already promoted yourself to Magister. Is Father dead then?"

Eli assessed Devi with cool interest. "He's as alive as your latent whore." His nose wrinkled. "The stubborn old bastard won't die. She seems to suffer from the same streak of obstinacy, but I can fix that problem for both of them."

Mal had sagged visibly at the news his father still lived, but now his spine stiffened. "I can't let you do this, Eli."

Eli laughed. "You think you can stop me? You're an inept warlock. Go back to your little apartment in Hollywood, playing your mediocre music and fucking a different human woman every night. Walk away from coven business, just as you have all your life, and I'll let you live. You're no threat to me, but I will destroy you if you force me to."

Devi winced at the words, torn between sadness that Eli's words affected Mal, though he was good at hiding it, and anger from imagining him in bed with a different woman each night. It was far too easy to visualize that being the case, as desirable as Mal was.

"Can't you give this up, Eli? Is whatever you think you're gaining with this coup worth losing Father? He loves you."

"Wrong!" Eli's cool facade slipped, showing a trace of the rage he must have bottled up for years. "He needs me. One of his offspring has to carry on for him. I have been forced into this path, shaped and molded all my life. Saul loves you, and he loves Sabine. He gave you the freedom to choose."

Mal took a step toward his brother. "Father loves you, too,

Eli. You know that. He's pushed you, sometimes too hard, but only because he wants you to be ready to become the Magister. Can you imagine yourself doing anything else? You were the one who chose this path. I remember how you used to sneak into his library to read the forbidden magic books. You begged Father to teach you everything. He saw the interest in you and nurtured it. He no more forced you to become his heir than he forced me to love music."

Devi eased closer to Eli when she saw him hesitate. He seemed on the verge of an epiphany, but she didn't trust that it would lead him to ending his attempted takeover.

After a moment, the spark faded from his dull eyes, and he was again the cold, calculating man he'd been before. "Think what you like, brother. If it allows you to avoid feeling guilt for leaving me to carry this burden alone, keep those thoughts in your heart. I know the truth. So does Saul. As he dies, he'll be thinking of how he orchestrated the events that led to his demise."

"Don't you dare blame Father for what you're doing here," Mal snapped. "He never nurtured this psychotic streak you're embracing."

Without warning, Eli attacked, beaming a band of energy at Mal. He narrowly sidestepped the surprise assault. The sneakiness of Eli's actions made Devi act without thinking. She lunged at him, tackling Eli. He grunted at the impact, stumbling. She clawed his neck and face with her new talons. With a scream, he tried to throw her off. The movement upset his precarious balance, and he fell to the floor. Devi lost her grip and slid several feet along the marble floor.

She gained her feet quickly, turning in time to see Mal and Eli lock bands of energy. The opposing powers made a sizzling sound, and the air pressure dropped. The hairs on her neck stood up, and she had to quell the urge to vomit.

Cords in Mal's neck bulged with his exertion, and a primal cry issued from him as he managed to break the band, grazing Eli in the process.

"I'm impressed," said Eli, sounding out of breath. He dabbed at the incision on his cheek. It was deep, but instantly cauterized. Mal's power had scored a clear-cut groove in his brother's flesh, one as precise as if he'd used a laser.

The sight turned Devi's stomach because it was sickening, but also because she couldn't stave off mental images of Eli using his powers in a similar fashion against the man with whom she was falling in love.

"There's more to you than I expected, Mal. I guess I am going to have to destroy you." He didn't sound broken up by the possibility.

"If you can." A flash of energy arced from his hands, engulfing Eli.

Devi had seen the same type of energy field almost instantly subdue several of the people they had faced. Expecting the same result, it was a nasty surprise to see Eli practically shrug it off and return a similar burst. It hit Mal in the chest, and he folded to his knees. She shook her head, wanting to deny what she witnessed. As Mal crumpled to the ground, the light still encompassed him, making his entire body glow with faint silver energy. He lay without moving, eyes wide-open. It was impossible to determine if he was alive or dead.

Devi didn't know what to do. She wanted to run to Mal, but knew Eli wasn't finished with her yet. Instinct had served her well thus far, so she surrendered to it, allowing it to lead her. She reached Eli about the time he became aware she was behind him. Once again, her heightened senses had exceeded her expectations, allowing her to move lightning-fast and silently.

As she grabbed Eli around the waist, he directed a burst of energy toward her. The beam hit her arm, and she cried out, but didn't release him. Adrenaline fueled the strength she expended in spinning him to face her, making him turn so fast he almost fell. Devi punched him, riding high on the rush of battle. She was invincible, with more strength than she could have ever imagined.

He grabbed her wrist, and his hand scorched her flesh. The sizzling sound, coupled with the agony, cut through her delusions of superpowers. Yes, she had increased strength and agility, but she was no more experienced at fighting than she had been before the transformation. Not to mention, the man she faced was probably a lot more powerful than she was with his magic figured into the equation.

"Why are you here? You have nothing to do with any of this." Eli squeezed her wrist harder as he cupped her chin with his other hand. Devi barely suppressed the urge to whimper as his fingers seared her skin. "What do you hope to gain?" When she didn't answer, he shook her like a rag doll, lifting her off her feet by her chin. "Speak, latent."

"I'm a vampire now, asshole." Devi raked his cheek with her nails, making him howl as she gouged the furrow Mal's magic had left.

Apparently, the pain wasn't devastating enough to force him to release her. Eli held her suspended, legs kicking. The muscles in her neck were aflame from the strain of her position, and she teetered on the edge of blacking out.

"What can you do for him as a vampire? You were only

useful as a latent." Eli shook his head, his eyes mirroring his contempt. "Once again, Mal screwed up. If he thought you could be of any use, he was wrong."

Devi bit her tongue, refusing to divulge the details of their plan in case maybe they could still defeat Eli and reach Saul before it was too late. If that happened, she hoped fervently that she could save his father, or Mal would be shattered. She knew him well enough to know he would internalize the failure, blame it on his lack of magical education, and carry the scar on his soul for the rest of his life.

"That still doesn't explain why you're here." Slowly, Eli brought her closer, lifting her higher until their faces were level. "I assume Mal asked you to come, so you're here for Mal." An icy laugh escaped him. "How sweet. Have you fallen in love with my brother? Surely, you must have, or you wouldn't be here."

She squirmed, trying to pull away when he kissed her nose. "Don't touch me."

Eli smiled, but no emotion registered in his eyes. "Don't worry, my dear. I'm not interested in your lovely body. That was simply a gesture of pity, I suppose. You must realize by now that Mal had no interest in you personally? He chose you because of the power you had inside you. Any body would have done for his needs. Yet, here you are, standing by your man." He laughed again, his gaze raking her from head to toe as he put distance between them. "Or should I say, swinging for your man. Soon, you'll be lying beside him, but not in the way you'd hoped."

His obvious delight in her heartache stoked Devi's anger, which in turn fueled her confidence. Determinedly, she blocked out the pain his hands inflicted. The sense of helplessness that had frozen her fled, and she swung a leg forward. Her foot connected with Eli's crotch, and it was her turn to enjoy his pain. He dropped her as the air hissed from his lungs. Unsteady, he swayed before falling to his knees.

He had instinctively cupped his testicles, and she took advantage of the moment to kick him again, this time in the chest. Eli muttered something as he fell backward, and coldness swept over Devi. She blinked to clear the gray fog settling over her eyes. His whispered sounds penetrated the haze, and she realized he was casting a spell on her.

"No!" The denial, issued in a shout, helped dissipate the effects, and she leaped forward before the magic could renew its hold on her. Eli's lips still moved, and she clapped her hand over his mouth. "Shut up. I've had enough of your damned magic. If I never hear another word about magic again, I'll be thrilled."

His eyes widened, warming with a spark of fear as she raised her fist over his head. A feral part of Devi encouraged her to slam it through his chest, rip out his heart, and bring it to her mouth in order to drain the organ. The ferocity of the idea startled her. Maybe the conversion to a vampire wasn't completely a wonderful thing after all.

Shaken by the urge to commit such violence, Devi deliberately repelled the idea. Instead, she hit Eli in the temple with the meat of her palm. His eyes shifted out of focus, and he went limp. She hovered beside him, not certain if she could safely turn her back on the man to check Mal.

Devi looked up as a hand settled on her shoulder. Her eyes widened with her surprise at seeing Mal up and looking only mildly disheveled. "Are you okay?" The inane question led to a torrent of words she couldn't hold in. "Of course you aren't okay. I saw him freeze you…or whatever. You couldn't move. Now you're up? What's going on?"

"I couldn't move, but I could hear and see. As soon as Eli lost consciousness, any active spells he'd cast degenerated. As soon as the energy field faded, I was able to get up." He rubbed absently at his chest. "Not easily, but I'm up."

She nodded, unable to speak as she struggled to suppress tears of relief. Mal's fate had been unknown to her for too long, and she had feared the worst from seeing his lifeless form. Finally, she managed to choke back the ball of moisture in her throat. "What do we do about him?"

Mal hesitated for a long moment, his struggle visible in every twitch of his features. After a time, he said, "I'll bind him for now. If Father recovers, I'll leave him to deal with Eli."

"If he doesn't?" she asked softly. Perhaps it was too soft for him to hear, or maybe he didn't know the answer, because he didn't reply.

Mal took her hand, helping her to her feet. He grimaced as he examined her wrist. "I think you'll heal without a trace of the injury. Vampires rejuvenate quickly, so there shouldn't be a scar." He brought the burned flesh to his mouth, pressing a gentle kiss near the injury. "I'm sorry he marked you, Devi."

Discomfited, she tugged her hand free from his grasp. The show of concern and display of affection confused her, bringing up emotions and questions she didn't want to sort through at the moment. "I'm fine. We should find your father, Mal."

He nodded. "Maybe it isn't too late."

To her surprise, he took hold of her hand as he led her down the hallway. They approached tall wooden doors, carved with intricate designs and inlaid with silver replicas of the symbol she had seen Eli wearing. Once again, the celestial emblem inspired a mix of awe and terror that she had to push away forcefully.

Mal turned a knob, cursing when he found it locked. A second later, his lips moved, and the offending silver fixture went flying down the corridor. He shoved open the heavy wooden panel, and she followed closely behind him. She had expected to find someone else guarding Saul, but the room was deserted, save for the still form lying on the massive bed.

She couldn't help appreciating the Victorian furniture and luxurious fabrics as Mal rushed to the bed, half dragging her behind him. As soon as she saw Saul, all thoughts of the interior decorating fled from her mind. He was pale and drawn. In the prime of health, no doubt Saul was an older version of Mal, and a more vibrant copy of Eli. At the moment, his skin was paler than the off-white sheet tucked under his arms. His gray hair, spread out on the pillowcase, only emphasized the gray tinge of his complexion. The hollows in his cheeks and bruises under his eyes revealed his exhaustion.

"He looks like a ghost." Mal's voice broke, and he turned from his father, as if unable to look at him in that condition. "It's too late. We're too late, Devi. He can't possibly survive the transformation."

Gently, she grasped his face between her hands. Her voice was firm when she said, "We already agreed to try. He's going to die if we don't."

"He will anyway." A tear leaked down Mal's face. "This is all my fault."

"No, it isn't." She squeezed his cheeks with enough pressure to get him to meet her gaze. "You did everything you could, Mal. If your father doesn't make it, you have only one person to blame, and that's Eli. But if we don't try to save him, you will carry that burden forever. Let me try. Okay?"

After a second, he nodded. A ragged exhalation left him, and he straightened his spine. "All right."

They turned simultaneously back to Saul. Mal sat on the bed beside his father, lifting his frail frame into a sitting position. Braced against Mal's arm, his father looked like a shriveled old man, decades beyond what his actual age must be. She prayed she could help Saul, not just for Mal's sake, but for his own, as well. Even in his current condition, traces of the man he must have been were evident. His shoulders suggested he always kept them back, head held high. There was wisdom and dignity remaining in the lines and wrinkles of his sunken face. He commanded respect, even as he was.

"Master Shol didn't have to bite you, Devi, because of the wound Eli gave you. You'll have to access my father's blood somehow." He looked faintly queasy. "Do you think you can bite him?"

The thought was abhorrent to her conscience, but the new, primal side of her relished the thought. Devi nodded, not wanting to talk through the process with Mal. She had no desire to tell him how much she both dreaded and anticipated feeding from his father. Now that the moment was at hand, her stomach growled, and Devi was aware of just how ravenous she was. This hunger was different from any she'd ever experienced. It tore through her, leaving her weak and frantic. Was she going to have to contend with this for the rest of her life now that she was a vampire?

Devi knelt on the other side of Saul, leaning forward to bring her mouth against his throat. The skin sagged, and she had to feel for his carotid artery with her finger. Once she found it, beating so slowly as to be barely detectable, she immediately placed her mouth to the spot. Devi analyzed her forthcoming actions, trying to play out events in her mind. Before she got further than sinking her teeth into his flesh, she was biting him. Instinct had taken over, and she followed.

Her fangs sank through his skin like a hot knife through butter. Hot blood spurted into her mouth, and she almost withdrew. The foreign, coppery taste made her mentally recoil, but her body responded enthusiastically. She licked at the wound as the blood flowed, until a steady amount flooded her mouth. Devi swallowed quickly, trying to keep from losing any of the precious liquid. Inevitably, it flowed down her chin anyway, and she wiped without breaking suction.

Abruptly, her hunger eased, and she no longer wanted the blood. Devi lifted her head, slightly sickened at the sight of Saul's neck bleeding copiously. A glance at the mirror showed her an equally repulsive sight—her own face smeared with blood. She looked away and forced the bile down. "Now what?" she asked in a thick voice.

"Give him your blood. Master Shol dripped some of his own into your wound, so I don't think Father has to drink your blood."

Devi nodded, somehow knowing he was right. Perhaps it was her vampiric senses speaking to her, or maybe it was logic. After all, she hadn't awakened with the taste of blood in her mouth after Master Shol changed her.

Her teeth had become conveniently sharp when she was about to feed, but they had receded once more to normal length. Devi concentrated on forcing her fangs to extend, but nothing happened. After a moment, she gave up. There was a lot to learn about her new life, once she parted ways with Mal.

"Do you have something sharp?"

Mal looked around, as did Devi. Before she had seen anything that would work, she heard glass shattering. A look over her shoulder revealed Mal had broken the nearest lamp. He extracted a shard of the Tiffany glass and held it out to her. Devi extended her palm. "Do it for me. I can't."

His lips firmed, and he slashed her palm with the glass. It stung, but also yielded a surprising surge of desire. Devi blinked at the reaction. It was so intimate to have him cut her, though she didn't fully grasp why. Maybe it was the measure of trust involved. She had known he was going to hurt her, but had trusted him just the same. It was eerie to feel so bonded to him, and she ruthlessly reminded herself it was foolish, too. Mal didn't love her and never would. The sooner she accepted that, the easier their parting would be.

Returning her focus to the process of converting Saul, she brought her palm to his neck, pressing the wound to the one her teeth had left in his skin. Their blood mingled, and she experienced a curious tingling sensation that spread throughout her body. Power surged through her, and she was euphoric.

Head spinning, Devi collapsed onto the bed beside Saul, unable to think clearly. Her body hummed with energy, flowing through her veins. It seemed to grow exponentially, and she had no outlet. A sense of pressure squeezed her from the inside out. She was going to explode because the energy had nowhere to go. She opened her mouth to tell Mal, and a beam of light shot from her mouth. It hit the ceiling forcefully enough to singe the mural, forever burning away the image of the classically beautiful woman that had been immortalized there.

As quickly as it happened, it was over. Drained, she sagged into the bed, finding it impossible to keep her eyes open. Vaguely, she heard Mal say, "Dawn is coming, Devi." She knew that was dangerous to her and Saul, if he survived, but couldn't force herself to move from the bed. Through a slitted eye, she watched Mal close the curtains and whisk blankets from the bed. They hovered briefly in midair before flying to the windows, under the direction of Mal's power. The room darkened significantly, and her eyes closed. Blackness claimed her, and she sank into oblivion so deep that she wondered if she would ever find her way back from the abyss. That was her last thought before the void swallowed her.

Chapter Six

Devi woke in unfamiliar surroundings. The room was completely dark, but her eyes saw the details of the room as clearly as if the lamp were on. It wasn't Saul's room, where she had fallen into unconsciousness. Sometime during the day, someone had moved her to this room. She imagined it was Mal.

Devi knew it must have been Mal when she pushed aside the covers and realized she wore only her underwear. More out of habit than necessity, she reached for the lamp to click it on. A visual scan of the room showed no sign of her clothes, but unfamiliar garments lay over the back of a wing chair. She left the incredibly soft bed and padded to the chair. The deep fibers of the carpet cradled her bare feet, and she sighed with pleasure at the luxury.

The garments were a flowing patchwork skirt and white peasant blouse. Devi wrinkled a nose at the style, but decided beggars couldn't be choosy. When she lifted the blouse, the scent of its owner wafted to her nostrils, still detectable under the stronger scent of detergent. Her newly enhanced sense of smell discerned nuances she wouldn't have noticed before. They left the impression of someone who was cheerful, giving and carefree. Deducing the clothes belonged to

Mal's sister made it much easier to slip them on. The idea of wearing something one of his previous lovers had worn was too distasteful to contemplate.

Once dressed in the borrowed items, Devi left the guest room. She was in an unfamiliar wing of the house, but recognized the second floor when she went down the stairs. Making her way to Saul's room, she paused at the doorway to listen. Voices spoke in low tones, but didn't sound sorrowful or grieving when she strained to hear. With a deep breath, she knocked on the door, preparing herself for whatever she would find on the other side.

After a moment, the door opened, and a beautiful blond woman stood in the doorway. The light from the chandelier framed her, giving her an angelic glow that perfectly matched her exquisite features. Devi grunted with surprise when the diminutive woman hugged her. It wasn't often she came across someone shorter than herself, she thought dazedly as she absently returned the hug.

"Thank you so much for saving Father," said Sabine as she released Devi from the embrace, but still kept her arm to draw her into the room.

That answered her unasked question just before she caught sight of Saul. He sat up in the bed, but looked like he didn't need to be resting. He was the picture of health, and just as imposing as she had imagined him to be when he wasn't gravely ill. His hair hung neatly to his shoulders, supple and as shiny as the silver pendant around his neck. He wore a fresh robe, the same sapphire shade as the one Eli had worn, and seemed to be in deep conversation with Mal. She hung back, reluctant to disturb them.

Sabine had no such qualms. She compelled Devi forward, only releasing her to grasp Saul's hand. "Father, this is Devi."

Saul stopped speaking and looked up, his gaze locking with Devi's. She resisted the urge to tremble under his solemn assessment, reminding herself it didn't matter if she passed whatever inspection he imposed. After tonight, she would never see any of them again. After a moment, he gave her a short nod, and his green eyes darkened slightly. "Welcome, Ms. Madigan."

Her smile was only a little shaky around the edges. "Thank you. You're looking well."

He inclined his head. "I have recovered from the poison. I fear it will take quite a bit longer to adjust to certain changes."

Devi licked her lips, wondering if she was being overly sensitive. Had he really sounded chastising, or was that her imagination? Though she had done nothing that should cause her to be defensive, it was difficult to quell the urge to defend her actions. "I am still adapting, as well," she settled for saying.

After a moment, Saul looked away from her, returning his attention to Mal. He made no effort to lower his voice. "Where is Eli now?" No one asked Devi to leave, but she was uncomfortable remaining during the discussion of family business. Still, curiosity kept her standing near the bed, since she wanted to know what had become of Eli.

Darkness shaded Mal's eyes. "I have him confined to his room. Aunt Merelda reinforced my confinement spell to ensure he couldn't escape."

The only visible sign of Saul's distress was the way he bunched his fists in his lap. "I see. That should do for this evening. I'll turn him over to the Council tomorrow, along with the Rippa scum locked in the basement."

Sabine shook her head. "Please, Father, isn't there another way?"

With a hint of reluctance, Saul said, "No. The Council must deal with all lawbreakers, Sabine. You know that. Your brother will have to face the punishment of the Council alongside those with whom he conspired. I can't protect him."

"What will you do now? Who will succeed you?" Devi was surprised to hear herself ask the question, but hadn't been able to stop herself. She couldn't stand the thought of Saul forcing Mal into taking his brother's place against his will.

The Magister seemed equally surprised by her audacity. His silence indicated he wasn't going to answer, and she flushed with embarrassment. Unexpectedly, he started speaking after studying her for several seconds. "Sabine will replace me."

Sabine looked stunned. "But, Father, I can't."

Saul looked at her, his gaze stern. "Why not?"

"I'm a woman. The Magister is always a man. It's been that way forever."

Her father shrugged. "Just because it is tradition doesn't mean it is right. You have the ability and the interest. I have seen it in you all along, but chose to ignore it because of tradition. Instead, I drove Eli too hard, pushing him to accept a role he was never meant to assume. His interest was always in the darker spells and augmenting his power. Forcing myself to ignore those traits caused this." Saul's voice broke. "Tradition and my bad judgment led to the current predicament. Both are now rectified. You will come home from Paris and begin studying to take over my position when I am ready to step down."

Sabine nodded meekly, but Devi saw the sparkle of excitement in her eyes. "Yes, Father, if that is your wish."

Saul turned his gaze on Mal. "As for you, son, well done. I won't pretend that I like being a vampire, but it's better than the alternative. I don't know where you found your young lady, but I thank you." He looked at Devi. "Both of you."

She nodded when their gazes locked. A flush of warmth from the new respect in his eyes spread through her. It buoyed Devi as she stepped into the background. Once the family had continued with their conversation, she backed to the door. There was no place for her among them, and she had to leave before she overstayed the welcome they had issued. The last thing Devi wanted was to make Mal feel like he had to accept her or owed her something for saving his father. Much as she wanted to be with him, she couldn't live with their union if it was under those circumstances.

It was better to make a clean break and not prolong their parting. Her pride was all she had left, and she wasn't going to sacrifice it in order to spend a little more time with Mal.

They were strong words and made sense, but offered only cold comfort as she walked away from the Nixa mansion without looking back.

♣ ♠ ♥ ♦ ♣ ♠ ♥ ♦ ♣ ♠ ♥ ♦

Chapter Seven

Devi stumbled at the sight of Mal standing outside her shop when she closed up the next night. In her surprise, she dropped the keys and bent down for them at the same time Mal reached for them. Their fingers touched, and she jerked away as if burned. In truth, his touch was hot and as dangerous to her common sense as an open flame. "Excuse me," she mumbled as she scooped up the keys and deposited them into her bag.

Shoulders squared, she started walking toward the parking garage of the Liege. "What are you doing here?"

"I wanted to say thank-you, and to explain a few things."

Devi didn't reply until they were at the elevators. After pressing the button, she turned to look at him. "There's no need to thank me. Saul already did."

"But you did it for me," he said with a disgusting amount of confidence.

Disgruntled, she glared at him as the elevator dinged before the doors opened. "Why does it matter why I helped your father? The outcome is the same." She stepped into the cab before he could respond. It was too much to hope he wouldn't follow her. Devi sighed when he squeezed in beside her, though there was plenty of room in the empty car. The button bore the brunt of her annoyance as she stabbed it with more force than necessary.

"Okay, so you're thanked. I'd still like to clear up a few things," said Mal.

"That isn't necessary." She didn't look away from the floor indicator. "I understand everything, Mal."

"No, I don't think you do." He pressed the stop button and blocked the panel when she tried to push the button for her floor. "Not yet, love."

Devi glowered at him. "Don't patronize me."

Mal blinked. "How am I doing that?"

Anger was making it difficult to think, and she took several cleansing breaths. "Look, I really do understand what happened," she said in a much more reasonable tone. "You did what was necessary to save your father."

He nodded, still not letting her press the button when she tried. Instead, he took her hand, holding firmly when she tried to snatch it away. "That's right. When I cast the spell, my only interest was in the closest latent vampire. I didn't care who or what you were. Hell, I would have seduced anyone, even a man, if that had been necessary."

"Yeah, I got that." She took another deep breath, finding it less effective for controlling her emotions when he stated the situation so bluntly. "Thanks for clearing it up, just in case I hadn't." It was all she could do to keep from rolling her eyes.

"I didn't expect to find *you*, Devi." He stroked her hand with his fingers, making her skin tingle with warmth. "You are passionate and caring, warm and vibrant. Even though I had betrayed your trust, you still helped me save my father. With your beautiful body and amazing sexual appetite, how could I ask for more?"

Devi wanted to believe him, but couldn't allow herself to be hurt again. She stiffened her spine. "This really isn't necessary. You don't owe me anything, least of all one last pity-fuck, or whatever you're here for."

"That's absurd." A hint of anger darkened his eyes. "Why are you being so damned cold to me? I'm trying to tell you how I feel."

"No." Her tenuous control snapped, and she poked him in the chest. "You're trying to tell me what you think I want to hear. You don't have to feel guilty for fucking me, or nearly getting me killed. Slimy as some of your actions were, I understand why you did what you did. I'm even grateful that you helped me discover a key part of my physiology. All I want from you now is for you to leave me alone."

In her tirade, she had driven him against the elevator panel and was standing much too close for her comfort. Coming to her senses, she started to take a step back, but his arms enfolded her. With her new level of strength, she could have thrown him off easily, but his proximity made her freeze, muffling the voice of logic and encouraging the madness of surrendering to Mal. What could it hurt to pretend he really desired her just one more time?

"I can't do that, love."

Devi licked her dry lips. "Why not?"

"'Cause I'm crazy in love with you, Devi. If you tell me to leave, I will, but I'd rather you just ask me to rip my own heart out and stomp on it. That'll be less painful." His eyes shone with sincerity.

"Don't be so melodramatic." Despite her flippant words, she weakened, not sure what to believe. Her body melted against his, but she tried to resist. "I just can't believe that."

Mal shook his head, his expression one of confusion. "Why not?"

"It's too convenient. What would you have found so appealing about me, Mal? Until Master Shol transformed me, I wasn't even average. A man like you couldn't have found me attractive."

"What do you mean, a man like me?" he asked with narrowed eyes.

She shrugged. "You're a musician, and you're gorgeous. There's a different woman for you every night, and you can have your pick of any of them. So why me?"

His mouth opened and closed a couple of times, as if he was formulating and rejecting different responses. Finally, he said, "I don't know. I can't explain why I feel the way I do. I just feel it. There hasn't been a woman, ever, who made me feel the way you do. I want to spend the rest of my life exploring every inch of your body. I want to get to know everything about you. Just being with you, even right now when you are so angry and rejecting me, makes me happy." Mal shrugged. "I don't know what else you want me to say. How can I convince you?"

"Make love to me." The words surprised her, but resounded with an echo of rightness. Only in the heat of passion would she be able to discern the facts. If he was telling the truth, she would know it. If he wasn't, at least she would have one more blissful moment in his arms. She ignored the voice whispering to her that she already knew the truth. Why would he go through such an elaborate charade if he didn't feel something? Did she really believe he would go so far with the pretense as to confess his love if he was just here out of a sense of obligation?

I don't know.

Yes, you do, whispered that annoying voice. *Tell him you believe him and enjoy each other for the right reasons.*

He deserves to suffer a little uncertainty after everything he put me through without mercy. I don't care what his reasons were. Ruthlessly, she refused to listen to her conscience. Devi closed her eyes, silenced the voice, and lifted her head to accept his kiss.

His lips were hot and moist against hers, and she opened her mouth, welcoming his tongue. She rubbed and stroked it with her own, matching his caresses as their tongues parried and thrust in imitation of the way their bodies would soon move. She gasped at the slight sting caused by him nibbling her lower lip, finding it more pleasurable than painful by far. As he swept the roof of her mouth, he hissed and recoiled. The taste of blood on her tongue had her checking her teeth, which had become fangs. Instinctively, she cupped her hand over her mouth. "I'm sorry," she said, voice muffled.

Mal dabbed at a place on his tongue, and his fingers bore a trace of crimson when he withdrew them from his mouth. With a crooked grin, he reached for her again. "One of the hazards of making love with a vampire."

Fear of hurting him had her resisting his attempts to embrace her again, and she tried to pull away. Her strength should have exceeded his, but perhaps his determination helped him keep her in the circle of his arms. She stared up at him, certain he could read the worry in her eyes. "I can't control this thing yet. I don't want to bite you." The words were difficult to discern with her hand blocking her mouth, but she was superstitiously frightened to drop her arm, as if she would suddenly attack him if her mouth wasn't covered.

He cupped her face in his palms, his expression serious. "I don't care if you do. Really. I'd prefer you feed from me than some random stranger. If that's part of our lovemaking from now on, I can accept that."

She swallowed, finally dropping her hand from her mouth. "You're awfully confident there will be more sex between us in the future."

A full smile bloomed on his lips. "I'm going to spend every day of our first fifty years together learning everything there is to know about your body. When I know it all, I'm going to start over and relearn every curve, mound and niche again."

Devi allowed herself to relax against him again, tentatively returning his kiss. Sealing her lips didn't keep his determined tongue from squirming between them to plumb the moist recess beyond. Her fangs remained extended, but he deftly maneuvered around them this time. Soon, the passion overrode her hesitation, and she enthusiastically returned his kisses once more.

Devi wanted his bare skin against hers, so she grasped his shirt and tore it open. He chuckled as she stripped the ruined fabric from his arms and let it fall to the floor of the elevator. Primal need ruled her actions, lust directing her to drag her nails down his chest and stomach. He grunted, but didn't withdraw. Her eyes widened when she broke the kiss to examine the result. Red scratches marred his perfect skin, and remorse needled her. She dipped her head to trace her tongue down the marks, soothing the sting. Mal shifted restlessly, clearly enjoying her tongue on him, and she went lower.

Her fingers were nimbler than ever, and she unfastened his jeans in seconds, peeling them down to his knees, along with the scrap of red he wore as a pair of briefs. Very briefs, she thought with a hint of amusement as she dropped to her knees. Devi looked up at him from her subservient position, never having felt more control in her life. "Have I told you how much I like your cock?" She stroked the length as she asked the question.

"Devi, this is supposed to be about you. You don't have to—"

"I know." Devi licked the head of his shaft, thrilled by the way his body stiffened in response. "I want to." She needed to. Not only did she want to taste his cock, to swallow his length again, she had to see if she could without losing control.

Devi opened her mouth wider and slid her hot mouth down his erection, taking him completely inside. At first, she bobbed her head slowly, enjoying the taste and texture of him inside her mouth. Gradually, she increased her pace, bobbing and sucking with more enthusiasm. Every few seconds, a spasm ran the length of his cock and transmitted to his body. He sagged against the wall, his ragged breathing the only sound in the cab, aside from her licking and sucking.

When he stiffened, she prepared for his orgasm. Mal's cock convulsed, and she continued sucking, lapping up every pearly drop of his release. Her own control was tenuous, and her fangs were out, but she managed not to bite or nick him. Relief surged through her, and she released his erection when the last twitch finished. He was still semihard, and she grasped his shaft, meeting his gaze. The naked love in his eyes took her breath away, and she couldn't doubt his words any longer.

With slow, gentle strokes and light squeezes, Devi coaxed his erection forth again. A light kiss on the tip of his head made his cock jerk in her hands, and she looked up. "Save the next round for inside me, Mal."

"And the next, and the one after that, too," he agreed as he took her arms and lifted her to her feet. Mal slammed his mouth over hers in a heated kiss, his tongue not at all shy about entering her mouth. Liquid heat ran down Devi's thighs, and she reached between them to push aside the panties chafing her so unbearably. Grateful she'd worn a short minidress that evening, she pushed it up to her hips and plunged a finger into her pussy to stroke her neglected core. She whimpered when he pulled her hand from her heated flesh. "That's my job, love." Mal licked her finger thoroughly before releasing her hand.

"Take off your dress." His commanding tone excited her, and she grasped the hem of the indigo denim sheath, peeling the garment over her head and discarding it near his shirt. The black bra she wore pushed her breasts together and up, maximizing her cleavage. "Come here." She stepped toward him, and Mal bent his head to lick the valley between her breasts. She trembled at the sensations his tongue evoked, and he steadied her with a hand on her back. The other busied itself with unfastening the front clasp of her bra. They sighed in unison when the closure yielded and her breasts spilled forth.

Mal traced a path with his tongue to one of her hard nipples. The bud pulsed with anticipation as his tongue neared, and she cried out at the first stroke over her nipple. He circled the nub in slow, maddening circles, gradually tightening his focus until he was flicking just the very tip. She arched against him, needing more. Mal complied by sucking her nipple into his mouth. He inhaled, sending ripples of pleasure through her breast, and then sucked again.

She buried her hands in his hair, wanting to hold him at her breast forever.

The ignored breast was hard and full, anxious for its share of attention, and Devi stroked her nipple, squeezing and pinching it as Mal sucked more vigorously on the other. Her clit twitched in time with her heartbeat, and her lower body rocked against his in desperate need of his cock to fill her empty slit. She gritted her teeth to hold in a scream of frustration when he abruptly lifted his head, leaving her in that revved-up state without a chance of release without the stimulation from his mouth. "Don't stop."

"I'm not, love. We're just shifting gears." He urged her backward to lie down on the floor of the elevator after he fashioned a makeshift bed from her dress and his shirt. Devi let him direct her, aching for completion and willing to do just about anything he asked of her. Mal took time to shed the remainder of his pants before kneeling between her spread legs. "Have I told you how much I love your pussy? I enjoyed it completely bald, but this—" he ran his fingers through the new growth of soft pubic hair that now shielded her folds "—is nice." Dipping a finger inside her, he rubbed her clit in a circular motion. "So is this. Your clit is very, very nice. Not as nice as your pussy, of course." He lowered his hand to push two fingers into her opening. "Nothing compares to the wet heat of your tight pussy around my cock."

"Stop torturing me." She arched her hips. "Fuck me, Mal. Please!"

He had the nerve to laugh. "I will. Be patient. First, I want another taste of your sweet cream, love." Mal parted her thighs wider to make room between them. She closed her eyes and balled her hands into fists with anticipation. His breath wafted across her hot cleft before his tongue breached her. Devi whimpered, her body shaking just from the light contact of his tongue on her clit. When he drew the bud into his mouth to suck gently, she cried out. "Easy, love," he said against her pussy, triggering more convulsions.

Mal twisted and circled his tongue around her clit, often straying downward to sweep inside her opening. Lost in the sensations, she grasped his hair and held on to him. He was her only anchor in the passionate maelstrom. When Mal sucked her clit into his mouth and feathered the tip as one finger entered her opening, and another probed her anus, even her anchor couldn't keep her centered. A scream of pure primal arousal escaped Devi as she came. Her pussy clenched around his hand and mouth as spasms racked her body.

The last traces of the orgasm hadn't yet dispelled when Mal shifted positions and plunged his cock deeply into her quaking pussy. Devi tightened her legs around his waist and drove her buttocks upward, taking in as much of his length as she could get. He grasped her cheeks in his hands, kneading her ass as he thrust into her. Their eyes locked, and his spoke volumes. Love shone from his eyes, and he seemed to make no attempt to shield his vulnerability. The last of her anger melted, and she crumbled. "I love you, Mal."

"I know, love, but it sure is good to hear you say it." He pistoned his lower body again, sinking into her heat and withdrawing slightly before adding, "You believe I love you now, don't you?"

Devi nodded, letting her eyes close again as ecstasy overtook her. A dragging sensation in her stomach told her release was close, and she concentrated solely on meeting each of his thrusts and matching his pace.

Dimly, the sound of the doors opening penetrated her hedonistic fog, and she blinked open her eyes, wondering who had overridden the emergency stop. Two men in the dark suits commonly worn by the casino's security team stood there, eyes wide. She knew she should stop Mal, but was in the moment, too close to orgasm to say anything. Instead, she closed her eyes again and continued to make love with Mal.

One of the men laughed softly, and as the doors shut again, she heard him say, "This happens a lot around here, Evan. It's best to just let them finish."

At that moment, she climaxed, her pussy tightening around Mal's cock. He bucked his hips, grunting as he came. Her eyes opened and collided with his gaze. Spellbound, Devi let the green in his eyes suck her in, binding her to him in a way completely different from the artificial binding spell he had imposed upon her before. This time, it was as though their souls merged, and she voluntarily gave herself to him, never wanting to part from Mal again. Whatever their future held, she had no doubt they would be together.

THE PROMISE

♣ ♠ ♥ ◆ ♣ ♠ ♥ ◆ ♣ ♠ ♥ ◆

Anya Bast

The Promise is a prequel to *The Deal*, which appeared in the first *What Happens in Vegas…* anthology, and occurs about one year before Cassidy's story.

For James. As ever, thank you
for your support and your love.

♣ ♠ ♥ ♦ ♣ ♠ ♥ ♦ ♣ ♠ ♥ ♦

Chapter One

"Come on, man. You're going to be late for your own wedding." Tom slumped down in a chair in Damian's bedroom and stared at his friend.

Damian glanced at Tom in the mirror he faced. "I'm hurrying, I'm hurrying." He knotted his tie, unknotted it and knotted it again for the twentieth time. "Damn it." The only person who could ever get it right was Cassidy, his fiancée…his soon-to-be-wife.

Fuck. He fumbled his tie again.

The thought that he'd be married in the next hour still made his hands tremble and created the sensation of a noose being slowly tightened around his neck until he couldn't breathe. "Just like this fucking tie," he growled, pulling the offending fabric off and throwing it to the floor of his bedroom.

Tom shifted in the chair. "What?"

"Nothing. Screw the tie."

"You can't screw the tie. You can't get married without a tie." He motioned with his hands in his agitation. "Don't be such an asshole, Damian. Cassidy is the best thing that ever happened to you."

Damian fought the urge to snarl at his friend.

He couldn't shake the feeling that something huge besides the wedding was about to happen—something bad. Something that would change his life forever. He'd dismiss the feeling as only fear about getting married, but he'd been having other "feelings" about things lately that later had come true. Damian was about ready to sign himself as one of the precog acts in the casinos. Maybe he could make some cash on the side, predicting events.

"Listen, we gotta go," said Tom, standing. "Stop talking to your clothing and let's get out of here. It's still a fifteen-minute drive across town and you should be walking down the aisle *right now.*"

Yes, he should be walking down the aisle of the White Wishes Chapel on Hamilton Street right now. Tom was right. Gee, could it be he was procrastinating about getting married? Damian studied his reflection in the mirror. No doubt on that score. His feet weren't just cold, they were blocks of ice.

But he'd made a promise. A promise to Cassidy to see this through.

Truth was, he should have broken up with her long ago. But how do you break up with the most perfect woman in the world? Damian didn't have any solid reason to do it, that was for sure. He loved her, maybe not as much as Cassidy loved him…but he loved her enough. And what was the alternative to marrying Cassidy? Just loneliness, that's what.

Damian had had enough of *lonely* to last him a lifetime. All his life he'd felt like he didn't fit in with his people, a round peg in a square hole. He couldn't ever lay his finger on exactly why he felt that way, only that he did.

Damian scooped the tie off the floor. "Okay, let's go."

"I don't know why you want to keep a woman like Cassidy waiting," Tom muttered, herding him out the door. "I'd kill for a girl like her."

"Cassidy is awesome."

"Yeah, she is. So what's up with dragging your feet?"

"I don't know, man." He shook his head and opened the door to his apartment. The traffic on the busy Las Vegas street in front of his apartment building hummed and honked. "It's just…the permanence of marriage, I guess. Losing my freedom."

Yeah, maybe that was it.

Cassidy was great, there was no denying it. She was beautiful and intelligent. She shared his taste in music and movies and when they were together they had a great time. They could talk about anything. He should be racing to the church to marry her and counting every one of his lucky stars along the way.

So why wasn't he?

He was ready to settle down. He'd just landed a job as an insurance agent, allowing him to leave his job as a poker dealer at the Gold Diggers Casino down on the Strip. He wanted to buy a house, have kids. Cassidy would be a great mom. He and Cass had been together for two years now. They were best friends.

It was just…

If he truly examined his feelings in this moment, he'd probably be happy if something prevented him from ever getting to the White Wishes Chapel today.

He followed Tom out the front door of his apartment and turned to lock it. A man stood to his immediate left outside.

Noooo…make that *two* men. One on either side of the door.

Big men.

Thugs. Oh, shit.

"Hey, guys," said Damian with a friendly grin. "How's it going?"

One of the men grabbed him by the throat and pushed him up against the wall. Another man grabbed Tom. Damian gagged and desperately tried to think of all the people he'd pissed off lately. Or maybe this was Tom's deal. He knew his friend had some gambling debts.

Then he noticed the man's eyes.

For a moment, they seemed to shimmer…like a fish cresting the top of the water on a sunny day. Molten silver, brilliant blue, green—then back to prosaic brown. Damian stopped struggling and stared, wondering if he'd really just seen what he'd seen.

"Stay still," the man growled.

Odd. He wanted to do as the man asked. In fact, his compulsion to do exactly what the thug had demanded of him was overwhelming. He knew he should be fighting, but he just…didn't want to.

The other thug holding Tom against the wall pressed his hand to his friend's chest and stared into his eyes. Tom went motionless, limp. "You will forget this incident. You will forget you ever came to Damian Porter's apartment this morning. This morning Damian called and told you he wanted to get ready alone. Now you will go to the chapel. When Damian doesn't show up for the wedding, you'll be as surprised as everyone else."

What?

The partial hold on Damian's will evaporated with a pop. He pushed against the guy holding him and brought his fist up in a hard and fast right hook. To Damian's total surprise, it connected. The thug fell backward to collapse against the railing behind him.

The other guy left Tom, who just stood there staring ahead as if caught in a trance, and came after Damian. They scuffled. Damian threw another punch and missed. By then Thug One had recovered and they were both on him. They yanked his arms behind his back and pressed him face-first against the wall.

Tom didn't even look at him. He just walked away, down the stairs and toward his car, parked in the lot below.

"Hey! What the hell, man? I thought you were my friend!"

"He can't hear you," Thug Two said. "Save your breath."

"What the fuck is going on? Who are you guys? How do you know me? I have a wedding to go to, goddamn it!"

"Not today. Not any day if your people have anything to say about it."

His people?

Thug One leaned in, holding his cheek where Damian had punched him, and grimaced. Damian was happy to see the thug's nose was bleeding and his lip was split. "It's your birthday, boy."

Damian made a scoffing sound. "It's not my birthday, you IQ-challenged ape. You have the wrong guy."

"Don't have the wrong guy," Thug Two snarled, hauling him away from the wall and pushing him toward the stairs. He gave him a good shove forward that made him stumble. "And don't make us do this the hard way. As long as you come along nice with us, we won't have to hurt you."

♣ ♠ ♥ ♦ ♣ ♠ ♥ ♦ ♣ ♠ ♥ ♦

Chapter Two

They loaded him into an SUV and took him to the Strip. Secreted in between two buildings and across from the Liege casino, was a nightclub that Damian had never noticed before. Not in all the times he'd been up and down this street. He'd been born and raised in Las Vegas; he thought he knew every stick and brick in this city. Yet, there it was, hidden away in an odd space that seemed to suck away and make disappear all the light around it. The club was aptly named.

Darkness.

The thugs parked the SUV on a side street and yanked him from the vehicle. They muscled him up to the front entrance of the building, pushing him through some unseen film of stickiness that made his stomach turn. It made him want to turn around and run the other way…even more than he already did.

Another thug opened the door and Thug One produced a card and flashed it at him. Damn. This was obviously an establishment of many thugs.

They pushed him inside.

"Look, guys, nice as this visit has been, like I said, I've got somewhere to be."

Thug Two pushed him forward again, into the club proper. "Elena wants to see you."

He spoke as if that answered everything.

Damian stumbled forward and caught himself against a chair. When he looked up, he gawked. The interior was done in all blacks and dark, deep red…bloodred. It looked like a place where Goths would hang out.

A bar lined the wall and the place was filled to bursting with tables and chairs. This time of day, he'd expect a nightclub to be closed, but this place was pretty packed…and these patrons were definitely *not* local. His eyebrows rose into his hairline as he examined the nightclub's unique customers. Some guy with pale skin and prosthetic fangs peeking from curled lips snarled at him.

"What is it, Halloween?" he mumbled as Thug One took him by the arm and pushed him to the left.

A tall, tattooed woman passed him, bared her teeth and hissed, her eyes flashing that strange silver sparkling whatever at him. Okaaaaaay. Yeah, this was a Goth club all right.

They prodded and muscled him through a door near the bar, then through a kitchen to another door at the back of that room. They pushed him through that one so hard, he stumbled and fell to his knees.

"Fuck! I'm really starting to get annoyed," Damian said, staring at the bloodred carpet he'd landed on.

Nothing. No response but the sound of a closing door. The thugs had left him alone.

Damian raised his head, looking up slowly. Standing in front of him with one hip cocked was the most beautiful woman he'd ever seen. That was not a good thought to be having on his wedding day, while Cassidy waited for him at the altar *this very moment*.

God, he was such an asshole.

He lowered his forehead to the carpet, closed his eyes and counted to five. Maybe this was all some kind of hallucination brought on by the stress of impending lifetime commitment. Maybe when he opened his eyes the next time, the Most Beautiful Woman In The World would be gone.

"You punched Hugo," his dream woman said in a liquid silver voice. "That's why they manhandled you. Otherwise, your trip to Darkness would have been uneventful."

Damian opened his eyes and stared into the red. Damn it, she was still there.

He raised his gaze. She wore fuck-me shoes of tooled black leather. From there things just got better. Her legs were bare, shapely and creamy pale. She wore a short black skirt, slit to show one mouthwatering thigh. Her shirt was a shimmering blue button-down, opened to show just a hint of cleavage. Long, dark brown hair tumbled around her shoulders and framed a heart-shaped face with a small, pointy chin, a longish nose and beautiful dark brown eyes. She wasn't tall, but she was curvy.

Full ruby-red lips parted and she spoke again. "Do you have a brain in your head? You haven't said a word."

She was pretty, but apparently not all that nice. And he was on his knees in front of her.

Damian stood. "Hey, Hugo grabbed me and pushed me up against the wall first. He had the punch coming. Who the hell are you people, anyway?"

"We are *your* people. We're the *thooahaw day dah nawn*."

Damian resisted the urge to say *God bless you*. He blinked. "The who?"

"The people of the goddess Danu," she replied patiently. "A lost race of Ireland thought by mortals to be only myth and so much legend." She paused a beat. "We're the fae, Damian, and you are one of us. I am one of the daughters of the king who rules here in the Las Vegas fae underground."

The Tuatha Dé Danann. That's what she was talking about. He remembered the term from one of the books on Irish history his sister had been reading. Suzanne was a nut for anything about the history of Ireland. The name and the story of the Tuatha Dé had captured his imagination and he'd read a bit about them after finding her book open on the kitchen table one night. He'd just never known how to pronounce their name.

His brief flirtation with faery tales wasn't something he'd ever told anyone about because that's what it was…a faery tale. As in not real. Anyway, that stuff was for girls so he'd never admit how much it had fascinated him.

"Though Hugo and Aaron, the men who picked you up from your apartment, are not fae, they're demons. We hire them once in a while."

"Elena? Is that your name?"

She nodded.

"Well, Elena, I think you're bat-shit crazy."

"I know you probably don't believe me yet," said Elena, casting her eyes down so that her eyelashes shadowed the peaches-and-cream skin of her cheek.

She really was pretty enough to be a faery. The thought bit into him with a good dollop of guilt.

"Yeah, you'd be right on that count, all except for the *yet* part. I don't believe you now and I never will. Now I don't know who you people really are or why you've brought me here, but I have to leave. This suit I'm wearing isn't just for show. I don't wear one of these every day. I'm supposed to be at a chapel marrying my fiancée. She's there, right now, waiting for me...*at the altar!*" He yelled the last part, his control finally shredded.

Elena jumped, but quickly regained her composure. "You're supposed to be marrying Cassidy Williams right now, I know."

"How do you know—"

She held up a hand. "Listen to me for a just a moment, Damian, please."

She didn't wait for his reply, which was good, because he had none. Elena walked to him and took his hands in hers. Her palms were warm and silken. As much as he wanted to deny it, the touch of her was good.

"You may not believe me yet about the Tuatha Dé, but believe this—I am a fae princess and I can see into your heart and soul, Damian Alex Porter. Don't ask me how, not yet, just accept that I can." She lifted a brow. "Don't believe me? I know how you really feel about Cassidy. I know what you've told no one else in the entire world. I know that you don't really want to marry her. I know you only asked because you thought you should, that you'd been together for so long it was a question of either marriage or breakup. I know you like Cassidy a lot and that you think she's a wonderful woman and you can't figure why you can't just love her like she deserves. You think that if you marry her the love will eventually come." She paused. "But it won't."

Damian opened his mouth, but she covered it with her hand. He was suddenly caught between wanting to bite it and wanting to suck every one of her slender, pretty fingers into the recesses of his mouth.

She continued, "Cassidy is the best of women, it's true, but she is not the one for you, Damian. And you are not the one for her. Don't blame yourself, but do let it go…let *her* go. If you marry Cassidy this day, you will be making the worst mistake of your life and of Cassidy's. If you marry Cassidy today, she will miss meeting the man she *should* be with, the one who will love her with all his heart and soul the way she deserves. Do you want to do that to Cassidy, Damian?"

"No." He couldn't say anything else. It *was* like she could see into his heart and soul. Guilt swelled.

"Cassidy will be all right, Damian. You should have broken it off before now and it's a pity you couldn't find the courage, a pity you were so afraid of ending up alone. She'll have a rough year, it's true. She'll doubt her ability to fall in love again and she'll fear it. She will suffer for the rejection you give her today. But in the long run, she'll be better off." Elena smiled. "You see, she's already met her true love—she just doesn't know it yet. And Damian?"

"Yes?" His voice was a rough, emotion-filled whisper.

"I'm sorry to put a chink in your ego, but it's not you. Don't go off and marry Cassidy when you don't really want it way down deep in your heart. It's not fair to her."

Damian stared into Elena's eyes. Her gaze hadn't wavered from his even once since she'd begun speaking. How did she know any of this? He'd never told anyone about his doubts. No one, *ever*. His family and friends thought he and Cassidy had the best of relationships, that they'd been made for each other.

Elena finally let go of his hand and walked to a table in the corner. Damian blinked. He hadn't even noticed the room beyond the carpet and the woman. It appeared to be a living room, but a bit more formal…more like a waiting room in a really fancy doctor's office. On the table, near a vase of expensive flowers, she picked up a phone. Then she walked back and handed it to him. "Press One for the White Wishes Chapel. I put it on speed dial."

Oh, God. He stared at the sleek black phone in his hand.

"You know it's the right thing to do. No matter how much it might hurt Cassidy today, it's best for her in the long run. You're best removed from her life to make room for another." Elena looked thoughtful for a moment. "His name is James, James Carter."

James. His best man. Why didn't that surprise him? He'd known James had the hots for Cassidy.

Oddly, it didn't even prick his ego—the thought of James and Cassidy together. He just wanted Cassidy to be happy and loved. James was a good man. He'd treat her well.

No, Damian didn't feel jealous or hurt. He didn't pine for Cassidy and want nothing more than to be at the chapel right now marrying her.

"Call her," Elena said again.

"And tell her what?"

She tipped her head to the side and gave him a sad little smile. "The truth."

♣ ♠ ♥ ♦ ♣ ♠ ♥ ♦ ♣ ♠ ♥ ♦

Chapter Three

He glanced up at her. "That two demons kidnapped me on the way to my wedding, brainwashed my friend and brought me to a nightclub on the Strip I've never noticed before—and I thought I knew *every* place on this street—where I was greeted by a faery princess? Yeah, Cassidy won't believe that. *I* don't believe that."

Elena lifted a brow. "The *other* truth."

Damian stared at the phone in his hand some more. He felt freer at the simple contemplation of calling off the wedding. And that, ultimately, is what made him give the phone back to Elena and take his own cell phone from his back pocket.

He called his best man.

"Where the hell are you, Damian?" James demanded as soon as he answered. "She's waiting for you."

"Can I talk to Cassidy?"

There was a lengthy pause before James handed the phone over.

"Damian?" Cassidy's voice was shaky.

"Hi, Cassidy." He paused and tried to form the right words. Emotion tightened his chest. "I'm sorry, but I'm not coming. It's not because I don't care about you that I'm doing this. I do care about you…and that's why I can't be there today."

"I—I don't understand." Cassidy's voice broke on a sob. "You unbelievable bastard!"

"Yeah, I am. I know I am, Cassidy. God." He sighed. This was the hardest thing he'd ever done. "You may not think so right now, but I'm doing you a favor." He closed his eyes. "Have a good life."

She hung up on him.

He turned off his cell phone and stared at it for a moment before repocketing it. He felt like absolute shit for hurting her, but he knew, *knew* he'd done the right thing. He was a total asshole for letting it go as far as he had. A coward.

Anger at himself billowed up from the bottom of his toes and exploded at Elena. He stalked toward her, looking menacing enough to cause her to take a few steps back. "You're going to let me out of here, lady," he growled. "You may have been right about all that, but that doesn't make you my friend."

She bumped against the table behind her. "I understand that you're upset."

He pinned her against the table and bracketed her there with a hand to either side of her luscious body. "And being right doesn't make you any less crazy. I want out. I want out *now,* so I can go home, lick my wounds and clean up the fucking mess I've made of my life and hers."

Elena's eyes widened and her lips parted. Damian tried hard not to stare, but the attraction he'd felt for her before seemed to have exploded with his rage.

Maybe it was stress. Maybe it was cutting that tie with Cassidy. Whatever it was, he fucking wanted the woman in front of him with a desire so deep it was nearly uncontrollable. He wanted to turn her around, yank up that silly, frivolous little skirt and bury his cock deep inside her silken pussy.

And from the flush on her face that seemed to have little to do with fear, Damian wasn't so sure she didn't want that, too.

He leaned in and kissed her.

She made a little whimpering sound, wrapped her arms around his neck and kissed him back.

Fuck. Sweet heaven.

He let his hands snake around her waist as he slanted his mouth across hers and forced her lips open with his tongue so he could take her hard and deep, just like how he wanted to fuck her.

And that's how Damian was spending his wedding day.

At the thought, he pushed from her and turned away, swearing under his breath.

"It's not your fault," Elena said breathlessly. "It's not your fault you're attracted to me. There's a reason for it and there's nothing you can do about it. There's nothing I can do about it, either. Don't beat yourself up, Damian. It's just bad timing."

Damian made a scoffing sound, went back and kissed her again. He was doomed to hell anyway, might as well enjoy himself.

His hands slipped over her curves, over her small breasts through the material of her shirt. Her nipples—God he wanted to taste them—puckered and hardened against his palms. Her hands slid over his shoulders, his back, as she kissed him with total abandon and complete passion. His cock was hard as a rock and he wanted her so badly he could hardly stand it.

She broke the kiss. Her eyes were heavy-lidded and her lips swollen. "You were born on January 16 at 11:25 a.m., right?"

His mind was so blurred with lust, the oddness of the question barely registered. "Yes."

Two strong hands yanked him back. Thug One, Hugo, pressed a syringe gun to his neck and pulled the trigger. Sharp pain followed the press of the cold metal.

Damian turned and threw another punch, but missed because whatever they'd injected him with was spreading like fire through his veins. He stumbled forward on the momentum of the punch and fell to his knees for the second time that day. The room swam, but he forced himself to stay upright. Voices were raised around him, but he couldn't understand what anyone was saying.

Damian bowed his head and shook it, bracing his hands on the thick carpet. Gradually the haze over his mind dispersed and the fire in his body leaked away. Sounds came clearer. His vision suddenly was better, sharper, more focused. He felt stronger…healthier.

"What the fuck?" he roared, coming to his feet in one strong move. "What the fuck did you just do?"

"We did you a favor," said Elena. Her eyes were shiny. "I'm sorry it had to be like that. You never would have accepted the activation and it had to be today. It had to be now. Otherwise it would have been too late."

Damian clapped a hand over his neck. "Late for what?" Hugo had disappeared while he'd been reeling on the floor, leaving him alone with Elena again.

She licked her lips in a clearly nervous gesture. "For you to realize your true self. For you to find belonging. It's what you've always longed for without knowing it. You don't understand yet, but you will."

"That's for sure. Was that kiss just a diversion, then? Were you trying to distract me so muscle-bound boy with the fish eyeballs could stick me? What a bunch of freaks." He turned, masking his terror at being injected with God-knew-what. "You'll be hearing from my attorney later today…after I go to the hospital to find what the hell you just put into me."

Elena followed him. "You can go to the hospital, but they won't find anything. We didn't hurt you, Damian. We would never do that. Damian—"

He stopped with his hand on the doorknob and turned.

"I wish you wouldn't go. I have so much to tell you. If you leave now you'll have lots of questions later and no answers."

"So why don't you just kiss me again, then have Hugo come in, knock me on my head and throw me into a locked room?" Sarcasm dripped from every syllable. "You can imprison me and tell me whatever you want."

"I won't keep you here against your will."

Damian laughed and opened the door. "You are all a bunch of freaks."

"You'll be back, Damian," she called at his back as he strode toward the front of the nightclub.

"Yeah," he threw back over his shoulder. "I'll be back with the police."

Elena stared at Damian's retreating form, her heart heavy. That had not gone well. In fact, that had probably been one of her worst inductions ever. But Damian would be back. With a vial of her blood acting as a catalyst, they'd managed to activate the fae DNA in him. He would be noticing changes in his body and his thought processes almost immediately. He would have questions to which only she held answers.

She felt bad that it had to happen on today of all days, his wedding day. Worse that she and Damian shared such an incredible attraction. The attraction had been a surprise. Elena had thought this had been an induction like any other, but it hadn't been. Not by a long shot. When Damian had looked up at her for the first time and their gazes had met, she'd been shocked by a deep soul recognition of him.

Heartstring.

Heartstrings were rare in the world of the fae. Two people sharing a heartstring were compatible in most every way for a relationship—for matehood. A person maybe had a handful of heartstrings walking around in the world; the chances of their paths crossing were astronomical. Damian was the only one of hers she'd ever met.

She and Damian had a romantic compatibility that went far beyond the ordinary.

And, wow, Reynolds was not going to like that.

♣ ♠ ♥ ♦ ♣ ♠ ♥ ♦ ♣ ♠ ♥ ♦

Chapter Four

Better.

Stronger. Faster. Clearer.

Had they injected him with some kind of illegal drug? No, it wasn't that. Damian wasn't sure how he knew the very important fact, he just did.

Damian hailed a cab on the Strip and told it to pass by the White Wishes Chapel on his way home. He wasn't going to the hospital. Damian knew whatever they'd given him wasn't harmful. He'd decided that…or known it, or whatever, only moments after leaving Darkness.

The taxi slowed in front of the chapel and Damian caught sight of Cassidy outside with James. "Stop for a minute," he told the cabbie. The vehicle pulled over to park on the side of the street across from the building.

She looked beautiful in her gown, like walking sunlight. Damian touched the doorknob to get out, go and talk to her, but just then James pulled her close and she rested her head on his shoulder, accepting the comfort he gave.

Images flashed in Damian's mind, so clear it was like sitting in a movie theater. Cassidy leaving Gold Diggers and going to the Liege to work as a shill where James was employed as a blackjack dealer. Cassidy upset, grieving their relationship, doubting her self-worth, doubting her ability to risk her heart again. Then…James. First as a friend, then as more. Eventually true love. Marriage. Kids. *Happiness.*

Damian shook his head, trying to clear it, and looked up at James and Cassidy again. That had been a glimpse of the future. He *knew* it.

Whatever they'd given him at Darkness, Damian liked it.

He directed his gaze to Cassidy again, guilt welling once more. But it was better he leave it like this. Better he let things take the course he'd just seen in his mind. Cassidy really *would* be fine.

"Okay, I've seen enough," Damian said to the cabbie. "Take me home."

He didn't call his lawyer, either.

He'd gone back to his apartment, to about fifty irate messages on his answering machine. There'd even been one from Tom, wondering what had happened and why he'd never shown up at the church. From the message it was clear that Tom remembered nothing about that morning.

Or maybe he was the victim of some elaborate prank put together by Cassidy and company? No…that wasn't her style, not on their wedding day. If it had been a practical joke it had really backfired. Or maybe there was a camera filming him right now and he'd somehow become the butt of some television program's practical joke? That seemed unlikely.

The only other explanation was insanity. How unpleasant.

Keeping that possibility in the back of his mind, but not quite ready to entertain it seriously—did the insane know they were insane?—he'd escaped his answering machine and the swear words issuing from it in the evening and headed to Cassidy's. She deserved an explanation.

Her mother had answered the door and let him in without a word. Damian had found Cassidy in her bedroom. She'd ranted and screamed at him for a couple of hours while he told her the truth about his feelings for her.

He'd told her she'd be okay. She'd told him he was an asshole and he'd agreed. Pretty much, they'd left it at that.

Damian knew that about a year from now he'd get a call from Cassidy, once she'd finally figured out she was in love with James and was better off for Damian having left her at the altar. When Damian got that call he'd have to act surprised…but he'd be expecting it.

Now it was midnight and Damian stood on the Strip watching Darkness shimmering eerily in its namesake across the street from him. How was it he'd never noticed it before in all the years he'd lived here? He'd always thought there'd been a wall there.

He grabbed a homeless man he'd seen walk this area for years. He dug out some bills and pressed them into the old guy's hand, then he pointed at the club. "That place new?"

The old homeless man squinted. "What place?"

"That place. Darkness. The club across the street." You couldn't miss it, it flashed with blue and orange lights on the facade.

"I don't see nothing there but a wall and shadows, kid, but thanks for the cash." The man ambled on.

Damian stared at the man's back. How strange. Or maybe not. Maybe the homeless guy was a little off his rocker.

Or maybe Damian was.

He shook the thought off, pushed his hands into his

pockets, and played Frogger to get across the busy street. Yeah, Elena had been right. He was back. He had questions. Damian wasn't sure she'd still be there. Maybe she'd gone back to her home under a toadstool for the night.

He approached the door and it opened. A thug… *demon?*…stood inside. "Card?"

"Card?"

"You need a card to get into Darkness."

"I don't have one. What is this, a private club?"

The muscle-bound man narrowed his eyes. "Are you a paranormal?" He sniffed. "You smell fae."

"What the fuck—"

Muscle-bound threw over his shoulder, "Hey, I think we have a stray."

"A stray?" Hugo appeared, gave him a once-over. "Nah, he's new. Inducted today. Probably doesn't have a card yet. Come in. Elena wants to see you."

Damian stepped over the threshold and followed Hugo, whose face was black-and-blue on one side.

"If Elena didn't have such a hard-on for you, I'd kill you and dump your body in the alley," Hugo growled over the thump of the driving music inside.

Great.

Damian watched Hugo stalk away, then turned left, figuring he'd find Elena in the same room she'd been in today. He *knew* she'd been notified of his arrival somehow and would be waiting for him. The club was crowded with all manner of…creatures. Damian did his best to look forward and ignore it all. Denial was a great coping strategy.

When he reached the room, Elena was sitting on the white sofa, wearing a silken blue bathrobe. Her feet were bare and her legs were crossed, revealing satiny-looking flesh. Her arms were crossed over her chest and she wore a wary expression on her face.

Damian stopped short at the threshold and his mouth went dry before he recovered. He walked inside and closed the door behind him. "Do you live here?"

"Sort of." She uncrossed her arms and looked a little uncomfortable. "I live beneath it." Elena paused, drew a breath. "In a pocket of reality created by my will, emotion and magic. All the fae do, from the Tuatha Dé Danann to the Twyleth Teg, both light and dark."

"Okay." He wasn't even going to ask. Damian walked a few steps closer. "I'm getting a little sick of feeling like I slipped down a rabbit hole every time I come into this place. I feel like my whole world has been standing on end ever since I met you."

"Rabbit hole." She smiled. "That's not an incorrect description of Darkness. It's secreted in a fold of reality."

"A fold of reality." He couldn't believe he actually said it with a straight face. But there was a point where you were presented with so much unreality, you just had to believe it. Or accept it, at the very least. Your mind had to bend, or it would break.

"You can't see it unless you're a paranormal." She hesitated at the look on his face. "Demon, angel, vampire or fae."

Well, that explained a lot. "I'm fae, so I can see it."

"Right."

Riiiiight. "What's a stray?"

"It's slang. A human, a nonpara, who can see Darkness for whatever reason. They probably have a drop of para blood somewhere, enough to let them see through the veil and into the pocket where Darkness exists."

"And you live here."

She nodded and stood in one mouthwateringly smooth move. "I do. Would you like to see? We can have some tea." She walked toward the wall.

"Sure, why not?" He shrugged. "I've never had tea in a pocket of reality with a fae princess before."

Her steps hesitated, but she kept going. She pushed the wall and a door opened. Secret passageways. *Of course* there would be secret passageways. A set of stairs led downward. He followed her.

"Centuries ago the Tuatha Dé's population dwindled to near nothing. We were forced to go underground, to hide from humans."

"I see you mean that literally," Damian said, examining the artwork on the walls. Images of the Wild Hunt and other fae legends cavorted in paint every few feet in between classy, expensive lighting.

"Well, yes, sometimes. We do live aboveground, too, but in every major city there are fae residences underground. The royal family, for example, always lives underground."

"Why were you forced to hide from the humans? The fae have all kinds of special powers, right? Why didn't they just take over?"

She turned her head and glanced at him. "You mean, why were we forced to hide? It was because our numbers grew so low the humans formed lynch mobs. No amount of special powers in the world would have helped us when our numbers were so drastically reduced. Our magic is limited to precognitive abilities and illusion, mostly. We can alter matter in pockets of reality—that's not illusion. Those pockets are faery and we rule there. But illusion in this reality construct is just a parlor trick and it doesn't do much good in a war. Plus, the humans had reason to hate us. Back then we weren't very nice to them, not a lot of us, anyway."

"What do you mean?"

"You've never read any faery tales? The Brothers Grimm, perhaps?"

"Sure."

They reached the end of the stairs and they found themselves in a long corridor. "Then you know we liked to play tricks on them. We used to lure mortals into falling into faery and some of the darker of us did cruel things to them there. Occasionally we even ate them. Think of the old woman who lured children to her house in the woods. That was based on a true story."

"You can't tell me that faery tales are for real."

Elena shrugged. "Believe what you will. Your beliefs don't make reality any less true."

She went through the third door on the right and he followed. Inside was a luxurious apartment. It was huge, far too big to be believed. The doors in the corridor had been close together. By all rights they should have entered a very narrow room. He stopped short, staring at the overstuffed, comfortable-looking furniture, the fire flickering in the hearth and the open kitchen at the far end of the room.

Elena turned. "It's a pocket."

"Of course it is. It reminds me of a clown car."

She laughed and went into the kitchen. "Would you prefer coffee to tea?"

"Always."

He wandered over to a table with a glass top. On it were displayed many different beautiful pieces of multicolored pottery. He picked one up and examined it. "This is really beautiful stuff," he said in admiration. He wasn't much for interior design, but these objects called to him. They were special in some way.

Elena peeked out of the kitchen. "The pottery, you mean?"

"Yes. I really like it."

She smiled—warm and bright. It made something around his heart squeeze. "Thank you. It means a lot to me that you like those pieces." She ducked back in.

He frowned. "Uh. You're welcome."

"How do you take your coffee?" she asked from the kitchen.

"Black."

Elena poured two mugs of black coffee. Then she came back and handed him one. "Sit down. We have a lot to discuss."

He sank down onto the comfortable couch and took a sip of the rich hickory blend. Damian had so many questions he didn't know where to start. "So what's the deal with my birthday?"

Elena sat down in a recliner near him and set her coffee on an end table after taking a sip. "I mentioned that the fae fertility levels have dwindled? That hasn't changed over the centuries. Sometimes our people get lost, go off on their own, have children with humans. Some of them, through some kind of subconscious attraction, find each other and have kids, not even knowing what they are." She paused. "Both your parents are Tuatha Dé. They just don't know it. That means you're a full-blood fae, though it's been diluted with human blood in your genetic line. It's very rare. Both you and your sister are full-bloods. Your parents were never located, not until it was too late to induct them."

"Uh, huh." *Yeah, sure.* He sipped his coffee.

She leaned forward. "The fae genes you carry have been mostly dormant…you've *forgotten* that you're fae. In order to make you remember we had to inject you with our blood, my blood, in this case, exactly one hundred and seventy-three days after your birthday. Over the next few days, you'll notice many changes as you become who you truly were meant to be. I'm just sorry it had to happen on your wedding day."

"How does all that work?"

She shrugged a shoulder. "It's magic."

"Magic, huh?" He looked into his coffee cup for a moment and then set it aside. "I don't believe in magic."

Elena smiled knowingly. "You will."

He looked up at her. "Why don't you show me some? I mean, you're fae, right? You should be able to pull a rabbit out of a hat or something."

She gave him a slow blink. "I can control fire, air, heat and light. I can throw illusion like nobody's business and I can create sensation, though that's a part of illusion, even here in this pocket of faery."

He leaned forward with challenge clear in his eyes. "Go ahead. Shock and awe me."

Elena grinned and leaned forward, too. "Are you sure you can handle it?"

Damian grinned. "I can handle anything you throw at me, lady."

She snapped her fingers and plunged the room into darkness. The fire in the fireplace flickered twice, then roared to renewed life.

Velvet stroked along his thigh. He jerked and yelped a little in surprise. "Holy—"

"Shhh…" Elena shushed him from the opposite chair.

"You asked for magic and magic you shall have." Her voice was softer and smoother than the sensation moving over his body and he responded to it involuntarily.

The magical touch continued up his chest and over his arms. It lifted the coffee cup from his fingers and took it away, and then pressed him back into the cushions, moving over his neck and then down his stomach. It undid his belt and slipped inside, moving over his hard cock.

Damian's breath caught and he closed his eyes, giving over to it. Maybe he should have been concerned, but he trusted Elena with strong irrationality. It didn't make sense, it just was.

He opened his eyes enough to see Elena watching intently from the other chair as her ghostly fingers of magic caressed him. Her eyelids were heavy and her breathing seemed shallow. She rubbed over his cock, harder and faster, making him go rigid and needy. The magic ruffled his hair, pressed against his lips.

Hell, this would make him come.

"Okay, I believe you," he murmured. "Now come on over here and give me the real thing."

♣ ♠ ♥ ♦ ♣ ♠ ♥ ♦ ♣ ♠ ♥ ♦

Chapter Five

Damn it all to hell. What was he doing? This was wrong on so many levels. For fuck's sake, he'd just jilted someone at the altar today!

Maybe it was for that reason that he suddenly needed Elena more than he needed to draw breath. Maybe it was the fact his world had been tilted on end, shaken, and then set back on its feet as though everything he'd ever known wasn't a lie. Maybe it was Elena's fae blood coursing through his veins, making him remember a promise his DNA had made without his permission or his knowledge.

Whatever it was, it was absolutely undeniable. He needed Elena and judging by the look on Elena's face, she needed him just as badly.

Elena rose and took a step toward Damian.

Gods, what was she doing? She was engaged! It didn't matter that she'd only once met the man she was destined to marry. It didn't matter that it was a loveless political match, or that she and Damian shared something much deeper and real than she'd ever have with Reynolds. A heartstring. A cursed heartstring, a thing so rare as to be nonexistent had fallen into her lap only days before her wedding.

How could the universe be so cruel?

Her father expected she marry Reynolds and that was that. The last thing she should be doing now was Damian Porter.

"We shouldn't do this." She licked her suddenly dry lips. Fae culture said she could sleep with any male of her choosing up until the day of her wedding, but still…to engage this way with a heartstring was dangerous.

But nothing, *nothing* in the world *or* the underworld could stop her.

"Yeah, I know." Damian stood and walked toward her. He moved her hair to the side, exposing her shoulder. His gaze lingered on her skin. "Let's do it anyway."

"Oh, gods," she murmured.

In a fit of good sense, she pushed past him toward her darkened kitchen. She stopped with her hands on her counter, staring at her kitchen cabinets as if they held all the answers about her life that she sought.

Damian approached her from behind. His heat radiated out and touched her through the fabric of her nightgown and robe. She turned to face him, but refused to raise her gaze to his. He didn't know—couldn't know what a heartstring was. All he likely felt for her was a confusing mixture of intense emotion and undeniable lust.

Her heart skipped a beat at the look in his eyes and she stepped to the side. He blocked her, caged her with his arms on either side of her. She considered her situation. If she wanted to get away, she could, but did she really want to?

No.

"Elena." His voice shook. "Have you woven a spell over me?"

She gasped. "I would never do such a thing—"

"I want you more than is reasonable, more than I can control. Elena, please, let me touch you, let me be with you tonight. If you tell me to go away, I will, but—"

"I don't want you to go away, Damian."

His eyes went dark with passion. He yanked her robe and nightgown up to her waist with a jerk, while his mouth came down on hers. He delved his hand between her thighs, felt her bare neediness, where she was wet and warm and creaming at his touch.

Elena gasped in shock and pleasure and Damian made a contented sound. He stroked her softly between her thighs until she moaned and her blood heated. Elena's clit swelled and became deliciously sensitive. When Damian touched her there, she ground herself against his hand, eager for more contact.

Damian made a frustrated noise and then pushed her robe off her shoulders and pulled her nightgown over her head. He seemed really impatient for this. She was, too. Elena knew it was the heartstring…tugging. Maybe this was good. They could scratch their itch, get each other worked out of their systems.

Yet, she knew that was a lie. There was no expunging the desire for a heartstring through mere sex.

Damian covered the mound of her breast with his hand. She had small breasts, but he seemed pretty happy with them. He lowered his head and sucked one, then the other into his mouth, licking her nipples like they were the best pieces of candy he'd ever tasted.

The delicious sound of Damian's belt buckle being undone penetrated the haze of pleasure that enveloped her. "I have to feel you," Damian murmured. "I have to feel you *now*." He swore. "I have no condom."

"We are fae, Damian," she whispered. "We make our own fertility. You don't need a condom right now."

"Sweeter words never spoken." He eased her thighs wider apart and set the smooth, broad head of his cock to her slick opening. Damian flexed his thighs and pushed up and into her. He did it slow—inch by wonderful inch.

Her breath caught at the sensation of him filling her. It had been a long time since she'd been with a man. She tended to be choosy about the men she slept with. To have a heartstring be the one breaking her self-imposed celibacy made it that much more profound.

Her fingers closed over the edge of the countertop behind her so she could steady herself for his slow, steady thrusts. They made her knees go weak and her toes curl. Maybe a bed would have better, but Elena wasn't sure anything short of magic could improve on having Damian inside her right now.

His warm breath brushed the tender skin of her neck and teased the fine hairs there. "You feel good to me, Elena. Does this feel good to you?"

"Yes," she breathed back.

"It's been a while for you, hasn't it?"

She could only manage a nod.

"I'm wondering why that is for such a beautiful woman." His mouth found hers and he kissed her deeply, his tongue playing against hers.

Her fingers curled around his shoulders. "Less talking," she murmured with a grin.

He nipped her lower lip and settled back into the delicious business of being the first man she'd been with in months. Elena felt her climax building. Pleasure seeped through every pore of her body as he drove her harder and faster until her orgasm exploded and washed through her body. She cried out as it overwhelmed her, nearly stealing her ability to remain upright.

As she shuddered under the pleasurable spasms of the tail end of her climax, Damian jerked against her, groaned and came. She slumped against him as he scattered kisses all over her shoulder, neck and mouth.

"Where's your bedroom, Elena?" he whispered. "I'm not even close to finished with you."

She shivered at the timbre of his voice—low, husky and filled with need. Elena took his hand and led him to the back of her apartment where her bedroom was. Once they arrived, he led her to the bed.

Damian stripped off the rest of his clothes with Elena's help. They were both impatient to feel each other skin-on-skin. After they were both bare and sliding against each other, he pressed her down onto the mattress.

She let out a little sighing moan that made his cock go harder. "Spread your thighs for me," he demanded in a low, soft voice. He wanted to explore every part of her body numerous times before Elena figured out her mistake and kicked him out of her apartment and her life.

He couldn't understand why he needed and wanted her so badly. Tonight he would've risked anything to be with her and it wasn't just about the sex—though that was great. It was a matter of connecting with her on an intimate level, becoming a part of her. It seemed odd he should want that so strongly with Elena; he'd only just met her. Yet, it was like he knew her and she knew him on a level that surpassed anything physical and went straight to metaphysical.

It was strange, but that went with his day.

Elena lay back against the pillows and dark blue silk sheets and opened her thighs. The soft light from the small lamp in the corner of the room caressed her small, pert breasts and their tightened, suckable nipples. Her beautiful pink pussy was aroused and swollen a bit from his cock. She'd creamed for him, ready once more.

Leaning down, he kissed the smooth skin between her breasts and then worked his way down. Her abdomen quivered under his lips and he drank in her response to him like a sip of the headiest alcohol. Needing to taste her, he trailed his tongue through her short, curly dark pubic hair and licked her swollen clit.

Elena buried her fingers in his hair and let out a long, low sigh. "Spend the night with me," she murmured.

He raised his head from between her legs. "You'd have to use magic to make me go away. Elena, touch yourself for me, baby."

A look of surprise crossed her pretty face. "What?"

"Touch your breasts, play with your nipples. Touch your pussy. Make yourself come while I watch. I want to see how you like to be touched."

"Really?" She paused. "That would excite you?"

"Oh, yeah."

Endearingly, she blushed a little. She was so formal, so elegant and a little bit reserved. Damian wanted to tear down the walls holding back her sexuality. He could sense a delicious wantonness in her and he wanted to let it off its leash.

Biting her lower lip and casting her gaze downward so her long sooty lashes shadowed her cheek, she reached up and cupped her breast. Her actions were unsure, tentative. "I'd rather have you touch me, Damian."

"Oh, I will, don't worry about that. I want to see you do it first." Damian knew she was aroused, knew that soon she'd give herself over to the excitement of the game and forget he was even watching.

She closed her eyes and settled back into the pillows, allowing her thighs to fall open a little more. Damian's fingers curled to touch her, but he resisted, wanting to see what she would do.

Her hands plumped her breasts and she rubbed her thumbs over the hard nipples until her breath caught and her tongue stole out to wet her lips. Gently, she pinched each in turn, just a little, and a soft moan of pleasure escaped her.

"That's right, pinch them. Roll your nipples, baby."

She did it again and her hips thrust forward.

"You want me to fuck you, Elena?"

"Yes," she breathed.

Her pussy looked like a beautiful, ruby-red fruit in its arousal. He had a full view of her perfect, excited, suckable clit and her pouting labia. If he leaned in now, he could take her labia between his lips, he could lick her little clit until she bucked beneath him and came.

"I want to fuck that pretty cunt of yours, and I will. Make yourself come for me first."

Elena flushed a little at the coarseness of his words. This woman needed some coarse in her life. She licked her lips and her breath caught. Talking dirty excited her.

She slid one hand down her stomach slowly and allowed her fingers to tangle through her pubic hair.

"That's right, Elena, touch your pussy. Stroke your clit a little. It looks like it's just begging to be petted."

She dipped her hand down and rolled the pads of her index and second finger over her swollen clit. Her back arched and her thighs spread even more. She rubbed her clit up and down, her soft, sexy moans falling into the quiet air around them.

"I can tell by the way you're moving your hips that you want my cock deep inside that pretty pussy right now."

"Yes, I do." Her voice caught, hitched.

"So put your fingers there, baby. Fuck your fingers and make yourself come."

Her hand still caressed her breasts, playing across the ruby-red nipple he so wanted between his lips. Then she dropped her hand to her glistening, aroused pussy and slid a finger inside herself.

Damian had to grab fistfuls of blankets to keep from jumping her right then and there. He watched in fascination as her finger disappeared and reappeared over and over, wet with her luscious cream. Soon she'd added a second finger and dropped the hand on her breast to her clit.

"What does it feel like?" he asked, his voice tight with the strength it took to just watch.

"Hot. Silky. Wet." Her breathing was heavy and her voice soft. She opened her eyes and held his gaze.

"Yeah, that's what I feel around my cock when I fuck you, baby. It's nice."

She rotated her fingers around her clit—rubbing the pads of her fingers up and down it—as she finger-fucked herself. Her hips rose and fell to the rhythm and Damian could tell she was getting closer and closer to a climax.

"Come, Elena. I want to watch you." He gripped the base of his rock-hard cock and stroked himself while Elena pushed herself over the edge.

Her back arched and she dug her heels into the mattress as she came. Gasps and shouts of pleasure filled the room, fading into soft sighs and heavy breathing as her climax ebbed away.

Unable to take even one more moment of just watching, Damian moved in on her. He spread her thighs wide again and buried his mouth in her pussy, making her yelp with surprise.

He couldn't answer. He was too overcome by the delicious taste and scent of her pleasure, the beauty of her sex laid before him. Her sweet come spread across his tongue and lips and he lapped it up like it was ambrosia. To Damian, it was. He licked her aroused clit and pulled her labia between his lips—everything he'd been dreaming of doing to her while she'd been bringing herself to orgasm.

God, she tasted so good.

Elena moved on the bed beneath him, moaning. "You're going to make me come again."

"Is that a complaint?" he asked when he took a minute to do something other than lick her.

"No," she sighed.

He took her hands from her pussy and drew them over her head and pinned them there. He forced her thighs apart with his knee and slid the head of his cock to the opening of her slick pussy and pushed all the way to the base. "Oh, yeah, I'm going to make you come again. There's no doubt about that."

"Oh, Gods," she shouted, her head falling back. "Yes, that's what I wanted. I wanted you inside me, Damian."

"What do you want, honey? Use the words. I know you want to, so don't be shy."

She opened her eyes and held his gaze. "I wanted your cock deep inside me."

"That's better. That's what I wanted to hear."

He lowered his mouth to her throat and gently bit her, just enough to leave the faintest of marks. Damian needed to mark her somehow, claim her as his.

His cock tunneled in and out of her pussy, harder and faster, until their bodies slapped together and their sighs and cries mingled in the air.

Elena's pussy convulsed around his cock, her muscles spasming in her climax. Pleasure exploded from his balls and he sank as deep as possible inside her to come.

They crashed in a satisfied, sweaty tangle on the bed and lay, both breathing heavy.

"Oh, my Gods," Elena whispered.

He chuckled and pulled her to him, burying his face in her sweet-smelling hair. "Well, that was unexpected."

"No, not really. I said you and I share a special attraction, Damian. I meant that."

"What kind of special attraction?"

She sighed and turned over to face him, licking her lips and taking her time in answering. "We're heartstrings, Damian. That means that we recognize each other through scent and on a subconscious level. We're well matched to be partners through life, matched in personality, in genetics to have children, in intelligence, everything." She paused and smiled. "Well matched sexually."

"We're soul mates."

"Not exactly. There are a handful of matches in this world for a person, not just one. Still, it's extremely rare to find one."

Damian kissed her forehead and exhaled slowly. He didn't

doubt her words. The attraction he felt for her was too strange, too sudden...too strong. "This is a lot to take in."

"I know it's hard, but the activation of the fae in your blood should be making it easier."

"It is. It's helping me accept this as reality, I guess."

"That's good."

Damian gave her puppy-dog eyes. "So when do I get magic of my very own?"

She laughed. "It's...*baking*...inside you right now. I guess that's a good analogy. It will come slowly, so don't push it. It's good it happens that way because you need to learn how to use it slowly. Do you think you will come to live here?"

Surprise jolted through his veins. "Here? As in behind one of the doors off this corridor? Can I?"

"Of course you can. The first thing I did after I inducted you was dedicate a door for you. You'll have your own apartment in faery, but there are common areas, too, where we all congregate."

He had no response. Live here? Wow. Damian had to admit that the concept was an attractive one. He'd be near Elena and that would be great, but he also craved contact with others of his kind. As odd as it was, Damian felt a bit like he'd come home.

A round peg in the square hole no longer.

He'd found the right size hole and oddly enough, it was in faery.

"So I'd have a little pocket of reality of my very own right here." He frowned. "But if my magic is still *baking,* what would my pocket look like?"

"Probably not much different than your current apartment.

The space will pull it from your subconscious, but once your magic gets stronger you'll be able to shape it any way you like."

"Okay, what the hell."

"We can go now and look at it, if you like."

Damian snuggled against her and sighed. "No way. I want to stay right where I am. I know what my apartment looks like already."

She smiled and kissed him. "Want to see if you've got any magic yet?" Elena actually sounded excited.

"You mean check the cake in the oven?"

She laughed and took his hand in hers. "Concentrate on the center of your palm, but look past it. You know those pictures they have at the mall that look abstract until you unfocus your eyes, revealing an image? That's a little like how you call magic. You should know how to do it instinctively."

Damian focused on his palm and yet…didn't. Letting his mind relax, he allowed his awareness to float somewhere that was neither here nor there. His palm tingled. He jerked and stared at a small whitish-blue whirl of something in his hand. It was gone as soon as glimpsed it. "Hey, was that—"

"It was!" Elena said excitedly. "You curled a bit of magic into your hand. Looks to me like you'll be heavily psychic. Psychic abilities are blue and white. Do you have any of those kinds of skills already?"

Damian thought back to numerous incidents in his life, culminating in the episode in front of the White Wishes Chapel. "Yeah, I have."

She kissed him. "I'm so happy for you. You've finally found your true self."

Yes, he had.

"So, how old are you, Elena? Don't fae, you know, live to be really old?"

"Yes, that's another thing. We are essentially immortal. Your aging will slow now to an incredible degree. Our average lifespan is five hundred and fifty years."

Holy shit.

He arched a brow. "Are you avoiding my question, Elena? How old are you?"

"I'm eighty-five."

Okay, he was *not* going to let that freak him out.

"You look damn good for a senior citizen." He rolled her under his body and kissed her all over until she was breathless with laughter.

Once they'd settled back down again, Elena nuzzled his throat and asked, "Tell me a little bit about yourself, Damian. About your family and where you grew up."

"There's not much exciting to tell." He shrugged and pulled her closer.

She inserted a long, slim leg between his thighs and his breath shuddered out in a sigh. He wanted her again. He'd just had her twice, but he wanted her, impossibly, a third time. Did the fae have some sort of natural Viagra coursing through their veins? He couldn't remember being this horny in…well, ever.

"That's okay. Tell me anyway."

"It'll put you to sleep. I come from a regular, middle-class family. My mom's a stay-at-home who just never went back to work once the kids were in school. My dad's an electrician. My sister is a complete nerd who's now working on her graduate degree in English literature." He rubbed his palm down her arm. "If you want to come over on Wednesday evening, my mom makes meat loaf. There's nothing even remotely exotic or otherworldly about my bloodline as far as I can tell."

"Only because your parents were missed, lost fae we call them. I bet they've gone their whole lives not quite fitting in, thinking there was something missing from their lives."

Damian shook his head slowly. He just couldn't imagine his good-natured, beer-swilling father or his cross-stitching, meat-loaf-making mother as anything more than they appeared.

"So my sister is fae, too," he said suddenly. That would make a little bit of sense. She'd always been fascinated with Irish and Welsh history, especially the ancient legends.

Elena smiled. "She is, but she's not ready yet. It will be a couple years before it's time for us to induct her."

"It sounds like I've joined a cult."

She laughed. "The culture of the fae is quite different, but in time you'll come to see that on your own. As far as your sister goes, her induction will be easier since you'll have already gone through it and will be there to guide her."

"Are you kidding? She'll love it. It will be a dream come true for her."

"Good. That's excellent news. It makes my job easier when they're like that."

"Do you do this often? I mean, induct people? I thought you were a princess. I didn't think they had to work."

She rolled onto her stomach with a laugh and a soft sigh. Studying the blue-and-green silk pillowcase, she took a moment to answer. "I choose to do what I do. Because of who my parents are, I don't get to choose very often. When I have an opportunity, I take it."

"I don't understand."

She sighed. "I come from the purest line of fae there is. We have no human blood in it at all, not a drop. I have five brothers and sisters. I'm the oldest. We're all expected to behave a certain way, do certain things. All of us are encouraged to be well educated, but not to work. We're expected to marry the right person and have a ton of kids in order to ensure the bloodline. We're told to wear certain clothing, eat certain things, befriend certain people. I had to fight to do the job I do here at Darkness. I've fought long and hard for everything that's mine." She laughed. "I know, poor little rich girl, right?"

"No, that's not what I was thinking." He kissed her shoulder. "There are things in life more important than money. Freedom is definitely one of them. It sounds so…feudal." He rubbed her shoulder. "Next you're going to tell me you have arranged marriages."

Elena looked away.

He stopped rubbing her shoulder and sat up. "Are you serious?"

She pushed up, holding the sheet up to cover her beautiful breasts. "In fact…I'm engaged, Damian."

Damian went motionless, mute. Then the numbness faded and shock rippled through his body. "What? That can't be."

It couldn't be because Elena was as close to a soul mate as he had ever met. It was…magical…this attraction and emotion between them. It simply wasn't possible that she be meant for anyone other than him.

Then anger set in. Funny that *he,* of all men, on *this* day, should feel betrayed by a woman. "If you're engaged, why are you here in bed with me, Elena?" His voice came out a low, angry whisper.

"You have to understand our culture is very different,

Damian. I'm here because I can be, up until my marriage and also because…I like you. A lot." She buried her face in her hands. "I've met my fiancé once. Trust me when I say it's not going to be a happy marriage." She lowered her hands and looked at him. "You never would have come to bed with me if I'd told you I was engaged."

Damian threw the sheet and blankets back and stood. "Yeah, you're right about that, Elena. I wouldn't have. Now, not only have I dumped my own fiancée at the altar on our wedding day, I've been fucking someone else's." He angrily pulled on his clothes.

"Damian, please don't go. It's true that there can be nothing but sex between us, but at least let's have that."

He rounded on her. "You want to use me for sex?" Why did it bother him that a beautiful woman like Elena wanted to hire him out for a while as a stud? Normally that would not have pricked his conscience. He searched his emotions…. Oh, yeah, because he'd actually felt something for Elena.

Apparently the reverse wasn't true.

"I want us to take what we can get." Her eyes were bright with unshed tears.

She looked lovely on the bed that way, so anguished. It took all his willpower not to go to her, push her back onto the mattress and make slow, sweet love to her. Damn the consequences or his bruised ego.

"Damn it, Elena." He looked from her to the door. "You're different to me than other women."

"You're different to me, too. I knew it the first time I met you."

"Great. That makes this suck all the more."

He turned on his heel and walked out of the room.

♣ ♠ ♥ ♦ ♣ ♠ ♥ ♦ ♣ ♠ ♥ ♦

Chapter Six

Elena stared out the window of her father's mansion. It was located in the heart of Darkness, in one of the many pockets of alternate dimension that had been built into the lower part of the structure. All one had to do in Darkness was open a door and step through to find oneself in a different part of faery.

This was the king's world. Her father, Theron Albert Evan's little pocket of reality.

When you stepped through his doorway (tenth on the right once you reached the bottom of the stairs), you found yourself in a rolling green landscape that stretched for miles. Blue sky dominated most of the time, unless her father was angry or depressed and he wanted the weather to match. When there were storm clouds on the horizon, it was best to turn and go back the way you came. Today her father was calm and happy. Birds twittered in the trees and a gentle, perfect breeze rustled the leaf-laden branches. A gravel-strewn path led to a mansion enclosed by a tall black iron fence.

Two of her younger siblings still lived in Father's house. By cultural law they were all supposed to live there until the day of their marriage, but as the eldest Elena had fought for her freedom and won. Since she'd successfully convinced her father that his children should have a certain amount of world experience, her brothers and sisters were now allowed to strike off on their own once they became of legal age, too. She was a family pioneer.

"So you're telling me that you and this common fae, Damian Porter, share a relationship resonance? You found a heartstring?" Her father turned from the tall window in his library, brushing the swank golden draperies.

His expression was stern, severe. Everything about her father was that way.

She finished chewing the bite of pastry in her mouth and set the rest of the sugary confection on her plate. The food in faery was delicious, but only edible to the fae. It would taste like ambrosia to any human who came here and also act like poison. "Yes, that's what I'm saying."

Elena had known she needed to tell her father about the resonance, or he'd find out himself the first time he saw her and Damian together. A strong heartstring like she and Damian shared was palpable to all fae onlookers.

Damian had returned to Darkness not long after their night together. It had been inevitable he would. Once inducted, the urge to be with his kind became irresistible. Since Damian had taken his rightful place in Darkness's underground, there was no way her father would not eventually encounter them together. It was better she revealed the truth beforehand so he could prepare himself.

"I hope you don't think this will change my decision about your marriage to Reynolds."

A weight settled in the center of her chest. Maybe she had, a little. She sighed and lifted her weary gaze to her father's uncompromising visage. "Of course not."

"Finding this heartstring now will only serve to make your impending nuptials harder on you. It's a pity, really." Her father turned, walking to a sideboard filled with food that had been placed out for her visit. Her father adored food and his waistline showed it. "Damn bad luck, I think." His voice was just a mutter. "Go your whole life never meeting a heartstring, then you find one right before your marriage."

Yes, it *was* bad luck. Her father was right. A part of her wished she'd never taken that induction assignment to begin with. Before she'd met Damian, she'd been resigned to settle with someone she didn't love for the sake of her family's honor. Accepting of it even though she hadn't wanted it. Having met Damian, she still had to marry Reynolds, but it would be much harder to find happiness now that she knew her heartstring was out there.

"Ironic, isn't it?" she murmured.

"The wedding is in a week. Are all the preparations in order?"

Her father had spared no expense, of course. She'd had a wedding planner and a budget that stretched into the stratosphere. It would have been great if she'd wanted it all…or the groom, for that matter.

She waved her hand dismissively. "The planner assures me all is ready." Elena had had little do with it. She'd laid down some basic ground rules—no puce, no peonies and no peppermint anything. Other than that she'd let the planner pretty much do whatever she'd wanted. Elena hardly cared and her mother didn't seem all that interested, either.

Elena's mother was busy most of the time playing bridge or corralling her youngest children. Her goal seemed to be to avoid her husband at all cost. Elena's parents' marriage was arranged and highly loveless.

Reynolds was a corporate attorney in the non-fae world. He lived in New York, where she would soon be relocating. Some of the truest, purest fae blood ran through his veins. Elena had been promised to Reynolds since she'd been five years old. She'd only met him once, though, at the betrothal party. He was okay. They'd had a nice conversation, but honestly, if she had her druthers she wouldn't care if she ever saw him again or not.

He hadn't seemed all that interested in marrying her, either, not on a personal level. But hell, she was a princess after all. Reynolds knew he would get the title of prince by marrying her and Elena knew that interested him. Marrying her would add to his prestige and his reputation in the fae world. It would also make his children heirs to the throne. What wasn't there to like?

She stood to leave, her obligation to her father fulfilled satisfactorily. "Well, I have a full schedule this afternoon."

"Your…*job,* no doubt?"

Her father hated that she worked. He considered her efforts at inducting common fae a waste of time and energy. "Yes. We have information there may be someone with the genes just west of the city. I have research to do." She walked to the door and turned.

The king's lip curled. "Yes, well, Reynolds will be arriving tomorrow morning, I am told, in anticipation of the nuptials. I hope you will take time from your…*work* to spend time with him."

Elena blinked. "Why would I want to do that? We'll be spending eternity together after the wedding. I see no reason to get a jump on things."

★ ★ ★

That evening, when she returned to her apartment, Damian was outside her door flipping a coin into the air. When the coin reached a certain height, it disappeared, then reappeared on its way down. Apparently he'd been practicing with his magic. He leaned against the wall, one leg bent, focused on the trick. He was so attentive that he didn't notice her approach, which meant she could drink her fill of him with Damian unawares.

He was a powerfully attractive man. His body was long and lean, muscular, but not in the overdone way of a body-builder. Damian's build was powerful without being over-powering. His dark hair fell across his brow in an attractive way, framing a face that wasn't quite as handsome as it was interesting.

Reynolds was good-looking in a pure-blood fae, corporate lawyer way. Damian was attractive in a dangerous alley-dwelling stray-cat kind of way.

Elena really had a soft spot for stray cats.

"I thought you weren't going to darken my doorstep ever again," she said as she approached him.

He lost control of the coin and it fell to the carpeted corridor floor. "I couldn't stay away."

She walked to within a breath's space of him, paused, and then smiled. "I'm glad."

"Anyway, I live here now." He pointed down the corridor. "Twentieth door on the right. I figured we'd run into each other eventually."

"I'd love to see your place."

He pushed a hand through his hair. "Yeah, well, I'm still trying to get a handle on this interdimensional magic stuff.

It's not very nice yet." He smiled with chagrin. "And it flickers occasionally."

She laughed. "It takes a while to get the hang of it. Your magic has to——"

"Bake a little more. Yeah, I get that."

The pockets allotted to those who lived under Darkness were shaped by the owner's magic. It wasn't illusion, but in fact reality created and formed by the owner's will and desire. The stronger the owner's magic meant the grander the space.

She unlocked her door. "Want to come in?"

"I was hoping for an invite, yeah."

Elena opened the door and he trailed her inside. The lights flickered on as soon as she entered and a fire poofed to life in the hearth. She threw her keys into the bowl on the table near the door and kicked off her shoes. It was good to be home and it felt perfect that Damian was here with her.

She watched him wander to her pottery again. He picked up a piece and studied it.

"I make it," she said, walking to him. "I have a pottery room here in my apartment. I even have a kiln. It's kind of a…hobby." She only wished it could be more.

He turned to her with raised eyebrows. "Made by your hands, with your heart?" He stared down at the bowl he held. "No wonder I'm drawn to it," he muttered.

"What?"

He set the bowl down and turned toward her. "So, this heartstring thing. Is that why even though I left here with every intention to avoid you for the rest of my natural life, I can't stop thinking about you?"

She suddenly became interested in the carpet.

He walked over and turned her to face him, forcing her

head up and her gaze to collide with his. "Is the heartstring why I can't stay away from you even though I know you're going to trample all over my soul? Is it why I dream of you, wake up thinking about you? Is it why when I inhale something that smells like you it makes my cock hard?"

Oh, gods… "Yes," she whispered.

"But this is slumming for you, right? I'm just a commoner. It must really suck for you to find a heartstring with a guy like me."

"Yes."

He turned away from her, stalking to the center of the room and running a hand over his unshaven jaw.

"Wait!" Gods, she was stupid. "I didn't mean it like that." She walked to him, touched his arm, but he pulled away from her. "Damian, let me explain."

Damian turned toward her, a pissed-off expression dominating his face. His eyes said, *go ahead and try.*

"It's inconvenient because of the pressure that's put on me to marry pure, that's all." She reached up and cupped his cheek. "I don't care that you're common. Gods, Damian, I'm not that way at all. This just…*sucks* because I want to be with you and I can't." She paused. "I can't, Damian, and that's going to rip me to shreds. Marrying a man I don't love while I know you exist in the world is going to devastate me."

He grabbed her hand and jerked her forward a step, right up against his chest. "Then don't do it."

"You don't understand."

He made a low sound of frustration. "No, I don't, Elena. You're right. *This* is all I understand."

His mouth came down on hers and met her tongue in a

tangle of need and impatience. It made her heart thump and her breath hitch in her throat.

Elena needed to feel his hands on her, his lips. She wanted that deep physical connection with him. Even though she'd only known him a short time, sex with Damian enhanced the emotion she felt for him. She wanted to bare herself to him, body and soul. She wanted him to touch her intimately. Over and over and over...

"Elena." His voice shook. "I need to be one with you."

Yes, that was it. Perfectly stated.

"I need that, too, Damian. Please."

♣ ♠ ♥ ♦ ♣ ♠ ♥ ♦ ♣ ♠ ♥ ♦

Chapter Seven

He pulled her shirt over her head, then reached down, undid the button and zipper of her skirt and sent the article of clothing sliding down her legs to pool at her feet. She was left in nothing but her silky bra and panties.

He made short work of those, too, and the cool air bathed her breasts, touched her heated pussy.

Damian groaned, his hands running over her curves. "Damn, you're pretty, baby. I want you to be mine." He growled the words, laden with emotion. "*Mine,* Elena. Not this guy…what's his name? Reynolds? Not his. Mine."

"For tonight," she murmured, her mouth against his, "I am yours." She placed his hand over her breast, her nipple pebbling against his palm.

"Not just tonight, Elena. I don't accept any limitations on what's developing between us." He laid his lips to her bare shoulder. His breath warmed her skin, his mouth brushed her as he dragged his lips over her collarbone to the place where her neck met her shoulder.

Elena opened her mouth to reply, trying to struggle up from the layers of need Damian was covering her with…and then he bit her.

His teeth scraped her skin and then bore down, not hard enough to actually hurt her, but enough to leave a mark. It was a sign of dominance, *ownership*. With that mark, it was as though he'd staked a claim on her. The action was primal and erotic.

Elena gasped and her fingers closed hard around his shoulders, feeling the bunch and ripple of his muscles. Her pussy plumped with need, her clit growing more sensitive as he bore down a little and gooseflesh erupted all over her body.

"Damian." His name sounded strangled coming from her throat.

His hand eased between her thighs and found her aching clit. With the pad of his finger, he brushed back and forth until her body tensed with the need to come.

Abruptly he released the hold he had on her neck. Blood rushed back to the area, making her feel tingly in more than one place. "Do you have a mirror in here?"

"What?" she asked, dazed.

"A mirror, one that's long and wide. I want you to see how pretty you are, Elena. I want you to watch us together. *Us,* making love. Not you and that other fuck. *Me and you.*" His voice was gruff, commanding, almost angry.

"This is my space—I create it any way I choose."

"Then create a mirror."

"Done." Her voice came out breathless. "In the bedroom."

He took her hand and dragged her there.

At the end of her bed stood a mirror, just as he'd asked. Damian led her there. She was completely naked, her clothes in a pile on the living-room floor. He was still fully clothed and standing behind her, looking aroused and just a little pissed off. "Look at us, Elena. What do you see?"

She studied herself in the mirror's reflection—lips swollen from his kisses, hair mussed from his hands. A faint mark marred the skin of her shoulder. Her breasts looked heavy, the nipples red and tight from her excitement.

"I see…lust," she answered honestly. Her gaze rose to his eyes and the way they warmed when they caught hers in the reflection. "I see the beginning of love." Her breath caught. "I see *potential*."

"What do you see when you look at your fiancé?"

She blinked and dropped her gaze from his for a moment. "Coldness. Duty."

"Which would you rather have?"

"There's no question about what I would *rather* have. That's not the issue."

"Stand up to your father."

"I would be the first in millennia to break this tradition, Damian."

"Times change," he growled.

"Damian—"

"Shhh. The last thing I want to do with you right now is argue." His voice had dropped into something dark and sinful, like warmed gourmet chocolate. He dropped his hand to her lower stomach and splayed it there. "I wanted to show you how pretty you are because I'm not sure you know."

He guided her back to sit on the mattress and spread her thighs so her sex was clearly visible in the mirror's reflection. Then covered her pussy with his hand. The heat of his palm warmed her and his hand looked so big and masculine between her slender, pale thighs.

"Touch me," she whispered.

"My current goal in life," he murmured. He slid a hand

up to cup one breast and glide his thumb over the aching nipple. While he did that, he also slid his middle finger deep inside her. Her muscles clenched around the invasion and she gasped his name.

He slid his finger back out, slowly, so she could see it in the mirror's reflection. Then back in. Her clit tingled and pulsed, wanting to be stroked. She tipped her head back and moaned.

"Elena, watch what I'm doing to you."

She tipped her head forward and met his gaze in the mirror.

"Don't look away. I want you to see that it's my hand giving you pleasure, my body bracing yours, my cock sliding into your sweet pussy. I want you to see that it's me who is giving you pleasure now." He paused a beat. "Not Reynolds."

Gods, she didn't want to hear his name now. Not ever.

Damian added another finger to the first, making her muscles stretch a little more and the pleasure more intense. She felt herself grow wetter, saw the gleam of her juices on his fingers on every downward motion. His other hand stroked her nipple, rolled and pinched it just hard enough to send ripples of ecstasy shooting through her.

"Have you ever watched yourself come?" he murmured in her ear.

She shook her head. Her mouth was a little slack, and her body tense. Her pupils were big and dark. Elena had never seen herself like this, so sexually excited. She barely recognized the woman in the mirror as herself, having given in completely to Damian and his command of her body.

He slowly dropped the hand on her breasts to her clit. There, he stroked her over and over, manipulating the bundle of nerves to bring her up to the edge of a climax. Fascinated, lost to her body's responses, she watched his big hands move between her thighs, working her pussy just right…

"Come for me, Elena."

Her climax shattered over her. It was hard to prevent her head from tipping back, hard not to close her eyes, hard not to cry out.

She kept her gaze on her reflection, watched the way Damian pulled her orgasm out longer and longer. The muscles of her pussy pulsed around his thrusting fingers and her knees went weak. That familiar lack of thought—sensation dominating her world—possessed her as her body rode out the waves of ecstasy until they gradually faded away.

The climax only made her want more. She wanted to touch him, see him experience as much pleasure as he'd just given her.

Feeling almost boneless, she sank down onto the plush carpeting at her feet and turned her back to the mirror, facing him. He stared down at her with a hungry expression on his face, his cock straining against his jeans.

Elena reached up and rubbed his shaft through the material. "Let's free him, shall we?" she purred with a lift of her brow.

She made short work of the button and zipper and soon had him naked from the waist down. Damian pulled his shirt over his head, muscles rippling and making her mouth water, and threw the article of clothing to the floor.

Her fingertips played down the length of him, exploring the heavy veins that traversed it. Damian tipped his head back, Adam's apple jutting, and groaned.

"Uh-uh," she chastised. "I want you to watch me, Damian.

See that it's my lips on your cock, my tongue licking up and down your shaft. I want you to see it's me giving you pleasure."

He tipped his head forward with a grin. "Do your worst, baby."

Licking her lips, she passed her thumb over the smooth head of his shaft, smearing the bit of precome that beaded there. She dipped her finger down and rubbed it back and forth over the frenulum, making him jolt with pleasure. Then she eased the crown into her mouth and sucked him down as far as she could, almost to the base.

Damian groaned her name and tangled his hands in her hair as she worked him in and out of her mouth. His hips thrust forward a little and his big body tightened. Gods, she loved rendering a strong man helpless to the touch of her lips.

He had her flipped and on her back before she could draw another breath.

Elena yelped in surprise as Damian's big body pinned hers to the carpet. So much for thinking she'd rendered him helpless.

"That was going to make me come," he rasped in a low voice, "and when I come I want my cock buried deep inside your sweet pussy and the sound of you calling my name in my ears."

Elena shivered.

"Is that agreeable to you, baby? Do you want me to fuck this pretty little pussy of yours?"

"Yes," she managed to answer.

He turned her head to the side so she could see their reflection in the mirror. "I want you to watch me fuck you, Elena."

In the reflection, her eyes were wide. A trill of excitement coursed through her. She wound her legs—pale, thin—around his narrow, tanned waist. Then she returned her gaze to his. "What are you waiting for?"

He leaned in, nipped at her lower lip. "On your stomach."

She rolled over and he pulled her up on her hands and knees, his hand snaking between her thighs to tease her clit. In the reflection, she watched his hands move back and forth, stimulating her. Then he pushed her feet apart and slid her rear into the cradle of his pelvis. The head of his cock jutted her pussy.

His expression was intense, his gaze running over the slope of her back and nip of her waist, his fingers trailing in its wake. He touched her like she was some rare and beautiful piece of artwork, something he could appreciate just for tonight and no longer than that.

Damian swore low and guided his cock into her pussy. The muscles of his thighs and buttocks flexed as he pushed deep into her body.

Elena bowed her head and hit the floor with a closed fist. "Yes, Damian, that feels so good." He was long and wide and stretched her muscles exquisitely, gave her the impression she was totally possessed and filled.

He held on to her hips and began to thrust. In the mirror's reflection she could see his shaft on every outward motion, glistening wet with her juices. Damian came down over her body, taking her harder and faster. Her breath caught on an inhale as another climax flirted hard with her body.

Damian reached around and slid his hand between her thighs to stroke her clit even as the head of his cock brushed her G-spot deep within her in this position.

"Oh, gods, I'm going to come," she breathed. "Don't stop. Please don't stop."

"Never."

Another orgasm took her over, made her head snap back and stars explode on the back of her eyelids. She lost all ability to remain on her hands and knees and Damian turned her to her back, remounted her, and began to slow his pace.

Elena panted, feeling sated and relaxed beyond belief.

"It's good between us, isn't it?" Damian murmured, his mouth a breath's space from hers. "We know how to touch each other." His cock slid in and out of her at a slower pace now. She could feel every massive inch of him deep in the heart of her body.

She touched his cheek, a heaviness settling in her chest. "Of course it's good between us. We're heartstrings. It's why I feel so comfortable with you."

Damian said nothing for a moment, then he dipped his head and kissed her deeply while his cock glided in and out of her. When he finally came, he did it with her name spilling from his lips.

♣ ♠ ♥ ♦ ♣ ♠ ♥ ♦ ♣ ♠ ♥ ♦

Chapter Eight

He stayed the night with her.

He put her in her bed and pulled her near, wrapping his arms around her. They stayed awake until the morning, talking about their families, their lives, getting to know each other.

For Elena it seemed retroactive, and she was sure Damian felt the same way. They already knew each other. They'd known each other from the first time their gazes had collided. To find out now that Damian's favorite ice cream was Chunky Monkey and for him to discover she absolutely loathed the smell of lavender seemed almost inconsequential. Like somewhere way deep down they'd already known these things about each other.

It was magic.

For the entire night, in the softly lit room, Damian touched her. His hands ran over her breasts, teased her nipples. He stroked her clit and delved deep inside her pussy. Twice more during the night he made her come, bringing her softly and easily again and then again.

He knew just how to touch her, just where, to bring her the maximum amount of pleasure. Close to dawn when

Damian's hands finally fell away and his breathing deepened to sleep, she felt his ghost hands still roving her body.

If only those ghost hands would remain on her body forever. They'd be a distant second to the real thing, but at least they'd be *something*. They'd be better than Reynolds's hands on her.

Elena closed her eyes against the bitter prick of tears. She couldn't imagine Reynolds touching her now. The thought made her shudder.

Eventually she drifted into a fitful, light sleep.

"Don't marry him."

She opened her eyes at the soft murmur. Damian was staring down at her, love warming his eyes. He stroked her hair. "Don't marry him, Elena," he repeated.

She swallowed against the lump in her throat. "Damian, you don't understand our ways yet. You don't understand—"

He forced himself up and away from her, swinging his legs over the side of the bed. "You keep saying that. I understand enough to know your ways are cruel and silly. If you don't love this man, don't tie your life to his forevermore, Elena." He drew a careful breath. "Please, don't take yourself away from me once I've finally found you."

Elena pushed up onto her elbows. "Damian." She squeezed her eyes shut and a tear slid down her cheek. "I've known I had to do this since I was a toddler. It's my duty to my race to marry Reynolds and bear his children. *I must.*"

"Bullshit."

"If I don't go through with the wedding, I will shame my family beyond belief. If you had grown up fae, you would understand this, Damian, and you wouldn't even ask…heartstring or not."

Damian stood and paced the floor. "Elena, don't you realize how special our heartstring is? Some people go their whole lives searching for that one person they can spend their life with. That one individual who will best fill in the parts they're lacking. You are that person for me, as I am for you. For the rest of our lives, we will never find another more perfect fit than we've found in each other."

"I know." Her lower lip trembled and sorrow squeezed her chest. He was what she needed in her life—something raw, a little bit unordered, primal, full of life and passion.

He turned to her. "I won't let you marry him, Elena. I won't. Consider that my promise to you." He shook his head. "I won't break it."

Her wedding day dawned bright and sunny.

Well, of course it did. It was in her father's massive pocket of reality. It was sunny because he willed it that way.

Elena allowed her five cousins and three aunts to fuss and primp her as she stared out the window of her dressing room in the mansion. Just steps away loomed the fae church, where she would be marrying Reynolds in just a short time. The Church of the Morrigan had floated to this reality for the day, at her father's behest. Fae of all sorts, even some vampires and demons, roamed the lawn of the mansion, making their way into the tall gray stone building to find their seats.

Elena's hands shook.

"There, there, dear," hushed her aunt Eloise. "All women are nervous on their wedding day."

Gah! Elena was drowning, dying, and no one noticed. No one cared.

She closed her eyes for a moment and pushed the self-indulgent thought and their accompanying emotions away. Along with it she banished the image of Damian that always appeared unbidden. She couldn't afford to think of him, not now. If she could she would banish him from her mind forevermore. To think of him after this day would only bring pain.

She would marry Reynolds today and do what her family required of her. Tomorrow she would pack her things and move to New York and the fae underworld there. She would forget her heartstring and try to make a life for herself as best she could. Hell, she'd be the toast of the New York fae, she'd have plenty to keep her occupied. None of it very appealing.

What Elena truly wanted to do, the thing her status and bloodline would not allow her to do, was make pottery and sell it. Inside her beat the heart of an entrepreneur. She wanted to make her pottery-making hobby more than that, but her birth and position in fae culture made that impossible.

But complaining about it was silly, not to mention ungrateful. Her father and her family had given her everything she'd needed in life as far as material possessions went. Elena had wanted for nothing. It was time she paid them back.

Don't do it.

Damian's voice echoed in her head. She squeezed her eyes shut for a moment and forced away the flood of emotion that clogged her throat. She opened her eyes and wistfully stared at her expression in the mirror.

"You look stunning," her aunt Millie declared.

Elena had fifteen aunts. All of them would offer an opinion on her appearance before they reached the church.

Millie turned her to face the lengthwise mirror, a smile

blooming across her age-weathered face. "Reynolds will drool when he sees you walk down the aisle."

He would drool and she would cry. It would be a festival of bodily fluids.

It was true she looked good, though. The fitted sheath ivory wedding dress she wore accented her slimness. The train trailing behind floated like a cloud. Her aunts had pulled her hair on top of her head in a sleek chignon— classic. Pearls dripped from her earlobes and nestled in the hollow of her throat. Elegant ivory gloves stretched to her elbows and her makeup was done flawlessly—understated to accentuate her natural beauty.

She sighed. "Very well, let's get on with it then. Is it time?"

Her aunts frowned at each other. "Yes," answered Millie. "It's time."

Great.

♣ ♠ ♥ ♦ ♣ ♠ ♥ ♦ ♣ ♠ ♥ ♦

Chapter Nine

Ethereal music wafted from the Church of the Morrigan, which only yesterday Damian could have sworn stood in Tibbing Square in the fae city secreted under Darkness (twenty-seventh door on the left). He didn't let the oddness of it slow his step. Life in the fae underground was odd at every turn; he wouldn't allow a spontaneously relocating church to get the better of him.

He was on a mission.

No, he didn't hold an invitation to Elena's wedding, the event of the season, by all fae accounts. The Underground had been atwitter for days.

No. No invitation. Instead he was going to crash this party and run off with the bride.

Damian was not going to let her get away from him. He didn't care about fae culture, or what Elena's last name was. He didn't care what kind of blood ran through her veins. She could be related to the King of the Las Vegas Fae, or Oscar the Grouch for all he cared.

All Damian knew was that beyond all reason, beyond all sanity, he'd fallen in love with Elena. And no one, not even Reynolds with his fake tan and his sparkling white teeth that looked like oversize Chiclets and his money and prestige, was going to stand in Damian's way of his happily-ever-after with her.

He'd so thoroughly worked himself into a self-righteous frenzy that when he burst the doors of the church open with his magic, he hit two men who'd been behind them. They careened off to the sides, swearing loudly. Luckily he hadn't hurt them too badly. Both men stood, rubbing their heads, and glared at him. No wonder Damian had hit them; the church was standing room only. It was *packed.*

All faces turned toward him. Pews squeaked. Someone coughed. Other than that, all was silent. Expectant.

Oh, shit. What was he supposed to do now?

At the front of the church, Elena also turned toward him. Even at a distance, he glimpsed shock on her beautiful face. She shouldn't have been surprised. He'd told her he wasn't going to let this happen, and he'd meant it.

Damian strode down the aisle toward the couple standing in front of an angry-looking fae clergyman. His boots squished flowers into the carpet. "I object to this union!" he called. "I object on the basis that Elena is my heartstring."

The crowd collectively gasped. Murmuring began.

"We've found each other, against all odds, and it's wrong to make her marry a man she doesn't love. I don't care who her fa—"

A man suddenly blocked his path, a man who'd come from nowhere. Damian stopped short. He recognized him, of course. It was the king. The force of the man's magic made him want to drop to his knees and bow his head. Damian refused to give in to the impulse, instead drawing himself up to stand taller.

The king knit his brows and scowled. "You mean to interrupt my daughter's wedding, you insignificant little fae foundling?"

Wow. Talk about elitist.

"What gives you the right?" the king asked.

"Love gives me the right."

The king laughed. "Are you a twelve-year-old girl? Our world doesn't work that way."

Elena had removed her hand from Reynolds's grasp and started down the aisle toward them.

"I know how your world works. You expect Elena—all your children—to marry fae truebloods and spend their lives as broodmares and studs in order to make more truebloods. It's wrong. I don't care how long the tradition goes back."

"Damian," Elena said in a warning voice behind her father. "Please be careful. You don't know what you're doing." His gaze locked with hers and he glimpsed deep worry in her eyes.

Reynolds came up behind her and pushed her to the side. Elena stumbled against a pew. Rage shot through Damian, hard and bitter. Her fiancé came to stand next to the king. "Give me permission to dispatch this common fae swine."

Damian couldn't wait to knock out those big Chiclet teeth.

The king took a step backward. "Please."

Reynolds stepped forward and punched him in the jaw.

Pain exploded through Damian's face and he flew backward, skidding on the floor of the church. Goddamn! That had been a teeth-rattling punch. Did Reynolds work out…or…*the bastard had used magic!* Damian could taste it faintly on the back of his tongue, glittery sweet.

He groaned and remembered hearing Elena shriek when

he'd fallen. He looked up and saw that Reynolds was holding her by the upper arm, keeping her from running to him.

Bastard.

Damian rolled to the side and forced himself to his feet slowly. Holding his jaw and split lip, he laughed the whole way. A raw, mirthless sound. It was the only noise in the church.

"Okay, so I see how it's going to be, attorney-boy. You're not very tough and you know it, so you're going to use magic to back your punches." He held up his hands when Reynolds protested. "Hey, don't worry. It's nothing to be ashamed of. We all feel a little *weak* sometimes."

Reynolds pushed past Elena and charged him. Damian took him full in the chest, but Damian was magic-laced, too, this time, so it was more like a being hit by a bus than a train. They both went careening backward and landed in a tangle of punching arms and kicking legs in the middle of the aisle.

Distantly he heard the scrambling of the wedding guests to get out of their way, heard their gasps and exclamations. Then he took a solid punch to the face and all he heard after that was ringing.

Damian brought his fist up and connected with Reynolds's jaw. His head snapped back and he rolled to the side. Damian had pricked his pride, which meant the pure-blood fae was no longer using magic to back his fists.

Now Damian could take him.

Damian jumped Reynolds and began to punch. He didn't stop until hands pulled him off and up. He glanced down and watched Reynolds roll to his side, holding his eye and cheek. Damian's fists burned.

"Damian!"

Elena's voice was the only one that broke through the

fog the fight had put him in. His head snapped to the side, to her face.

"What are you doing?" Her face was pale, her pretty lips bloodless.

The people around him were murmuring and talking excitedly. He caught the words *hae ilyium* several times.

"Trying to stop this damn farce of a wedding," he replied.

"Enough!" Boomed the voice of the king. Everything went silent. The only sound in the church was Reynolds groaning.

Elena cast him a worried glance. "Father, be lenient with him—"

The king held up a silencing hand. "You have no recollections of our people's laws?" her father asked her. His voice grew shriller with every word.

Elena frowned. "What? What—"

"If a wedding is broken on hallowed ground without the aid of magic, and if the challenger prevails, the challenger gains certain rights." The king looked utterly defeated.

"Hae ilyium," a man to Damian's left said. The old guy grinned and bobbed his head excitedly.

Reynolds groaned once more at their feet and then lay still.

"Hae ilyium," the king repeated as his shoulders rounded and slumped.

"Wait a minute, what does that mean, Father?" Elena asked.

The queen pushed past the king, a triumphant gleam in her eyes. "It means, daughter of mine, that your heartstring has a chance to save you."

Hae ilyium turned out to be something that had been neglected in Elena's schooling. Now that she knew what it meant, she could see why.

She looked from Reynolds, who lay unconscious on the floor, utterly defeated beyond a shadow of a doubt, to Damian. Damian's face was marked with blood, his lip was split and a bruise was already beginning to bloom on his jaw.

Hae ilyium was an ancient law, one from which not even those of noble blood were exempt. It was almost unheard of and Damian had accomplished it without even being aware. He'd goaded Reynolds's pride and forced him to drop his magic for the fight, then he'd jumped on Reynolds like a practiced barroom brawler and knocked him out within a minute.

If a challenger of a wedding bested the groom without the use of magic and that challenger was a heartstring…the strung couple would be given a chance to be together.

They had a chance. Elena could hardly believe it. However, they had to undergo a test that would force their hearts to show true. A true heartstring, it seemed, trumped all the political marriages in the world. There was a catch, though.

The test could kill them.

She twined her fingers with Damian's as her mother smiled, her father raged and the church dissolved into delighted shocked chaos. For the first time in a very, very long time, hope fluttered in her chest.

♣ ♠ ♥ ♦ ♣ ♠ ♥ ♦ ♣ ♠ ♥ ♦

Chapter Ten

Hae ilyium.

There were no two sweeter words in the fae language. Damian didn't know much of his genetic mother tongue yet, but that had to be true. He had never heard two more beautiful words in English, that was for sure.

Reynolds had tried to pick two fights with him since the incident in the church, but apparently that was against the rules of *hae ilyium* because some guys dressed in gray had corralled the big attorney the second time and hauled him off kicking and screaming to the gods only knew.

Reynolds was not happy that his societal meal ticket was being snatched from his jaws right as he was about to sink his Chiclets into it. No one was cueing the violins for him, though, not even the king, who had seen how Reynolds had roughly pushed aside his daughter in the church.

Damian had been a no-show at his own wedding, only to crash another one days later. The fact hadn't been lost on the fae residents of Darkness and he and the princess were the talk of the Las Vegas Underground.

He didn't care about anything—not about the strange twist his life had taken, not about Reynolds, not about the fae Underground. Damian only cared about Elena. Come hell or high water, he was going to make sure he spent the rest of his life caring about her, too. And the test—which hung over their heads like some shiny, well-polished guillotine—just might bring forth hell or a flood of high water, maybe both. They had no idea what to expect.

But while they waited and while Reynolds had been effectively muzzled, he and Elena spent every waking moment together.

He knocked on her door, balancing a stack of Tupperware containers under one arm.

She opened the door and stared at the containers.

"Picnic?" he asked. He followed her gaze to the Tupperware. "I didn't have a basket."

His magic was getting strong enough that he could manifest things within his quarters, in his little slice of alternate reality. However, when he tried to take those objects he created past the threshold of his apartment, they disappeared. He was told that was true for all fae, no matter the strength of their magic.

She smiled warmly and ushered him within.

Elena took the containers from him and he paused to consider her pottery. "If you make it through this test, will you be allowed go into business for yourself?"

She returned from the kitchen, licking frosting off her index finger. Apparently she'd found the cupcakes.

Elena leaned against the wall and crossed her arms over her chest. She wore a soft vanilla-colored sweater with sleeves a bit too long for her. Damian wanted to take it off. Clothing on Elena offended him, in general.

She tipped her head to the side, thinking. "I think *hae*

ilyium changes a lot of the rules. If I'm allowed to twine my life with yours, I'll be able to do lots of things I would have been forbidden before."

"That's great."

She smiled. "It's an added benefit. I want to be with you, Damian. The rest of it is just a bonus."

He grinned. "I'm the grand prize?"

"Better than a million dollars."

He held out his hand. "Come here and let me start living up to that."

She pushed away from the wall and walked into his arms. He twined his fingers though her hair and kissed her earlobe, closing his eyes and inhaling the scent of her. God, he loved her so much. The sensation of it filled his chest with lightness, made him almost dizzy. He couldn't give her up, not ever.

"I love you," he whispered into her ear.

She moved her head and stared into his eyes. "I love you, too, Damian. More than I can express with words."

He lightly touched his lips to hers—just a breath of a tease, a promise of more to come. "Then let's say it without words."

He took her hand and led her to her bedroom, stopping in the kitchen to gather a cold bottle of champagne and two glasses. Food could wait; Damian wanted to taste Elena now.

With roving hands and lips, nips to flesh here and there, they undressed each other. Damian loved undressing Elena. It was like Christmas every time. He dropped a kiss to the swell of her breast in the silky demibra she wore, then got rid of that, too.

Damian pressed her back onto her bed, noting there was a window in her bedroom today, an expanse of blue sky and grass beyond it. A willow tree dipped branches in front of the opening and a bird sang into the room.

"Wow, that's pretty happy-go-lucky," he whispered with a glance at the window. "I never noticed that before."

She smiled against his mouth. "Ever since the day in the church, my reality has been expanded, growing bigger and richer. It's like my magic has become more expansive with the love I feel for you and the chance at freedom that I'm getting."

Damian rocked back a little. "That's incredible."

"Yes, I think so, too. My father has been impressed, as well. It's making him rethink his harsh stance on purity. If our family members could increase the strength of their magic through happiness, it would mean more to our bloodline than pedigree."

He glanced at the window. "No one's going to peek in the window, are they? I have lots of kinky things I want to do to your sweet body."

"No peeking, I swear. Bring on the kinky."

"First, let's toast." He reached over and poured them both glasses of champagne. "To the possibility of freedom or death."

She laughed and their glasses clinked. "To freedom or death."

Damian drank deep, but didn't drink all of it. It went down sweet and cold—crisp. All food and drink tasted better in faery. He never wanted to eat anything when he was aboveground anymore. He sealed his mouth to Elena's and kissed her deeply, their champagned tongues meshing within the hot confines of her mouth, then he dropped lower.

His lips skated over her flesh, the gentle curve of her breasts and each delectable cherrylike nipple, the flat plane of her stomach and the soft hair of her mound. Damian forced her thighs apart and kissed the sensitive inner area on each, hearing Elena's breathing hitch and grow heavier.

"Do you want me to lick your pussy, Elena?" he purred up at her, breathing over the quivering flesh of her luscious cunt.

"Yes," she whispered.

"Tell me. Use the words."

She closed her eyes. "I—I want you to lick my pussy, Damian."

"Good girl." He rubbed her clit until she jerked and then moaned. "You taste good. I could do it all day." Gods, and he had. Since the day in the church, he'd spent whole afternoons between Elena's silky thighs, bringing her to orgasm with his mouth again and again.

He tipped the champagne glass and poured some of the cold liquid on her clit. She jolted, but he held her thighs down and apart, dribbling more onto her cunt. Elena gasped as it ran down and pooled at her entrance.

"Mmmm." Damian leaned in and licked it up. He explored every one of her folds with his tongue, then slid two fingers deep inside her and began to thrust while he settled his mouth over her champagne-flavored clit and sucked on it.

"Damian," she breathed. "You're going to make me come."

That was his objective. He wanted her nice and boneless for what was to happen next. He speared his fingers in and out of her creamy cunt again and again until her body stiffened and the muscles of her sex convulsed. He licked and sucked her little clit through it, until she cried his name at the top of her lungs and colorful stars exploded outside her window, making the bird fall silent.

"Oh, gods," she breathed when it was finished.

"I'm not done with you by half," Damian said, rising. His cock was hard as rock and he couldn't wait to slide inside her hot, perfect pussy—couldn't wait to make himself one with her in the most carnal of ways.

He sought his discarded jeans on the floor and the things he'd put into the back pocket.

Elena watched him curiously. "Lengths of rope?"

"You trust me, right?"

"Heart and soul."

He grinned. "Rope."

Damian gathered her wrists and tied them to the headboard, making sure not to bind her too tight. Then he tied each ankle to the headboard, too, bringing her knees level with her chin.

And completely baring her cunt for him.

Chapter Eleven

Elena's breath came faster and faster. She trusted Damian with all she was and yet she was completely vulnerable in this position. Her cunt was bared to his hand and cock and there was nothing she could do to prevent him from touching it.

Gods, it was exciting.

Damian caught her gaze. His eyes were dark with lust, his cock incredibly hard. He eased his hand down her pussy and speared his fingers deep inside. In this position, with her knees practically up near her ears, she could watch as those thick digits slid in and out of her, wet with her juices. Her clit was plumped and withdrawn from its hood, already red and swollen from the pull of his lips and the lash of his hungry tongue.

It wanted more.

Elena whimpered.

"What do you want, baby?" Damian asked, stopping to rub her clit until she moaned. "What do you want me to do to you?"

"I want you to fuck me." The words tumbled from her lips easily. Before Damian had brought out this naughty, dirty-talking side of her, she never would have used those words in bed.

He teased her clit back and forth. "Mmm…that feels good, doesn't it?"

"Yes." She licked her lips. "Don't tease me, Damian. Give me your cock."

"Where do you want it?" He speared two fingers deep into her cunt. "Here? You want my cock fucking you here?"

"Yes."

"My cock is better, isn't it? Thicker. Wider."

"Damian!" She slurred his name, drunk on pleasure.

He pulled his fingers free and stroked her clit again. She could tell this game cost him, too. His entire body was tight with desire. "Are you so impatient to have me inside you?"

"Please, Damian, yes."

He rose up and set the head of his cock to her entrance. "Then take me, baby." He pushed deep inside her aching cunt—all the way to his base.

Her breath left her lungs in a rush and she closed her eyes. It didn't seem to matter how many times they made love, or how many times she had his cock inside her, it was like heaven every time. She would never grow tired of it. Having Damian inside of her made him an extension of her and she wanted to experience that intimacy forever, every single day if she could.

"Fuck, Elena," Damian breathed, his head falling back and his eyes closing, "you feel so good."

And then he began to thrust.

She sank her teeth into her bottom lip as she watched his cock glide in and out of her. He shafted her slow, so she could see every inch penetrate her, come back out coated in her juices, and then slide back in. His cock seemed almost too big to fit inside her, yet he did—so perfectly stretching her muscles to that point where she could orgasm from penetration alone.

"Oh, Elena, that's so good," Damian breathed, grabbing the headboard above her head. "You're so wet for me, so hot and sweet. Are you watching me fuck you, beautiful?"

Elena couldn't even respond. Pleasure caught the words in her throat before she could force them into the air.

He increased the pace of his thrusts, his shaft plunging into her faster and faster. Elena watched every hammering downward thrust that stretched her so wide and filled her so well. He grabbed her hips and held her steady and he took her harder and faster, until the only sound in the room was the slick sound of their bodies coming together and the heaviness of their mingling breath.

Damian licked his thumb and set it to her clit, rubbing the small bundle of nerves as he fucked her. He knew just how to touch her, how hard to press, how fast to stroke her....

"I'm coming, Damian!" she cried. "Oh, gods, yes!"

It rolled over her like a freight train, stealing her breath and her thought. Ecstasy slammed into her body and forced a cry from her lungs. He kept up the pistonlike movement as she orgasmed. She pulled on the rope that bound her as he drew it out longer and longer, until she sagged, limp with exhausted pleasure.

Damian untied her, frantically working the knots free until she collapsed into his arms. His cock still glided in and out of her. "Touch me, baby," he whispered raggedly. "Hold me. God, I love you so much."

She wrapped her hands and legs around him, kissing his lips, face and throat. Her hands skated over the bunching muscles of his shoulders and back, slipped down to cup his buttocks as he thrust into her again and again.

He nipped the sensitive place where her shoulder met her

neck, the place he'd marked when they'd first met. "Ah, Elena, baby…baby." His cock jumped deep inside her and she felt the hot rush of his come.

Damian rolled to the side and pulled her up into the protective cradle of his body. His hands roamed her body territorially, as they were wont to do after sex. He kissed her shoulder. "Elena, you taste and feel so good. I love you, baby." His voice shook. "I never want to go a day without you."

A flare of happiness bloomed in her chest, making the blue sky outside her window even bluer. She closed her eyes and smiled. "Hopefully we'll never have to, Damian."

It was the very last door on the left. The very…last…one.

Damian had never walked the entire corridor. It was long, at least two miles, and simply lined with doors. Apparently every major city had a nightclub like Darkness and every nightclub had an underground like this one.

To his preinduction mind, it would have seemed unbelievable, fantastic, unreal. Now, however, after he'd found his place among his people and had honored that promise his blood had made without his knowledge or consent, it seemed perfectly reasonable. Not only that, it seemed right.

He glanced over at Elena, who stood with him before the very last fae door in the Underground's corridor. She seemed right, too, in a way he'd never have believed possible before. She fit against him like a smooth puzzle piece, snuggling into his life and blending into his personality—his heart, his mind—like a drop of water absorbed by the earth.

"Are you ready?" she asked.

"No."

She stared at the door. "Me, either."

He took her hand. It was warm and strong in his—like the woman. "I still want to do it, though."

"Then let's go in."

Together, they walked through the door.

Chapter Twelve

Grass cushioned their footfalls and trees, ringed by bushes, rose around them. They stood on a hill. It was just past twilight by the looks of it. Cool air, just enough to make Elena shiver, tugged gently at her shirt.

Their hands still intertwined, they waited, watching the full moon rise unnaturally fast over the crest of the hill and nightfall coat the ground around them.

Eventually the sound of footsteps on the grass, a gentle rustling, reached their ears. Over the rise of the hill came three people, dressed all in white. One of them was her mother, the queen. The other two men Elena didn't recognize.

The queen stopped in front of them both and smiled. "My daughter and her lover." She raised an eyebrow. "Heart-string, too. Perhaps after today he'll be your mate, Elena. Are you sure you want this? Have you considered what you'll be throwing away?"

She started in surprise. "Mother, I have nothing to lose and everything to gain in Damian. He's one of my best matches on this planet. If I don't have a chance at happiness with him, there is no hope at all for me."

"You have nothing to lose but your life, Elena." Her voice

cracked like a whip. The queen skewered Damian with her icy gaze. "You, too, could end up buried under one of these hawthorn bushes before the night is over."

"Well, yes, there is that," answered Damian, his full mouth twisting in a grin. "There is the possibility of death tonight, but I'll die anyway if Elena is forced to marry Reynolds. So, for me, there's not much of a choice."

Elena smiled and glanced at Damian, who stared back at her with an expression of tenderness on his face.

"Oh, gods," sighed the queen. "All right, let's get started then." She motioned to the men standing near her. "This is Marsden and Terry. They came from San Francisco to administer this test. *Hae ilyium* doesn't happen very often. This is their bit of faery and the test you're about to undergo is their creation. Are you ready?"

Elena glanced at Damian, alarm ratcheting up her blood pressure. "Uh, how should we be getting ready?"

"Actually, that was a trick question. There is no ready."

The two men in white waved their arms and the hill, and everyone on it, disappeared.

Elena stood in the middle of her father's library, wearing a dress she'd owned as a teenager—blue, designer, short. She hadn't been able to fit into this dress since she'd been eighteen.

That was her first clue that something was very, very odd.

Somewhere in the hallway, something crashed. A little boy screeched for his mother. Elena frowned. That sounded like her little brother, Tad, but Tad was a grown man.

"Tad, what are you doing? You tipped over your mama's favorite pedestal with your cavorting!"

Flashback. That was her nanny's voice, Hilda. Gods, she

was back in her parents' house and she was a—no! Elena ran to a mirror to make sure she wasn't sixteen again and sagged when she saw she *was*.

"Oh, gods."

She would do anything to avoid reliving her teenage years in her parents' house. Elena didn't even want to revisit that time, not for a moment.

From the corridor beyond the room, she heard her mother talking in low, chiding tones to her brother.

Invisible hands tightened around Elena's throat. She was back home.

It wasn't that she'd had a horrible life here, or that she'd been beaten or anything dark like that. It was just that her parents, with their strained, uncomfortable marriage, had choked her every day into doing things she'd never wanted to do. Her father had been especially bad, with his *duty! duty! duty!* refrain beating endlessly in her head. Her mother had mostly been distracted, trying to pick up threads of happiness in a life gone sour.

Elena had never wanted to end up like her mother, though she'd always known it was her destiny. Oddly, now she understood that her mother didn't want Elena to end up like her, either.

"Elena, you're here."

Elena's head snapped up from where she'd bowed it in defeat and she whirled around. "Mother."

Her mother swept into the room. "Loren has arrived. He's in the kitchen with Cook. You should go see to him before your father decides to have him poisoned." She waved her hand dismissively, as if she didn't care one way or the other.

Loren. Her very first boyfriend. Her first "love" or at least that's what she'd considered him back then, despite being promised to Reynolds.

"Where's Damian?"

Her mother frowned. "Who is Damian, darling? Gods, I hope you haven't picked up another commoner stray—your father will have an apoplexy."

"What kind of test is this? It's so strange."

"Test, dear?" said her mother, idly arranging the fresh-cut flowers in the vase on a nearby table.

"Test for the *hae ilyium*," she mumbled.

Her mother turned. "The *hae ilyium!* How wonderfully romantic. As for the test that goes with it, I've heard it's always something that looks into your heart, pulls out your greatest fears or failures and then bats you about the head with them."

*Bats you about the head…*well, that was for sure.

"I'll go see to Loren, then."

"You do that, dear."

Her feet felt heavy as she picked her way past her brother, still sprawled and whimpering in the hallway. Gods, she hoped she wasn't stuck here. The thought made her miss a step.

She walked down the stairs to the main floor, and glimpsed workmen in the grand foyer, up on a ladder and adjusting the chandelier.

Wait a minute. She stopped on a stair. She knew what was about to happen because she'd lived this day before. Now she remembered—her brother falling in the hallway, the chandelier…

"Hey, stop guys!" she yelled. "Make sure the piece on the right is holding properly. My…er…intuition is telling me it's loose."

One of the workmen took a look. "Yes, you were right. Thanks!"

"Not a problem. All in a day's work for a faery princess."

The workman laughed.

Once upon a time the piece had fallen and smashed on the marble flooring. She remembered it vividly because that was the day her father had…

"Oh, no, Daddy!" She hastened down the stairs toward the kitchen.

She burst into the kitchen to find her father bellowing at Loren, who appeared absolutely terrified.

Elena stopped short, remembering how she'd cowered right along with Loren in the face of her father's wrath, while inwardly seething about her lack of choices.

"I won't have you courting my daughter!" the king yelled. "You have no royal fae blood! Get out of my house immediately and never return!"

Loren's green gaze flicked to her and then at the door. "Of course, my king."

Back then, on the day that Elena remembered, she'd looked on in horror as her father had banished Loren from the house and put an end to all her dating (except those of royal blood) until she'd been an adult. She remembered how sick and helpless she'd felt in the face of her father's iron-fisted rule.

Elena had acquiesced back then. She'd submitted.

Not today.

Rage erupted from Elena. She clenched her fists and stalked up to her father. She'd changed the fate of the chandelier; maybe she could change her reaction to her father, too. It was past time she found her voice. If she had a chance to relive part of her past, she might as well do it right.

"Daddy, back off!" She marched up to her father and stood in front of him. The king looked at her as if she'd grown another head. "I like Loren and I want to date him. I don't care that he doesn't have royal blood! Frankly, every boy I've ever met with royal blood has been an egoistical ass—er—jerk who isn't worth a damn and who never treats me right. What do you care about more, Daddy? The preservation of your precious bloodline or your eldest daughter's happiness?"

The king sputtered. Loren had pressed himself up against the kitchen wall.

"You know the tradition, Elena," her father finally forced out. "You know our need to preserve the ancient bloodlines."

"On that, I cry bullsh—er—bull hockey! What's so special about royal blood? As far as I can see, fae is fae. We all have magic, so who cares about bloodline? I know lots of fae with magic stronger than the royal line, anyway. Stop being such a stuck-up elitist."

The king sucked in a breath of surprise.

"I want to open a pottery business!" she declared. Where the hell had that come from? "And I want to marry who I want!"

The king sputtered again.

"The bottom line is, do you love me, Daddy?"

"Of—of course I do."

"Then stop smothering me and dictating my life. Allow me and your other children to make their own choices. I guarantee they'll respect you more for it and they'll all make you proud."

Her father remained mute for several moments. "I don't know what to say, Elena."

"Say you'll consider what I said."

"I will…consider it."

Elena smiled, feeling more satisfied with herself than she had in a long time. Maybe her father would dismiss her concerns and go back to his old ways, but at least she'd stood up to him and said her piece.

Then she remembered that she was still trapped in the past and she'd already lived all of this. She remembered the test.

Pop.

She dropped to the floor and everything went black.

Damian staggered forward and fell to his knees. When he looked up, his heart skipped a beat.

Cassidy, beautiful, perfect Cassidy Williams—his ex-fiancée—stared down at him. "Are you all right?"

He pushed to his feet and became aware of the tinging and pinging of slot machines around him. Oh, hell, he was back at Gold Diggers. He was even wearing his work uniform. "Cassidy," he blurted. "Are you all right?"

She lifted a perfectly shaped golden brow. "Yessss, you're the one who tripped, Damian."

He glanced around in panic for Elena. What the hell? Was this the test?

Oh, gods, he was back in his old life!

His attention snapped to his open hand, where he tried to spindle a little magic. It didn't come. He didn't even get a tingle. Nothing. It was gone.

Had it ever been real?

Horror tightened a cold fist in his stomach. Was he trapped back here? Was he destined to relive this part of his life over? Was that his test? If so, maybe he wouldn't be inducted this time and he'd be forced to live his life as a round peg trying to valiantly fit into a square hole.

Even more horrifying was the notion that perhaps Darkness, Elena, and the fae didn't exist at all. Maybe he'd dreamed it as a reaction to wedding stress. Maybe he had a brain tumor. Maybe he was in a coma and his body was lying in some hospital bed right now while he dreamed all this!

Delusion. That was the only possible explanation. Or a psychotic break.

"Why are you staring at your hand?" Cassidy asked, linking her arm with his. "And why do you look so disturbed all of a sudden?"

"Uh." What had he just been thinking about? All of a sudden everything having to do with Elena and Darkness…the fae, it all seemed so hazy and unreal. Like a dream. Fading…

Gone.

"Damian…Damian?" Cassidy shook his shoulder. "You're starting to freak me out. Why the hell are you staring at your palm?"

Yes, why was he looking at his palm? And what had he just been thinking about? He frowned, and then shook his head. "I think I'm going crazy. I can't remember the last two minutes of my life."

Cassidy laughed. "You had too much to drink last night, is all. Come on, we'll be late clocking in if we don't hurry."

Oh, yeah, that's right. They'd been out with James and their friends last night, down at a bar on the Strip. They *had* drunk a lot and he did have a bit of a headache. Maybe that accounted for stopping like an imbecile in the middle of the casino and staring at his palm for a full minute.

They clocked in. They worked their shifts. It was a day like any other day.

And then, after he and Cassidy had clocked out, he saw *her*.

Damian stopped short and stared at a woman sitting at one of the casino bars with a man. She seemed so familiar, so…beloved. How strange. The way she tipped her head to the side and smiled, her long dark hair cascading over her shoulder, it reminded him of something. What was it about her that resonated in his blood? It was almost as if he could remember what her creamy skin tasted like, how it felt under his lips and hands.

"Damian."

He snapped out of the second daze he'd found himself that day. "Sorry." Damian shook his head and laughed. "Me and Jack Daniel's have parted ways for good. I better never drink again. Tonight I'm going straight home to sleep."

"That's good, since tomorrow is all about wedding planning. You said you'd come over so we could decide some stuff, remember?"

The wedding. Yes. It never fully left his mind. Cassidy was a wonderful woman, perfect. Beautiful, intelligent, funny. He had absolutely no reason to want to break it off with her. Hell, that's how he'd ended up proposing to her. They'd reached that part in their relationship where The Question had been the only place to go and he'd had no concrete reason to end the relationship.

Maybe he feared being alone. Maybe that was the real reason he'd asked her to marry him. And yet, it wasn't fair to Cassidy. He didn't love her like he should.

That had been on his mind a lot lately. What if there was a man out there who could love her better? Cassidy needed that.

Cassidy deserved that.

Damian stopped in the hallway of the casino and let the truth of that crash into him. There was no denying it. He was doing Cassidy, and himself, wrong.

It was time to make things right.

"The wedding, yes." He took her hand and walked toward the door of the casino. "Do you have time to talk?"

She tipped her head to the side and smiled. "Sure."

"Great."

This was going to be the hardest thing he'd ever done.

"What if I told you that marrying me would be the biggest mistake you'd ever make?"

Cassidy tipped her head to the side, the warm evening breeze playing with tendrils of the blond hair curling around her pretty face. She smiled a little sadly. "I'd say you were being silly." Her voice was a little tight.

Tread carefully.

"You may think I'm being silly now, from this vantage point, but what if a year from now you meet a man who is far more suitable than I am, Cassidy? Someone you'd be happier with, who would love you better than I ever could?"

Cassidy stared hard at him. "Are you breaking up with me, Damian?"

Damian swallowed the lump in his throat. His fear rose. God, he didn't want to hurt Cassidy. Maybe it would be better to just go on the way they had been. After all, he had no concrete reason to not want to spend his life with her. Any man would—should—be thrilled to have Cassidy as his wife.

Any man but him.

Oh, sure, there could be a comfortable, lukewarm marriage. They would be happy, but not deliriously so. He wouldn't be alone. But that would be selfish of him, no matter how painful doing this now might be.

He *had* to do this. So, maybe it was better to do it fast, like pulling off a Band-Aid. She'd heal and be the stronger for it in the long run.

"I am, Cassidy."

Her eyes went wide and her face pale. Damian's heart lurched in his chest. He plunged ahead. "I know you won't believe me, but I'm breaking up with you because I care about you. I want you to have a man who's right for you. I want you to have a strong and everlasting love. I know that person is out there somewhere for you, Cassidy. I can feel it in this odd intuitive way." He paused. "That person is not me."

"You care about me, but you don't love me?" She sounded completely shocked.

"I do love you, Cassidy. I just don't love you enough."

She stared at him in stunned horror for several seconds, then she simply turned and stalked off down the sidewalk.

Damian watched her go. A vise of misery slowly constricted around his chest. In a way, he was relieved. He'd *known* he'd had to do that and now it was done. At the same time, now he was alone.

He shifted his gaze to the Strip, where cars and buses whizzed by. Damn it. He'd done the right thing for Cassidy, even though she didn't see it that way right now. But had he done the right thing for himself?

The doors of the casino opened and the woman from the bar exited. Damian watched her, frowning and trying to figure out why she seemed so familiar. Something about her drew him so strongly, almost as if like called to like. Fuck, he was stupid. He'd just broken off his engagement. Now was hardly the time to be watching other women.

The lady stepped out into the street to hail a cab…right in front of a bus.

Damian didn't think about it, he just acted. Somewhere deep in his heart, he knew he couldn't watch this woman die, no matter what it cost him. He dove from the sidewalk and into the street, crashing into her and pushing her forward hard, out of the way of the bus.

Damian hit the asphalt. Tires screeched. The grill of the bus came toward him.

Searing pain. Breaking bones. Exploding organs.

Blackness.

Damian's eyes came open. He lay on his back in the grass, staring up at the night sky. His breathing came shallow as memory flooded his mind. He wasn't dead. He'd just been tested.

"What…the…fuck?" he shouted.

Near him someone moaned. Elena.

He turned on his side and saw her lying about four feet away. His arms ached to hold her. It was all he could think of. He crawled to her and took her into his arms. She fought him for a moment, seemingly disoriented, then recognized him and tucked herself against him, nuzzling her head into the crook of his neck.

Damian closed his eyes and sighed in absolute relief. Thank God it hadn't been real. Thank God he wasn't stuck back in the past, his memory erased…without Elena.

Someone was clapping.

He and Elena disentangled themselves to find the queen standing over them. She smiled widely. "Congratulations, you both passed."

Damian collapsed back to the grass.

"Elena, I am so proud of you for standing up to your father. I've wanted to see you do that your whole life."

"Thank you, Mother."

The queen fixed her gaze on Damian. "You have proven your heart is worthy of our daughter. Her hand is yours if you still desire it."

"I do."

The queen's smile widened. "The king will be so…pleased."

Damian propped himself up on his elbows. "That wasn't real, was it? It was just illusion…faery magic. I didn't really go back into my past and right a wrong, did I?"

"No, Damian," answered the queen. "We don't have the power to change the past. You still jilted your fiancée at the altar. Believe me, try something like that with Elena and you'll find yourself in an illusory hell you'll never break from."

Damian swallowed hard.

"But," continued the queen, "you showed that if you were given a second chance, you would do the right thing. Also, you knowingly sacrificed your life for Elena's, proving you value her more than yourself. Reynolds would have failed that test." The queen smiled warmly. "That's enough for me to welcome you to our family, Damian. It should be enough for the king, as well."

Elena's gaze had snapped to him and held as soon as the words *sacrificed your life for Elena's* had been uttered.

"What would have happened if I'd failed the test?" Damian asked.

The queen's smile faded. "Somehow the bus would have hit you and you never would have regained consciousness here on the hill. You'd have died."

"Ah."

"You sacrificed your life for me?" asked Elena, stunned pleasure on her face.

"Painfully, yes." He paused, thinking. "Hey, you didn't have to sacrifice your life for me during your test?"

"No."

"What?" Damian looked at the queen. "How come she didn't have to be hit by a bus for me?"

The queen just laughed, snapped her fingers and disappeared.

Elena laughed and tackled him, covering his face with kisses. "I would throw—" *smack* "—myself—" *smack, smack* "—in front of a bus—" *smack* "—any day for you."

Damian rolled her over and kissed her, his tongue sliding between her lush lips to find hot, sweet heaven.

Damian pulled Elena back against him and kissed her bare shoulder and neck as his hands played over her body. Her breath came fast and heavy. Around them the rain slowed to a light drizzle.

She wasn't cold, not at all, not with Damian's strong arms around her. In that moment, she fully gave herself over to the wonderfulness of it. He made her feel so cherished and protected. She knew that—unlike so much in the world of the fae—what they shared was no illusion. Damian loved her; he would *die* for her.

"I'm so happy right now, I feel like I could burst," she murmured.

"Mmm…" He nuzzled the nape of her neck. "Don't do that, it would be messy."

She chuckled and turned to face him.

He stared at her with intense love in his eyes, then kissed her slowly. "I know what you mean," he whispered against her lips. "During the test I lost my memory of Darkness, the fae…even you. In contrast, I can't believe how unhappy I was before I met you, Elena." He paused and closed his eyes. "You are *everything* to me." His voice shook with emotion.

She smiled and tears pricked her eyes. "Ditto."

"Will you marry me, fae-style? With the removable floating church and the demons and all that?"

Elena laughed. "I'll marry you any style."

He kissed her again. "Okay, now let's go home. I'm getting pruny out here in the rain." Damian stood, helped her up and they dressed.

Elena pulled her shirt over her head. "Hey, that begs the question, where are we going to live? Your place or mine?"

He shot her a look of incredulity. "Mine, of course."

"Yours?" She hopped on one foot while she slipped on a boot. "Mine is a million times nicer. Your magic isn't strong enough to create adequate housing."

He gaped for a moment in mock offense. "I resent that implication, even if it's true. The female always goes to live in the male's home."

She swatted him with her other boot. "That's totally ridiculous and chauvinistic."

"Is not."

"Is, too!"

They argued all the way to the door. Right before they opened it, Damian pulled Elena to him and kissed the top of her head. "I was just yanking your chain. I'm coming to live at your place, my love. I already came home a long time ago. That happened the day I met you."

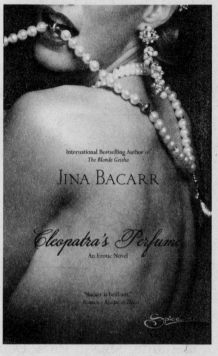

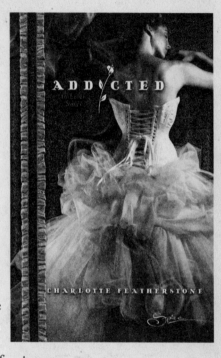

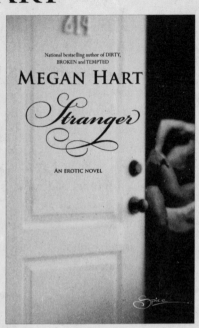

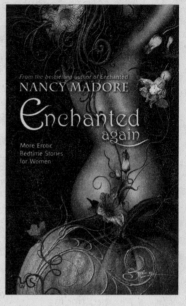